REDROVER
PERDITION GAMES

BY L.E. FRASER

Also by L.E. Fraser

Red Rover, Perdition Games

Skully, Perdition Games

Simon Says, Perdition Games

For my mother
who taught me that reading was a pleasure not a task.

PROLOGUE

IT WAS A gorgeous spring day, and Roger had decided to cancel his Friday psychiatric patients so he could attempt a little cognitive behavioural exercise. The objective was to practise spontaneity, something he usually avoided. His unannounced visit would thrill his lover almost as much as his uncharacteristic impulsiveness.

Forty-five minutes after leaving his Cabbagetown home in downtown Toronto, he pulled off the highway and into the city of Vaughan. Not wanting to arrive empty-handed, he found a flower shop and bought a bouquet of yellow roses before continuing north along a country road toward Brenda's farm.

Just as he spotted the left turn into her gravel lane, a burping tractor popped into view on the decline of a small hill on the opposite side of the two-lane country road. Roger sat impatiently with his indicator ticking off the seconds. He cursed when he spied a line of traffic approaching from behind the tractor. A Ford truck led the procession and was travelling fast, closing the distance. If the damn farmer hurried up, Roger figured he'd have just enough time to make the turn. He leaned forward, grasped the steering wheel, and waited for his opportunity.

"Come on! Move it!" he yelled.

The second the tractor cleared the driveway, Roger hit the gas and sped into the left lane, confident that the approaching pickup had plenty of time to slow down. Too late, he realized the asshole wasn't reducing his speed. In fact, the heavy vehicle had accelerated on the hill's decline. Second-guessing himself at the last minute, Roger slammed on the brakes. The car stalled. Trying not to overreact, he quickly pressed the start button and fumbled with the gears. His foot slipped off the clutch, and the car stalled again.

A horn blared. Brakes squealed in protest. The truck's locked tires howled against the asphalt, and a sickening odour of burning rubber assaulted Roger's nose. His heart galloped in his chest as he grasped the steering wheel and frantically jammed his finger against the start button. Turning his head, he saw the front of the giant pickup swerve as the driver tried to steer away from the imminent collision. Frozen, Roger watched in horror as the truck skidded sideways but continued rushing toward his Audi. Drywall flew off the truck bed, breaking against the road. A chunk bounced off the windshield of his convertible and struck him in the face. The back of his head bounced against the headrest, and he flung his arms over his head and closed his eyes with a moan of despair, waiting for the sound of crunching metal as the truck sideswiped him. When the crash didn't occur, Roger opened his eyes and saw that the pickup had stopped less than an inch from the side of his car.

Blinking rapidly and trying to catch his breath, he looked behind the Ford. One car was in the ditch. Two more had managed to stop on the side of the road. People were climbing from their vehicles and shading their eyes against the sun in an effort to see what had happened. The old man behind the wheel of the Ford leaned on his horn and flipped the bird through his open window.

Roger wiped a trickle of blood from his forehead with a shaking hand and managed to start the car. Anxious to avoid an ugly scene with the other driver, he sped into Brenda's long laneway, hoping that the hillbilly truck driver wasn't going to follow and confront him.

There were two cars and a truck in the gravel yard, but plenty of room for his Audi. Wanting to surprise her, Roger parked on the far side of the decrepit garage where she wouldn't see his car from the house. He got out, peered into the side mirror, and dabbed a tissue against the cut. Satisfied that it wasn't serious, he reached into the car for the flowers. Bouquet in hand, he strolled to the back of the property, chuckling as he imagined Brenda enthralled by his story of the near miss.

Since he was usually sneaking in and out, he'd never had a good look at the farmhouse and had never been in the backyard. Enjoying the warm spring sunshine, he turned his back on the ugly stone house, and his eyes scanned over the land to the north. Clusters of tall maple and sycamore trees dotted rolling green fields, and colourful wildflowers bloomed in the overgrown brush where crops had once thrived. A charming location and it was hard to believe that downtown Toronto was less than an hour away.

The illusion of beauty shattered when Roger's eyes drifted to the south where a decaying barn perched about ninety metres from the back of the house. He shuddered and imagined rats scurrying to filthy nests. About forty metres to the right of the barn was a pus-yellow shed. The outbuildings were garish scars against the bright blue sky and emerald fields. Nature only compensated for so much. Brenda may as well squat in a condemned building in the Garden of Eden.

Turning in a semi-circle, he studied the back of the dilapidated farmhouse and the falling-down garage beside it. In spite of the demolition costs, the land's resale value would be well over two million, more if they sold to a developer. It was a damn shame Brenda's obstinate husband refused to sell.

The idiot had moved his family of five from the city with the intention of renovating the house and three outbuildings. A reasonable man would recognize the futility of trying. Besides, according to Brenda, her husband wasn't handy. He started projects and left them half-finished, which might explain the blue tarp that covered a portion of the garage roof.

In Roger's professional opinion, Graham suffered from the Dunning-Kruger effect, a cognitive bias that made him believe he possessed superior skills compared to everyone else. If she couldn't convince her moronic husband to sell the money pit, winter would be a freezing nightmare of despair. How could the man subject his family to such squalor? It was selfish, vindictive... stupid. Roger should have no problem outsmarting a man like that, and yet, here he was, skulking around in the middle of the day like *he* was the bad guy.

If he lived like this, he wouldn't want anyone to know. He chewed his lower lip. Maybe he should go around front and pretend he hadn't seen the mess in the backyard. In fact, maybe he should leave. On the other hand, he'd been inside the house on more than one occasion. Now that he'd seen the entire property, he could genuinely sympathize when she complained.

Decision made, he headed for the back door, a journey that required agility because of the broken cement stones that were an inch elevated in places along the pathway. At the back entrance, he hoped his knock wouldn't bash in the screen door that dangled precariously from a single hinge. His fist stopped in mid-air as he heard voices enter the kitchen on the other side of the door. Angry voices.

"She has an active imagination." Brenda. "You should be proud of her." She sounded frustrated.

"What are you talking about?" a male voice asked incredulously. "You didn't even look at it. I'm telling you, there's something wrong."

Graham was home. Brenda had told him yesterday that her husband was going away for the weekend. Unpleasant surprises like this were why Roger avoided spontaneity.

"The only thing wrong with her is her brother," Brenda was saying. "Are you going to do something about Jordan?"

"It was a joke. Lighten up. Isn't that what your precious Dr. Peterson told you to do?"

Roger jumped at hearing his own name enter the argument.

"Don't start!" Brenda yelled. "Every time I bring up Jordan, you turn the conversation around and accuse me of cheating on you."

"Tell me why Dr. Peterson turned you over to another head-shrinker," Graham demanded. "Let's see, was it a twisted shot at ethics?"

"Graham, I'm warning you. If—"

"*You're* warning *me*?" Graham laughed. "How do you think the College of Physicians would discipline a psychiatrist who re-assigned a patient so he could fuck her?"

Roger's blood ran cold. Another complaint would ruin him. He slid out of sight, glancing around for an escape route. There wasn't one. Graham would see him from the kitchen window.

Before their friendship had progressed to a sexual relation-ship, Brenda had introduced him to her husband. All six feet, four inches and three hundred pounds of him. Hard muscle had loosened and fallen to flab, but the man was still threatening. He'd played football with the Toronto Argonauts until three years ago when he'd blown his knee out as an offensive lineman. Now he was a stereotypical embittered alcoholic who guzzled beer and relived the glory days with friends.

Over the past year, Roger's opinion of the odious bully had shifted from indifference to dislike to outright hatred. He had no doubt that the arse would lodge a grievance against him, espe-cially if Graham found him snooping around with a bunch of posies clutched in his hand.

He jumped off the back porch to a patch of dirt alongside the house and pressed his body against the fieldstone wall under the window. How had he gotten into this mess?

From inside the house, the arguing was still going strong and their voices drifted out of the open window. He'd missed part of the discussion, but they were back on the subject of the children.

"Oh, right—*boys will be boys*," Brenda mimicked in a drawl. "What happened in the city was not okay. What happened at the high school was criminal. When are you going to open your eyes?"

"Nothing happened!"

The voice was directly to Roger's right, in front of the screen door. If Graham glanced outside, he'd see him skulking under the window. Roger repressed his instinct to bolt, stood still, and held his breath.

"The only problem with this family is you," Graham yelled. "You're setting such a great example, whoring around with your psychiatrist."

"Look around you!" Brenda shrieked. "We're living like animals. The basement is flooded with sewage."

"You're exaggerating."

"And you're unbelievable. You're okay letting the kids—delights that they are—live in raw sewage like gutter rats."

Something smashed on the floor. Roger jumped. Was the argument escalating to physical violence? He had to do something.

"There's no sewage! It's the sump-pump or the receptacle. Give me a chance to fix it."

"Don't you get it? *You* can't fix anything," Brenda shouted.

"I'll figure it out!"

"When? When are you going to *figure it out*? I married a football player. I didn't marry a farmer. I hate you for forcing me to live like this!"

"So leave." Graham's voice moved away from the door and into the kitchen. "Who's stopping you? Run off with your darling doctor."

The voices drifted further away from the kitchen, and Roger missed Brenda's response. He had no trouble hearing Graham shout, "Good! Let's see how happy you are with him when he loses his licence. Let's see how many people buy his self-help books when I out him as a cheating fraud." A door slammed inside the house.

Roger stood on his tiptoes and peeked in the kitchen window. The room was empty. He quickly turned and picked his way across renovation waste piled against the side of the house. Once he reached the path, he broke into a jog. He could get to his car from the other side of the garage. So long as Graham hadn't exited the house through the front door, Roger knew he could escape unseen.

He couldn't let the vindictive arse accuse him of seducing a patient. He'd had no idea Graham knew the truth. Why hadn't Brenda warned him? Roger stopped abruptly beside the garage. He was short of breath, his chest felt tight, and his hands shook. Perspiration poured down his face but he felt cold. He pulled his hair hard, trying to ward off a panic attack. Slowly, the pain in his chest eased and his breathing evened out. He paced in a circle, taking frantic, jerky steps. If the media discovered he'd slept with a patient again, the scandal would ruin him. He had to do something.

Focused on his musings, Roger didn't notice the young man until he bumped into him. Dressed in football gear, the teenager held a scuffed helmet that was a frightening map of brutality. Mixed with stains of ground dirt were smears of dried blood. The knuckles on the hand that gripped the helmet strap had ugly bruises and bloody scrapes.

The teenager clenched his square jaw, and his eyes narrowed menacingly. "Who the fuck are you?"

No wonder Brenda had complaints about her eighteen-year-old son, Jordan. Roger's temper rose to a breaking point and dancing black dots distorted his vision. "Watch where you're going," he retorted.

The kid looked down at the flowers in Roger's hand, and his lips pressed together to form a tight smile. "Right. I get it." The smile turned to an ugly smirk. "No fun playing with the cow when the bull's in the yard, eh?" The kid leaned into Roger's face. "I know who you are," he said in a singsong voice.

Without thinking, Roger shoved him hard in the chest with both hands, but the burly teenager barely moved.

Jordan laughed and held up his hands in mock submission. "Assaulting a high school student on his own property. What do you think that'll get you, doc? Some time in prison is my guess." The kid brushed by with a swagger and a nasty chuckle. He disappeared into the house, slamming the back door behind him.

Standing motionless, Roger tried to steady his breathing again. Cloying sweetness from the roses wafted up and his stomach somersaulted. He tossed the bouquet into the garden.

Roger envisioned a media headline and heard a disgusted broadcaster's voice in his head. *Bestselling author and renowned psychiatrist caught seducing a patient and assaulting her teenage son.*

Seeing the flowers discarded on the ground, hearing the arguing that still pierced the air from inside the house, and imagining the end of his life's work, he snapped. He didn't know what he was going to do, but he had to do something.

Before he could lose his nerve, he marched back to the door and peered inside. He couldn't see anyone, but it sounded like the voices were coming from below him. He opened the screen door and stepped into a small foyer. The kitchen was to the right. Straight ahead, about five feet from the door, was a staircase. Ten or twelve steep steps led down to a landing with a wall. A second set of stairs descended to the left of the landing, presumably ending in the cellar. The angle of the split staircase prevented him from seeing into the actual cellar.

He hesitated and swiped his hand across the moisture on his brow. Blood coated his fingertips from the cut on his forehead. He didn't have a tissue and thought again about going back to the car.

Just then, he heard the heart-stopping sound of flesh smacking flesh, followed by Brenda crying out. Her voice propelled him into action. He tore outside and frantically searched the yard for a weapon, settling on a rusted pipe that lay in a pile of renovation waste on the right side of the porch. He grabbed it. It weighed maybe ten pounds. He swung the pipe, adjusted his grip, and sprinted back up the porch steps to the door. Above him, the outdoor light flickered and went out. There were loud footsteps in the kitchen, the sound of crashing furniture, smashing glass, and the clatter of falling objects.

Roger leaped off the porch and stood on his toes to peer through the kitchen window. Jordan was leaning against the open fridge door, drinking from a milk carton. Two chairs lay on their sides and the contents of a utensil drawer littered the floor. Judging from the amount of broken ceramic on the floor, someone had smashed most of the dishes. As Roger watched, Jordan hurled the milk to the ground and stomped out of the room. Angry footsteps thumped on the stairs. An upstairs door slammed. The house was silent. Gripping the pipe, Roger returned to the porch, quietly opened the door, and stepped inside. He stood in the entry, straining to hear any sound from the basement. Nothing but silence.

Perhaps Brenda had also come upstairs when he was outside hunting for a weapon. Maybe he could find her and get her out of the house without having to confront Graham. He crept through the main level of the old farmhouse, and the pipe grew slick in his perspiring hand. Heavy metal music now blared from somewhere upstairs. Brenda wasn't on the main floor. Roger snuck to the back door and took a hesitant step down the first step to the basement landing. Did he hear a whimper? He took another step, leaning down to better hear. Someone was weeping. It had to be Brenda. She was in the cellar.

He tiptoed down the stairs. Halfway to the landing, his foot slipped out from under him. A jolt of panic engulfed him. His left hand hit the wall, but there was nothing to grasp. His feet scrambled against the edge of the narrow stair before he fell to his ass and slid down to the landing.

He remained perfectly still, barely breathing, and waited for approaching footsteps. Nothing. Slowly, he climbed to his feet. His tailbone throbbed and his elbow stung. He turned to face the second staircase that descended into gloom. He could smell the stench of sewage. From below him, he heard an irregular clanging that sounded like metal hitting metal. Graham must be fiddling with the sump-pump.

Worried about losing his balance again, he looked around for something to hold onto so he could lean into the staircase to get a sense of how far it descended. Perched on the landing wall was an electrical box, and the rusted metal door was open. He shifted the pipe to his left hand and tugged on the door. It seemed firmly attached to the box so he grasped it, leaned into the stairwell, and peered down. Beneath the fifth step was pitch black. Impossible to guess how many stairs remained before reaching the cellar floor. He couldn't risk using his cell to light the staircase because he didn't know exactly where Graham was working. The clanging echoed in the old cellar and seemed to be coming from every direction.

He let go of the breaker box door and transferred the metal pipe to his right hand. Slowly, he descended. He counted seven stairs. The suffocating reek of sewage was stronger, and he struggled not to gag. Two more stairs and he reached the bottom. Cold liquid sloshed across the top of his shoes. He didn't want to imagine what floated in the water. A flashlight beam illuminated the back wall, about ten metres from the stairs. He could just make out Graham crouched in front of a sump-pump.

Roger's breath came in small gasps. He could just go back up those stairs, assume that Brenda was safe, and hope her abusive husband wouldn't act on his threat to ruin him. Against the darkness, he imagined the looks of disdain on the faces of his esteemed colleagues. A public accusation by an irate husband would be the demise of all of his hard work and dreams. Years of medical school for nothing. Massive legal bills to defend his reputation would leave him penniless. He'd lose his house, his car, his friends. Sniggering ridicule would follow him for the rest of his life. He gripped the pipe in both hands and licked his lips, telling himself that it was only a matter of time before Graham seriously injured Brenda, maybe even killed her. He had a responsibility to protect her. He swallowed hard. His mouth was dry. He had to decide what to do. Any minute, Graham could turn around and see him.

Roger took a deep breath and made his decision, knowing it would change his life forever.

CHAPTER ONE

REECE

AT SEVEN-THIRTY on Saturday morning, Reece was wandering through the crowd at the St. Lawrence Market on Front Street. Unable to sleep again, he'd left the loft at five a.m. and walked the sixteen blocks to the Saturday farmers' market. He'd learned to leave the car at home. No parking. Anywhere. Ever.

He mumbled "excuse me" and "pardon me" as he tried to carve a path to the organic butcher kiosk. He didn't need to visit the butcher, but there wasn't any reason to race home. Sam was swamped with PhD work and spending the day at the university. Reece didn't have any friends in the city, and a boring weekend alone stretched ahead of him. Again.

After moving to Toronto last year, the market had become his favourite place in a city he hated. The building was over two hundred years old and housed a ton of artisans selling gourmet wares from stalls set up in a vast space with steel-beamed ceiling rafters and cement floors. His eyes roamed across the crowd; a throwback to being a cop. Spring sunlight streamed through the many windows set high against the old walls. Reece wished he were outside in a backyard doing lawn work. Instead, he was stuck in a gigantic city hoping a scumbag wasn't lying in wait to mug him.

It wasn't Toronto specifically or Torontonians that Reece distrusted—it was any metropolitan area. He was a country boy at heart, and quiet towns suited him better. But he'd tendered his resignation as an inspector with the Ontario Provincial Police at the Uthisca detachment to be with Sam, a private investigator from Toronto. Being in love with an urban dweller meant adapting. For Sam's sake, he was trying. It wasn't going well.

What Reece hated was the lack of parking, constant crowds, indifference, and noise. He felt disconnected from people and nature but was trying hard to find positive attributes about city living. Watching Abigail—the only one of Sam's friends Reece liked—dance with The National Ballet of Canada was fun. So was the historical tour of the city he and Sam had taken. That was about it. Along with his dissatisfaction with city living, he also wasn't keen on PI work. He had an offer on the table from Toronto Police Services but wasn't sure homicide detective was his destiny either. Truth was he didn't know what he wanted to do with the rest of his life. Living in a state of limbo sucked.

With a sigh, he reminded himself that the only problem he needed to solve today was how to plot a course to the butcher on the west side of the crowded market. He wished Abigail had been available to meet him. The ballerina's ethereal beauty caused mobs to part in awe. Abby was a sweet woman who seldom spoke and had tremendously sad eyes. Reece hadn't met her girlfriend, Talia, and hoped he'd hit it off with the Canadian Armed Forces officer when she returned from overseas. Having some friends might help him settle into Toronto.

He finally reached the butcher kiosk, feeling flustered and out of sorts. His phone chirped. Reece dug it out and glanced at the caller ID. Unknown number. With a frown, he answered and barked, "Hash."

"*The dew of the morning, sunk chill on my brow,*" an unfamiliar voice quoted. "Early rising is a residual effect of country living, I presume. Regrettably, I called Sam first and woke her." The man chuckled. "She dispatched an eloquent reprimand prior to furnishing me with your cell number."

Reece didn't have a clue who would call him to quote poetry. "What's going on?" he asked.

"I call on bended knee to implore you to assist me. How are you with a hammer?"

"Who is this?"

"Roger."

It took a minute before it clicked. Roger Peterson, a psychiatrist friend of Sam's. She'd introduced him months ago at a Christmas party, and Reece had immediately labelled the man an ostentatious stuffed shirt. "I'm at the market. Didn't recognize your voice." He refrained from adding, *which should be a given since we only met once.*

"Ah, the next contestant on *Master Chef.*" Another chuckle.

"What's up, Roger? That one," he added in response to the butcher's question, pointing at a lovely duck.

"A barn raising. Well, a deck raising, at my place. Cold beer on ice and steaks on the lunch menu. I know that it's short notice, but I do hope you're available this afternoon," Roger said primly. "I'm also inviting Jim Stipelli. You two get on well, I believe?"

"Yeah, Sam and I worked for him on a murder case a few months ago," Reece said.

Jim was great when he wasn't around his harridan wife. Lisa Stipelli, Sam's best friend, was a passive-aggressive woman who milked sympathy by portraying herself as a hapless victim. Worse, she treated everyone who enjoyed a glass of wine with dinner as an alcoholic. It was impossible to get a word in edgewise, busy as she was lecturing you on your shortcomings. If you tried to defend yourself, she'd snipe about how you monopolized the conversation. Reece couldn't stand her, and it baffled him that Sam was friends with the hateful woman. More bewildering was why Roger, a passionate professional in self-help, tolerated Lisa's antics. The last thing Reece wanted to do was to hang out with Lisa.

"Sorry, Roger, we can't make it. Sam's tied up today," Reece said.

"I know. She told me she's spending the day at the university, which works because I was planning a boys' afternoon." Roger paused and then added, "Lisa won't be here."

Reece handed over his cash, accepted the bag, and waved at the butcher, who ignored him as usual. The next man in line hip-checked him out of the way and shouted his order. A woman loudly objected, insisting it was her turn. Reece picked his way through the crowd to the back wall of the building.

"Why the short notice? If you want to build a deck, it'll take planning," Reece said.

"The project's planned. Listen, Sam told me you might be at loose ends today. I've been meaning to invite you over for weeks.

I'd like to get to know you." He laughed. "After all, you never know when I might need the services of a private investigator."

Jim Stipelli was Toronto's top defence attorney. Why was Roger inviting a criminal lawyer and an ex-cop to his house without notice?

"Roger, is everything okay?"

The man's response was a bit fast. "Sure. Everything's fine. Come on, it'll be fun."

"Well… okay," Reece agreed, curiosity getting the getter of him. "I picked up wild mushrooms that I'll bring over to go with the steak. I have to drop by the loft first though." Roger lived downtown, he knew. Reece checked his watch. "How's eleven o'clock?"

"Great. I'm in Cabbagetown on Wellesley Street East—"

A rude shopper plowed into Reece, and he fumbled for his phone before it smashed onto the cement. He caught it and brought it back to his ear. "I'll get the address from Sam, no worries. See you later."

After he hung up, he gazed at the chaos before him.

Yeah, he thought, *a change of scenery would be good right about now.*

THE CIRCA-EIGHTEEN-HUNDREDS homes on Roger's street were striking. The charming neighbourhood had been part of the historical tour Reece had taken with Sam. Protected by the Cabbagetown Preservation Association, the area on the east side of downtown Toronto was a spectacular example of one of the largest Victorian housing districts in North America.

Gentrification had begun in the 1970s, and many of the restored semis, row houses, and detached homes on the narrow streets now sold for millions of dollars. Remarkable, considering impoverished nineteenth-century Irish immigrants had grown cabbages on their front lawns to feed their families.

Roger's home was a two-and-a-half-storey brick structure with elaborate cornices. A peaked roof capped the dormer attic window, gorgeous dentils decorated the facade, and rounded columns supported a delightful second-storey portico. Elegant ivy hugged the stone around a protruding bay window. It was, in a word, stunning.

Reece pulled into Roger's lane and manoeuvred his Toyota beside a brand new Audi convertible. Nice ride, but much too fancy for Reece's taste. Squeezing his six-foot-three frame out of his car to avoid even touching the Spyder, he cursed the city and its tight spaces.

"Salutations, Reece."

Reece jerked at the sound of his name and looked over at Roger, who had opened the gate in the back fence.

"Great house," Reece said. "Architecture is a hobby of mine, and she's a beauty."

"Most visitors park on the street."

Nice welcome, Reece thought, glancing up and down the street. There wasn't any available parking. Annoyed by Roger's rudeness, but not wanting to get off on the wrong foot, Reece asked, "Is there a side street you'd recommend?"

"You may as well leave it," Roger said with a sigh of annoyance. "I'm surprised you failed to see the sign."

Reece had indeed seen the sign but assumed it was to protect the parking pad from strangers, not to prevent the homeowner's guests from parking there.

Instead of going through the gate, Roger walked to the front door and held it open. When Reece entered the house, a sense of déjà vu engulfed him. Hemlock floors ran throughout the open main floor, and the wood had the same unusual grey stain as those in the loft he shared with Sam. The walls were the same shade of grey with smoky white trim, and even the modern, minimalistic furniture style was similar. He trailed along behind Roger and stopped to gawk at the kitchen. Carrara marble countertops, identical to the stone in Sam's kitchen. Same cabinetry and backsplash. The light fixtures were different, but the similarities between Roger's decor and Sam's were striking. Creepy, in fact.

"Something wrong?" Roger asked.

"Ah... no. Nice place. Did you design it yourself?"

"Not entirely. I bought it six years ago," Roger said. "The den is my creation." He gestured to the left of the eating area at the back of the kitchen.

Reece crossed the room and peeked through the door. A masculine space with a brown leather sofa, a heavy walnut desk, and plaid curtains. It didn't match the sleek, minimalistic design of either the front room or the kitchen. It also didn't fit Roger, who was a bit effeminate. He was a short man, maybe five-seven, with a slight build and blond hair styled just so. He wore expensive designer clothes and purple paisley socks. Last time Reece had seen Roger, the socks had been orange with white polka dots. Sock fetish aside, Roger reminded Reece of Niles Crane from the show *Frasier*. The resemblance was in part because Roger was a psychiatrist, but also because of his prissy appearance, persnickety mannerisms, and condescending tone.

Reece wandered back to the kitchen where Roger was fussing with an elaborate coffee machine. "It's amazing how similar your house is to Sam's loft," he said.

"Really?" Roger looked surprised and pleased.

"Haven't you been to her place?"

He shook his head. "In what way is it comparable?"

"The floors, paint colours, fixtures, stuff like that. How come you've never been to the loft?"

Roger shrugged. "Sam's protective of her space and privacy. She isn't fond of entertaining."

Correct on both counts. Still, it was peculiar she'd never invited one of her five childhood friends in the three years she'd lived there.

"Well, we'll have to have you over for dinner sometime," Reece said.

"What a delight it would be to partake in the culinary enchantments concocted by such a gifted chef. I dabble in the kitchen myself. Check out the steaks, they're in the fridge."

Resisting the urge to roll his eyes at Roger's highfalutin way of speaking, Reece opened the fridge and took in the array of expensive foodie delights. The three Wagyu sirloins were a thing of beauty.

"Geez, those must have set you back a few bills." He closed the fridge and accepted a mug of coffee.

"You can have two, if you have a large appetite. Regrettably, Jim isn't available to join us."

"That's too bad." Reece had been looking forward to hanging out with Jim without Lisa.

"There's imported white wine vinegar and fresh tarragon, if you can handle Béarnaise with sufficient technique to avoid breaking the sauce." Roger blew on his coffee. "Otherwise, I can execute it with ease."

Anything you can do, I can do better, Reece thought. It was childish, but he couldn't squash his growing distaste for the pompous, condescending man. Last time they'd met, Reece had had the same reaction to Roger but had decided to give him the benefit of the doubt. Seemed his first impression had been right.

In response to the suggestion of Béarnaise sauce, Reece landed a shot of his own. "Come on, only a novice would smother spectacular beef with a rich sauce."

"You think?" Roger shook his head with a smile, as if Reece's comment amused him. "Classically trained French chefs would beg to differ, but I suppose that's neither here nor there." He raised a perfectly groomed eyebrow. "From what Sam has said, you're a fine chef. It's a surprising observation, coming from her. I've never considered her to have a discerning palate or much interest in the culinary arts."

Reece wasn't getting into a pissing contest with Roger. He tried a different line of conversation. "So, how did you and Sam meet?"

"She attended school with my younger sister. Jim and I are six years older than Sam and Lisa," Roger said curtly, clearly not interested in the topic. "How about we start on the deck. You can let me know what you think of my new grill."

Grilling the steaks would take away some of the sting of having to suffer Roger's company. One of the drawbacks to living in a downtown loft was a lack of barbecue. Reece took his coffee and followed Roger outside.

Displayed on a cedar deck was a brand new barbecue—flashy cooking surface, gas and infrared burners, warming ovens, and a stainless steel woodchip smoker. Reece knew the price tag for the sleek grilling beauty was well over ten thousand dollars.

"What do you think?" Roger asked with a pensive gaze, as if he wasn't proud to own one of the best barbecues money could buy.

Pretentious and superfluous, Reece wanted to say, but instead replied, "It's something." He looked around, a little confused. "I thought you wanted to build a deck."

"That's right."

The large hexagonal deck, ringed with benches and stairs that led to a small garden, was pristine.

"What's wrong with this one?" Reece wasn't sure he wanted to hear the answer.

"Not a thing. You're tasked with constructing a lower deck on the grass."

"Tasked? You said you wanted *help*." Reece took a deep breath and tried to rein in his growing temper.

"Pish posh," Roger said dismissively, handing him a magazine. "It looks easy."

Reece studied the picture of the ground deck with elevated gardens in *Dream Decks and Patios*. It didn't look at all easy. "Do you have plans?"

Roger tapped the magazine picture with a manicured finger. "Right here."

"I can see the damn picture, Roger. I'm talking about building plans."

"A depiction suffices for talented carpenters. Don't you concur?"

"No, I don't," Reece retorted, his temper beginning to get the better of him.

Roger's expression implied that Reece was stupid and unreasonable. "Well, perhaps it's a project best left to a professional. There's no reason to become confrontational." His tone was one of exaggerated patience. "I was under the impression you could do it since you're a man's man." He dropped the magazine to the table and sat on a swanky teak patio chair.

The man clearly didn't want or need a new deck. It pissed Reece off that Roger had fabricated a ruse to get him over to the house. He was beginning to feel like he was the butt of a bad joke.

Reece remained standing. "I'm not being confrontational. I'm trying to understand what's going on here."

"Come now, you sound paranoid." Roger chuckled. "Nothing is going on. It's a beautiful day and I wanted to get to know you." He sipped from his coffee cup and winced. "Cold. Perhaps it's time for a beer. Shall we partake and get to know each other?"

"You said on the phone that you might need a PI someday," Reece said. "You want to tell me why?"

Did Roger's face pale? Reece wasn't sure, but something changed in the man's demeanour. Roger stood abruptly and fussed with a potted tulip plant on the table. His movements were flustered, but he'd lowered his head and Reece couldn't see his expression.

"It was a figure of speech," he said, without meeting Reece's eyes.

"Why am I here, Roger?" Reece didn't care that he sounded confrontational now. He couldn't tolerate lies and hated hypocrisy. Roger had some reason for inviting him, and Reece wanted to know what it was.

Wide eyes filled with earnestness met his steely gaze. "Well, I assumed you could assist. I'm afraid I'm more suited to intellectual pursuits." He glanced at his watch. "It's almost noon. Shall we grab a beer and grill those steaks? It would be sacrilege to waste Wagyu beef. I don't suppose you've ever tried it."

By his expression and tone, it was clear he thought *a man's man* ate squirrels and roadkill.

Reece walked across the deck to the back gate. "Thanks for the invitation, but I'm not staying."

Roger followed him. "Look, I'm sorry I've offended you. It wasn't my intention. I really do want to get to know you. Sam and I have been close friends since childhood. Please stay. You can initiate the grill and enlighten me on your gastronomic opinion."

Reece eyed the barbecue. He *was* itching to discover if it was worth the money. Those steaks had looked damn good, too.

"Please stay and we'll give this another try." Roger held out his hand.

It would be petty not to accept the apology. Might as well enjoy the luxury grill and the food. With a sigh, he shook Roger's hand. "Sure. What can I do to help?"

"How about you deal with the mushrooms you brought?" Roger suggested and went into the kitchen.

Unable to shake the feeling he had accepted the Judas kiss, Reece reluctantly followed.

Over the next half hour, they cooked and kept the conversation light. In spite of himself, Reece began to have fun. The man was brilliant, and Reece found his work in recovery interesting. The craft beers Roger had stocked were delicious, and he told Reece about some independent breweries around the Greater Toronto Area that offered tours.

Outside, the afternoon sun felt like June rather than early May, and the grill lived up to its reputation. Controlling the heat to get the proper char was easy and being able to transfer the meat to a reduced heat zone to obtain the perfect medium rare temperature was handy.

Roger set the outdoor table while Reece tented the steaks. As the meat rested, Roger grilled Romaine hearts for Caesar salad, and Reece finished the wild mushroom crostini with imported goat cheese. The food was fantastic, the day was beautiful, and Reece felt satisfied with his decision to stay.

The sun was hot, and Roger swiped his hair off his forehead, holding long bangs flat against the crown of his head. With his hairline exposed, Reece noticed a bandage over an ugly bruise.

"Ouch, what did you do to yourself?" he asked.

Roger looked startled and dropped his hand. He ran his fingers through the longish sweep of hair that covered the left side of his forehead. It fell into a perfect wave that Reece immediately suspected resulted from a curling iron.

"Nothing. I mean, just bumped my head getting out of a friend's car. No big deal. Let's get the table cleared and grab another beer."

Hitting his head might explain the cut on his forehead, but Reece had also noticed a nasty scrape on his elbow. The man clearly didn't want to talk about it, and it wasn't any of his business so Reece dropped it. He collected his plate and utensils from the table and followed Roger into the kitchen.

After they cleared the table and tidied the kitchen, they returned to the patio.

Reece was examining the labels of the craft beers that remained in the outside fridge when Roger asked, "If there's a home accident involving death, are police involved?"

Reece straightened, holding a bottle of coffee-flavoured ale in his hand. "Sure. Any time there's an unexpected death, police investigate." He took the bottle to the table and sat. "Did someone you know die?"

Roger shook his head. "No, I'm just curious. Sometimes I treat patients with severe survival guilt, you know, when there's a fatal accident. How intensely do the authorities investigate a home mishap?"

"They're very thorough. You'd be surprised how many accidents turn out to be something more nefarious."

Roger played with a teaspoon and chewed his lower lip. "Before that mess in Uthisca, how many murders did you investigate with the OPP?"

Canada had few serial killers and mass murders. After what had happened at Bueton Sanctuary two years ago, people frequently asked him similar questions. Roger didn't strike Reece as the type of person who would have such a macabre curiosity though.

"More than I care to remember," he replied obliquely and looked around for the bottle opener.

"So you have experience with police procedures in murder cases?"

Reece frowned. "Yes. Why do you ask?"

Roger dropped his eyes and picked a piece of lint off his slacks. "Just making conversation." He stood, walked to the back gate, and opened it. "Thanks for coming."

"Ah... no problem." Reece put the unopened beer on the table and dropped the opener. He stood and met Roger at the gate. "Lunch was great. Thanks for inviting me," he said, confused by the urgency to see him out.

"Next time," Roger said, "I'd prefer it if you parked on the street."

With that, the gate closed in his face, leaving Reece standing on the parking pad with his mouth half-open.

CHAPTER TWO

SAM

"DO I LOOK okay?" Reece asked.

Sam was watching *Better Call Saul* on Netflix and she glanced at Reece, who was standing at the base of the ladder staircase that led up to the bedroom loft. His sky-blue eyes were a little wild, and he was fidgeting with his belt. It was rare for Reece to be nervous. Instead of laughing, she turned off the television and stood to face him, twirling her finger with a grin. He frowned but spun around. His ass looked marvellous in his new jeans, the black T-shirt showed off impressive abdomen and bicep definition, and he'd had his thick black hair cut in a way that tamed the cowlick above his left eye. The crooked tooth in his otherwise straight white teeth was showing, and the dimple in his right cheek puckered when he smiled at her. Her partner in life and in business was amazing in every regard. Sam enjoyed a moment of smug self-satisfaction. Her mother would swoon.

Even the thought of her mother caused Sam to wince internally. How was she going to get through an entire evening with the woman? It didn't matter that other people would be at the party she and Reece were attending. Other people's presence did little to curb her mother's sharp tongue. In fact, an audience gave

Grace, who was anything but gracious, plenty of opportunities to make her daughter look like a troll. For over three years, Sam had cut her out of her life. Now she had to introduce the heinous woman to her fiancé. Thinking about the next few hours made her stomach roll with anxiety.

They'd planned to visit over Christmas, but Sam's stepfather had taken Grace to Europe to meet with an Alzheimer specialist. Since returning, Harvey and Reece had both been pestering her about the introduction. It was stupid to have ignored them. If she'd arranged to go over for a drink, they could have had a short visit and escaped. Instead, poor Reece would be stuck at a party all night with Grace telling nasty stories about what a miserable brat her daughter had been.

Since Lisa grew up next door and knew her family dynamics, going behind her back and inviting Grace and Harvey to the party was a crappy thing to do, In fact, everything Lisa was doing these days was shitty. Reece disliked her best friend, and Sam couldn't blame him. He'd never seen the warm, caring side of the beautiful Italian artist. This new Lisa was a stranger. It was as if an alien had transformed her childhood friend into an unrecognizable bitch.

The whole situation sucked and Sam was dreading the party. At least there was nothing negative Grace could say about Reece. Mother Dearest would love everything about him.

"Is it too much black?" he was asking, and she tried to focus on him rather than worrying about the hideous party. "Should I wear a button shirt? Maybe the T-shirt is too tight." Reece tugged at the sleeves and frowned.

Sam was about to tell him how fantastic he looked when her eyes fell on the watch he was wearing. His dad's Rolex never left the safe deposit box.

"You look great." She took his hand and ran the fingertips of her other hand across the face of the watch. "Your dad's watch looks great on you, too."

He licked his lips and swallowed. "Yeah, well, you know. Since I'm meeting your mother for the first time..."

She smiled. "You wanted a piece of your family with you."

"Stupid, eh?"

"Not at all," she said. "You know, your dad would be proud of you."

His face crinkled with distaste and he shook his head. "No, he wouldn't. On top of not finishing law school, I left the OPP." He turned away to pick up his jacket.

Dumb, dumb, dumb. Why hadn't she kept her mouth shut? His father had been a federal court judge, and, from what Lisa's lawyer husband had told her, Justice Hash had ranked judges followed by lawyers at the top of the law enforcement pack. Federal police, provincial police, and municipal police followed. PIs didn't rank at all. According to Justice Hash, they were useless organisms, slithering around in the muck, impeding intelligent people's attempts to avoid anarchy within the masses. Although he'd never said, Sam imagined a young Reece calling his father "My Lord" rather than "Dad."

"So, before we go, is there anything you need to tell me?" Reece asked.

Fair question. Last year, she'd told him her mother was dead. They had almost broken up when he discovered the truth—

well, that and a few other lies that blew up in her face. Sometimes late at night, she still woke in a cold sweat over how close she'd come to destroying their relationship.

"Yes. My mother is a bitch."

He laughed. "Something you *haven't* already told me."

She sighed. "With the exception of Talia, you've met everyone who'll be at the party, so no surprises there. Remember, Grace has a habit of using the Alzheimer's as an excuse to be mean. My stepfather told me last week she's had amazing success with a trial drug for early onset. Don't let her bamboozle you."

"Well, people change when they face serious illness." He picked up his phone and put it in his pocket. "I'm excited to meet her."

A nasty prickle of apprehension scurried up her neck. Evil people did not change but she held her tongue. "Remember your promise," she said instead.

The response was a dismissive hand gesture. "I'm the Starship Enterprise with a non-interference directive. I'm not going to try to force you to mend your relationship." He paused. "Even though it's important to sort through the pain. You don't want regrets."

Amazing how couples always circle back to the main personality difference between them. Reece was a "confront the past and work toward closure" personality. She was a "do it and be done with it" type. Time to change the subject.

"Be warned," she said. "Lisa has theme parties."

Reece went to the front door and held it open. "Geez, I hate those. Why can't adults get together to celebrate something without turning it into a kids' party?"

"Well, you said earlier that you're starving. You'll like the food. It'll be catered by some up-and-coming chef." She couldn't help rolling her eyes. "It always is at Lisa's parties. Me, I'd prefer burgers on the barbecue. I've never understood the purpose of things like micro-greens."

Reece laughed. "They're pretty. We eat with our eyes."

Sam picked up her keys and wandered around the loft, bending to give Brandy, their golden retriever, a pat.

"Stop dawdling," Reece said. "I'm activating the alarm. You have sixty seconds to get your butt out the door." He keyed in the code.

With a sigh, she shuffled over and he kissed the top of her head. "It won't be that bad. I'll protect you from your mother."

She wrapped her arms around his waist. "We could stay home and have alone time," she suggested, with what she hoped was a seductive smile. She wasn't good at seduction and wasn't surprised when he laughed at her.

"Fine," she said with a sigh. "Let's get this hell over with."

"THEY AREN'T COMING," Lisa announced the second they'd walked through the door of the High Park house. "So stop bitching at me for inviting a guest to my party without asking your permission."

From the corner of her eye, Sam caught the disappointment on Reece's face.

"Why not?" she asked.

"How should I know?" Lisa glanced at Reece with a sour expression and didn't acknowledge him.

Oh boy. This is going to be a fun evening.

"Hi Lisa, nice to see you." Reece leaned in and pecked her cheek. "Thanks for inviting us."

In lieu of a greeting, Lisa said, "It's an urban animal theme."

That explained the squirrel costume.

"Where's my gorgeous goddaughter?" Sam asked, peeking over Lisa's shoulder to the family room.

"Staying overnight with my brother and Janice. Kira wants you to take her to the zoo on Saturday," Lisa said. "Can you please call her? She doesn't understand why you aren't around." She shot Reece a scathing glare. "Her feelings are hurt."

"Sounds fun," she said, ignoring Lisa's guilt trip. "So long as it's just me and Kira."

Typically, Lisa's sister-in-law pawned her three little monsters off on Lisa. Sam always referred to her friend as having "kids"— plural rather than singular—and she wasn't fond of Lisa's nephews. She wasn't taking them to the zoo, where they would wreak havoc and she wouldn't be able to corral them. On the other hand, she adored her five-year-old goddaughter. She wasn't keen about gawking at animals trapped in cages outside their natural habitats, but maybe she could coax Kira into staying around the petting zoo and stuffing her chubby cheeks with treats.

More guests had arrived and Reece was speaking to an owl. Because of the costume, Sam couldn't tell who it was and wandered into the living room. Lisa had decorated it as a city park. A woodland mural hung against the long wall that divided the front room from the formal dining room, and a couple of inflatable trees sat beside papier mâché rocks. Cheap synthetic grass covered the gorgeous Persian carpet. It was ridiculous, but Sam couldn't help but laugh when she spied a park bench covered with graffiti.

In jarring contrast with the childish party decorations, formal servers dressed in black pants and starched white shirts strolled around the room with trays of hors d'oeuvres. A bartender operated a corner bar that displayed a vast assortment of booze, and catering staff was setting up an elaborate buffet in the dining room. The big prime rib roast was a welcome sight. Sam always feared that one of Lisa's avant-garde chefs would reveal some disgusting delicacy, such as bull penis.

She chatted with a chipmunk, a bat, two birds, and a deer. The chipmunk was already drunk, and Sam didn't blame him. None of the urban animals looked happy.

When she returned to the entry to fetch Reece, she found him holding two paper bags.

In answer to her unasked question, he dolefully said, "Costumes."

Lisa popped her head back into the hallway. "I rented them because I knew you wouldn't. You can change upstairs." Her tone was judgemental when she added, "I'm sure your boyfriend is dying for a drink." With that, she flounced away with her bushy tail wagging behind her.

"Is there a reason Lisa thinks I'm an alcoholic?" Reece asked. "Every time I see her, she implies I drink too much."

Reece didn't drink much and the comment wasn't about him. "Her dad was an alcoholic," she told him. "She's sensitive around people she doesn't know well and booze."

"Then she shouldn't serve it at parties." He tugged her into the corner of the stairwell. "Why did she rent us costumes?"

"It's just in fun." Sam kept her tone cheery.

His jaw jutted out stubbornly. "We're not five years old. I'm not wearing a bloody costume."

"Abigail and Talia aren't here yet, and Talia won't wear a costume." She flicked the brown bag. "If you don't want to wear it, it's not a big deal. At least take a look, okay?"

"Is Roger here?" Reece asked.

She shrugged. "Not that I noticed, why?"

"I am a little curious to see that fusspot in a costume." He grinned at her.

She laughed and led him up the stairs to the bedrooms.

In the guest room, he handed her the bag with her name on it and opened his own.

Slowly, he extracted a black costume. "At least it matches my clothes." He turned the fabric over in his hand. He froze and his eyes widened.

"What? What is it?"

He held it out but she couldn't tell.

Once he turned it around to face her, she felt her own eyes widen.

"Oh."

A long white stripe ran down the back of the black jumpsuit from the collar to the tip of a fluffy tail.

Reece dropped it on the bed. "I'm not wearing it," he said with a composed tone but ugly expression.

It took her a minute to figure out what her brown suit with the white front was. When the animal came to mind, her cheeks flushed with anger.

Reece's expression shifted to curiosity. "Well, what is it?"

"It's... a weasel."

He burst into laughter.

There was a knock on the door, and Sam yanked it open to find Jim the coyote and Roger the raccoon standing forlorn on the other side.

"I'm not wearing it," Reece told Jim.

Jim draped a paw across Reece's shoulder. "It's over the top, I'll give you that. I warned Lisa, but, when she gets an idea, she's a pit bull with a kitten locked in its jaws."

"What did you get?" Roger asked Sam as he tugged at the neck of his raccoon sweater.

"A weasel."

Roger's groomed eyebrow rose. "An oblique metaphor perchance?"

"Of course it is." Reece waved his hands at the costumes. "She specifically chose these. It's an insult."

"You're reading too much into this," Jim said in his persuasive courtroom voice. "You don't have to wear it. My wife has taken the theme too far. It was poor judgement, not a personal attack. Come on, let's get a drink."

Sam wasn't positive it was unintentional. She ran the weasel costume through her fingers before dropping it to the bed beside Reece's skunk.

Roger put his hand on her shoulder. "A word before you go, Sam."

"Sure."

After Reece left with Jim, Roger said, "I'm concerned about Lisa. She's acting very disagreeable."

"I know."

He fussed with his raccoon gloves. "It started five months ago, after their Christmas party. That's also when I became aware of the way she interacts with Reece. Lisa doesn't like him." He picked up the skunk costume. "This is her way of driving home her point. Did something happen between them?"

Before she could answer, someone started to shout obscenities from downstairs. It sounded like Talia, but Sam wasn't sure. Alarmed, she followed Roger downstairs. The front door was wide open, and Talia was in the entry, looming over Lisa. Talia's face was a mask of rage, and Lisa was screaming at her but wasn't making any sense. Something about not knowing and how it wasn't her fault.

Party guests stood in the doorway between the front foyer and the living room. Everyone wore shocked expressions, and it stunned Sam to see a few of the women crying. Reece exited the bathroom, looking confused by the crowd of people in the entry.

When Talia saw Reece, she pushed Lisa aside. What Sam glimpsed in the soldier's eyes terrified her. Not understanding what was going on, she immediately felt a need to protect Reece and stood between him and her friend.

"It was you!" Talia screamed at Reece. "All those walks around the city. You sick motherfucker."

Jim wrapped his arms around Talia. He was crying. Even as kids, Sam had never seen Jim cry. A ribbon of fear unravelled in her stomach, and a sharp cramp nearly doubled her over. Something had happened. Something terrible.

"I promise it wasn't me, and it wasn't Reece," Jim said. "You're distraught. Let us help you."

"How could you do this to me, Talia?" Lisa yelled through tears. "How could you say such a terrible thing to me?"

Someone had shut off the music. Stunned servers stood stationary among the sobbing guests.

Sam grabbed Lisa's upper arm. "What's going on?"

"It's Abigail." Lisa's voice trembled. "She's dead."

"What? How?" Sam's eyes darted between Lisa and Talia. Shock prevented her from accepting what she'd just heard. "When? I don't understand."

"She was pregnant!" Talia screamed, fighting against Jim's grip. "She killed herself."

Sam couldn't breathe. Her chest felt tight, and there was a ringing in her ears. She slid down the wall and landed with a thump on the floor. Reece rushed to her side, helped her up, and gripped her shoulders, forcing her to look up at him.

His voice was calm—a cop's voice. "I'm so sorry, Sam. But you know Abby and I were never together that way."

"She was afraid of men!" Talia screamed. "You're the only men she'd ever trust. One of you knows who violated her!"

Lisa's face drained of colour. She was gripping Roger's hand so tightly he was wincing.

"I know it wasn't you," Sam whispered to Reece. "Get rid of everyone. Get them out of here."

He nodded and left to herd people to the door. Jim dragged Talia into his office. Lisa followed and slammed the door closed behind her.

Sam leaned against the wall, clamping an iron fist around the pain and shock. She'd known something was wrong. Abigail had always been fragile, and Talia's second deployment had crushed her. The signs of depression were so obvious now.

Talia's accusations still ringing in her ears, her eyes fell on Roger, sitting on the stairs with his face in his hands. Roger had offered to counsel Abigail four months ago. Disgust and anger took the place of the pain.

No, he wouldn't. He couldn't have.

But he had before. Years ago, he'd taken advantage of a patient. She'd seen it with her own eyes. He'd lost objectivity and had given in to his attraction, harming his patient in the process. This time it wasn't just a patient. It was Abigail, whom he'd known for nearly three decades. Why would he develop feelings for her now?

It's a symptom of physician burnout, a voice whispered in her head. *Just like last time.*

Reece's voice drew her from her miserable thoughts. "Babe, Lisa asked that we leave. Jim is trying to talk to Talia and thinks it's best if everyone goes."

"I never attended Abigail's performance," she said. "I didn't see her dance with The National Ballet. Now I'll never see her dance again."

"I know."

Tears burned behind her eyes and she pushed him to the door. "Go, I need a minute."

Reece went outside, and Sam turned to stare at Roger.

His expression was cold as his pale blue eyes held hers. "Accuse me again, Sam, I'll ruin you."

CHAPTER THREE

REECE

TWO DAYS HAD passed since Abigail's funeral, a week since the terrible news. It was two-thirty in the afternoon, and Sam was in bed. The amount she slept worried Reece. She hadn't cried in front of him, not once. That scared him. Out of desperation, he'd dropped by Roger's house to ask for help. All he suggested was to listen and not to push her in a direction she wasn't ready to go. Sam needed to process the grief and work through the steps, Roger had said.

The fact that the psychiatrist was a mess didn't instill confidence. Something about Roger's attitude during the short visit made Reece suspicious. It didn't feel like grief so much as fear, but he didn't know the man well enough to judge.

Reece didn't know where Talia was. She'd refused to speak to any of them at the funeral. Cocooned in a shell of anger and grief, the soldier had stood dry-eyed at parade rest during the service. At the end, she'd accepted the ashes without a word and left.

Reece was having his own issues dealing with the suicide. He should have recognized Abigail's desperation and done something. Intellectually, he understood that suicide was a personal choice that had little to do with anyone else. He'd called a friend at Toronto Police Services and asked for a copy of the Coroner's findings, and Abigail's autopsy report had driven home the deliberation behind her act.

She'd slit the inside of both forearms from the heel of her hand to her elbow. There were no tentative, hesitant cuts. The toxicology report noted a high amount of acetylsalicylic acid in her blood. In addition to consuming Aspirin over the course of several weeks to thin her blood, she'd killed herself in a bathtub filled with warm water to increase exsanguination. She'd been nineteen weeks pregnant.

The day before her death, Abigail had packed all her clothes, sorted out her personal belongings, and called Goodwill to pick up everything. She had sold her car two weeks before she died and transferred all her money into a co-signatory account she shared with Talia. Their condo was spotless, and Abigail had paid all the bills. She closed her social media and email accounts. Although she'd wiped and formatted her computer, police IT specialists recovered the hard drive and found nothing of interest. On the bathroom sink was a copy of a life insurance policy and her will, which she'd had drawn up a month before her death. In the document, she listed the funeral home she'd chosen and had settled the account for her service and cremation. In death, as in life, Abigail hadn't wanted to be a bother. Everything about her suicide fit Abigail's meticulous, considerate nature to a T. Everything except for one detail that Reece could not understand—why hadn't she left Talia a note?

The hardest part for Reece was that he couldn't talk to anyone about his feelings. Sam and her friends had known Abigail since kindergarten. In his mind, their grief took precedence over his own—he'd known her for six short months.

The one-thousand-square-foot loft felt like a prison cell. The walls were closing in on him. Brandy hadn't had a decent walk for days, and they would both benefit from getting outside. As Reece attached the leash, the old dog gazed up at him with mournful eyes.

"We're going to get through this, girl," he promised. But he wasn't sure, and Brandy's head tilt and droopy tail suggested that she wasn't sure either.

After a long walk, he felt a bit better. As he approached the door to the loft, a long-haired man came down the hall wearing a kimono style robe and a tattered pair of slippers. His eyes were glassy and he stunk of pot.

"Hey man, this your crib?"

"Yeah, why?"

"Got a piece of mail for you. We had a gig in Detroit. Just got back." He handed Reece a thick, creamy envelope.

Reece thanked him and went inside, hoping Sam would be up and doing something—anything.

She wasn't. He checked and found her asleep. Strawberry-blond curls stuck to her damp forehead. When he ran his fingers across her cheeks, he felt tears and it broke his heart that she was crying in her sleep.

Back in the kitchen, he glanced at the envelope addressed to him and tried to think of anyone he knew who was getting married. The weight of the stationery implied it was an invitation. No return address on the front. He turned it over. The back was blank. He tore it open, didn't recognize the handwriting on the letter, and flipped to the last page. His heart stopped and he fell into a chair. Slowly, he shuffled the sheets to the first page. The date on the top was the day before Abigail had killed herself.

Dear Reece,

Thank you for your kindness. For how you never forced me to talk. How you never asked questions or offered advice. How you never touched me, not even gently on my arm. You never made me feel broken. I want you to know how much I looked forward to our Saturday morning market trips and our walks around the city. For those few hours, I was able to forget and to live again.

You are a sweet man, the only man I ever met who never asked for anything from me. You are an accepting man, a man whose personal journey will allow him to understand that my death was inevitable. And so I write to you because these words will not destroy you.

My death will hurt Sam. She will entomb the pain in layers of brick, but acid will erode the stone until her heart is hard with poison. Promise you won't surrender to her attempts to drive you away, for she loves you and that love frightens her because it makes her vulnerable. You are her salvation and she is yours. Your souls entwine. Please do not give up on each other. Love is a tangled root that twists through the soil in search of nutrients, but it is the foundation of the tree of life.

My shame is no longer a burden too heavy to carry. It's a palpable entity. The heartbeat relentlessly hammers at me like a hundred drums that beat to placate a vengeful god. The persistent pounding drives me forward to the lips of the abyss. My world has become microscopic, constricting me with bleakness until even dancing has become unbearable. I see only black and crimson when I close my eyes now. I hear only Satan howl as his demons call me over, but I will never break through their line to find peace again.

Unimaginable horrors haunt my dreams, and I understand that, be it on this earth or be it in a different dimension, hell is my destiny. But here on earth, Talia must bear witness. I will not damn my love to stand wretched and consumed by her impotency. With the last of my strength, I will prevent her from pursuing me through the darkness. This is the kindest thing I can do. This is the greatest gift I can offer.

My skin burns from the caress of his hands. I can't wash the stench of his body from my flesh. At night, I feel his seed inside me and know I'm damned. It was a single second of unbearable loneliness—a tiny moment when my desire to experience something beyond despair ascended in defiance. But I cannot look at the horror through a victim's eyes this time. I was complacent and I am culpable. I will forever exist behind the silhouette of iniquity, where the light of forgiveness can never reach.

I implore you and Sam to help Talia. She must live and learn to find joy in life. You and Sam survived great tragedy. You both found your way through perdition's maze. And so I beseech you to revisit the abyss to save my love. Pull Talia from the banks of hell and bring her home. Do everything within your power to give her what she needs to find peace.
With my everlasting gratitude,
Abigail

Reece read the letter three times, shielding it from his tears. The flowery prose that matched Abigail's love of poetry again showed Reece the determination and planning she had put into her suicide. Now, he thought he might understand why she hadn't written to Talia. Shame over cheating on her girlfriend had made it impossible. Abigail was asking an objective observer to help her beloved girlfriend understand that shame.

A red mist coated his eyes when his sorrow inexplicably morphed to rage. Some bastard had defiled his friend. Some bastard had betrayed Talia while she served the country.

"What's that?"

Sam's voice caused him to jump, and he snatched the pages from the table.

She sat and studied him. A ring of red lined her swollen eyes, and her freckles were brash spots of colour on a face that was gaunt.

He didn't know what to do, didn't know if he should give her the letter or if it would make things worse. When she plucked the thick envelope from the table, he realized the decision wasn't his to make. Abigail had made it for him. The only way he could help Sam would be to allow her to read her friend's final words.

Sam gazed at the writing on the front. Her throat worked and she blinked rapidly. She stared at him with naked desperation, her eyes wide and her pain etching deep furrows in her forehead.

She threw the envelope on the floor, and her eyes dropped to the sheets of paper he clutched in his fist. "I can't read it. I won't read it. Don't ask me."

He took her hand to prevent her from bolting from the table. "I'm not asking you," he said. "Abigail is."

For a moment, she didn't move. Her face became a battleground between her desire to hold onto her friend and her implacable grief that commanded she protect herself from further pain.

"I could read it to you," he offered, sliding his chair over so he could wrap his arms around her and pull her close.

She leaned her head against his shoulder. They sat together in silence, and Brandy put her snout on Sam's leg, whimpering in sympathy.

Her throat worked as she repeatedly swallowed, fighting tears. She pulled away and sat rigid on the chair with her shaking hands clasped tight in her lap. "I need to do this alone," she whispered. "I need you to leave. Please."

Slowly, he stood and shuffled to the door. Leaving her alone and in pain was the hardest thing he'd ever had to do.

CHAPTER FOUR

REECE

REECE AND BRANDY returned an hour later. No Sam, but a wrinkly mess of creamy stationery was on the table. She had apparently crumpled the pages into a ball, then reconsidered and smoothed them out. The ink had run in places from her tears. The crystal vase from the kitchen island was shattered. Scattered among the shards of glass were bruised hydrangea blossoms. But he heard the shower running in the ensuite bathroom in the bedroom loft above him. And Florence and the Machine played from wireless speakers hidden in the ceiling throughout the thousand-square-foot loft.

Sam's laptop was on the table. She'd retyped Abigail's letter in Word, highlighted phrases, and added comments in the margin. Beside *I hear only Satan howl as his demons call me over, but I will never break through their line to find peace again* was more than just a comment. A whole paragraph read:

Abigail hated red rover. She'd cringe beside me on the playground, terrified they'd call her name. The boys targeted her because she was so tiny. They could always get through the line at her point of defence. The public school banned the game after an asshole broke Abby's arm when he charged through her. The school suspended Jim for a week because he beat the snot out of him. Lisa said it was the moment she realized she'd marry Jim someday. In her speech at their wedding, Abby said she'd break every bone if it meant her friends found true love.

Reece hadn't realized that Abigail's reference in the letter was about the game red rover. The first and last time he'd tried out for high school football in grade nine, the coach had used red rover to pick linebackers. It had been a humiliating experience. Reece hadn't made the cut and had taken the walk of shame off the field with a broken thumb.

Sam had refused to speak at the funeral, saying she didn't want to remember anything—the good or the bad. She'd out-right banned Reece from speaking Abigail's name again. That pitiful paragraph of type, recounting a mixture of good and bad memories, signified hope. To Reece, it meant that Sam was ready to face her grief.

When she came down the ladder staircase from the elevated bedroom suite, she looked better. Not great, but better. At least she was dressed. Her curly hair was wet, and her T-shirt showed off the hours she spent in the gym.

In the kitchen, she put a T-Disc in the Tassimo and some bread in the toaster. When her coffee and toast were ready, she crossed the room to the living space that ran in front of the floor-to-ceiling windows on the south wall.

"Tell me everything you know," she said curtly.

He frowned.

She patted the seat beside her on the leather sofa. "Don't lie. I know you. You've spoken to your police friends and read the in-vestigation reports. Tell me everything."

By the time he'd finished, her coffee and toast were gone.

"I have to tell you something," she said. "I didn't tell you before because I wanted you to form your own impression. Regardless, because you're so anal over honesty, you're going to consider it a lie."

"You had a relationship with Roger Peterson and bought the house in Cabbagetown with him," he stated.

She looked stunned. "He told you?"

"No. I figured it out a couple of days after I went to his house to help him with a deck he didn't have any intention of building."

"How?"

"Because the decor is the same as in here. Roger told me he bought the place six years ago but only decorated the den. You designed this loft three years ago, but you finished your master's degree six years ago. You never said where you lived for the other three years, and since you loathe your mother, I figured it wasn't with her and Harvey."

"Well, look at you, Sherlock Holmes. Still, that's not much to go on," she said. "You must have had other clues."

He laughed and it felt wonderful. He was enjoying the admiration on her face. Sam herself was a damn fine investigator.

"Have I ever mentioned how impressive the stain is on the hemlock flooring?" Reece crossed his legs and leaned against the back of the sofa. "I took a picture and a contractor told me it's tough to get this shade of grey without the red in the wood ruining it. He said it was a remarkable feat." He chuckled at her expression. "Roger's floor is the same custom colour."

Reece gestured to the L-shaped kitchen in the northeast corner of the open space. "Your glass and stainless backsplash is unique. Art, in fact. It's your design. The one in his kitchen isn't identical, but it's close. Then there's the Carrara marble. Marble isn't practical in a heavily used kitchen. It doesn't hold up well under rigorous chopping. You didn't care. Remember last year when I moved in and you told me it was a 'decoration to be appreciated but never used'?"

Her smile widened and she flopped against the back of the sofa. "And Roger thinks he's a gourmet chef. He'd never pick marble. Is that it?"

"Also the way Roger kept one-upping me when I was over and the condescending way he tried to put the country bumpkin in his place. Based on his posturing alpha behaviour, I assume you left him."

He raised his eyebrow, knowing her well enough not to ask for details. After coming close to breaking up last year because she'd lied about her past, he'd learned to give her space. People had different comfort zones.

"Oh yeah." Her nose crinkled with dislike. "It was the day after I killed the Crips gang member who shot my partner. You know about that."

He did. The shooter had been fifteen and supported by gangbangers, but the public outcry that followed a Toronto police officer killing a boy wasn't pretty.

"The Internal Affairs investigation wrecked me," she said. "I went home in tears and found Roger in bed with a patient. We had a terrible fight. I left, resigned from Police Services, and the rest is history."

"A patient?" he sputtered.

She nodded. "Yup. From his point of view, it wasn't a breach of ethics because he'd referred her to another psychiatrist."

"That's ridiculous and self-serving," Reece said. "He should have lost his licence to practise medicine."

"Well, I reported him to the College of Physicians, but it was his first complaint and they didn't rule it as an ethics breach. They felt Roger suffered from burnout and mandated counselling. It took him a long time to forgive me for making an official complaint that could have destroyed his career. In hindsight, I reacted the way I did because I was angry. It wasn't one of my proudest moments."

Reece didn't care if personal reasons had motivated her complaint. A doctor who took advantage of a patient didn't deserve to hold a medical licence. Period.

"What happened to the woman?" he asked.

"Her name was Heather. They dated for about four months. She was a chef and went to France." She paused and looked away. "That was after she attempted suicide twice."

A question had been weighing on him since reading Abigail's letter. "Roger treated Abigail for a while, correct?"

Her eyes were grim. "Yes, and I wondered the same thing but it doesn't make sense." The music had stopped and she glanced at the audio system. "Can you pick another CD?"

Instead, he found her iPod and put it on the docking station. Alter Bridge's album *Blackbird* was first in the queue, and Myles Kennedy's voice streamed through the wireless speakers.

When he sat back on the sofa, Sam was chewing on the corner of her lip, tapping her fingertips against her knee. "Roger treated Abigail as a little sister. A broken little sister, after what happened when she was sixteen."

Reece knew Abigail had been a victim of a violent crime. He assumed it involved a man—sadistic crimes against women usually did—but he didn't know the details. "What happened to her?"

Sam lowered her eyes and her lips thinned. After a few moments, she looked up. "It was summer fourteen years ago. There was a street party," she said. "Our families all lived on Vero Beach. It's sort of a boot-shaped boulevard along the Humber River and a cliquey little community. Everyone attended the party—Jim's and Lisa's families, my folks, Talia, and her parents and brother. Jim, Roger, his older sister, and my sister were all home from university. You know that Jim and Roger are six years older than us, right?"

Reece nodded. At first, it had excited him that Roger and Jim were the same age as he was. He figured they'd have a lot in common. That was before he had gotten to know Roger.

Her voice was wistful when she continued. "The girls and I were sixteen, and we wanted to drink. Roger and Jim were twenty-two and could have gone to the liquor store, but Roger coaxed Abigail into sneaking home to steal a bottle of vodka from her parents' bar. Around the same time, although none of us knew it yet, a group of men had been breaking into houses. Five men. They were in her house." She gazed into the distance and fiddled with her empty coffee mug. "They raped her. All of them."

Reece had figured it was something along those lines, but the depravity of gang rape shocked him. "Did they catch them?"

She nodded. "Dad swore he'd never stop hunting and he didn't. He caught the last one a month before he died. Abby had just turned twenty-one."

"I'm so sorry." Reece pulled her into his arms.

"Talia never left her side. Abby stayed in hospital for three months. They beat her, raped her, and sodomized her." Sam's voice filled with hate. "Broken bones and internal injuries. Excruciating operations and cosmetic surgeries. Doctors said she'd never dance again. But she did. The pain must have been unbearable." She lowered her eyes and picked at a thread on her jeans. "I always felt she wanted the physical pain as punishment because she'd planned to steal the booze. Her parents and their rabbi couldn't get her to understand that what happened wasn't her fault."

"Were Abigail and Talia a couple back then?" Reece asked.

"I don't know. I mean I knew they were gay, but they never said anything so I never talked to them about it. None of my business. After high school, Abigail stayed in Toronto to study dance and Talia attended Royal Military College in Kingston. When the military posted her to CFB Petawawa, an hour outside Ottawa, Abigail moved in with her. Truth is I don't know much about Talia's military career. She was a sniper at one time, but not now. I know she's with the Canadian Special Operations Regiment. Abby told me Talia's goal is to get to Syria. She has extremely strong feelings around stopping ISIS."

Reece knew enough about the armed forces to know that CANSOFCOM were highly trained military personnel responsible for responding to terrorism and threats to Canadians. Talia would have to be one hell of a soldier to be part of the regiment.

How was he supposed to help a woman like that deal with her lover's suicide?

"How'd they end up with the condo downtown?" he asked.

"Abigail came home when Talia was deployed overseas about five years ago. Last year, The National Ballet accepted her, and Talia wanted her to be close to the Four Seasons Centre for the Performing Arts." She looked sad. "It bothered Abigail that they were separated so much."

Reece saw the many layers of Abigail's life that could have driven her to such a desperate choice as suicide. What he couldn't see was how to honour her wish and help Talia, a woman he'd never even met before the party.

He put his elbows on his knees and rubbed the palms of his hands against his face. "I don't know what to do about that." He looked up and pointed at the letter on the kitchen table. "How can I possibly help Talia?"

Sam squeezed his hand and stood. "By asking her what she needs. We're going to show her the letter."

Reece wasn't sure that was a good idea. Abigail would have written it to her girlfriend had she wanted Talia to read it. He stood but didn't move.

Sam wrapped her arm around his waist. "I know why you're concerned, but trust me on this. I know Talia well."

Releasing him, she picked up the letter and tucked it into the pocket of her hoodie. At the front door, she bent to tug on her sneakers.

Reluctantly, he followed. "Do you know where she is?"

"I know where she'll be in an hour. I texted and asked her to meet us for an early dinner."

When she straightened and faced him, her green eyes blazed with anger and her expression was determined. "Talia thinks you're the father. This letter proves you aren't. And we're going to find the son of a bitch who was."

CHAPTER FIVE

SAM

WHEN THEY ENTERED the restaurant in Greektown on Danforth Avenue at Pape, the owner rushed over with a huge smile.

Sam raised her hand before he could engulf her in a bear hug, which—she knew from experience—he'd follow with wet smacks on each cheek.

"So good to see you," the man gushed, and the sincerity was genuine. He grasped her hand in both paws and smooched each of her cheeks.

From her fifth birthday until his death nine years ago, her father had taken her to eat at the restaurant once a month. All her favourite childhood memories included the red bar with the hidden lights and the wood-beam, stucco walls of the quaint Greek restaurant.

"I'm starved," she told Obasi and was surprised to find it was true. Her appetite had returned.

"Excellent." He snagged the arm of a passing server. "Tirokafteri on table 15, please." He turned back to Sam with a broad smile. "Dolmadakia to start, followed by Exohiko, yes?"

Just like Pavlov's dog, her mouth watered at the image of grape leaves stuffed with ground beef and rice, smothered in hot, whipped lemon sauce. Exohiko—chicken, peppers, tomatoes, feta and graviera cheese, wrapped in filo pastry—had been her go-to dish as a child.

Obasi clapped Reece on the shoulder and spoke in rapid Greek, chuckling at the end and winking at Sam.

Reece, who didn't speak Greek, stood nodding with a bemused smile.

They crossed the restaurant to the same table Sam had sat at with her father on the third Saturday of every month for sixteen years. Beside her Reece muttered, "Every time Obasi speaks to me in Greek, I fear I'm agreeing to something awful."

Sam laughed. "That's why he does it."

"Not because he thinks I'm Greek?" He threw a baleful glance over his shoulder.

She tucked her hand into the crook of his arm. "Not with your baby blue eyes."

Sam took the seat in the corner so she could watch the door. Heads turned as Talia entered the restaurant, glanced around, and marched to their table. Everything about the military officer was intimidating. She was a five-foot-eleven, muscular Black woman with a regal posture and short-cropped hair that highlighted her elegant cheekbones. Today she was wearing a crisp white T-shirt, a pair of jeans, and short-heeled black boots. No makeup or jewelry, but the metal chain of her dog tags was visible around her neck. As usual, her face showed no discernible emotion.

Talia pulled out a chair. "Why am I here?" Her tone was frosty.

Without ceremony, Sam put the letter on the table. Unfolded, so Talia could see the handwriting.

Her eyes widened, but her neutral expression remained in place. While she read her lover's final words, a tiny vein throbbed in her smooth forehead.

"Excuse me." Talia stood, pushed in her chair, and walked to the front of the restaurant where stairs led up to the bathrooms.

After ten minutes, Reece asked, "Think you should check on her?"

"No."

The server brought platters with tendrils of steam rising from the fragrant food. Starved, Sam dug in without ceremony and grabbed a stuffed grape leave. She closed her eyes in pleasure as she chewed.

Another ten minutes passed before Talia returned. Her eyes were dry, but bloodshot.

"We ordered," Sam said. "Help yourself."

"No thank you." Talia's face showed nothing but placid interest when she locked eyes with Reece and asked, "Why do you think she picked you to write to?"

He finished his mouthful of food, put down his fork, and shrugged. Sam was proud that he held Talia's eyes. "Because I'm not historically connected to your group is my guess."

Keeping her attention fixed on Reece, Talia spoke in a robotic monotone that did little to hide the pain that radiated from her like the steam that had risen from the food. "You aren't the father. Do you know who was?"

He shook his head.

"What did you and Abigail talk about when you went to the market and on those walks?"

"Sometimes she'd talk about food and television series." He took a sip of his beer, and Sam could tell he was struggling with his own grief. Under the table, she took his hand.

"She liked *Fortitude*," Reece said. "Thought the Arctic Circle scenery was amazing." He cleared his throat and reached for his beer again.

Talia continued to stare at him. "Will you honour her wish?"

He answered without hesitation, but Sam detected a flicker of doubt in his eyes when they darted to her face. "Yes. What do you need?"

Talia ignored him and turned to Sam. "Do you think Roger's the father?" she asked directly. "He has a history of poor decisions when it comes to attractive patients. When I left for the Middle East, he was counselling Abigail twice a week." There was no accusation in her tone, but the cold expression was probably the same as in the days when she'd peered through the scope of her sniper rifle.

"I don't think he would betray you and hurt Abigail that way," Sam said.

"Roger is an arrogant man," Talia stated dispassionately. "Egotistical men do things for their own pleasure. Conquering a lesbian, as he would see it, would be quite an achievement for him."

"But Roger would have to face the consequences," Sam said. "What you're describing is someone who could walk away and never see Abigail again."

Talia held her eyes. "Remember what he did to his sister years ago. It isn't unusual for Roger to act without considering the consequences."

Sam was aware of Roger's low impulse control and bursts of anger. Still, that weakness had nothing to do with what happened to Abby. She just couldn't see him seducing Abigail behind Talia's back.

"Could it be a man she met through ballet?" Sam asked. "Did she ever mention anyone?"

Talia didn't answer. Instead, she asked, "Do you know Roger's a person of interest in a police investigation?"

Sam frowned. They hadn't read the papers for a few days or watched the news. "Why?"

"A man, Graham Harris, an ex-Argonauts player, died in what authorities first thought to be an accidental mishap." Talia took out her phone, looked something up, and passed the device to Sam. "Now it's a murder investigation."

Sam read the article and handed Reece the cell.

Mr. Harris had died at home, trying to fix a faultily wired sump-pump in his flooded basement. Authorities believed his death had resulted from electrocution when he failed to kill the power to the receptacle, but the autopsy revealed suspicious circumstances. The article didn't list the evidence. It only reported that York Regional Police were treating it as a homicide and that the wife was acquainted with Dr. Roger Peterson, the famous self-help author. Mrs. Harris was catatonic and hospitalized.

"What's Roger's involvement?" Reece asked, handing Talia the phone.

"Given the fact that Brenda Harris is catatonic, I suspect she suffers mental health issues. Roger is probably her psychiatrist." Talia held Sam's eyes. "Does Reece know about your past relationship with Roger and what happened with his patient a few years ago?"

Sam nodded, annoyed that Talia asked in front of Reece.

"We can agree that Dr. Peterson has a history of inappropriate behaviour with attractive female patients. Now, Abigail is dead and Brenda's husband is dead," Talia stated. "I want to know why the police are speaking with Roger."

Frankly, so did Sam. She was curious why Roger hadn't called and sought her advice about being involved in a homicide. "The staff inspector of homicide is the brother of Reece's friend." She turned to him. "Can you talk to Bryce and see if he'll show you any love?

"Sam, I doubt he'll speak to me about an active investigation, especially one outside his jurisdiction." The look in Reece's eyes was a silent plea to drop it.

"Since he's trying to recruit you for his squad, he might." She didn't like pushing him, but she liked the anger in her friend's eyes less.

Reece turned to Talia. "Can you tell me what you hope to accomplish?"

"If he's involved, it will give me leverage."

"For what?"

"A paternity test."

She wanted to know who the baby's father was. Sam didn't blame her. "Have you asked him to do the test?"

"He refused."

Not good, but Sam knew Roger well. He'd refuse out of principle, not necessarily out of guilt. And Talia wouldn't have asked, she would have ordered. Roger did not deal well with controlling people. Since his IQ exceeded one fifty-five, his assumption was correct: he was the smartest person he knew. What Roger didn't recognize was that his information-focused personality hindered his social skills. Roger was a rude son of a bitch, in addition to being a pompous ass. During her years of psychology studies, Sam had discovered that many brilliant psychiatrists shared the same flaw, which was a weird paradox in a profession that required talking to patients.

"I suppose he was angry you asked," she ventured.

"Very." Talia turned to Reece, her tone softening just perceptibly. "Abigail trusted you to help me. This is what I'm asking, and you said you'd honour her dying wish."

Disquietude shadowed Reece's eyes while he fiddled with a teaspoon. Sam suspected that he didn't want to get involved because he feared he wasn't objective. She didn't blame him. But the only way Talia would find peace was with the assurance that a friend wasn't culpable in Abigail's suicide.

Finally, Reece said quietly, "I'll see what I can find out."

Talia smiled but it was faint and tinged with sadness. "I owe you an apology. My conduct at the party was unacceptable." She held out her hand and Reece shook it. "The letter is yours, but I'd like to keep it. It's important to me."

Reece nodded and she picked up the letter, stroking the writing on the envelope. "I picked this life. Abigail didn't. It isn't easy for the ones you leave behind. I would have forgiven her, if she'd only told me."

Sam reached for her hand. "I know."

Talia squeezed her fingers and her eyes filled with tears. "Thank you." She stood, again tucking her chair under the table. She crossed the restaurant and they watched until she disappeared through the door.

"I don't like this, Sam. It feels like a witch hunt," Reece said.

"I know, but we don't have an option."

"Why?"

"Because I know Talia," she said. "If we don't find out what's going on in the Harris investigation, I suspect she'll leak Abigail's pregnancy and her association with the famous Dr. Peterson to the press, while implying he had a connection to another patient's murdered husband. Abigail was a National Ballet dancer, Graham played for the Toronto Argonauts, and Roger's three books were on the *New York Times* bestseller list. The press loves a juicy scandal, especially an inside exclusive. If Talia goes to a tabloid, they'll have a field day."

Reece continued to stare at the empty doorway of the restaurant. "Would she taint her girlfriend's memory that way?"

Sam shrugged. "She'd consider retribution a fair trade. The dead can't be hurt. The living can."

"Pity help Roger if it turns out he was the baby's father." He shuddered and slid his plate to the centre of the table.

A sense of foreboding blanketed her. "If he's a person of interest in a homicide investigation," she said, "Roger has bigger problems than Talia."

CHAPTER SIX

SAM

THE NEXT DAY Sam and Reece slept in. It had been a rough night, but she'd made progress in dealing with Abigail's suicide. Speaking with Talia had been part of her journey toward healing, but Reece was the real catalyst. He held her while she cried, soothed her when she ranted, and continued to show his love and support.

His love today was in the form of a delicious mushroom and pancetta frittata he prepared for brunch. She ate half the pan. Then she ate a chunk of his.

"Time to get back to the gym." She patted her bulging belly and moaned. "Wanna meet me there after you talk to Bryce?"

"Sure, text me when you're done with Roger. What time is he expecting you?"

She checked her watch. "Ten minutes. I'll have to grab a cab. I hate trying to find parking on his street, and he freaks out if you park on his parking pad."

She gave him a quick kiss and raced out to Queen Street to hail a cab.

ROGER DIDN'T ANSWER the doorbell, so she wandered around back and peeked over his privacy fence, which required hoisting herself up by her arms. At five-foot-three, she wasn't tall enough to see over the top of the high fence.

With her forearms holding her body weight, she hollered, "Unlock the gate!"

He glanced at her over the rim of his coffee mug. "The fitness queen can't scale a privacy fence?"

She could and she did, dropping to the other side and marching to the deck. "We aren't twelve, Roger."

The smile didn't reach his eyes. In fact, he looked like hell. His pale, bumpy complexion was the texture of ricotta cheese, and a tuft of greasy hair stood up at the back of his head. He'd bitten his fingernails to the quick, and there was a bloody scab on the side of his left thumb.

"How are you doing?" she asked. "I haven't heard from you since Abby's funeral."

He rotated his hand. "*Comme ci, comme ça*," he replied. "And you?"

"Getting there."

"Sam, I'm sorry about what I said at the party."

She was glad he'd brought it up before she had to. "You mean about ruining me if I tattled on you again?"

He blushed. "I wasn't myself."

"I know. But I thought we'd made peace over the complaint I lodged. You said you understood. In fact, you thanked me, because it was the catalyst to addressing your burnout."

He sighed but didn't respond. A few moments passed before he said, "How about some coffee?" He checked his watch. "Or a drink? The sun is over the yardarm somewhere in the world."

She laughed. "Well, in this time zone, it's eleven o'clock in the morning." She sat and studied him across the top of a potted tulip plant on the centre of the teak table. "Abigail wrote to Reece." She handed Roger a copy of the letter she'd photocopied before giving the original to Talia.

He glanced at the handwriting. His jaw clenched and he looked away to gaze up at the sky. After a few minutes, he read the letter and then stood abruptly, almost knocking over the heavy teak chair. "I'm getting that drink."

She waited for him to return and raised an eyebrow when he came out with two glasses and a bottle of Johnny Walker Black Label. Having witnessed alcohol's destructive properties in his practice, Roger seldom drank hard liquor.

He poured and took a long swallow. She left her glass on the table. In the distance, she could hear a woodpecker tapping on a tree.

Roger brushed away a tear that had rolled down his cheek. "Childhood trauma lives forever in the heart of our inner child."

"Did she talk to you about how desperate she'd become?"

He ignored the question. "She abandons *us*," he said, "forcing her friends to exist under the umbrella of ineffectuality. But Reece, ah, *he's* special. A man whose stellar reputation one must protect at all costs. Abigail's dying wish was to clear Reece of any assumed guilt regarding the pregnancy. It must be complicated for Reece to be so perfect," he scoffed.

"It was kinder to write to him," Sam said believing the words. "He's a more objective observer."

Roger laughed and rubbed a bump on his cheek that might be a bug bite. It turned crimson under his assault. "Is that what you think romped across Abigail's sick mind in the hour before she filled the bathtub?"

Sam lowered her eyes.

"I've offended you with my anger." He held his hands up in mock submission. "One must not speak ill of the dead. Much too high a risk of expulsion from the herd should people whiff anger, and what a calamity that would be." He took a swig of his whisky, sloshing it around in his cheeks before swallowing.

"Healthy anger is an oxymoron these days," he continued in a lecturing tone. "The antithesis of stability in this era of entitlement and self-indulgence. Perhaps your mother was on to something." His wide smile was a caricature. "Repress socially taboo feelings. Let all the bitterness and resentment simmer until you're on the clock tower with a sniper rifle. People's ignorance is tiresome."

Sam ignored the reference to her mother's hypocritical habits. "Anger is an important stage of grief, you know that." Her concern was that Roger didn't always process anger in healthy ways. She reached for his hand, but he removed it from the table and placed it on his lap.

"Society ostracizes angry people and empathy is a lost art. It amazes me how inept humans are at recognizing the misery we cause others, while being so quick to see the trespasses against us." He pounded his fist on the table and the tulip pot shuddered. "Goddamn her! Why didn't she talk to me? I could have helped her." He hurled the letter to the deck. "Instead, she takes hours to write *that* to a relative stranger! Why didn't she say who the man was? Why did she leave us to suspect each other?"

Sam understood his anger. He'd tried to help Abigail. For a psychiatrist, suicide was tantamount to a surgeon making a mistake that resulted in death.

"This isn't your fault, Roger."

The rest of his drink disappeared in a single gulp, and he leaned against the back of his chair. "Are you sure about that?"

Deciding to get to the point of her visit, she said, "We talked with Talia yesterday."

"Ah, yes. I suppose she enlightened you on her theory that I am the father of Abigail's baby." He tapped the letter with his foot. "Especially since Abigail so kindly exonerated Reece of culpability. How gracious of her to protect him. You know Jim is out of the running."

"I wasn't aware he was *in* the running."

Roger poured another three fingers of whisky. "He was, hence the reason for Lisa and Talia quarrelling at the party. He isn't now. Jim submitted to the degradation of a DNA test."

Sam took a minute to choose her words. "I suppose because he wanted to give Talia peace of mind. Abigail was terrified of men. Talia's suspicion that the father is one of their childhood friends is rational. Isn't the test a small thing to do?"

Cloudy eyes studied her over the rim of his glass. "If you discount how repugnant it is to ask. You won't cajole me into taking the test, so don't waste your time."

Something occurred to her that made her shift the conversation. "You don't have patients today?" He hadn't shaved and was wearing a stained and misbuttoned shirt, so she was fairly certain he wasn't working.

"Not today, or yesterday, or the day before."

"Why's that?"

He grinned and laced his fingers behind his head. "Things to do, people to see."

"Roger, what's going on? Is it Abigail's suicide or is it something else? I'd like to help."

He uttered an admonishing scoff. "Come on, Sam. Don't gaze at me with your green eyes filled with compassion and expect me not to see the cunning glint that lies beneath. You are a talented liar. I give you that." He tapped his forehead with the tip of his finger. "But I am a gifted psychiatrist and know you well. The ease with which I can read you is frightening. You know the other piece. You've read the papers." His smile was tight. "And your clever mind is running on the hamster wheel connecting dots."

"I don't know what you're talking about."

"Up and to the left. A classic unconscious reaction that reveals a lie, and it's one you've failed to control and conquer. Congratulations, it means you aren't a sociopath."

"Fine," Sam said calmly. "Graham Harris, the ex-Argonauts player. I read about his murder. I know the police are talking to you. Can you tell me what his murder has to do with you?"

"I was in the vicinity at the time of his death."

Sam felt her eyes widen. "But he died at home, at a farm north of Vaughan."

"I had the dubious distinction of being there. Two witnesses will testify to that unlucky happenstance. Assuming the driver who nearly hit me wants his fifteen minutes of fame. Regardless,

Graham's son will most certainly tell police I was there. The bouquet of posies littered in their front garden will offer fingerprint substantiation. The florist will confirm the time of purchase. I used my credit card. An unintelligent error, had I conspired to murder. Nevertheless, the police will grasp at what's far too obvious while congratulating each other on their astute deductive reasoning."

She sat back in her chair. With a heavy sigh, she reached for her glass. "You need to tell me what happened."

When Roger finished his story about his spontaneous visit to his friend's house, Sam took a moment to process what she'd learned.

"Did you enter the house?"

"Not on that occasion."

Meaning he'd been in the house at one time. Unless Brenda and Graham were obsessive cleaners, forensics would find his fingerprints on the premises. There was nothing wrong with her deductive reasoning. Roger was knee-deep in shit.

"Have you spoken to the police?"

"Brenda's at Mount Sinai Hospital, psychiatric ward," he replied. "She's catatonic. A condition police suspect is counterfeit. In partnership with her attending psychiatrist, I attempted to enlighten the detectives on the complexity of her case. Their questions immediately twisted to why I referred her to another doctor two years ago." His laugh was ugly. "I can well imagine the Neanderthal innuendos that flowed between them when they meandered to the donut shop."

Since her father had been a homicide detective and she'd been a police officer, his speech offended her. She swallowed the rebuttal on the tip of her tongue and asked, "Have you heard from them since?"

"They were here yesterday. I'm a person of interest, or so they say." He laughed bitterly. "A polite euphemism for suspect." He licked his lips, his eyes intense as he scrutinized her. "Talia knows, doesn't she?"

Sam nodded.

"Ah, the dear officer smells blood in the water and is circling her prey. What's her plan? Let me guess, full disclosure to the sleaziest tabloid journalist she can find. A heart-wrenching narrative of misconduct by a perverted monster and the victimization of a beautiful, mentally fragile ballerina."

"Probably along those lines," Sam replied. "If you take the DNA test, Talia goes away."

He tore the scab off the cuticle of his thumb and reached for the bottle she'd moved to her side of the table. "I didn't seduce Abigail. I can promise you that."

"Were you sleeping with Brenda Harris?" She didn't want to hear the answer.

"I was but she wasn't my patient. The College may discipline me, but I won't lose my medical licence. I might even benefit from a smear campaign." He winked at her. "Readers love infamous authors. My books will once again grace the *New York Times* bestseller list. What a treat!" The raw panic on his face undermined his sarcasm. A scandal would ruin him, and they both knew it.

"There are thousands of women in the world, Roger. Why would you become involved with someone who was receiving mental health care? A married woman no less."

When he did it before—cheated on her with a different patient—her pride had been hurt and his unethical conduct had infuriated her, but the actual break-up hadn't devastated her. On a cowardly level, catching him with another woman had given her the excuse she'd needed to end the relationship. She'd always loved Roger as a friend, but she'd never been in love with him. Now that she was with Reece, Sam understood the importance of that difference.

"I have a proposition." He leaned forward and put his elbows on the table. "One that will protect Abigail's saintly reputation."

Sam had a feeling she knew what was coming next but remained silent, hoping she was wrong.

"You and Reece could help me," Roger said. "I'll make it worth your time. *Quid pro quo*, as your stepfather's fond of saying."

"Roger, I—"

"Don't decline in haste. My proposal comprises three things you covet." He held up his index finger. "First, if you help me, I'll take Talia's DNA test." He held up his middle finger. "Second, I'll transfer my discipline to psychiatric research and never treat another patient. No need for you to worry about Dr. Peterson ever becoming romantically involved with another patient." Up popped his ring finger. "Third, I'll help you prepare and defend your doctoral dissertation at the oral defence examination, and I'll write a recommendation and advocate for any internship you desire for your clinical practicum. In order for that recommendation to be worthwhile, you will need to ensure my reputation isn't tarnished."

Roger's lunch invitation to Reece a week back suddenly made sense to Sam. He hadn't wanted a new deck. What he'd wanted was to establish a friendship so Reece would be on board to help investigate Graham Harris's death. She thought about the dates. Roger had invited Reece over on Saturday. Based on the news reports, Graham had died on Friday afternoon. Less than twenty-four hours after the death, Roger had predicted that police would rule the accident as suspicious.

He must have read the distrust on her face because he added, "It's an attractive proposition. Last time you were here asking for my help with your PhD, it bewildered me how a person with your intellect could traipse around idiocy with such obliviousness. Your methodology is flawed, your research fails to support your hypothesis, and you haven't a hope against the scrutiny of gifted minds."

There wasn't much to say to that. He was right. She was in trouble with her PhD and knew it.

He reached into a pocket of his pants and removed a cheque, which he put in front of her. "But I'll up the ante. Your usual fee and expenses, plus this."

It was for ten thousand dollars.

"I can't take this." She slid the cheque to his side of the table.

"You can. In the event you set up a private therapy practice when you're awarded your PhD, which you will not obtain without help, you'll need money."

"Because of our past, it's a huge conflict of interest."

He nudged the cheque closer. "Private investigators are not limited by the same regulatory rules that bind the hands of police officers and lawyers." He smiled. "And doctors." He reached for the bottle again. "I have every confidence in your ability to remain impartial. Speak to Reece. It isn't a conflict for him. Talia will get her DNA test. Reece will savour the satisfaction of honouring Abigail's wish and achieving yet another golden token for admission through the pearly gates of heaven." He looked up at her. "And you, my dear, will receive what you've desired since you caught me with Heather years ago. I'll stop treating patients."

She chewed on her lower lip and considered the offer. "If we agree to investigate Graham Harris's murder, you'll have to take the DNA test right away."

He shook his head. "To quote the illustrious Stephen King, 'No bounce, no play.' Apropos, considering my life has become content for horror fiction. The DNA test is my only guarantee Reece will toil diligently to establish my innocence." He again poured from the bottle and waited for her to respond.

When she didn't, he added with a knowing smile, "I understand you're far too high-minded to be coerced by personal gain." He gazed at the garden against his fence. "But that PhD you've lusted after for years is tough to ignore." His eyes shifted back to hers. "How satisfied you'd be to gain your doctoral degree before your mother's Alzheimer's renders it a futile achievement. Perhaps you'll eke out a nod of approval from a woman who has always viewed you as her greatest disappointment."

You dick, Sam thought bitterly.

"I never thought I'd descend to this," Roger remarked. "I'm sincerely remorseful, but this is survival."

Sam glared at the rhododendron and azalea bushes. They were in full bloom, and she'd admired their beauty when she'd arrived. Now they were garish.

"At some point, you're going to have to admit you treat people like shit to push them away before they follow your father's example and abandon you." She struggled to keep the pain from her voice. "You may know me and all my crappy family history, but don't forget I know you. I know what you did to your sister. I know what you're capable of doing to protect yourself."

Roger stood unsteadily, put the bottle of whisky under his arm, and picked up his glass. "The gate locks behind you," he said haughtily. "Call me with your decision."

CHAPTER SEVEN

REECE

REECE WAS FIFTEEN minutes early for his meeting with Bryce Mansfield, the staff inspector of the homicide squad. He'd planned to be early so he could admire Eldon Garnet's *Serve and Protect* sculpture collection outside the Metropolitan Toronto Police Headquarters. He circled the building's exterior, enjoying the warm spring sun and pausing at each piece of art. His favourite was the granite block pyramid and brass police officer sculpture. Something about the focused expression on the constable's face as he leaned over the pyramid with his trowel touched Reece and made him proud to have been a cop.

He wasn't sure what he thought of the postmodern building though. Officers referred to the twelve-storey, octagonal structure as the "pink palace." There were a few less complimentary nicknames, such as "pink whorehouse." The colour reference was due to the rose granite cubes used to construct the structure. Reece stepped onto the sidewalk and viewed the building from a different angle. He shaded his eyes against the sun and studied the high elevator tower capped with a blue dome. Artistic, he supposed, but the neo-eclectic angles of the front entrance and the multi-levelled tiered roofs looked like haphazardly stacked building blocks. The architecture was unique, but a tad chaotic for his taste.

He held the door open for a woman with a baby and then strolled toward the elevators, admiring the ten-storey-high atrium flooded with natural light.

Behind him, he heard a voice. "Reece, you're early."

Turning, he found Bryce strutting toward him, balancing a large tray of Starbucks coffees. Reece always felt uncomfortable greeting Bryce, who was demonstrative. They exchanged an awkward bro-hug, complete with manly thumps to the back, and Bryce led the way into the elevator and then to the homicide division.

They crossed the bullpen, Bryce distributed coffees, and Reece chatted with a couple of detectives he'd met over the course of his year in Toronto.

Instead of a sense of belonging, he felt like a guest who was happy to visit but eager to go home. It gave him pause because it was the first time he felt certain he didn't want to join the squad. Police work was in the past. The epiphany saddened him and made him anxious about his future.

Once they settled into his office, Bryce asked, "What brings you in? Have you decided to join the homicide squad?"

"Considering it." The lie stuck in his throat but now wasn't the time to reject the offer. "Today, I need your help with something." He squirmed and crossed his legs. Abigail's sad eyes filled his memory and he soldiered on. "A friend of Sam's is a person of interest in a York Regional homicide case."

Bryce leaned back in his chair. "North of my jurisdiction."

"It is, but I thought you might have some insight. Have you read about the ballerina who committed suicide?"

Bryce straightened in his chair, looking confused. "Are you saying Abigail Schwartz had something to do with a homicide?" There was disbelief in his voice.

Reece shook his head. "Not that I'm aware. Abigail was a close friend of Sam's from childhood. Now, well, another of the group has some trouble. You know Sam. She copes better with information."

Bryce was nodding. "Yup, she sure does, which was one of many things that made her a good cop. I was sad to read about Abigail's suicide," he said. "No reason you'd know, but my partner and I were first on the scene fourteen years ago after her attack. Hell of a thing." His eyes darkened, but he didn't elaborate on the effect it had had on a young cop to find a woman brutally beaten and gang-raped. "I met Colin McNamara because of his personal interest. He was a good man and a great detective."

Reece uncrossed his legs and cleared his throat again. "Well, I understand this is unorthodox, but I was wondering if you could look up the details on York Regional's case and let me know what they have."

"You're right," Bryce said. "It is unorthodox." He studied Reece solemnly and tapped a pen against the side of his desk. After a minute or so, Bryce dropped his eyes and leaned back in his chair. "What's the case?"

"Graham Harris, the ex-Argonauts player."

Bryce typed on his keyboard and picked up the phone. "Let's see what the lead detective at York thinks."

After a bit of back and forth, Bryce turned to Reece. "Detective Alston is asking who you know in connection to the case."

"Dr. Roger Peterson."

Bryce relayed the answer, listened intently, and covered the phone. "Reece, how about you step out for a minute."

Reece nodded, and then left the office. He stood outside the door, shuffling his feet and avoiding the sideways glances of the curious detectives. He had the ridiculous feeling of being a high school student again, waiting outside the principal's office to explain some juvenile indiscretion.

A few minutes later, Bryce opened the door. "Thanks. Come on back in."

"Bryce," Reece said directly, "I'm uncomfortable asking, and it's understandable if York is holding their cards close to their chest."

Bryce studied him solemnly. "I'm not sure you're aware of how stellar your reputation is. Going after Mussani in Australia after that cult horror garnered you professional support. Sam, well, she was a good cop. She got a raw deal." Bryce lowered his eyes. "Her father was a great man and a respected detective."

"I wish I'd met him before he died."

Bryce nodded, circling his desk to the chair behind. "Colin would have liked you. If Dr. Peterson is a friend, are you and Sam taking the case?"

Reece took the seat he'd previously occupied. "I don't know if he's hiring private investigators or not. Sam's talking to him now."

"Okay, Detective Alston has agreed to share a few facts." Bryce pointed his finger at Reece. "But if you two investigate, he expects the information road to run both ways."

"It always does, but you have my word."

Reece knew that the police would soon disclose to the media whatever information Bryce chose to share today. They weren't really offering Reece confidential details on the investigation, just giving him early access. It didn't matter. At least he'd be ahead of the game.

Bryce typed on his keyboard and read the monitor. "Okay, the eighteen-year-old son, Jordan Harris, called 911 after returning from football practice to find his father dead in the basement. The wife, Brenda Harris, suffers from mental illness." He caught Reece's eye. "I suppose you know that."

Reece nodded.

"Well, that isn't Dr. Peterson's only connection, but I'll get to that in a minute," he said. "First officers and paramedics believed the cause of death was electrocution. Mr. Harris was wading around in water trying to fix the wiring to an old sump-pump. Power to the house wasn't cut."

"Can you tell me why it's being considered a homicide?"

"Autopsy showed feces and urine in his lungs as well as the electrical burns on his body." Bryce crinkled his nose. "Sewage had backed up from the septic to the main water line and through the overloaded basement drain. The electrical burns showed the entry and exit points and the pathway of the current. Nasty but not deadly."

Reece leaned forward and put his elbow on the desk. "If he fell into the water after the shock, it makes sense."

"It would, except for the bruising pattern on the back of his neck." Bryce took a sip of his coffee. "Size eleven rubber boot imprints."

Reece tried to image persnickety Roger wadding around in sewage and holding an ex-footballer's face under water. It was a reach. Not because of the size difference between the two men—the electrical shock would have incapacitated Graham, rendering him unable to defend himself. Reece's issue was with the unpredictable method of the homicide. Perhaps it was a fatal accident during a vicious disagreement rather than premeditated murder.

"Any sign of a struggle or a fight?" he asked.

"In the kitchen, and there were smears of blood in the stair-well leading to the cellar."

Reece pieced together the scenario Bryce was outlining. "So, Graham fought with someone in the kitchen. Then he went downstairs to fix the sump-pump. He must have seen the other person leave the house and thought the fight was over."

"Unless the perpetrator lived in the house," Bryce said.

Based on the bit of research Reece had done, Graham's property was worth a chunk of change. He didn't have the details of the estate but assumed Brenda Harris inherited. Money ranked high on the motive list, and spouses high on the suspect list.

Bryce continued to read the file, clicking now and again to switch pages. "Graham's uncle lives next door. He claims he was in his field behind their barn when the lights went out. Graham has old lights mounted on ten-foot posts around the barn, wired to the house. The uncle noticed because he'd told his nephew not to fool with the existing box and to get an electrician, even offered to lend him the money."

"Would the shock generate a power surge that fried the box?"

"Maybe, but the power was on when EMTs arrived, which is why they assumed he'd failed to disengage the main switch. The house has an ancient fuse box without a ground fault circuit interrupter, and Graham had overloaded the box by tying new receptacles into existing circuits." Bryce threw his empty coffee cup into the trash. "He must have thought the sump-pump issue was with the receptacle. He'd taken it apart."

Reece frowned. "You'd have to be an idiot to work with live wires."

"And the box wasn't damaged. There was no reason the lights would go off, unless Graham had shut off the power."

"Someone turned on the power when Graham was in the water," Reece said. "Where's the box located?"

"Landing on the stairs. It's a split staircase. The first half runs from the back door foyer to the landing. To the left of the landing, a second staircase leads down into the cellar, which was the flooded section. The killer could access the box without being in the water and without Graham seeing."

Reece got up and paced the small office. A good lawyer could argue manslaughter, based on impulsively flicking a switch under duress and without forethought. Going into the water to check for signs of life and using an ulterior method to ensure death made it premeditated first-degree murder.

He stopped pacing and faced Bryce. "Any motive?"

"Several and that's where your friend enters the party." Bryce waved at him to sit down. "Pacing makes me nervous," he said with a chuckle.

Once Reece had sat, Bryce continued. "The uncle nearly sideswiped a car entering the Harris farm about an hour and a quarter before the cops got the call. He got a good look at the car and a partial on the plate."

"Roger's car," Reece guessed.

Bryce nodded. "The son, Jordan, ran into Dr. Peterson when he came home from school. Claims he caught him 'creeping around the house,' and there was a bouquet of yellow roses in the garden with Dr. Peterson's fingerprints on the wrapping. He'd bought them on his Visa from a Vaughan florist ninety minutes before the 911 call."

"Putting Roger on the scene," Reece said with a sigh.

"Peterson doesn't deny that he went to the farm on the day of the murder but claims he didn't enter the house. His explanation for his fingerprints in the stairwell is that he was in the house in the past." Bryce spun the pen between his fingers. "Cops recovered a rusted pipe buried under some renovation waste in the backyard. Your friend's bloody fingerprints were on it."

The blood confused Reece. "Wait a minute. If the perp electrocuted Graham before drowning him, where did the blood come from?"

Bryce studied him with a professional lack of emotion. "Best guess, Peterson. According to Alston, your friend had a facial wound when he was interviewed a couple of days after the murder. He refused to volunteer a blood sample. Alston is waiting for a judge to sign a warrant."

Reece's mind flashed to the cut on Roger's forehead and the nasty scrape on his arm that he'd noticed when they'd had lunch. The day after the murder. He considered the evidence. Roger wasn't a person of interest. He was a prime suspect. He had opportunity and means, and there was sufficient direct evidence pointing at him.

One thing didn't make sense. "What would his motive be?" Reece asked.

"The daughter, Jordanna—Jordan's twin—told police that Dr. Peterson was a regular visitor when her father wasn't around."

"If Brenda and Roger wanted to be together, why didn't she leave the marriage?" Reece asked.

"The property Graham inherited last year is worth millions because of the land," Bryce explained. "Extended family told us his wife wanted to sell but Graham refused. Under the terms of his grandparents' will, if Brenda filed for divorce while Graham held title, a prenuptial agreement protected the physical property from inclusion in a divorce settlement. But if Graham sold while cohabitating with his wife, the capital gains reverted to a family asset, divided if they divorced in the future."

People could set up clauses in their wills to cover anything they liked, but it made Reece curious why the grandparents felt the need to protect their ancestral land from Graham's wife. If Roger was the culprit, something else didn't make sense.

Leaning across the desk, he said, "Roger Peterson is wealthy. He didn't need to kill a man to steal his estate."

"Well, the wife might," countered Bryce. "Family claims the marriage was bad, and the financial analyst says Brenda doesn't have any money of her own. Graham received a monthly stipend from a trust his grandparents left, but the prenuptial protects the trust. If she divorced him, spousal support would be based on his income, which was negligible."

She had the means, the opportunity, and the motive. Boot size meant nothing. She could easily have slipped on a pair of ill-fitting boots. But evidence put Roger on the scene, which made him a probable witness or an accomplice to murder. It was tough to believe the arrogant, self-centred man would risk his freedom to help a lover commit murder. It was possible Roger had been in the wrong place at the wrong time. He could have stumbled onto the murder unawares.

"What does Brenda have to say?" Reece asked.

Bryce shrugged. "Not a thing. She's still at Mount Sinai, catatonic. EMTs found her sitting on the basement stairs, soaking wet. She hasn't moved or spoken since. Her primary psychiatrist says she suffers from," he glanced at the monitor, "schizoaffective disorder, bipolar type. Episodes of catatonia aren't unusual, if she'd stopped taking her meds."

Or she was a hell of an actor and—with a little help from her psychiatrist lover—was faking the catatonic state. Reece squirmed in the office chair, wishing he could walk around. He always thought better on his feet.

"Just the twins or do they have more kids?" he asked.

"Jennifer, she's sixteen." He frowned and read something on his monitor. "Alston made a note that Jennifer was at her great-aunt's house. They talked to her, but Rachel Harris, the great-aunt, wouldn't leave and censored the questions."

"Where are the kids now?" Reece asked.

"At the farm. With the twins over the age of majority and family next door, Children's Aid felt it best for Jennifer to stay at home and in school." Bryce glanced at his watch and stood. "I need to get to a budget meeting." He scribbled something on a piece of paper and handed it to Reece. "Here's the name and number for the lead detective at York. He's not fond of PIs, so if you and Sam end up investigating this, give him a courtesy call."

Reece stood and took the paper. "Will do." He held out his hand. "Thanks, Bryce, appreciate the time and information."

Reece waited in the hall while Bryce grabbed a file folder and locked his office door. While walking to the elevator, Bryce stopped. "I suppose Jim Stipelli will be Dr. Peterson's defence attorney."

"Does he need one at this point?" Reece asked.

Bryce shrugged. "From my experience, people like Peterson always lawyer up. Have a good day, Reece. Let's grab a beer sometime." He turned back. "Don't forget to call Alston. I don't want my nuts in a vice over this."

CHAPTER EIGHT

SAM

REECE'S FACE WAS tight after Sam finished updating him. She'd thought she'd done a solid job glossing over the nasty bits. Apparently not. But Reece had excellent situational awareness, could read people well, and already had a negative opinion of Roger. It wasn't surprising that the man's manipulative tactics pissed him off.

"It sounds like coercion, which doesn't surprise me when it comes to Roger." Reece stepped off the treadmill and pointed at the abdominal crunch machines. Sam followed and they chose their equipment.

It was true that Roger's behaviour earlier that day had annoyed her, but she knew her friend. Much of his pompous facade masked insecurity. Because he'd been an effeminate nerd who hated athletics, high school was a nightmare. Once, when Sam was in grade four, she'd walked across the park on her way home from basketball practice. A group of grade twelve boys had pulled down Roger's pants and were grinding his face in a pile of dog shit. They recognized her, knew her father was a cop, and took off. Roger had been in grade ten, and it still pained her to recall how mortified he'd been to find her witnessing his humiliation. When she tried to give him a bottle of water and a towel from her backpack, he screamed obscenities at her and ran way. People didn't endure that type of trauma in their youth without deep scars.

"He's scared and he's desperate," she told Reece. "Roger amps up the arrogance when he feels out of control."

She was about to declare he wasn't a violent man, though. Before the words left her mouth, Veronica's face flashed in her mind. Positioning her forearms on the armrests of the crunch machine, she grasped the handles and hid her face.

Reece adjusted the resistance up on his machine prior to moving into position. "He's playing you."

"I don't disagree, but it's a question of how badly we want him to take the DNA test," Sam said, finishing a short set and deciding she'd had enough. She'd spent an hour on the treadmill, running at a faster speed than his because she was a competitive person at heart. Stupid because now she was tired and wouldn't be able to keep up with him.

On his machine, Reece pulled his knees up and began working his abs.

With amusement—tinged with a bit of jealousy, if she was honest—Sam watched a busty blond woman enter the room and stop in mid-stride to ogle Reece.

When he finished his set of fifty reps, Reece asked, "Is Roger right? Do you need his help with your PhD?"

"I do need a solid recommendation to obtain a worthwhile internship for my clinical practicum," she conceded. "I also need more guidance on the thesis than I can receive at the university."

She sighed. "Truth is this PhD is harder than I thought it would be."

They moved to the free weight section of the gym. Sam wasn't pleased to see Sporty Barbie playing with the weights.

"It's a chunk of money," he said, moving over to select his weight discs and a bar.

Sam almost laughed aloud at the busty woman's attempt to get Reece to engage with her. Sam had caught his eyes widen at the sight of the enormous, artificial breasts. He ignored Sporty Barbie, loaded a bar with the weights he'd selected, and rejoined Sam at a bench press.

"We can't discount the money, especially with everything up in the air." He sighed, put his loaded bar on the posts, and settled on the bench. "Between your PhD requirements and my indecision on my career, we need to hire help for the business. Someone to do paperwork, research, background checks—gofer stuff."

She stood behind to spot him while he pushed up the bar that held a crippling amount of weight compared to what she could lift.

"I don't believe Roger's the father of Abigail's baby," she said. "But knowing for sure will give Talia some closure. The DNA test is the main incentive for taking on the case, in my opinion."

Reece finished twenty reps and took some of the weight off the bar, waving at her to take the bench.

"The motivation for me," he said, as Sam lay on her back and reached for the bar, "is he'll stop treating patients. There should be a way to have his licence revoked. He seduces patients for Christ sake."

She finished ten lifts and waved at him to indicate she was done. Her arms were burning.

"Calf press?" he asked over his shoulder, already headed in the direction of the machines. Reece was fresh as a daisy, barely even sweating.

"This isn't fair. You aren't challenging yourself," she said, wishing they could leave. Her stomach was starting to feel upset, and a headache throbbed at her temple.

"Sure I am."

"Then why aren't you all sweaty and panting?"

He laughed. "Because, unlike you, my workout is about maintenance, not showing off."

Not much to stay to that. She was trying to show off, in part because Sporty Barbie was breaking a sweat with a ten-pound weight. Sam refrained from commenting and trailed behind him to the calf press equipment.

People occupied all the pieces of equipment and they had to wait. Sam wasn't sorry for the break, but Reece looked a bit impatient.

She handed him a bottle of water. "The issue is Brenda wasn't a patient." Holding up her hand to ward off his objection, she continued, "It's shitty and unethical, but the discipline might not be severe. Brenda hadn't been under his care for two years. It's a grey area."

He snorted in disgust. "Not to me it isn't."

"Well, if we help him, he'll take the test, and we'll help Talia, which means you'll honour Abigail's wishes," she said. "Besides, he's going to be slaughtered in the court of public opinion. He isn't going to be able to stop the media train headed his way. He's involved in a homicide."

Reece sighed. "This isn't the type of help Abigail had in mind when she wrote the letter. If she'd wanted Talia to know the identity of the man, she'd have told someone."

What bugged her was that if the man were a stranger, Sam was sure Abigail would have told her. Abby shared everything with her and Lisa. Between work, school, and settling into her new life with Reece, she hadn't had much time for her friends over the past six months. Maybe Abby had tried to talk to her and she wasn't available. It was a horrible thought.

"I'm leaning toward taking the case," she said. "This isn't just about Roger or Abby. It's about Graham Harris. Whoever did this knew the shock from a household receptacle might not be sufficient to ensure electrocution. Drowning him in sewage is disgusting and degrading. If the detectives fix their sights on Roger, the actual murderer might walk."

"You could be right," Reece said with a sigh. "They'll be satisfied and search for evidence to prosecute, blinding them to other suspects."

She shrugged. "It happens more often than people know. Graham deserves justice. How do you feel about taking the case?"

"There's hard evidence implicating Roger," Reece said. "How objective can you be if we find more proof of his involvement?"

"It depends on what we uncover. Right now, it feels circumstantial to me. He isn't denying he was at the farm. The thing is that I can't see a man as smart as Roger killing someone in such a sloppy way."

"From what Bryce said, it doesn't feel premeditated. My instinct is that something unexpected happened, and the murderer acted out of desperation."

"I suppose, but Roger's a deliberate person. If he wanted to murder Graham, he'd plan it. He'd certainly do a better job covering it up."

"Talia said Roger did something to his sister. What's that about?"

He must have seen something cross her face because he took her hand. "Full disclosure, if you want me to take this case."

"It was a long time ago." Sam released his hand and sat on a bench, running a towel across the sweat on her forehead. "Roger was home from school for the summer. He had a job in construction with Lisa's father. Veronica, his older sister, was at the house visiting their mother. She came outside when Roger was unloading tools from Mr. Altieri's truck. Veronica confronted him about something—I don't know what—and he lost his temper." Her mouth felt dry and she licked her lips.

"How?"

"It's hard to explain. It'll sound worse than it was."

"What did he do?" There was a hard edge to Reece's voice.

"He attacked her with a hammer. Jim was mowing his parent's lawn. He pulled Roger off before he hit her more than once or twice, but he broke her nose and one of her ribs. Roger and Veronica haven't spoken since."

"Jesus." Reece ran his fingers through his hair and turned away.

"You have to understand that kids bullied Roger most of his life," Sam rushed to say. "Veronica and her boyfriend verbally abused him all the time. Not that what happened was okay, it just doesn't show an unprovoked proclivity toward violence, you know?" She sounded defensive and delusional to her own ears.

He turned back to face her. "If we do this and discover something awful about Roger," he paused with a cringe, "something more awful than what we already know, will you relinquish the friendship?"

He wasn't only talking about Roger, she knew. Many times over the past six months, he'd advised her to dump Lisa. Making and keeping friends wasn't a skill she'd mastered. Her candour and lack of tact made her a human repellent. Without her childhood friends, she wouldn't have any. If Reece spent more time with them, she was certain he'd grow to see their redeeming qualities and form relationships. Well, maybe not with Roger.

"Will you keep an open mind?" she asked, sidestepping his question. "This is about getting to the truth. It can't be a personal agenda to steamroll Roger because you find him objectionable as my friend."

He studied her intensely. "I'm not going to manufacture evidence, if that's what you mean."

"Don't be absurd. I'm not suggesting that," she said irritably. "I'm just saying that it's difficult to be objective when we don't like someone."

A flicker of anger crossed his eyes. "Innocent until proven guilty. If the evidence doesn't implicate a suspect, I don't allow personal feelings to interfere with my investigation."

Trust him and drop it, she warned herself.

"Where should we start?" she asked.

He rolled his eyes and crinkled his nose. "With the Harris kids."

She laughed. "Oh boy, you and kids. This will be interesting."

CHAPTER NINE

REECE

REECE CHECKED HIS side mirror to see how far Brandy's head was out the window. A while back, he'd read a nasty story about an eighteen-wheeler decapitating a dog when the owner tried to pass it on a highway. He moved to the right lane of the highway, closed the left back window, and opened the right halfway. Brandy moved over, stuck out as much of her head as fit, and panted with pleasure.

"Ideas on how to handle this?" he asked Sam, who was fiddling with her phone in the passenger seat.

"Divide and conquer," she replied, putting her phone in her pocket and glancing out the window. "That's your exit coming up. Stay right and head east."

"How do we do that? There are three kids."

He'd interviewed a few adolescents in his days with the OPF, and, during their last case, he'd been the one stuck interviewing Gabriella LeBlanc's bratty kids. Interrogating teenagers was never a pleasant experience. Hormones wound them too tight. It was tough to judge their reaction to questions and discern the truth from a lie. When adults jumped to the defence or responded in anger, you typically knew the question had hit a nerve.

With teenagers, anger was their favourite expression. You could ask them what they wanted to eat for dinner, and half the time they'd rage at you. Under the age of eighteen, you had to deal with helicopter parents. That wouldn't be an issue this time at least, since Brenda was in hospital, but Bryce had said the great-aunt was problematic when the cops tried to speak with Jennifer on the day of the murder.

"You take the boy and I'll take the girls," Sam was saying, completely at ease.

Reece sighed. While working on her master's degree, Sam had counselled juvenile delinquents in a lockdown group home. She actually liked teenagers, even law-breaking, screwed-up ones.

"Any suggestions on how to start?" Reece could feel her eyes on him. From his peripheral vision, he thought she might be smirking, amused by his lack of confidence.

She patted his thigh. "He plays football. Start there."

"Geez, I don't remember anything about high school football."

"Same rules as the CFL and NFL. Instead of men frolicking after a pigskin ball, they're boys. Turn left. I'll watch for the lane to the farm."

"What should I ask?"

She laughed. "Same stuff you'd ask an adult who was a material witness. Build some trust by chatting about casual things. When he's comfortable with you, move to questions about what happened." She paused. "Don't talk too much."

"What?"

"Teenagers don't like being talked at. Adults lecture them, and they hate it. If you want him to talk to you, listen."

Reece envisioned sitting in uncomfortable silence with a petulant teen. "What if he doesn't say anything?"

"He will." Her confidence was annoying. "Talk about stuff he likes."

"I don't know anything about him."

"Sure you do, he's a quarterback on the football team. I did some research. The twins attend King City Secondary. Grade twelve, so they're seniors. The football team is the Lions. Oh yeah, grade ten kids installed solar panels that operate a pump to a synthetic pond on the school grounds. Cool, eh?"

Reece knew diddly-squat about solar panels.

Sam's phone rang and she dug it out of her pocket. "Hi Lisa."

Reece could hear the shrew's high-pitched scolding from the other end of the phone.

"Shit, I forgot. I'll make it up to her. I promise."

Another pause. This time, Sam had to hold the phone away from her ear with a cringe.

"I know, but we're going to interview Graham Harris's kids. Reece and—"

A moment later, she disconnected. "Lisa's pissed. I promised to take Kira to the zoo and totally spaced. Jim took her. Let's stop at a toy store on the way home. I'll pick up that llama stuffy she wants." She sighed. "My sweet goddaughter never holds a grudge. I'm worried about Lisa though. Maybe we should hit a florist, too."

Great, Reece thought, *and Lisa will blame me for the missed zoo trip.* The day kept getting better.

He pulled the car into the lane and drove to a two-storey stone farmhouse.

"Yuck," Sam murmured. "What a dump." She jumped out of the car.

Grudgingly, Reece shuffled to the front door with Brandy trotting at his side.

A stern woman answered the door, her grey hair in a bun so tight it pulled up the corners of her eyes. She glared at them. From the deep furrows around her mouth, Reece surmised frowning was her resting facial expression. She was at least six inches taller than Sam was and loomed over her like a vulture. The woman had a bony frame and wore a dull housedress that matched the frocks his great-grandmother had worn in the morning before she dressed for the day.

Sam had a card ready and passed it to the woman. "Hi, Mrs. Harris. I'm Sam McNamara. This is my partner Reece Hash. We spoke on the phone this morning."

Instead of greeting them, the woman's scowl deepened. "*Do not neglect to show hospitality to strangers, for thereby some have entertained angels unawares.*" She paused. When neither of them replied, she barked, "Hebrews 13:2."

Based on her expression, she disbelieved either he or Sam had entertained angels during their tenure on earth. Sam had warned him about the woman's odd personality after speaking to her earlier in the day, so Reece smiled politely but kept his mouth firmly shut. His shoulder was touching Sam's as the two of them crowded together outside the door.

"Have you accepted Jesus as your personal saviour?" Beady eyes scoured Reece's face.

"Why yes we have!" Sam exclaimed with a wide grin.

Mrs. Harris nodded, apparently satisfied, and gestured them into the house.

"Oh, I brought my dog." Sam smiled demurely.

The woman glared at Brandy, who stood on the front porch looking up with trusting eyes and a tail wag. "Animals are dirty. They don't belong inside."

"Of course not," Sam assured her. "How about we chat with the kids outside."

"Get to the kitchen."

It took Reece a second to realize the woman was speaking to a pretty girl standing behind her inside the front foyer. The girl ignored her great-aunt, shoved by her, and came to the door. "Hi, I'm Jennifer."

Actually, she was more than pretty. Wavy blond hair framed a heart-shaped face with large almond-shaped eyes below arched brows. Her nose was small and slim, and her lips were full. She had a gorgeous smile and was tall and willowy.

Without any outward sign of discomfort, Sam extended her hand and smiled. "Hi, I'm Sam, he's Reece, and this golden beauty is Brandy."

"Oh! I love dogs. I have a cat, Midnight, but I always wanted a dog."

She stepped out onto the front porch. Her great-aunt grabbed her by her earlobe and shoved her into the house.

The woman turned back to address Sam. "I'll allow you to speak with Jordan and Jordanna." Judging by her sour expression, the notion didn't please the woman. "Jennifer is too young. Wait here. I'll get the twins." She shut the door on their faces.

"Off to a great start," Reece murmured.

"I got an earful about talking to Jennifer when I called to set up the meeting." She patted Brandy. "I figured if we brought the dog, we'd have a better chance of talking to the twins without Mrs. Harris around."

"So we've accepted Jesus as our personal saviour." He raised his eyebrow at her. "Don't be surprised when she invites us to attend a revival."

She laughed. "We may as well sit down and wait for Jordanna and Jordan."

Reece eyed two ancient wicker chairs on the decrepit porch. "I'm not sure the porch or the chairs will hold us."

The front door opened and a male teenager stepped out. He slammed the door shut behind him and folded his arms across his chest.

Sam got up from the wicker chair and introduced herself and Reece. The kid tilted his chin in Reece's direction but didn't speak. As they waited for Jordanna, Sam chatted to Jordan about football, university, and the recent Blue Jays game against the Red Sox. Reece wandered down the front steps with Brandy and looked across the fields.

Eventually, a girl came around the corner of the house from the back. She wasn't pretty like her younger sister. Jordanna's features were sharp and set close together. Heavy-lidded, small eyes drew attention to a hooked nose, and thin, straight hair did no favours to a big forehead. She wore a pair of hip-riding shorts that didn't fully cover her ass and a sleeveless T-shirt with a slit cut into the neckline so that it barely concealed her huge breasts. Her father must have had his hands full with her.

At least Jordanna's expression was pleasant, which was more than Reece could say about her brother.

Seeing his sister, Jordan jumped off the porch and whispered something in her ear that Reece didn't catch.

Joining them on the front yard, Sam said to Jordanna, "How about you show me around the property? Brandy could use a walk."

She agreed and they strolled off with Brandy, leaving Reece alone with the surly young man. He gestured at the porch and Jordan followed him up the stairs.

Reece cautiously eased his butt into one of the rotting wicker chairs. He cleared his throat. "I hear you play football."

Jordan was better looking than his twin was. At least he would be if he didn't look so disagreeable. His blond hair was long and shaggy. It curled around his neck, and he kept flipping it out of his large hazel eyes. There was a tiny crop of pimples on his prominent chin, but the rest of his complexion was clear. He had broad shoulders with impressive bicep definition and wore a tight white T-shirt with *Property of* in black letters and *King City Lions* in yellow. The khaki shorts he was wearing showed off muscular legs.

"Quarterback," Jordan muttered, leaning against the side of the house and crossing his arms against his chest. His lips formed a tight slash across his face, and he avoided Reece's eyes.

"I tried out but didn't make the cut." Reece wished the kid would sit down. "Ever hear of the game forcing the gates?"

Jordan shrugged.

"You know, they test the strength of the candidate by getting him to run at the line and break through," Reece prompted.

"Red rover."

"Yeah, that's another term. Does your football coach use that drill?"

Jordan's lip curled into a sneer, as if Reece was the stupidest person he'd ever met. "It's banned. Everyone knows that."

Grasping for a conversation topic that would stick, Reece examined the ink on the kid's left forearm. An elaborate design with intricate details. Well-drawn and expertly coloured.

"You like tattoos? That's something else."

"I drew it. It's Sharpie. What do you want?"

So much for establishing rapport.

Reece decided to cut the bullshit and treat it like any other interview. "What happened the day your dad died?"

A vein throbbed in the kid's forehead and his frown deepened. "He got fried. Didn't know what the fuck he was doing." He looked down, rummaged in one of the pockets of his shorts, and withdrew a phone.

"Wasn't good with electricity, eh?"

Jordan gestured around him. "Hashtag loser. Graham sucked at everything."

"Must have been tough to change schools. Think your mother will sell the farm and move you guys back to the city?"

"Probably in with the dude she's banging." He focused his attention on the phone, typing.

"Do you know the man?" Reece asked.

Jordan didn't look up from the phone. "The headshrinker from Toronto. Brenda's nuts."

"Have you met him?" Reece asked.

"He was creeping around when Graham bit it."

"Do you know what he was doing here?"

Jordan laughed. "What do you think he was doing? Looking to get laid."

"Did you talk to Roger the day your dad died?"

"Yeah, he was freaked out and his pants were soaked." Jordan glanced up from his phone. "Threw him some shade, went inside, found Brenda zoning, and Graham dead. Called 911. End of story."

"Did you see anyone else?"

"Nah." He looked off into the distance and shuffled his feet. "Couple days before, some creepy dude was here. He was freaking out over dollars Graham owed."

What? Reece felt confused. This was a big piece of information. Bryce hadn't said anything about the police looking into a dispute that had occurred a few days before the murder.

"Did you tell the cops?" he asked.

Jordan shrugged. "Can't remember."

"Do you know why your dad owed him money?"

The kid sneered at him. "Cards, horses, games, whatever."

"Gambling debts?" Reece was even more confused. If the man gambled, there could easily be another person with a motive to kill him.

Jordan shrugged.

"When you returned from school the day your dad died, were the lights on?" Reece asked.

Jordan stared down the lane to the main road. "I dunno."

"Did you go straight into the basement?"

"I dunno. Can't remember."

"Where were your sisters?"

This question pissed him off. "How the fuck should I know?" He jammed his fists against his hips and glared at Reece. "What do I look like, a babysitter?"

Talking to the kid was frustrating. Jordan was an indecipherable, seething lump of animosity. Maybe Sam was having better luck with Jordanna. Reece decided to take a different approach.

"What was your dad like?" he asked.

"What do you think? His woman was hooking up behind his back."

"He knew?"

A shrug. "When he took his head out of the bottle."

"Big drinker?"

"Hung with his squad so he didn't have to be here." He laughed in a mean way, but his eyes filled with tears. He swiped the back of his hand across his eyes and turned his back on Reece. "Like I blame him. Place is a hot mess."

A car pulled up with music blaring from the open windows. Jordan hopped down the porch steps and headed for the car. He stopped halfway to the car and turned back to face Reece.

"You wanna know about Graham, talk to his squad. They hung with him more than we did."

BACK IN THE car, Sam—cheerful and a bit smug—asked him how it went.

"Well," he said, "I learned how much teenage slang has changed. What hasn't changed is that teenage boys are angry, uncooperative creatures."

"Vernacular lesson aside, did he tell you anything interesting?" Sam asked.

"All I got was that Graham—he calls his parents by their first names—was a heavy drinker, hung out with his friends more than he was at home, and knew about Brenda and Roger. Roger was here, his pants were wet, and Jordan—" he paused, trying to remember the kid's wording, "threw him shade."

"Gave him attitude," Sam translated, patting his hand.

He put his blinker on and merged onto the Don Valley Parkway. "What was interesting was that Jordan claims a man visited the farm a few days earlier and argued with Graham over money. His sense was gambling debts."

Sam was nodding. "Jordanna said the same thing."

"I don't think they shared that with the cops. If they had, Bryce would have said something. I'll call Detective Alston at York Regional when we get back. Let him know we're working the case and fill him in," Reece said.

"The kids were probably in shock when the police interviewed them," Sam said. "It's not unusual to forget to mention things that turn out to be important."

"Or they lied."

"I have a bookie contact I've used in the past," Sam said. "He has his hand in most of the Toronto action. I'll give him a call and see if he recognizes Graham's name. He'd have to owe a chunk of change if someone hunted him down to collect."

"Well, they wouldn't kill him. They'd break bones. You can't collect from a dead man."

Sam nodded. "They wouldn't stage it as an accident. Anything else?"

"Jordan thinks Brenda plans to move them into Roger's place," Reece said.

"So the relationship is serious. That's not the impression I got from Roger. Overall, what's the kid like?"

"His only redeeming quality is he's an amazing artist. Or would be if he used paper as his medium rather than his skin." He sighed. "When Jordan and his squad are in prison someday, he can earn dollars inking inmates. Don't ask me to engage with kids again. That heinous exchange validated my suspicion that teenagers aren't part of the human race."

Normally he felt a bit sad leaving the country and heading into Toronto's bumper-to-bumper traffic, but not today. Adaptation or a strong desire to get back to adults? Reece wasn't sure.

"The kids are traumatized," Sam said. "Jordan's attitude and language is a defence mechanism to deal with loss he's too emotionally immature to process. His dad died less than two weeks ago, and his mother is in hospital. Their extended family is sketchy. It's a frightening time, and teens react with anger when they lose security."

"Jordan did not strike me as traumatized. Didn't seem to care at all," Reece insisted. "He's a scary kid. How'd you make out with the other one?"

"Actually, I talked with both girls," Sam said. "Jennifer snuck away from her great-aunt and joined us, but she didn't speak much. I think she's shy. Jordanna did most of the talking. She's very charming, Jordanna I mean. She was at school when it happened. The cheerleaders were planning an after-game event for the football team. Jennifer was with their religious indoctrinating great-aunt. When Jordanna arrived home, a social worker took her next door to her great-aunt and -uncle's place."

"You're sure it wasn't superficial charm?" he asked.

"Why?"

"Football is played in the fall. No football in May. Your charming princess lied."

"Maybe it was an off-season event..." She sounded doubtful.

He patted her hand. "Don't feel bad. Kids lie when they're traumatized." Reece laughed at her eye-roll. "Anything else?"

"Jordanna said Brenda has an office in the barn. I wouldn't mind having a snoop."

"Did she know about Roger?" Reece asked.

"She came home early from school once and met him. Figured they were having an affair, but she didn't blame Brenda. Jordanna said Graham drank and partied, so we have confirmation on that point. They were having money problems, and she overheard an argument. Brenda wanted to sell the farm."

He pulled off the Don Valley Parkway and headed west on Queen Street to the loft. "When you called Roger to tell him we took the case, did you ask how Brenda's doing?"

"He says he talks to her and thinks he's getting through but she's unresponsive. He told her he hired us," she said. "How about you follow up with Graham's donkey pals and I'll see about talking to Brenda?"

"Sounds good. Let's get cleaned up and go out for dinner," he said. "You pick the place, just nowhere with kids."

CHAPTER TEN

SAM

AT MOUNT SINAI Hospital on College and University streets, Sam entered the Second Cup coffee shop on the ground floor and texted Roger. Having visited "9-South" during her psychology training, she knew non-family admission to psychiatric patients required doctor's consent. She ordered a basic coffee and a chai latte from the barista and settled at a corner table to wait.

Roger wasn't normally one for demonstrative affection, so she choked on her coffee when he leaned down and hugged her.

"What was that for?" She wiped a coffee dribble from her chin with a paper napkin.

"A discomfiting endeavour to apologize for being an arse." He sat and removed the lid from his drink. "I'm an insufferable bore and astonished you tolerate me."

"Forget it," she said, eager to get past the awkwardness. "You weren't yourself last time we talked." She updated him on Reece's discussion with Bryce and their interview with the twins.

When she finished, Roger looked pensive. "So, Graham was a gambling man."

"Brenda didn't mention it?"

"I knew they had financial troubles," he said. "I loaned her money on a couple of occasions."

"How much?"

He blew on his chai latte and fiddled with the plastic lid. "Oh, about twenty grand, more or less."

The amount stunned her. "For what?"

"I felt it impertinent to ask. It's curious Jordan thinks they're all moving in with me." He frowned and looked a bit alarmed.

"You don't think your relationship is headed in that direction?" she asked.

"No." His Adam's apple bobbed as he swallowed hard, and he nibbled on his tattered thumbnail before dropping his hand to the table. "There's... intellectual distance between us." A flush of colour crept up his face.

Sam laughed. "There's intellectual distance between you and most people. Brenda's not the brightest crayon in the box?"

He cleared his throat. "Brenda can't even follow *Game of Thrones*. The plot is too complicated. She dislikes classic literature and music, and the Royal Ontario Museum bores her."

Sam could hardly fault Brenda for not being able to follow *Game of Thrones; many* people couldn't. Silently, Sam reviewed her conversation with Jordanna. The girl was scary smart.

"Was Graham bright?" she asked.

"Not that I noticed, why?"

"Have you met their kids?"

"Jordanna once or twice. Jennifer more often." Roger lowered his eyes. "Jordan the day his father died."

"Jordanna is smart." She refrained from adding "and manipulative." A quick call to King City Secondary had confirmed the cheerleaders weren't planning a school event on the afternoon of Graham's murder. Reece was right. It pissed her off she hadn't caught the lie. It made her wonder what else Jordanna had lied about, and what she'd been up to on the afternoon her father had died.

"Jordan is also brilliant," Roger said. "They're top of their grade twelve class and received acceptance letters to every university they applied to. University of Toronto, McGill, and UBC have offered scholarship incentives." He paused. "Jennifer is a genius. Her IQ is higher than mine."

Sam laughed at the dour expression on his face. "Did Brenda tell you that?"

"She asked me to do a neuropsychological assessment," he said.

"Why?"

"The school recommended it last year because Jennifer's marks don't reflect her abilities. The hypothesis is a learning impediment they lack resources to diagnose. I never finished the neuropsych testing. Graham found out and was livid."

"Why?"

"He claimed that tests label children and force them to conform to a diagnosis, which stifles natural development." Roger frowned. "But he lied. That wasn't the reason. I don't know what his real concern was."

"The affair," Sam said bluntly. "Having you, of all people, test his daughter behind his back wouldn't have landed well with Graham. Can you blame him?"

Roger shook his head but didn't look convinced. "I considered that but there was more to his objection. It felt like fear."

"It probably was. He's right about the issues associated with labelling," Sam said. "When adults tell children they differ from their peers, the child's perception is negative. They want to belong to the herd. Nice kids?"

"Jennifer is. She's sweet and charming. Has a way about her. I didn't spend enough time with either of the twins to judge. Brenda had complaints, but we didn't speak about the children after I stopped treating her."

Meaning he wouldn't breach confidentiality by discussing what she'd revealed during therapy.

"Can you give me a single word to describe her complaint?"

His stare was intense as he held her eyes with his. "Jordan and Jordanna are cruel."

Teenagers were notorious for cruelty, especially around their parents. The description didn't surprise or alarm Sam, who had counselled families. Once, when Sam had to schedule an evening meeting with a troubled teen and her mother, she'd stepped off the elevator to the deserted fifth floor of the empty building and had heard a woman screaming and pounding on a door. The fifteen-year-old had locked her claustrophobic mother in a dark janitor's closet. Sam had found the girl sitting passively in a chair outside her office. The teenager had defiantly stated it was a joke and that her mother needed to lighten up.

"Jordan and Jordanna said their dad liked to party," she ventured. Having caught Jordanna in at least one lie, Sam was hesitant to believe anything the girl had told her.

"Extensively, as I understand it," Roger said in agreement. "Graham would leave on Saturday morning and not return until late Sunday night. Because of his erratic business schedule, he dawdled about the farm during the week. Brenda found his idleness and ineptitude off-putting." He crushed the plastic lid from his chai latte, and his knuckles turned white. His eyes were dark with hatred, and his tone was low and gruff when he said, "His family lived like animals."

The rabid anger in Roger's eyes reminded Sam of his expression on the day he'd bludgeoned his sister with the hammer. She didn't understand why he had such strong feelings about a man he claimed he didn't know well. It didn't make sense.

"Did Graham ever confront you about the affair?" she asked.

Roger looked startled. "No. Of course not. I... I didn't even realize he knew."

"Well, he did. The kids knew, and they both said their father also knew."

Roger didn't respond. He dropped his eyes and started tearing the crushed plastic lid.

"What did Graham do for a living after leaving football?" she asked.

Roger looked up. His expression had shifted from raw hatred to mild interest. "Oh, some guest spots with The Sports Network," he replied airily, dropping the crushed and torn plastic lid to the table and sipping daintily at his tea.

His about-face was disconcerting—it was as if he'd hastily popped on a mask to hide his true emotions. Sam watched him in silence, and a nasty feeling of suspicion washed over her. She'd known Roger for over twenty-five years, ever since her parents had bought the house on Vero Beach when Sam was four and her father had left London Police Services to join the Toronto force. Today, it felt like she was talking with a stranger.

"Graham was competing for a coaching job with the Toronto Varsity Blues," Roger continued in a pleasant tone. "I'm not certain if that came to fruition, but he was pushing his son to attend U of T and play football. Jordan didn't want to. He wanted to go to UBC. Graham threatened to cut off financial assistance if his son didn't comply and stay in Toronto. Their relationship was ugly. Contentious."

Reece was following up with the Argonauts to get a list of Graham's acquaintances. Sam added TSN and the University of Toronto to the list she was making on a memo app on her phone. She thought about Roger's statement that Jordan was at odds with his dad before the murder. A disagreement over where to attend school wasn't exactly solid motive to off your father. But money was and she'd have to find out the details of Graham's estate.

"Does Reece know our history?" Roger's earnest eyes held hers.

"Yup."

He gazed across the café. "I want to speak with him and apologize. My hospitality left a bit to be desired when I invited him for lunch the week before last." His eyes drifted back to hers. "I want you to be happy. After everything we've been through over the years, you may not believe me but it's the truth."

The last thing she wanted to do was rehash ancient history. There wasn't any point. It was what it was and it was over.

"Come on. Take me up to see Brenda," she said.

"This is a waste of time. She hasn't spoken and doesn't respond to external stimuli. Her primary prescribed Risperidone." He stood, leaving his garbage littered on the table. "But I don't concur that schizophrenia is the correct diagnosis. She witnessed something in that cellar."

Sam gathered up the trash and dumped it in the can. "Atypical antipsychotics are gaining ground in treating post-traumatic stress," she reminded him.

"Perhaps."

"Isn't the main objective to pull her from catatonia?" Sam followed him to the main elevators.

"Yes, but my concern is Risperidone will impede psychogenic amnesia treatment. We may never find out what happened."

Memory loss was a possible side effect of the drug. If witnessing her husband's murder had caused the mental break, recovering the episodic memories would be hard. Harder if a psychotropic drug blocked a therapist's efforts.

"Maybe it's not what she saw," Sam suggested. "Maybe it's what she did. Could Brenda have killed Graham?"

Roger didn't respond. They rode the elevator in silence. When they reached their floor, Sam grabbed his arm to stop him from exiting. "Roger, could Brenda have killed her husband?" she repeated.

He sighed, shrugging his arm out of her grasp and stepping out of the elevator. "They argued and it escalated to violence sometimes. On more than one occasion, she admitted to striking him after he hit her." His hand twitched at his side. "The marriage was a war zone. I wanted her to leave."

He'd just told her he had no interest in pursuing a serious relationship because Brenda wasn't an intellectual giant. Why would he urge her to leave the marriage? Either he hadn't encouraged his lover to end her marriage, or he was more serious about Brenda than he'd admitted. Either way, her friend was lying to her. A dark knot settled in her stomach.

They hiked down a long corridor to a set of locked double doors, and a nurse buzzed them through. Changing the direction of her questions, Sam asked, "When you were at the house that day, did you hear anyone other than Brenda and Graham?"

"It sounded like more than two people arguing." He thought for a minute. "I assumed Jordan was in the basement. After—" He rubbed his eye and cleared his throat. "When I looked through the window, he was in the kitchen. I couldn't tell for sure if he'd been in the cellar and had come upstairs or if someone else was downstairs with Graham and Brenda."

Patients in robes, nurses, and orderlies flowed around them. Roger was motioning at her to move, and Sam followed him from the centre of the hallway to a wall between two room doors.

"How about cars?" she asked, and leaned against the wall. "When you pulled in, was there a car you didn't recognize?"

"Two, in fact. Brenda's was at the top of the driveway, but there was a truck and an old BMW in the yard. I don't know what Graham drove." He paused before rushing to add, "Brenda has a history of socially unacceptable behaviour."

Sam frowned. "What?" That last statement seemed to have come out of nowhere.

"I was working with her on controlling incidents of extreme rage, followed by impulsive yet calculated behaviour," he replied calmly. "The week before, she'd had a disagreement at a grocery store. She waited in the parking lot for the other woman. Then she followed her home, tailgating and utilizing intimidating behaviour." He held her eyes. "It wasn't the first time Brenda felt victimized and retaliated."

The knot in Sam's stomach tightened. Now he was throwing his lover under the bus. It felt like deflection, a means to shift attention off him.

"On the day of the murder, did you go into the cellar when you heard yelling?" she asked.

He continued walking down the hallway. "I did not enter the house."

A lie.

"Roger, police found your fingerprints in the stairwell, and Jordan told Reece the bottoms of your pants were wet. If you hadn't been in the cellar, why were your pants wet?"

He stopped in the corridor and she nearly ran into him. He turned to face her, his eyes angry. "Jordan's lying! I saw him in the backyard when he arrived from school. Brenda and Graham were arguing inside. He's trying to incriminate me! My trousers weren't wet and he's a liar."

Fingerprints didn't lie. He had been inside the house in the stairwell that led to the crime scene. But he hadn't denied being in the house in the past. Maybe the fingerprints weren't recent. If the blood the police found on the cellar stairs and on the landing wall turned out to be Roger's, that would confirm that he'd been in the house on the day of the crime. They'd know soon enough.

Deciding not to challenge him on his declaration that he hadn't been in the house, she asked, "Do you remember what you were wearing?"

"Of course." Roger continued walking down the hall with long strides.

Sam had to jog to keep up with him. "A lab can confirm the absence of biodegradable waste," she said. "Sewage had backed into the standing water that flooded the cellar."

He stopped with his back to her and his shoulders stiffened. "I had my trousers dry cleaned."

"Doesn't matter. We're having them tested," she retorted. "Negative results will prove to police that Jordan lied and you weren't holding Graham's head under the water."

Without turning, he asked over his shoulder, "Why would the pants be wet? The culprit wore rubber boots, which proves Jordan is lying."

She didn't recall telling him forensics had matched the boot print on Graham's neck to rubber boots. Police hadn't released that detail to the press. Perhaps the detectives had mentioned it to Roger during their interview.

She grabbed his shoulder to turn him to face her. "I want the pants."

Roger exhaled impatiently. "Then you shall have them." He stopped at a closed door. "Can we not talk about this in front of Brenda? Although she's unresponsive, we don't know how much she hears and comprehends. It's important not to upset her."

Sam nodded and stepped through the door Roger held open.

Brenda was sitting in a chair by the window. Her blue eyes were wide and blank. She was indeed a beautiful woman. High cheekbones, wide-set eyes, and a straight nose were symmetrically set in a milky complexion. Wispy bangs veiled her eyebrows, and her straight hair was a shiny sheet down her back, ending just before her waist.

Sam stood in the doorway, watching with confusion as Roger held Brenda's hand and chatted to her. Although she couldn't hear the words, there was an intimacy in the exchange. The show of affection felt contrary to the negative remarks he'd just shared in the hallway. While Roger stroked Brenda's cheek and whispered in her ear, the woman didn't move or indicate awareness. Sam watched the hypocritical picture with unease.

After a few minutes without any response from Brenda, Sam accepted that there wasn't any point in trying to talk with the woman. The lights were on, but Brenda Harris wasn't home.

CHAPTER ELEVEN

REECE

THE TORONTO ARGONAUTS defensive coordinator had kept in touch with Graham after he'd left the team. The man gushed about Graham's generous nature and kind disposition. According to him, the ex-football player had visited sick children in the hospital, delivering free season tickets and footballs signed by the team. In response to Reece's query about friends, the man provided him with contact details for someone he said Graham had brought to meet the team last summer. Reece figured it was a good start to tracking down Graham's squad.

Claude Malletier's office manager directed Reece to a Habitat for Humanity site on Dalton Road in Sutton, an hour north of Toronto on Lake Simcoe. The site was buzzing with construction activity, and Reece stopped at a trailer to ask for Claude.

While he waited, he wandered around the site, chatting with volunteers and learning about the project. They couldn't have broken ground too long ago, because they hadn't poured the foundations. The *beep-beep-beep* of cement trucks backing up rang in his ears, along with loud guffaws of laughter that came from the groups of men and women who stood around the house lots, holding shovels and waiting for the trucks to dump the cement.

The idea of volunteering to build family homes intrigued Reece. His fondest childhood memories included the large Tudor style house in Windsor where he had grown up with his brother. This summer marked the twelfth anniversary of the accident that killed his parents and brother. Not a day passed without Reece grieving the loss of his family.

The volunteers were nice and welcomed him when he stopped to ask questions. One of the on-site engineers showed Reece the architect's plans, explaining how they maximized their budget to produce high-quality homes. The houses would be simple, no fancy fixtures or finishes, but they would be solid and functional.

Helping to build them might be fun. Reece could swing a hammer and was good at following directions. Giving back would be nice. Maybe Sam would want to volunteer and they could make some new friends together. It wouldn't disappoint Reece to see the back end of her current group, especially Lisa and Roger.

A man's cheerful greeting startled him, and Reece turned to find a middle-aged man walking across the packed dirt toward him. The man removed his white construction helmet and wiped sweat off his sunburned, bald crown. His smile exposed stained yellow teeth, and a calloused hand pumped Reece's arm with enthusiasm.

"My office called, said to expect you. Claude Malletier at your service." His bow made Reece laugh.

"Reece Hash, Toronto PI. I'm involved in the investigation into Graham Harris's murder." He handed Claude a card.

The man shook his head. "Damn shame. I still can't believe it. Come on over to the picnic tables. Whatever I can do to help."

"How did you know Graham?" Reece asked.

"Here. Well, not this site, we only broke ground a month ago. The Brimley site in Markham last year."

Settling onto the picnic table bench across from Claude, Reece said, "So Graham volunteered."

"You bet, for about two years. He was on the Brimley project from start to finish. Was here for the groundbreaking ceremony and on the roster for this tour of duty. Hard worker. When it comes to working with their hands, some men won't admit they're up shit creek. Not Graham. He'd ask for help. Everyone liked him. He'll be missed."

That was what the Argonauts had said. Graham was a great guy. It didn't fit with what the family or Roger claimed. Maybe these outsiders hadn't known Graham well.

"How often did he volunteer?"

"Every weekend, in like clockwork. First one to arrive, last one to leave. Worked on the interiors during the winter. He stayed with me a couple of times. Wife liked him, and she's a crusty old c—" He caught himself with a sheepish grin and cleared his throat. His expression turned serious. "Makes me damn mad what happened."

Maybe Graham had a second squad. One he didn't wear his public face around. But participating in Argonauts charity events, volunteering every weekend building homes, and working for TSN didn't leave much time for Graham to cavort with his buddies.

"Did Graham ever bring anyone with him to the job site?" Reece asked.

Claude's expression hardened and his lips pressed together. After a moment he mumbled, "Yeah, his boy once."

"Just the once?" Reece prompted.

"Once was enough." He snorted. "The apple fell far from the tree with that kid."

"You didn't like him?"

"The kid is an asshole," Claude said. "If he were mine, I'd be smacking the smug grin off his face."

"Jordan doesn't appreciate what you're doing here, eh?"

Claude rolled his eyes. "Doesn't have an ounce of human kindness in him. Embarrassed his old man by making fun of the houses. He even made snide comments about the people we're building them for. Graham never brought him again."

"Did you and Graham ever go out drinking after work?"

"Nah, Graham never touched the stuff, even beer. Working in the sun, I bring cases for the end of the day when we're roofing. Graham stuck to soda and water."

Hiding a drinking problem was tough. It was doubtful that the man could have spent every weekend working with Claude without touching a drop of booze.

The Argonauts defensive coordinator had also told Reece that Graham didn't drink. It seemed that Roger had lied to Sam. But Roger admitted that he didn't know Graham, so the more likely explanation was that Brenda had lied to Roger. Maybe she wanted people to believe her husband was a hard-drinking, abusive man to excuse the fact she was cheating on him. That didn't explain Jordan's comment to him or Jordanna's to Sam. The more Reece thought about it, the more convinced he became that Graham's family were intentionally sullying his reputation.

Claude was looking impatient and Reece asked, "Was he skilled at construction?"

The man held out his hand and rolled it side to side. "He could follow directions, but he couldn't think outside the box, if you know what I mean. Thing was, Graham got it, you know? He didn't fiddle with shit he didn't understand. He'd back off and wait for reinforcements. Never had a problem tearing something out and redoing it."

If that was true, Graham must have thought the electrical problem in the basement would be easy to fix. A crossed wire in the receptacle maybe.

"How was he around electricity?"

"Didn't touch it here. We only use licensed trades. I can introduce you to the others. Rajah is here. Ran into him an hour ago. Thirty years' experience as an electrician. He and Graham got on. Raj taught him some simple stuff for his house." He shook his head sadly. "Great property, but they needed to pull down the buildings, especially that old barn. They should have stayed in the city and worked on the farmhouse part time."

"Why *did* he move his family, do you know?"

"He said something happened and the move was good for the kids." Claude shrugged. "Never said what."

"Did you visit the farm?" Reece asked.

"Sure. Met the little woman and the girls. The youngest is a cutie-pie, sweet as sugar. And his wife, *mamma mia!*" He fanned his face with his hand and grinned. "Wouldn't mind coming home to her."

"Did Brenda and the kids know he was volunteering here?" Reece asked.

"I guess so." The man peeked at his watch. "They knew we were from Habitat for Humanity."

"I'll take you up on that offer to speak with people who knew Graham," Reece said, standing and circling the table to Claude's side.

They walked around the site, and Claude introduced a dozen men and women. Everyone said the same thing: Graham Harris was a hard worker, a dedicated volunteer, and a great person.

Graham hadn't been out drinking and gambling every weekend. He'd built houses for disadvantaged people and tried to learn how to fix up his ancestral home. He was either the most misunderstood man in the world, or his wife and kids were misleading people. Dead people couldn't defend themselves, and it made Reece's blood boil that Graham's family was tarnishing his memory.

It was time to meet the woman behind the man. Reece texted Roger to see if he could visit Brenda. There wasn't any point in heading home if Roger was available to meet him. He'd go straight to the hospital. Reece sat in the driver's seat with the car door open and watched the activity on the site, again wondering if he wanted to volunteer.

After about ten minutes, Roger responded, *If U can B here B4 3. Need to talk /w U.*

Reece started the car and headed back to downtown Toronto, curious over what Roger wanted to talk to him about. If they were lucky, Brenda was lucid.

CHAPTER TWELVE

I SIT ALONE and think. My mind scampers along, popping with electrical signals from the billions of neurons. But in the mirror, my face remains calm. My heart thumps at a perfect sixty beats per minute. Then I think about her. In the mirror my pupils contract. The pulse in my neck quickens.

"Control," I whisper to my reflection.

My mind clears and becomes blank. I try again. This time, I envision blood pouring from her neck and relish the warmth when it washes over my hands. I picture the light as it fades from her eyes and the glassy haze of death that dulls the green of her irises. Satisfaction and peace replace the rolling wave of desire.

Pretending is second nature to me now. Just as I have learned to control physical signs, I have learned to control interaction. I watch her and know she doesn't see me for what I am. I can play with her before I kill her. But before she dies, she'll suffer. I will take from her the one thing she loves because I can.

She is a bit like me. I feel it deep inside on a primal level. It's surprising that she hasn't recognized what I am, but I suspect she will soon. She's hunting now. Instead of fear, there's a sense of arousal that's primitive. A hunger I must feed.

CHAPTER THIRTEEN

REECE

REECE ARRIVED AT the office he and Sam shared in the Palmerston district at three o'clock. As usual, there wasn't anywhere to park. Frustrated, he trolled along College Street and then Palmerston until a smart car pulled out. Only sheer determination and assertiveness got him wedged into the snug spot. Horns blared and drivers shrieked obscenities while he jammed traffic. He'd grown a thick skin over the past year and ignored the indignant shouts, but, when he tried to exit the car, a truck nearly took off his door. That was tougher to ignore, and he took a deep breath to quiet his galloping heart. Toronto parking was a beast he wasn't certain he'd ever master.

Before going upstairs, he popped into the Italian bakery on the street level of the building where their office occupied a small space on the second floor. Reece bought a lime Gatorade from Maria, who ran the family bakery in the two-storey building she owned with her husband. Having witnessed his parking adventure, his landlady put him through some good-natured teasing that he accepted with a chuckle.

Reece went out the front door of the bakery to an external side entrance that accessed the upper level. At the top of the narrow stairwell leading to the offices above, the Gatorade slipped out of his hand and bounced down the stairs. It hit the glass door to the street and spun around on the floor. Reece trudged back downstairs with a sigh and knelt to grab it. As he straightened up, he caught a glimpse of someone walking by who looked an awful lot like Jennifer Harris. He yanked open the door and stepped onto the sidewalk. The girl—or perhaps woman, he couldn't tell from the back—had crossed the street and entered a coffee shop. He was about to follow her when his phone rang. Reece checked the caller ID. Sam.

Keeping his eye on the coffee shop across the street, he answered, "Hey, what's up?"

"I'm drowning in background checks," she said with an exaggerated moan. "Where are you?"

The woman came out of the shop with a coffee in her hand and continued down the street in the opposite direction. From this angle, it didn't look as much like Jennifer as he'd first thought. A streetcar stopped and the woman got on.

"Reece? Are you still there?"

"Yeah, I'm on my way upstairs," he told her. "See you in a minute." He disconnected, and turned back to the door.

When he finally arrived at the office, the door stuck on the archaic orange shag carpet, and he had to fight to get into the disgusting three-hundred-square-foot space.

Sam looked up from her side of their old, scarred partner desk. "Hey you. How's your day been?"

"Busy and aggravating. I thought I saw Jennifer Harris outside. Was she here?"

Sam shook her head. "Are you sure it was her?"

"No. I only caught a glimpse of her. How was your day?"

He almost knocked over the rickety wicker table that held their ugly bar fridge and circa-1980s coffee machine. With some gymnastic moves that put his parking manoeuvres to shame, he managed to get to the chair on his side of the desk. The chair was lovely because he'd bought it himself. Everything else looked like it came from a junkyard. The orange plastic visitor chairs with rusted metal legs were plain gross. Moving to new digs was a constant bone of contention. Part of Sam's resistance about leaving was her close relationship with Maria, but the real issue was that she didn't like change.

Maybe with the money from the case, they could reach a compromise. Last year, when Reece had talked to Maria about the sad state of the upstairs office, she'd offered to deduct the cost of renovation material from their rent. The problem was that Reece didn't feel capable of tackling the project. A construction expert, such as Claude Malletier, might be able to do something. If they threw everything out and gutted the space, a carpenter could add custom built-ins. New drywall, baseboards, doors, flooring, and a new window—without the hideous orange metal blinds that were so bent they wouldn't close—would improve things. He'd read about small air conditioning units that could be ceiling-mounted when central air wasn't an option. That would just leave the matter of no parking.

Sam filled him in on her day and finished by saying, "So I heard back from my bookie contact. He can't find any trace of Graham Harris placing bets. The thing is people often use a pseudonym. But he asked around and couldn't find anyone who recently paid a visit to a client up in Vaughan."

"After talking to people who knew Graham, I don't believe he gambled," Reece said firmly. "The twins overheard an argument between their father and a stranger. They thought it was about money. They drew their own conclusions."

"Why would Brenda lie to Roger and tell him Graham gambled?"

"A ploy to garner sympathy so he'd give her the money?" he suggested.

"I guess," Sam said but looked dubious. "Assuming the catatonic state breaks, we can confront her about why she needed so much money. Roger's meeting me here. I'm going with him to get the pants."

She was obsessed with those damn pants.

"I know." Reece turned on his laptop. "He mentioned it when I left the hospital."

"Oh, you saw Brenda? Any change in her condition?"

"No, I couldn't get her to respond to me." He sighed and ran his fingers through his hair, trying to find the words to express his gut impression at the hospital. "I don't know how to explain it because nothing she did supports my suspicion, but I felt like she knew I was there."

"I didn't get that sense at all when I saw her," Sam said. "Patients can't fake catatonia, Reece. Humans have too many uncontrollable psychological responses to stimuli."

Reece supposed she was right, but he couldn't shake the feeling that Roger was protecting Brenda. "Wouldn't Roger be the one doing the tests?" he asked.

Sam shook her head. "No, he's not the attending psychiatrist."

He opened his Gatorade, took a long drink, and updated her on his meeting with the Argonauts and Claude Malletier, finishing by saying, "So Brenda and the kids are lying about Graham being a big drinker."

"Okay," Sam said slowly. "That's strange. Maybe the kids parroted Brenda's impression, and she's lying to deflect blame for cheating."

"Yeah, I considered that. Still, I think the twins lied with intent and I'd like to find out why." He entered his password to unlock his laptop and leaned back in his chair. "What do you think about volunteering with Habitat for Humanity? It might be fun. Something we could do together."

"I'd love to, but time is the enemy," she said. "Speaking of which, can you finish these background checks for me?"

Disappointing response, but maybe he'd be able to talk her into it after the case ended.

Roger popped his head through their open door. It had to be open when two people were in the room or the heat rose to an insufferable temperature. Unless it was winter. From December to March, the office was so cold Reece could see his breath.

"Hello there!" Roger's tone was jovial, and he perched himself on one of the orange chairs. The rusted metal legs creaked when he sat. He looked down in alarm and shifted in the seat. After a moment of cautious bouncing on the chair, he appeared satisfied that the legs weren't going to collapse. He leaned back and stared at Sam with a strange expression that Reece didn't like.

Reece cleared his throat. Loudly. "How's it going?"

Roger's attention shifted to him. "Lisa is on the warpath." He rolled his eyes. "She thinks you thwarted Kira's zoo plans and ruined her daughter's day out with Auntie Sam."

"That's ridiculous. I'll talk to her." Sam stood and tried to squeeze by Roger's chair to reach the door. "Let's go get your pants."

Roger frowned but stood.

"See you back at the loft?" she asked Reece.

"Sure, I'll make dinner."

"Oh, I thought Sam and I would have dinner together," Roger said. "You could join us, if you want."

"Perfect," Sam said.

Reece stood. "A minute before you go." He motioned her to follow him into the corridor. When she did, he pulled the door shut and took her to the stairwell for privacy.

"I don't want to have dinner with Roger," he stated bluntly.

"Do you care if I stay?"

"I do, in fact."

She looked up at him, not saying anything for a few seconds. "Is there a problem?" she finally asked.

"No, I just want alone time with you tonight."

But there *was* a problem. Reece hadn't liked the look in the man's eye when he'd checked out Sam. At the hospital, Roger had apologized for his attitude during the Wagyu steak lunch fiasco; he'd claimed he was happy Sam had found someone to share her life with. Reece wasn't buying it. Roger had feelings for Sam, and it made him damn uncomfortable. Stupid, maybe. He trusted Sam. But there was something slimy about Roger.

Sam was studying him with a small smile, and Reece felt colour flood his face. She knew he was jealous and found it funny.

She kissed him. "Okay, but how about takeout? I'm not in the mood for fancy."

Reece nodded, knowing she'd change her mind when she tasted the beef Wellington he was making.

They returned to the office, and Roger and Sam left Reece alone to finish the background checks. Frankly, he doubted the hapless interviewees would want to work for a company that conducted sneaky background checks on applicants. These weren't standard police checks. The client hacked social media accounts and dug deep enough to skirt privacy laws. It left a sour taste in Reece's mouth and was one of many aspects of a PI's job he loathed.

After the checks, he found a YouTube video on how to prepare Gordon Ramsey's famous beef Wellington. He stopped the video to zoom in and scrutinize the pastry wrapping technique. From behind him, he heard a girlish voice.

"Hi, Reece, right?"

He glanced up from the screen to find Jordanna in the doorway.

"Hello," he said, more than a little surprised. "What brings you here?"

Her nose crinkled with distaste when she looked around the office. "I was in the city and wanted to talk to Sam." She closed the door behind her.

Reece gestured to the chair Roger had vacated. Maybe she'd taken the trip to speak with them in private. "Sam's not here, but I can help. What's up?"

She removed her jacket and tucked it on the back of the chair. Reece's eyes widened. She was wearing a sheer blouse without a bra. Her breasts were huge and the nipples pressed against the see-through fabric.

Jordanna sat and crossed her legs. Her tight black skirt rode up her thigh, and he caught a glimpse of white panties.

She ran the tip of her tongue across her upper lip, tilted her head to the side, and regarded him coyly. "Do you want to go and grab a drink?"

Embarrassed by her attire and flirtatious manner, Reece circled the desk on the other side to avoid having to brush by her. "How about I grab you something from downstairs."

Her eyes dropped to his Gatorade. "That'll work. I'll have the same as what you're drinking."

At the bakery, he exhaled forcefully and texted Sam. *Where are you?*

Streetcar, heading to the loft. No pants. Pissed off. Tell you later.

It would take her twenty minutes to get back to the office. This was idiotic. Was he prepared to hang around the bakery stalling until his fiancée arrived to rescue him? He could handle a flirtatious teenager, but teenagers didn't accept rejection well. Sometimes they lied. Reece gnawed on his lower lip.

"Maria," he said, approaching the counter, "can you come upstairs for a minute?" He felt foolish but believed in trusting his gut, especially where scantily clad women were concerned.

Maria smiled knowingly. "I see girl," she said in her thick accent, taking off her apron. "Angelo! Take the counter."

Her twenty-two-year-old son came out and waved at Reece. He sat on the stool by the cash register and buried his nose in a book.

Maria swatted the book from his hand. "I clean the bathroom. You with customers, not with book."

She took a pail filled with cleaning supplies from under the counter and pushed at Reece. "Get on. Girls don't bite."

"That one might." Angelo snickered. "I saw her go up. Ooh la la!"

Maria yelled something in rapid Italian and marched to the stairs. Behind her back, Angelo winked at Reece and grinned.

In the stairwell, they ran into Jordan storming down the stairs.

Reece stared at him in confusion. "Where did you come from?"

"Back door open," Maria stated and continued up the stairs, glaring daggers at Jordan until he squeezed against the wall so she could pass.

"Tell Jordanna I'm peacing in ten. *Bye Felicia*," he said with a sneer, then slammed the glass door behind him as he left the building.

Reece didn't need an urban slang dictionary for that one. The expression on Jordan's face said it all. Whatever *bye Felicia* meant, it wasn't a compliment.

Jordanna was exiting the washroom when they reached the top of the stairs. She smiled at Reece and sashayed to the office without acknowledging Maria.

In the office—with the door wide open and Maria humming across the hall while she scrubbed a clean bathroom—Reece handed Jordanna the bottle of Gatorade. "Your brother said to tell you he's leaving in ten minutes."

She rolled her eyes but stood. "I was hoping he'd peace when I went to the ladies. At least he went downstairs instead of lurking in your office." She sighed. "I better go before he comes up again."

"Is Jennifer in the city, too?" he asked.

"No. She's in school. Jordan and I cut." She looked at her watch. "She's probably with Rachel by now. Why?"

"I thought I saw her outside," he said.

Jordanna looked confused, took out her phone, and made a call. "Hi, is Jenny there?" She paused to listen and flipped her hair across her shoulder. "Okay, just checking." She paused again and rolled her eyes. "Whatever. See you in a couple of hours."

She tucked her phone into her purse. "Jenny must have a doppelgänger. She's with Rachel. Any news on Daddy's murder?"

"Did you know that your dad built homes for Habitat for Humanity?"

"I guess." She batted her eyelashes. "Is it a clue?"

"Did you tell Sam when you talked with her?"

"I don't remember her asking." She picked up her jacket.

"Where were you the afternoon your dad died?" he asked.

"At the school."

"No, you weren't. We checked."

Her lip lowered to what she probably thought was a sexy pout. "Daddy didn't like me being out alone with boys."

I bet he didn't, Reece thought. "You were with a boy?"

She smiled. "Maybe."

"I need his name," Reece said firmly.

She paused and Reece prepared himself for an argument. Her lips puckered and she leaned over the desk, thrusting her arms against the sides of her breasts to accentuate the cleavage. "Do you have to talk to him? He's a computer geek. I don't want anyone to know I'm into him."

Reece nodded. "I do. Give me a name and number."

She took out her phone, looked up a number, and reluctantly passed him the device.

Reece jotted down the number for someone named Steve.

After putting her phone in her purse, she said, "I have to go before Jordan ditches me and I can't get home. See you later."

Reece stood at the window and watched her exit the building. Jordan was slouching against an older model BMW, smoking. They chatted for a few minutes, and Jordanna took a drag from her brother's cigarette. Before she got in the car, she stared up at the window and blew Reece a kiss.

Teenagers... he didn't understand the creatures and firmly believed he'd never been one.

She'd left the Gatorade unopened on the edge of the desk. He popped it into the fridge, finished his own, and rinsed out his empty bottle with soapy water. Maria insisted they wash the recycled bottles and cans. She had a phobia of long-tailed friends and cockroaches. The bakery was pristine, and she was adamant the building stay that way.

After disposing of the bottle, he printed his recipe and checked to ensure he had the ingredients. Reece couldn't remember the last time he and Sam had enjoyed a quiet night alone. A romantic evening was long overdue—the perfect end to a day fraught with frustration.

CHAPTER FOURTEEN

SAM

SAM WAS IN a foul mood. Instead of going straight home from Roger's house, she'd headed to the gym, thinking that strenuous exercise would clear her head. She hadn't wanted to ruin a nice evening with Reece by bitching. An hour on the treadmill hadn't helped, and the rush-hour streetcar ride back to the loft wasn't improving her ill temper.

The missing pants were the reason her disposition had turned toxic. Roger claimed the dry cleaner forgot to include them with his pickup. No big deal, he'd go back tomorrow. His lackadaisical reaction to a messed-up dry cleaning order was totally at odds with how anal he was about his belongings. There was no way he hadn't checked every item in his pickup. He always did.

An objective person would suspect that Roger didn't want a lab to test the pants. There could only be one reason for his reluctance. He'd been in the cellar the day of Graham's murder. If this were any other case, she'd have marched directly to the dry cleaner and questioned the owner. She hadn't done that and wasn't sure why. She feared it could be misplaced loyalty to an old friend.

At the hospital, when she'd mentioned having a private lab test the pants, Roger had stiffened up. And he'd lied about being in the house. Being in the house didn't mean he was busy committing murder, but Roger was hiding something. No matter how she reasoned with him, he refused to comprehend the investigative importance of those pants. Or, he understood perfectly. He'd destroyed the evidence and blamed the dry cleaner.

Her other issue was how uncomfortable she'd felt alone in the house with him while he pretended to look for the pants. It may have been a subconscious reaction to Reece's jealousy when they left the office, but Roger had felt like a stranger to her. From the corner of her eye, she'd even caught him ogling her. When she turned to face him, his expression had morphed to placid boredom. For the first time in their lifelong friendship, he struck her as unstable.

And there was the intimacy between him and Brenda. Roger was a gifted psychiatrist, and Sam had to admit that Reece was right. If Roger wanted the catatonic diagnosis to remain unchanged, he could coach Brenda. That would explain why he was spending so much time in the hospital despite his suggestion that the relationship wasn't going anywhere serious.

Unable to cope with the crowded streetcar a second longer, she got off two stops early, trudged down the sidewalk to her building, and up the three flights of stairs to the loft. Her mood took another nosedive when she entered to find Reece fussing around the kitchen.

"I thought we were doing something simple, like McD's," she complained.

"'eef 'ellington," he mumbled.

"What?"

He murmured something else and swayed into the kitchen island, knocking over a bottle of olive oil. The contents spilled across the marble and dripped down the side of the island to the floor. The kitchen was a disaster. The mess was unusual for Reece, who was typically a clean cook. The disarray pissed her off even more. Reece cooked and she cleaned up. In addition to not being in the mood for a gourmet delight, she didn't want to spend an hour cleaning the kitchen.

A bottle of Italian Amarone sat on the counter. Empty. Reece had a half glass in his hand. He muttered undecipherable words and wine sloshed out of his glass.

"Did you drink that entire bottle?" She read the label. "Reece, it has over fourteen percent alcohol."

"Sauce."

"You're slurring. You're pissed." She put her hands on her hips.

"Not drunk. Have a headache. My stomach hurts." He rubbed his side.

"Did you take something? Did you mix pain meds with booze? What's wrong with you?"

"Didn't. Sauce."

Annoyance surged over her. "You're drunk," she insisted.

A lump of half-cooked pastry was on the cutting board. Blood ran from slits in the top of the dough.

"What," she said very pointedly, "is that?"

"Beef Wellington." His forehead wrinkled with the effort it took to form the words.

"Christ sake, Reece!"

"Didn't turn out," he said mournfully.

"Of course it didn't. You're drunk! Now I'll have to grab a shower, clean the kitchen, *and* go get food. You need to eat." She scowled at him. "And go to bed. So much for our fun night together."

"I'll go." He staggered to the entry and tumbled over while trying to put on his shoes.

"Are you kidding me? You can't go out in this condition." She stomped up to the bedroom loft, pulling off her clothes along the way.

In the two years they'd been together, she'd never seen him drunk. Underneath her frustration and anger was fear. She didn't like being around intoxicated people. Growing up, Lisa's father had been a mean drunk and it was terrifying. Sam remembered two occasions when her dad had had to restrain Mr. Altieri so Lisa's family could escape the house. The man has been sober for five years, but the psychological damage he'd perpetrated against his daughter was permanent. Lisa's three brothers had survived relatively unscathed, but she'd spent years in therapy.

Sam peered down the stairs. Reece was sitting on the floor trying to navigate the daunting task of tying his shoes. His face was sweaty and he was panting, gulping air through his mouth in rapid succession.

Goddamn it! He's going to hyperventilate.

She grabbed a robe and was halfway downstairs when the door slammed shut.

"Shit!" She raced upstairs and snagged some clothes, scrambling to get her legs into her pants. She pulled a T-shirt over her head as she ran back down the stairs and out the door.

When she reached ground level, Reece was nowhere in sight. Maybe he hadn't even gone to McDonald's. The multitude of take-out options in Corktown was high.

Frustrated, she turned in a circle on the sidewalk, trying to decide what to do. Some fresh air would do Reece good. It certainly wouldn't be the first time that a downtown McDonald's— or any take-out joint for that matter—had to deal with a drunken customer. Maybe the evening would improve after a walk sobered Reece up and he got some food in him.

She went back inside, and, after a quick shower, she attacked the kitchen. It took over an hour to get everything scrubbed and put away to her obsessive-compulsive satisfaction. Still no Reece. Maybe he was angry with her and had hit up a bar instead of going for food. But that was so out of character. It would be more like him to go to the gym to try to sober up.

No response to her text. She called his cell, heard it ringing, and found it on the coffee table.

Another hour passed, and her anger had firmly shifted to worry. A call to the gym confirmed Reece hadn't been there. She tried Lisa and Jim. They hadn't heard from him. Regardless of how silly it was to believe Reece would visit Roger, Sam picked up her phone to call. It rang in her hand. Roger.

"Sam—"

She cut him off. "Is Reece with you?"

"Where are you?"

"Home. Have you seen Reece?"

"Go downstairs and find a cab."

"What? Why?"

"Do it. Now. Stay on the phone with me and get in a cab. Please."

Her heart thumped in her chest, and the muscles in her stomach clenched in fear. She put the phone on speaker, grabbed her wallet, set the alarm, and ran out to Queen Street. She raced into the middle of the road, waving her arms at an approaching cab. Short of running over her, he had no option but to stop.

The cabby yelled that he was off-duty and ordered her out of his cab.

Roger shouted through the speaker, "I'll pay you fifty dollars to bring her to Toronto General, emergency entrance. Get here as fast as you can."

Goosebumps popped out on her arms and blood rushed from her head, leaving her dizzy. The cabby glanced in the rear-view mirror. She didn't realize she was crying until she felt tears dripping off her chin. In the mirror, the driver's glare softened. He put the cab in gear and pulled into traffic, cutting off a car trying to turn off Sumach and narrowly avoiding a streetcar. Outside diners at a bistro patio stared at the taxi as horns blared, and a biker careened onto the sidewalk to escape the speeding vehicle.

"Roger, what's going on?" It had to be Reece.

"EMTs brought Reece in ninety minutes ago. He had my card in his wallet but no phone or emergency contact numbers. They thought he was a psychiatric patient and called me."

Why would they think he was a patient? Why hadn't he asked them to call her?

All the saliva in her mouth dried up. Déjà vu. Racing to the hospital to see her father and knowing it was too late. He'd died at the scene. On the side of the road like an animal, with the drunk driver blubbering that it wasn't his fault.

She couldn't do this again. She couldn't lose someone else without the opportunity to tell him he'd made her life worth living. They were moving in slow motion, although indignant horns blared while the driver sped around cars and pedestrians.

"He's in critical condition," Roger said. "Reece collapsed at McDonald's. One of the girls had CPR training and kept him alive until help arrived. EMTs thought it was a heart attack. ER doctors thought it was alcohol poisoning. How close are you?"

They were pulling up. Roger was pacing outside the ER doors. When he spied the cab, he pocketed his phone and handed the cabby a fifty-dollar bill for a fourteen-dollar fare. Roger dragged her into the ER.

"Where is he?" She looked around frantically. "Where's Reece?"

"They moved him up to ICU just after I called. Come on." He took her to the elevators and pushed three people aside to get her in. "He's still alive," he said, "but we need to hurry."

His voice came from a vacuum. Her vision became blurry, like she was looking through a fish-eye lens of a camera.

He's still alive. But.

"What happened? Was it an accident? How bad it is?" She clutched Roger's hand and he put his arm around her waist. "I can't lose him. He can't die."

Roger tightened his arm around her. When the elevator doors opened, he slipped the lanyard with his hospital credentials around his neck, held the badge up for the duty nurse to see, and waited for her to buzz open the doors to the Intensive Care Unit.

Critically ill patients occupied beds that crowded the open space. Nurses tended to several, while others lay miserable on starched white sheets. Many were unconscious, and a few had sobbing people surrounding their beds. The room reeked of fear and desperation.

Sam fell against the side of Reece's bed and gripped the sheet in her fists. He was unconscious, pale as the pillowcase his head rested on. His black hair made the contrast jarring. Tubes ran out of his arms to an intravenous pump, and a clamp on his finger sent his vital signs to a beeping machine. Accordion tubes lay across his chest, and the end of one disappeared down his throat, held in place by a strap around his jaw. A ventilator pumped oxygen into his lungs, making a sucking noise each time it depressed.

Because of the equipment and medical personnel, she couldn't see a way to get to him. Her need to touch him, to sense the warmth of his living flesh, was overpowering.

"You're family?" a doctor asked.

Her mind was cloudy, and she could barely understand what he'd asked. Mutely, she held up her left hand. The square diamond engagement ring twinkled in the fluorescent light.

"Does Reece have any allergies to food or medication?" the doctor asked.

She shook her head and stared at Reece's long eyelashes lying against his pale skin. *Wake up,* she willed. *You can't leave me here alone.*

"Is he on any medication?"

She shook her head again. *Please, wake up.*

"Any pre-existing medical conditions or past surgeries?"

"No," she croaked. "What's wrong with him? Why isn't he awake?"

"We've sedated him."

"What's that?" She motioned to the intravenous pump.

"Fomepizole," the doctor replied calmly, making notes in the chart he held. "If he ingested the poison less than twelve hours ago, he stands a chance."

"I don't understand. He ate something toxic?"

He glanced up with his pen poised over the paper in the metal chart. "Ethylene glycol." His eyes dropped back to the chart and he made another notation.

Sam wanted to snatch the chart from his hand and throw it across the room to force him to focus on her. "What is that?"

"Antifreeze. Fomepizole is the antidote," the doctor said, closing the chart and hanging it on the bottom of Reece's bed. He tucked his pen into the pocket of his lab coat. "If it weren't for Dr. Peterson, we might not have figured it out in time."

She looked up at Roger.

"A patient once tried to commit suicide by drinking antifreeze," he explained. "I recognized the symptoms and asked the toxicologist to test for ethylene glycol. It presents as intoxication, accompanied by headache and gastronomic discomfort. Often it's confused with stroke or aneurysm."

"It was lucky Dr. Peterson pieced it together," the ICU doctor said. "Police are outside. They want to speak with you."

"I'm not leaving." Sam shoved him aside so she could get to the head of the bed and take Reece's hand in hers. It felt cold.

Roger's phone pinged and he took it out to glance at the screen. "Lisa and Jim are here," he told her. "It'll be a couple of hours before Reece wakes."

If he wakes. That's what Roger meant. Sam could see it in his eyes.

She refused to budge, and Roger had to pry her hand away from the bed's dropped side bar and drag her from the unit.

Two uniformed officers waited outside the ICU. They asked useless questions she couldn't answer about what Reece had eaten during the day. They asked if he suffered from depression, or had a history of mental illness or suicide attempts. They wanted to know if she kept antifreeze or de-icing products in her home. She couldn't keep up with their barrage of questions, and when they asked about the state of their relationship, Jim stepped in and shut them down.

Sam managed to find a business card and the words to tell them to contact Bryce Mansfield. Recognizing the homicide staff inspector's name, they glanced at her card, then at each other, and left.

Lisa bundled Sam in her sweater and took her down to the cafeteria. They sat with hot chocolate and bowls of soup. Neither touched the food. Lisa talked non-stop for three hours. All about the drama in her own life. Maybe she was trying to be supportive by showing her life wasn't perfect either, but it was annoying and Sam wished her friend would shut the hell up.

When Lisa began the story of how she couldn't go to university because of her father, Sam couldn't stand it a second longer.

"I know," she snapped. "I was there. I went through it all with you. Can we just sit quietly?"

Her friend bristled. "I'm trying to keep your mind off things."

"Could you grab me a coffee? Caffeine will help." There was a nice size queue at the counter. The wait would take up at least five minutes, and she'd have the chance to breathe and to settle her raw nerves.

Lisa glowered but stood and smoothed the fabric of her dress. "I'm trying to help. That's why I came. I had to wake my brother to take Kira so I could be here for you."

"I appreciate it and coffee would be a big help."

"Reece is strong." Lisa laid her hand on Sam's shoulder. "He's going to be okay. We're all going to be okay. You'll see."

She returned with the coffee at the same time Roger texted that they'd settled Reece into a private room. Eight hours had passed since his admission. He was awake and wanted to see her.

CHAPTER FIFTEEN

SAM

"STOP FUSSING," REECE said when she tried to stuff another pillow behind his head. "If you add one more, my head will be in my crotch." He winked at her. "We don't want to give the nurses ideas on how to speed up my recovery."

She sat on the chair, but kept his hand grasped in hers. From the moment the doctor had assured her Reece would recover, she hadn't been able to stop touching him.

Roger had taken Brandy over to his house, and Sam was sleeping in the hospital. Last night, she'd crawled in beside him on the single bed, curled her body around his, and spooned him until a gruff nurse came in and ordered her out of the bed.

Lisa had arrived with a stunning acrylic she'd painted of Uthisca's main street, the town Reece loved, where he had worked as an OPP inspector. The thoughtful gift impressed Reece, and at the time, Sam had hoped it was a positive step toward friendship. Now, she wasn't as confident. In less than a week, Lisa's manner had shifted back to antagonism, and every word out of her mouth held an insulting subtext. It wasn't just the nasty disposition. Dark circles ringed Lisa's eyes, she'd lost weight, and Sam couldn't remember the last time she'd seen her smile. It added an extra layer of worry to Sam's already-crippling burden.

Roger had brought a PlayStation, of all things, and the prospect of taking it home and hooking it up in her living room didn't appeal to Sam. Talia visited the day before she shipped out to join the Canadian Special Forces in Syria under Operation Impact. Regardless of Talia's assurance that Canada's role was primarily advisory, Sam had clung to her old friend, trying to fight the premonition that she'd never see her again. For the first time, she experienced the utter misery Abigail must have faced every time the military deployed Talia to a war zone.

"Someone poisoned me," Reece said, pulling her from her thoughts. "We need to find out who did it and why. Any idea when I can get out of here?"

"A couple more renal tests." Reece had been on dialysis to remove the ethylene glycol from his blood, but he wasn't out of the woods.

"Whoever did this must have put something in a drink," he said.

"Let's start from the morning," she suggested.

He grinned. "Well, I had breakfast with you. Maybe I kept you up snoring, and you laced my orange juice with antifreeze in retaliation."

She rolled her eyes. "Be serious."

"I visited the Argonauts' office but I didn't eat or drink anything. Then I drove to the Habitat for Humanity site. Nothing to drink there."

"You went to the hospital to visit Brenda," she reminded him.

"And bought a banana smoothie. I had it in her room."

"Was it out of your sight?"

His expression was grim. "Yeah. Roger wanted to do a few tests and asked me to step out. I forgot the smoothie. He came out, we chatted, and a nurse went into the room. Roger and I waited in the hallway. When the nurse left, we went back and I stayed for about ten minutes. Brenda wasn't responding, so I left."

"So Brenda was alone in the room with your smoothie?"

"Yeah." His stare was intense. "So was Roger."

For the moment, Sam ignored the implication and asked, "How could Brenda get antifreeze? She's on a locked-down floor."

"Someone would have to bring it to her." His blue eyes drilled into hers. "Someone who had regular access to her. The doctors said one-hundred-fifty millilitres could be fatal. Depending on what it was contained in, I wouldn't taste it."

Reece had clearly decided Roger was behind the poisoning, either by enabling Brenda by supplying the antifreeze or by adding it to Reece's drink himself. That didn't make any sense to Sam, and she needed him to focus on other possibilities.

Instead of challenging him, she asked, "If there was half a cup of antifreeze in your drink, wouldn't you notice?"

He shrugged. "Antifreeze is sweet and banana would mask it."

"But the level of the drink would increase significantly," she argued.

"Not if they poured out some of the liquid and replaced it with the poison," he said. "But I don't think they used that much. The larger the dose, the sooner I would be symptomatic. I didn't feel ill until I was making dinner."

The fact Reece was healthy and in outstanding physical condition had contributed to his recovery. But he was correct. The higher the quantity consumed, the sooner he'd have felt symptoms. "That means they didn't want to kill you or were interrupted before they'd added enough."

"I bought a Gatorade when I got back to the office," he said. "Lime. I wouldn't have tasted antifreeze."

She frowned. "But you were alone."

"No, Roger was there. You and I went in the hall. I closed the door so we could speak privately, remember?" His eyes were hard. "He was alone for at least five minutes. All alone with my Gatorade."

"But Roger was the one who told the ER doctors to test for ethylene glycol poisoning," she argued.

"Convenient he thought of that prognosis." His tone was bitter. "Maybe he decided against murdering me, or he didn't intend to kill me. Just make me sick enough that we dropped the case."

"Why would Roger want us to drop a case he convinced us to take? It doesn't make sense."

"Maybe we're on to something he didn't think we'd find."

They contemplated their own thoughts.

"Jordanna visited after you and Roger left," Reece said.

"What?" she asked with surprise, leaning forward in her chair.

"That's why I texted you, remember?" he asked.

"Yeah, but you asked where I was. You never told me she was there."

"Well, she was." Reece raised his eyebrow at her. "You should have seen what she was wearing. It was beyond uncomfortable sitting in that office with her."

"Why didn't you ask me to come back?"

"Maria bailed me out," he said. "She went up to clean the public washroom, and I left the office door open."

Sam smiled. "Maria is the mother I never had and always wanted. But how would Jordanna find an opportunity with you in the room?"

"I texted from the bakery. She wanted a drink and I wanted to escape to clear my head."

"And you left your drink upstairs?"

He nodded. "When Maria and I went up, Jordan was coming downstairs."

"Jordan was there, too?" Sam was completely confused.

"He'd come through the back door."

"Through the alley? How did he find the correct door? They aren't marked in the back."

"I never thought of that," Reece said. "Maria said she'd left it open. But you wouldn't guess it accessed our office."

"You would if you'd done some reconnaissance," she said slowly. "Planned an impromptu visit. Maybe used your sister as distraction."

"When I returned upstairs, Jordanna was exiting the washroom. She said she'd left Jordan in the office, hoping he'd leave."

"Interesting," Sam said. "So Jordan was also alone with your drink. Why was Jordanna there? What did she want?"

"Nothing, best I could tell," he said. "Maybe she wanted to speak with us privately but her brother figured it out and interrupted."

"Maybe," Sam said.

"Another weird thing. Jordan's car was in front," Reece said. "I saw them from the window. There was no reason for him to be in back, and Angelo and Maria saw Jordanna enter the building, meaning she used the front door. Why would her brother go around back?"

"Because he didn't want anyone to see him," Sam said. "Maybe he intended on eavesdropping."

"But she caught him when she went out to the hallway to access the washroom," Reece said.

"So Brenda had opportunity, but we aren't sure about means," she said. "Jordanna and Jordan both had opportunity and could have brought the antifreeze with them."

He held her eyes. "And Roger. Roger had opportunity, means, and motive."

She sighed in frustration. "Fine, I understand that you're positive it was him, but what's his motive for trying to kill you? He's the one who begged us to take the case."

"He's still in love with you, and I'm in the way."

"No," she said firmly. "What happened to you is because of the case. Whoever did this wants us to drop the investigation. At the very least, they want to stall us. Roger needs us to find out who killed Graham. Don't you see? It doesn't make any sense."

Reece slapped his hand on the bedrail and exhaled loudly.

He was clearly annoyed at her but Sam refused to back down, waiting out his silence. If he could remove the personal aspect and look at the facts objectively, she had faith in his ability to stop forcing assumptions to fit his suspicions.

After a few minutes, Reece's facial expression changed from annoyed to contemplative. "Okay, you may be right. If so, then that means we're getting close to something. Any ideas?"

She thought about it. "It's time to learn more about Brenda, Jordanna, and Jordan," she said. "And to find out if Brenda could leave her room without detection."

CHAPTER SIXTEEN

IT WASN'T MY intention to kill him, not from a distance. The time will come, but, when it does, I'll be close and witness the moment when recognition dawns in his eyes. At first, he'll negotiate for his life, and his breath will turn sour with fear as his eyes plead for mercy. But as the hours pass, acceptance will surface, and he'll debase himself and beg for death. An animal goes limp before its captor's teeth tear into its throat. The broken wings of a bird lay still before the predator rips the meat from its body. That moment, the instant when denial fades, is the deepest pleasure.

Cats play with mice. It isn't the hunt. It's the pleasure of the game. He's a distraction, not the end game. He is only a means to hurt her on an emotional level that physical pain won't reach. Killing the dog would be poetic, but I've always liked dogs. An oddity, I suppose. Felines and feral animals are a different story. Dogs are too trusting; their fear isn't rewarding. It's too simple. I'm many things, but simple is not one. I'm a complicated creature. I live for the game.

Tick, tock, tick tock. How much time does my lovely have?

CHAPTER SEVENTEEN

REECE

HEARING A KNOCK, Reece dropped the *Architectural Digest* he was reading on the kitchen table and headed to the front door, tripping over an excited Brandy who was clearly eager to greet her keyless mistress.

Reece gave an exasperated little chuckle as he yanked open the door. "You know babe, if you'd leave your keys on the altar by the front door, you'd—"

"Be able to find them?" Jim finished with a grin.

"Oh, hey Jim, come on in." Reece stepped back.

Jim strolled into the thousand-square-foot open space, squinting in the sunlight that streamed from the floor-to-ceiling windows on the exterior south wall.

"Jesus, you need sunglasses in here."

Reece laughed. "It's fantastic on a sunny day in the winter. What brings you by? Want coffee?"

"Cream and two sugars, if you have it."

Jim examined the antique church altar by the front door. He whistled and ran his fingers across the wood. "Gorgeous. Eighteenth century?"

"Yup, circa-1792 was the appraiser's best guess. It's from a Quaker church in Uthisca. The town demolished the church six years ago, and I rescued the piece from the site."

"Wasn't the church protected by a historical association?"

Reece handed him a mug of coffee, studying the altar with affection. It was one of his favourite possessions. He was especially proud of the restoration job he'd done by himself.

In answer to Jim's question, Reece said, "No such thing as a historical association in Uthisca." He cringed. "You should see the modern monstrosity they built in place of the quaint original."

Jim sat at the kitchen table, stretching his legs out and crossing his ankles. "Bet Sam hates it."

"That's putting it mildly."

"Differences make relationships interesting." He eyed the pot hanger dangling above the large island. "Let me guess, you installed that when she wasn't home."

"It's growing on her."

"She's not here?" Jim asked.

"At the university. I suggested she meet with her adviser to see about changing her thesis proposal. Did you need to speak with her?"

"No. I was driving down Queen Street from the Don Valley Parkway. Nabbed a parking space out front, so I figured I'd drop in to see how you're doing."

Reece took a quick sip of his coffee and waved his hand dismissively. "Good, thanks, everything's great."

Talking about his health was uncomfortable, and he wished everyone would move on. Victim wasn't a suit he wore well.

"Any suspects?" Jim asked.

"Several but no evidence," Reece said, glad to get off the topic of his health. "Police checked the Gatorade bottle. No fingerprints except for a few smudged partials and mine. I'd rinsed the bottle out in warm water before recycling it. They didn't find any trace of antifreeze."

"Are you sure it was in the Gatorade?" Jim asked.

"No, it could have been in a smoothie I had at the hospital with Brenda and Roger." The insinuation hung between them.

Jim sipped his coffee. "You know they released Brenda."

"No." Reece put down his coffee too hard and some sloshed out. "When?" He got up and grabbed a paper towel to wipe up the spill.

"Two days ago." Jim held up his hand before Reece could interrupt. "She doesn't remember anything. Her psychiatrist says it'll take time. I'm surprised Roger didn't mention it."

It didn't surprise Reece at all. Roger's protective nature around Brenda was disturbing. But there was some good news, for a change. If the hospital had discharged Brenda, it would be easier for him and Sam to interview her without Roger's meddlesome interference.

Since he had Jim to himself, Reece decided to drill down and get some background on Roger from a male perspective.

"You're the same age as Roger, right?"

Jim nodded.

"Were you friends in high school?"

"We ran in different groups. I was athletic, Roger not so much." Jim picked up the *Architectural Digest,* flipped through the pages, and stopped to peruse an article.

"But you lived on Vero Beach with Sam, Lisa, Talia, Abigail, and Roger."

"My sister and Roger's older sister were friends." He didn't raise his eyes from the magazine. "I dated Sam's sister."

"Oh." Sam rarely spoke about her sister and Reece was curious. "What was Joyce like?"

Jim looked up from the magazine with a raised eyebrow. "High maintenance." He chuckled. "My mother found her manipulative and controlling. Besides, my parents had a hopeful eye cast in Lisa's direction." He laughed. "A suggestion I found disgusting since I was eighteen and Lisa was only twelve at the time."

"How long have you been married," Reece asked.

"Six years. She was twenty-four and I was thirty. I'd finished law school and was on the fast-track to becoming partner in one of the biggest criminal firms in the city." He sighed. "I worried that Lisa was too young to understand the number of hours I'd have to work. It's hard on her to be alone so much."

Kira was five, turning six, and Reece immediately wondered if Lisa had been pregnant when they married. It wasn't any of his business.

Reece kept his tone conversational when he said, "Well, for thirty-six, you've done remarkably well in your career. So has Roger. I'm curious, why did he pick psychiatry?"

Jim put the magazine down slowly. "Didn't Sam tell you?"

"No."

He didn't say anything more, so Reece remained silent. Sometimes, silence grows uncomfortable and people talk.

Finally, Jim asked, "Do you know about his sister?"

"I know he has an older sister, Veronica." *Whom he attacked with a hammer.* Reece kept his face impassive.

"No, I mean the younger one, Suzanna. Did Sam mention her?"

Reece shook his head.

"She got in with the wrong crowd in grade ten. Ended up with a drug problem. Roger had her admitted to rehab twice, but she overdosed at twenty. Heroin, I think."

That explained Roger's fierce passion for recovery work. Unable to save his sister, he was trying to save other families from a similar fate. Regardless of his low opinion of the man, Reece felt a tug of sympathy.

Jim finished his coffee. "After Suzanna's death, Roger's mother had issues," he said. "There was an unfortunate incident between Roger and Veronica just before they institutionalized their mother. They haven't spoken since."

Unfortunate incident was a gross understatement for attacking someone with a weapon.

"A year later," Jim continued, "Mrs. Peterson died. Roger was doing a speciality in cardiovascular surgery and changed his discipline to psychiatry. I suppose his family problems were part of the decision, but Roger never recovered from what happened to Abigail."

"You mean the home invasion attack?"

Jim nodded. "You see Roger blamed himself. If she hadn't been in the house or if someone had gone with her..." He gazed across the room and sighed. "Regrets, life's full of them. I think about Abigail every day. So much tragedy." His eyes returned to

Reece. "Why are you asking about Roger?" Hardness had crept into his tone.

"Trying to understand the group dynamics. You may not have noticed, but I'm not fitting into the gang too well."

"I've noticed." Jim's expression softened. "Everyone's reeling from Abby's suicide. It's a difficult time. You liked Abigail," he said, "but it's not necessary for you to share all of Sam's friends. People are different. Just because you don't mesh with someone, doesn't mean it should affect Sam's relationships. We're all adults."

The scolding tone of the last sentence was off-putting, but Reece kept quiet, hoping Jim would offer some insight into why Lisa disliked him.

"Sam's important to my wife." Now Reece heard a definite challenge in Jim's voice. "Sam's very important to my daughter."

"I'm not stopping Sam from spending time with Kira, and I'm not interfering in her relationship with Lisa," Reece retorted.

Jim raised his eyebrow. "Aren't you?"

"No, I'm not. And your implication that I would prevent my fiancée from seeing either her friend or her goddaughter is offensive." He took a minute to settle his nerves. "I wish your wife would cut me some slack," he continued. "Do you know what her problem with me is? Maybe if I understood I could find a solution."

Jim's face tightened and his eyes narrowed in anger. "Has it occurred to you that Lisa has her own issues right now?"

It was hard to imagine her *without* a life crisis. The most frustrating part of dealing with Lisa, in Reece's opinion, was that she didn't see the problems she created for her friends. She was always so self-absorbed.

Reece had plenty of experience with drama junkies. Having witnessed the ravaging effects real drama had on families who survived violent crimes, he had no tolerance for people who manufactured drama. Life was unpredictable. Enjoy today because fate could heap misery on your head tomorrow. But he understood it wasn't the right time to engage in a philosophical discussion about attention-seeking pessimists—especially when the man across from him was married to one.

"Does it really matter if you and Lisa get along?" Jim was asking. "The thing is, Reece, there are always going to be people in our partners' lives whose company we don't enjoy. It doesn't need to affect us. The key to cohabitation is respecting choices, rather than endeavouring to twist your partner's perspective to match yours."

"Are you saying I'm controlling?" It was a struggle to keep his face neutral.

"Yes, I am. You're a cop." He waved his hand in a flippant gesture. "Maybe not at the moment, but I suspect you will be again. Cops are black and white. The thing is that people aren't. Sam and Lisa have history, and it's tough to come into a play in the third act and expect to follow the story."

"I'm not interfering in their friendship," Reece repeated brusquely.

Jim ignored him. "Take Roger, for example. Lisa likes him but I find him an odd duck."

Now this topic, Reece found more interesting. "How so?"

"Oh, I don't know. Working with the clients I do, I form judgements."

Jim was one of Toronto's top defence attorneys. At least two of his clients—that Reece knew of—had been stone-cold killers, murdering for profit. One had been a serial rapist. Was Jim lumping Roger in with those character types?

"Are you defending Roger, if he needs representation?" he asked.

Jim folded his arms against his chest and his lips narrowed. "Whenever you're a person of interest in a police investigation, it's advisable to have counsel," he replied. "But my schedule is full so I referred him to another attorney."

Having worked with Jim in the past, Reece knew he seldom declined high profile cases. The murder of an ex-Argonauts player and the involvement of a *New York Times* bestselling self-help author were right up Jim's alley. Lots of media attention.

Jim dropped his eyes to the magazine and fiddled with his tie. "Do York Regional Police suspect him?"

"I'm not privy to the direction Detective Alston is taking his investigation." It was time to stop dancing around. "Do you believe Roger is capable of murder?"

"No," Jim said slowly, gazing out the window. "But he also might not say anything if he knew who did murder Graham. He might keep that nugget to himself." His face darkened.

"You don't like him." Reece made it a statement to gauge Jim's reaction.

"Doesn't matter. My wife likes him. I don't object to including him in things." He stood. "I should hit the road."

At the door, he turned back. "We're having a dinner party on Saturday. Hope to see you there."

The last thing Reece wanted to do was suffer through a dinner party with grouchy Lisa. It seemed to Reece that the selfish woman was only happy when she was the highest priority, with everyone's lives pivoting around her needs. It wasn't fair to Sam, and Reece wasn't going to support the parasitical relationship. Period. It would thrill him if Sam ended the friendship. If that made him unreasonable and controlling, so be it.

And now, after Jim's reprimand, Reece wasn't keen on spending an evening with him either—or chatting up Roger, a probable murderer.

"Let me talk with Sam." Reece didn't bother to disguise his reluctance.

Jim studied him with a slight frown before reaching for the door. "Consider what I said. Thanks for the coffee."

CHAPTER EIGHTEEN

SAM

"DO YOU THINK I'm controlling?"

Sam kept her eyes glued to the road as she drove and tried to think of how to frame her answer. The question annoyed her because you shouldn't ask a question if you couldn't deal with an honest answer. People did it all the time. Sometimes they ask because they have limited self-awareness, in which case a truthful answer can incite a defensive response that escalates into a vicious argument in a heartbeat. Other times they ask because they're insecure and seeking validation, in which case a candid reply is hurtful. Reece was neither unaware nor insecure, so Sam wasn't sure what motivated his loaded question.

"You love me," she said cautiously. "Sometimes love can be a tad controlling. It's not a big deal. You aren't a dictator." Hoping to change the topic of conversation, she rushed to add, "When we get to the Harris farm, let's interview Brenda together. Based on her reaction, we'll figure out who'll lead."

"Controlling how?"

Oh boy, he's not going to drop it.

"Well... My thesis." She kept her eyes on the road as she drove. "You didn't like the premise and strongly suggested I change it."

"What! That's not true," he argued. "I said it would be difficult to find evidence to support the hypothesis. I offered guidance and advice." He folded his arms and frowned. "I was *not* controlling your decision."

He *had* told her to change it. He wanted her to pick something outside Roger's discipline so she wasn't beholden to him for help.

"Well," she said, beginning to get a bit pissed off, "you want me to dump my friends."

The truth was that she was struggling to find a balance between work, school, friends, and their relationship. She'd figure it out, if everyone could get along and give her a chance. Lisa's cranky attitude and constant blaming, along with Reece's dislike toward Lisa, was driving her nuts.

When he didn't respond, she said, "Look, you're welcome to voice your opinion. After all, manipulation only works when one party is unsure of her own mind or lacks confidence to stand up for her rights."

He grunted. "Doesn't describe you, so I guess we're okay."

He fiddled with the phone charger. Because she drove a 1973 Grand Am, the cigarette lighter powered the charger. It was hit-and-miss at the best of times.

"The charger isn't working again," he grumbled.

"There's a portable one in the glove box. It's a red tube, about the size of your index finger."

He took it out, connected his phone, and put the entire bundle into his pocket.

She glanced over at him slouching against the car window. He looked upset and unhappy.

"I have a confession," she said in an effort to cheer him up. "I went behind your back two weeks ago and tossed your old magazines into the garbage. In my book, that's the definition of controlling." In her peripheral vision, she was pleased to see him smile.

"So that's what happened to my back copies of *Gourmet*," he mused. "I thought I'd misplaced them. There was a recipe for beef back ribs I wanted to try."

"That's what the Internet is for, Grandpa. Nowadays, we youngsters look stuff up on the interwebz."

He chuckled. "Maybe I am a bit controlling. But I worry about you getting hurt. Your plan about handling Brenda sounds good."

"Are you saying that so you don't seem controlling?" she teased.

He laughed and placed his hand on her leg.

"I spoke with Roger last night," she told him. "Brenda is indeed lucid and stable on the meds. But she can't recall her husband's death. The last clear memory she has is an argument about Jordan."

He stiffened up in the passenger seat and removed his hand. "Did you tell him we were interviewing her?"

"No."

Reece relaxed. "If she doesn't remember, this will be pointless. Too bad Jordan and Jordanna will be at school. I'd like to see them with their mom. Get a sense of how they interact."

"Speaking of school, I called to get background on the twins. Even though they're eighteen, the administration wouldn't talk to me. It was weird."

"Weird how?"

"Sort of defensive. Anyway, I'm hoping Brenda can give us the names of some teachers. Get the impressions of people in authority, you know?"

"Neither of them poisoned me." He clenched his jaw and stared out the front window, avoiding eye contact.

Reece *still* suspected Roger. It was so frustrating. Roger had no reason to try to kill Reece. Besides, if Roger wanted to poison someone, he wouldn't use antifreeze. A doctor with medical expertise and access to medication could select an untraceable drug to simulate a heart attack.

She pulled the car into the laneway to the Harris farm and followed the long gravel driveway to the house. It was a relief not to find Roger's car. Reece would have had plenty to say about that. The ugly barn loomed in the distance and reminded her she wanted a private opportunity to snoop. Jordanna had said her mother had a makeshift office in the barn. Maybe she'd drafted a murder mystery on how to electrocute her quarry. Murderers sometimes made stupider mistakes.

Sam remembered responding to a robbery one time when she'd been a beat cop. They'd found the perpetrator's government health card outside the alley door of the clothing shop.

Apparently, he'd tried to jimmy the lock with his own picture identification before giving up and smashing in a window.

At the front door of the farmhouse, Sam knocked, waited, and had to knock three more times before Brenda answered. The woman had lost weight since she'd seen her in the hospital. Purple circles ringed her eyes, which were glassy from her medication, but she welcomed them and escorted them into the living room. In contrast to the ramshackle house, crumbling plaster walls, and scarred wood floors, the furniture was nice. The decor was a little too "furniture store showroom" for Sam's taste, but the pieces worked together. She and Reece sat side by side on a brown leather sofa, and Brenda perched on a matching recliner across from a gigantic television that monopolized the back wall.

Brenda spoke first. "Roger tells me you're helping with the investigation into my husband's accident." Her voice was high and had a singsong quality to it. She focused her eyes on Reece, so Sam let him respond.

He spoke earnestly. "We're sorry for your loss."

"I told him to hire an electrician." Her expression was calm, emotionless.

The response confused Sam. Did the woman think her husband's death was accidental?

"Was Graham alone in the basement?" Reece asked.

"I think so."

"Was anyone visiting the day he died?"

She shook her head and her eyes darted back and forth between them. "No one was home. Just me and Graham."

Now Reece also looked confused. "Okay," he said slowly. "Then who do you think called 911?"

"I don't know." Her voice was shy of a whisper.

Unbelievable, Sam thought. Of course, she knew her son had called the police. It was ridiculous to plea a loss of memory over something so insignificant.

"It was Jordan," she retorted, not bothering to mask her annoyance. "Have you talked to him about what happened?"

"No," she said quickly, twisting the fabric of her skirt between her fingers. "We're trying to move on."

"Do you remember anything about the afternoon Graham died?" Reece asked.

Brenda's gaze remained on her lap, but at least she reacted this time, though only by shaking her head.

"Did you know Roger was here?" Reece asked.

Brenda shook of her head again.

"What about Jordan," he asked. "Do you recall him coming home?"

Her shoulders slumped. "No."

Reece paused, took a breath. "How did Graham get along with the kids?"

Brenda looked up. The tip of her tongue flicked out and ran across her dry lips. When she released the coiled fabric from her hands, a nest of wrinkles decorated her lap. "He was glad Jordan was on the football team. Graham used to go to his games." Her eyes dropped back to the ground.

"How about around the house? Did he spend time with his son?"

"Jordan has lots of friends. Players from the team, classmates." Hair fell across her face and she brushed it aside without shifting her eyes from her feet. "Graham thought one boy was a great linebacker. He taught them a game. They'd link hands in a line and take turns trying to break through."

"Red rover," Reece said.

Brenda nodded. "Jordan was jealous of the boy his father complimented. He took the game too far and someone got hurt. My husband was mad. He wouldn't practise with his son after that."

Reece caught Sam's eye, inviting her to interject.

"How does Jordan do in school?" she asked.

"He has good marks," Brenda answered. "So does Jordanna. Jennifer, well, she's different." She clamped her lips together and picked at the wrinkles on her skirt.

"Have Jordan or Jordanna experienced any problems in school?" Sam asked.

"No."

"Really?" Sam smiled and raised an eyebrow. "Teenagers usually have one or two issues."

Brenda shuffled her feet and crossed her legs. "Well, a teacher accused Jordan of something last year."

"What?" Sam asked.

"I don't know. Graham handled it. I'm not good with things like that." She spoke quickly and looked up for the first time, meeting Sam's eyes. Her head tilted to the side and she covered her mouth with her knuckle.

Classic signs of lying, Sam thought, curious over what Jordan did that Brenda didn't want to share. "What's the teacher's name?"

Colour flushed Brenda's face. "I don't remember. It wasn't serious. She doesn't teach there anymore."

Another lie. Some people were terrible liars and Brenda was one of them, apparently. Annoying, but Sam knew she'd be able to find out the names of last year's grade eleven teachers. With that, it would be easy to cross-reference which ones had left the high school this year. Since Brenda had referred to the teacher as female, that would shorten the list somewhat.

"You borrowed a substantial amount of money from Roger before you moved out here," Sam said. "Can you tell us what it was for?"

"Graham's gambling debts," she mumbled.

Sam shook her head. "No it wasn't. We checked." She paused but Brenda didn't say anything. "What was the money for?"

Brenda was silent for so long, Sam figured she wasn't going to answer. When she finally cleared her throat and spoke, her voice was unsteady. "There was a misunderstanding with a Toronto neighbour. Instead of, ah, going to court, we settled privately."

Like pulling teeth. "And what misunderstanding was that?"

She shrugged and looked up at Sam. "Graham handled it. An easement dispute, I think. I'm sorry I can't remember anything about the day Graham died." Her wide blue eyes shone with sincerity that Sam didn't believe for a second. "If there's nothing else, I need to lie down. The medication makes me tired."

Before Reece or Sam could get up, Brenda had hastened to the stairs. She paused, her hand on the railing, and then spoke softly without turning. "Life is easier when you sleep through it."

They watched as she disappeared up the creaking staircase. Once she was out of earshot, Sam snorted. "Well, that was weird. Twenty thousand bucks for a property dispute? Bullshit."

Reece stood. "Interviewing people with mental health issues is seldom productive. I'll visit their old neighbourhood and see if I can find the neighbour. Want to explore while we're here?"

Better to ask forgiveness than ask permission, Sam thought. "May as well." She stood and stretched. "I'll take the barn."

"I'll take the basement and meet you out back."

Outside, Sam spied someone sitting on the grass under the canopy of a group of maple trees about fifty metres from the back door of the house. She headed over, and, as she drew closer, she recognized Jennifer.

The sixteen-year-old wore a pair of white shorts with lacy edges and a cropped pink T-shirt. She was sitting cross-legged, staring into space with her arms hanging limply at her sides. A black cat lay in her lap.

Sam leaned against a nearby tree trunk. "Not in school today?"

Jennifer's eyes remained fixed straight ahead of her. When a breeze ruffled her hair, leaving a strand across her eye, she barely blinked.

"Jennifer?"

The girl didn't acknowledge her. Something was wrong. Seriously wrong.

Sam knelt to get a closer look at Jennifer. When her hand touched the cat, Sam froze. There was a moment of stark horror mixed with repulsion. Slowly, she turned the cat's face away from Jennifer's naked midriff. One dead eye stared back at her. The other socket was empty.

Shocked, she snatched the corpse from Jennifer's lap, carried it behind one of the larger trees, and placed it on the grass. In addition to the eyeball gouged from its cavity, something had torn open the belly. A piece of intestine hung from the gaping wound. No rigor mortis. The muscles would have stiffened within a few hours of death, the same as all mammals. It would take twelve to twenty hours before the body became flaccid and decay set in. Now the cat was upwind, she could smell it. Based on the stench emanating from the carcass, the cat had died several days ago.

Something tickled the back of her hand. She glanced at it and cried out, shaking both hands in disgust. Maggots dropped from her fingers, and she flicked fat white bodies from her forearms.

Backing away from the mutilated corpse, she returned to Jennifer. The girl still sat gazing sightlessly across the field. A tear dripped down her cheek now. Blood stained the lap of her white shorts and pulsing worms crawled across her bare stomach. A string of grey clung to the lace on her shorts. Several maggots fell from the hem of her cropped T-shirt to wallow in the dark puddle of clotting blood pooled in the crease of her bent thighs.

"It's okay," Sam said shakily. "You need to come with me." She reached out to take Jennifer's upper arm and try to lift her into a standing position.

The girl jerked suddenly and yanked her arm away. Something strange flashed across her eyes. The fleeting emotion was too fast for Sam to recognize. In an instant, it had vanished but Sam suspected that shock over discovering her dead pet was transforming into something else. A confusing mixture of repulsion, fear, and anger that the teenager's mind was too young to process.

Jennifer stood in slow motion. Her eyes dropped and she gasped, swiping the feeding larva from her thighs. She was crying in earnest now. "I wish my brother would die," she whispered and shook her blood-covered hands manically at her sides.

The teenager turned and ran toward the house. Reece was walking toward them and he had to jump aside to avoid having Jennifer tackle him in her haste to get away.

"Was that blood?" He turned to look over his shoulder.

"Yeah. From a dead cat." Sam led him behind the tree to the animal's corpse. "She was holding it."

"Jesus. Is she okay?"

Sam shook her head. "No. Can you imagine how awful it would be to find your pet mutilated?"

He glanced over his shoulder again with a troubled expression. "Should we go after her and tell Brenda?" His eyes shifted back to hers. "Maybe you should try to talk to Jennifer."

Sam thought about the look on the girl's face when she'd tried to touch her and shook her head. "No. Anything I do right now would be intrusive. Her father just died, and it's understandable that she thinks someone hurt her cat." She looked around. "But this is the country. A wild animal could have done it."

Reece knelt and picked up a twig. He used the tip of the stick to pull up a section of flesh. "No," he said slowly. "This looks sliced, not torn."

A blood-covered maggot wiggled out of the guts. Saliva filled Sam's mouth and she gagged.

Reece stood. "Take a few deep breaths," he said and rubbed her back

"Maybe they're claw marks?" she suggested, swallowing hard and breathing through her mouth.

I wish my brother would die, Jennifer had said.

"Animals kill because they're threatened or hungry." He waved the stick behind him before dropping it and wiping his hands on his jeans. "Anything that could do that to a cat wouldn't be threatened. A coyote would have consumed it. If an owl had tried to grab it and dropped it, the talons would have left distinctive wounds, same with a raccoon's claws."

"You're saying the predator was human."

Reece shrugged. "An animal can't pluck an eyeball without wounding the face. Have you got a garbage bag in the car?"

She nodded.

"Let's take the body. I'll call Brandy's vet and have him take a look before we reach a conclusion."

Reece walked toward the car and Sam was struck with the unshakable feeling of someone's eyes on her. She turned in a circle. The fields were empty. Reece had his back to her, talking on this cell. She stared at the house. The sun's glare reflected off the windows and she couldn't see inside. But she detected a wink of bright light. Binoculars.

Someone was watching.

CHAPTER NINETEEN

REECE

WHEN REECE FIRST joined Sam's investigation firm, he filed articles of incorporation for Lanteka Consulting Inc., a dummy corporation. Toronto Chamber of Commerce listed it, Lanteka had an excellent rating with the Better Business Bureau, and an in-bound call centre live-answered the business number. A lovely website boasted an array of marketing services with glowing testimonials.

The marketing consulting company would pass base-level background and credit checks. Reece and Sam paid a hacker a hundred dollars a week to maintain the illusion of legitimacy and to push the social media side. Easy money, once everything was in place, but they frequently hired Behoo to dig around online to obtain intel on cases.

Behoo's activities on the deep web most certainly breached Canadian privacy and cyber laws. Sam didn't care, but Reece hoped they were never in a position where they had to speak to authorities over how they'd obtained information. He also worried that Behoo's activities would eventually be of interest to the police. All Reece could do to try to hide their association with the hacker was to pay him in bitcoin to add a layer of cryptocurrency protection.

Neither Reece nor Sam had ever met the man and didn't know his real name, but the hacker had never given Reece any reason to mistrust him. In fact, last year, when he'd forgotten his credit card at a restaurant, Behoo had called within the hour to ask if he'd had a sudden urge to spend thousands of dollars at Chanel Boutique in Yorkville. Reece trusted the hacker and did his best to respect the man's obsessive need for anonymity.

Behoo and Lanteka had come in handy on more than one occasion. Today was one of those days.

A quick comparison of last year's King City yearbook against the current staff list confirmed that Sally Alistair had taught grade eleven math the year before. The Board of Education no longer employed her and she'd left mid-semester.

Using Lanteka's telephone number and contact details, he'd called the high school for a business reference, stating that Ms. Alistair had applied for a position with their market research division. The principal confirmed the dates of employment and the subjects she'd taught but declined to answer subjective questions or to comment on the teacher's abrupt departure.

However, the man was curious about Lanteka's hiring process. His daughter had graduated from a marketing program at Humber College. Reece directed him to the website and they had a lovely conversation about intern opportunities. Appetite whetted, the principal opened up to Reece by confidentially sharing that Ms. Alistair had had an unfortunate incident with a student. Her moral fibre was questionable, and he couldn't recommend her to such an innovative organization as Lanteka. He did hope Reece would repay the professional favour and put in a good word for his daughter. After a bit of coaxing and some empty promises, the principal gave Reece Sally Alistair's address.

Toys littered the front yard of the two-storey brick house, and a swing hung from the low branch of an apple tree laden with late spring blossoms. Beneath the tree was a group of trilliums, the provincial flower of Ontario that signified peace and hope. Digging them up from indigenous woodland areas not protected by the *Ontario Trillium Protection Act* wasn't illegal, but people frowned on transplanting the wild flowers. It was a rebellious choice to display in a front garden.

Reece was lifting his hand to knock on the screen door when a man ambled by from inside the house, glanced over, and jumped.

"You startled me," he exclaimed as he opened the door. "Can I help you?" Brown hair flopped into his eye, and he shoved it aside.

"Eric Alistair? Reece Hash." He dug out his wallet and opened it to his investigator licence. "I'd like to ask you and your wife, Sally, a couple of questions."

Eric opened the door and stepped out to the porch. He was a couple of inches taller than Reece, close to six-foot-five. His build was wiry and thin with slouched shoulders, as though he'd gotten so used to bending over, he didn't bother to straighten up any longer.

His expression was neither friendly nor hostile when he asked, "What about?"

"A student she taught."

Eric's eyes narrowed. "What student?"

There wasn't any reason to be cryptic, and Reece answered honestly. "Jordan Harris."

Eric's nose scrunched with distaste, and he folded his arms across his chest, taking a step back to block the door. "What about him?"

"His father—"

"Was murdered. I know. I read the papers. What's that got to do with my wife?"

"We're trying to get some background on the family," Reece explained, curious about Eric's sudden antagonism.

"Are you working with the cops?"

Reece settled on a small white lie he felt would put Eric at ease. "I'm collaborating with Detective Alston at York Regional Police," he said.

That was not exactly true, as Alston had in fact been openly hostile when Reece had called to inform him that they'd taken the case. Reece wasn't going to fret over semantics though.

Instead of soothing Eric, Reece's comment aggravated him. "We've nothing to say to the police," he stated briskly and turned toward the door.

Reece hurried to say, "Yes, but I'm not with the police. A man by the name of Dr. Roger Peterson hired my firm."

Eric turned back and faced Reece, looking baffled. "The guy who wrote those books on recovery and living life on your own terms?"

"That's right."

"My wife read them. She's into self-help stuff. Peterson's a shrink, right? Did they get the monster into therapy?"

Unsure which "monster" Eric was referring to, Reece kept his answer vague. "Dr. Peterson knows the family, yes."

Eric ran his tongue across his bottom lip, thinking. After a minute, he entered the house and held the door for Reece. "My wife is in the living room."

A tall, thin woman with short brown hair and large brown eyes was standing beside a fireplace, holding a child in her arms. The baby was sucking her thumb against her mother's shoulder. Eric spoke to his wife, but Reece couldn't hear the exchange. She glanced at Reece, whispered something to her husband, and nodded at his response.

"Tommy needs to go down for his nap," she said to Reece on her way by.

Oops. Boy baby, not girl baby.

Sitting on a canvas-covered sofa to await Sally's return, Reece gazed around the living room. He liked the bright colours and homespun country finishes better than the stark lines and grey, black, and white decor of the modern loft he shared with Sam.

The walls were painted blue, the shade of a shallow lake on a warm day. The trim was pale yellow. Handmade shelves, crafted from cut terracotta tiles that supported sheets of plywood, covered the walls on either side of the brick fireplace. The coffee table was a rectangular piece of glass perched on two pottery urns decorated with a swirling, abstract pattern. A sunflower rug covered the scratched wood floor, and a reproduction of Van Gogh's *Sunflowers* hung above the fireplace. Handcrafted picture frames, decorated with shells and dried flowers, held photos of Tommy in various stages of development. He looked like a girl in every snapshot.

A Steinway grand piano took up the entire dining room. On top of the closed lid, above the keys, were sheets of paper and four mechanical pencils. A good starting point to establish some rapport.

"Are you a musician?" Reece asked Eric, who had taken a seat in one of two stout chairs covered in aqua-striped fabric.

Eric nodded. "I compose for a theatre troupe downtown, and a production company commissioned me to do the score for an upcoming movie."

"That must be interesting. What's the movie?"

"Oh, just a sci-fi. No big deal." Eric looked toward the stairs.

Having not receiving an enthusiastic response from Eric regarding his work, Reece decided on another approach. "Nice house. Did you paint the coffee table urns yourself?"

That evoked a bright smile. "No, Sally gets the credit." Eric pointed at the Van Gogh copy above the fireplace. "That's her work, but she's a talented artist in her own right." His voice rang with pride.

Eric glanced to his right and stood as his wife entered the room. "Sally, this is Reece Hash. Reece, my wife."

Reece expected Sally to be shy and reserved. No reason for his assumption other than the demure way she'd interacted with her husband earlier.

She surprised him when she announced in a confident voice, "The Board of Education suspended me without pay for hitting Jordan Harris. Later, they asked for my resignation under the threat of termination. I have no regret or remorse over striking him. I wish I'd knocked his teeth out." Her voice was a beautiful mezzo-soprano. It was at odds with the ugly, aggressive expression on her face.

Reece waited for her to explain what Jordan had done. She didn't elaborate and sat beside her husband on the matching chair across from Reece.

"Last fall, I went to a convenience store," Eric said. "Tommy was asleep in his car seat, so I didn't wake him. I could see the car at all times. A cop pulled up, woke Tommy, and scared the shit out of him. When I ran out, he charged me with reckless endangerment of a minor because I'd left a crying baby in the car."

Reece had no idea what that had to do with anything. He remained silent.

"Police dropped the charges," Sally added.

Reece didn't care. He did care why she hit Jordan Harris. "What happened with Jordan that made you so angry?"

"Sally tried to do the right thing," Eric said. "When the school turned against her, she tried to speak with Brenda and Graham."

"We also asked for help from the cops," Sally added quickly. "Because of what happened with Eric and the baby and the horrible things the school said about me, the police disregarded our concerns."

"Jordan did something that required the police?" Reece asked, trying to coax them back to the subject that interested him.

The couple exchanged a guarded look.

"It would help me to understand, if you could say what happened between you and Jordan," Reece said patiently.

"Tell him," Eric said.

Sally held his eyes and then turned to address Reece. "He hurt younger kids. Only around me. Never in front of any other teacher. I'd escort Jordan to the office where he'd deny everything," Sally said. "When forced to confront him, his victims balked and wouldn't corroborate my claim. Eventually, the principal accused me of taking an unprofessional dislike to the school's star quarterback and fabricating allegations." Her lips were a tight slash across her face, and she was clenching her hands into fists.

"What exactly did he do?" Reece asked.

"At first, it was intimidation," Sally said as she unclenched her hands. "Mean stuff like crowding grade nine boys against a locker or throwing their books on the ground. He'd make fun of their size and embarrass them in front of bigger kids." She stopped and her lips pressed together again.

"So Jordan's a bully," Reece stated, growing impatient.

Popular kids were often the "mean" kids in a school hierarchy. But answering violence with violence wasn't a disciplinary strategy he endorsed, and he supported the school's decision to dismiss her for striking a student. This was a waste of time.

"But then it shifted to girls," Sally said. "Last year, I was at the school late. Jordan was in the hallway. He was sweet as pie, asking if I wanted him to escort me to my car. I declined and he left. When I finished what I was doing in the classroom, I went outside and found Jordan with a grade nine girl, away from the cameras. One hand was over her mouth, the other held her throat to keep her body pressed against the wall." She choked up and had to stop, putting her hands over her face.

When she lowered her hands, tears were filling her eyes. "She was gasping for air, clawing at the hand around her throat. He'd torn off her hijab, ripped her leggings, and her skirt was up. He was... Jordan was raping her."

"You caught Jordan *raping* a fourteen-year-old girl?" Reece asked in stunned disbelief.

She nodded and wiped the tears off her cheeks with the knuckle of her index finger. "I pulled him off her. He... he grabbed himself and asked if I wanted some. He... ejaculated on my leg. I hit him, locked the girl in my car, and called 911."

"Jesus," Reece muttered.

"The girl called her mother and sister who arrived before the cops. By then, Jordan was gone."

"Did the girl confirm he'd raped her?"

Sally shook her head. "No. She's Muslim and terrified of her father and brother. Her mother took her home before the police could question her. When they went to the house to interview her, she denied it happened. Her mother claimed she'd come straight home from school. There wasn't any evidence to support my testimony."

"What about your clothes? Any semen on your skirt?" Reece asked.

She dug in her pocket and took out a tattered tissue. After she'd wiped her nose, she said, "No and I scrubbed my leg with antibacterial wipes I had in the car. It never occurred to me it was evidence. I threw them out."

Eric cleared his throat and leaned forward in his chair. "Then we started to have issues. The football coach harassed Sally at work, accusing her of all sorts of shit, and the principal took his side." He sneered. "Old boys club alive and well, goddamn it."

"One night, the garage caught fire," Sally said. "The fire department told us if we hadn't had the home security system, the smoke and fumes could have killed us. Our master bedroom and the nursery are above the garage."

"Did they figure out the cause of the fire?" Reece asked.

"Solvents had spilled and combusted. But we didn't keep solvents in the garage," Sally said. "And the telephone calls came night after night. A freakish robotic voice, singing a depraved version of *Up in the Cradle*. The caller would shriek, 'and down will come baby, covered in blood.' Then there'd be this macabre hoot of laughter." She reached out and grasped her husband's hand.

"There were childish pranks, too," Eric said. "Car tires slashed, windshields smashed, a rock through our front window. Jordan complained to the football coach that I threatened him. The cops treated me like the criminal."

"Did you tape the calls?" Reece asked.

Sally shook her head. "It was random and late, like two or three in the morning. We'd prepare, but the calls wouldn't come. We'd relax and it would start again. Sometimes on our landline, sometimes on one of our cells. We changed our numbers and unlisted the home phone. A week later, we received a call. On the home phone. Whoever it was had the unlisted number."

"They got into our computer," Eric said. "Uploaded malware and wiped out our hard drive. A remote access tool, the cops said, and they didn't consider it a big deal. They said it happens all the time." Eric's cheeks flushed with anger. "I lost all my compositions."

It surprised Reece he hadn't backed up his files. Then again, it might not have mattered. Hackers could install a remote access tool—a RAT—via a USB stick the hapless user inserted into their computer, or from a link attached to an email using a recognizable address that overrode spam detectors. The hackers could access whatever they wanted whenever they wanted. They could download malware that would affect anything connected to the computer, such as a remote hard drive or USB stick that backed up files. One of many reasons experts recommended not leaving backup devices connected to a computer.

"They sent pornographic emails to everyone in our contacts," Sally was saying. "They accessed our bank accounts. Before we realized what was happening and cancelled our credit cards, they'd maxed out everything, including a fifty-thousand-dollar line of credit." Tears welled up again in her eyes. "We'll never get out of debt. If the house wasn't in my parents' name, we'd have lost it."

For the first time, Reece began to wonder if they were lying, or at least exaggerating. Credit card companies generally have excellent anti-fraud systems in place, and Reece had no idea how anyone could access a fifty-thousand-dollar line of credit without the bank's involvement.

"That's when we suspected it wasn't Jordan," Eric told him.

"Who did you think it was?"

"His mother," Sally said bitterly. "You see, everything with Jordan happened after she came to my classroom and wanted to take Jordanna out of school in the middle of the day. She caused a terrible scene, screaming accusations about Jordan and threatening me. I had to call security. The next day, I talked to Jordan about what happened and offered to set up an appointment with the school psychologist so he could talk out his feelings."

"I take it therapy didn't interest him," Reece said.

Sally laughed weakly. "He freaked out, claiming I was gossiping about his business. He was cold as ice when he told me no one made a fool out of him."

"Jordan's smart," Eric added. "But it's hard to believe he's as smart as his mother."

Brenda didn't strike Reece as smart. "What makes you think Brenda is intellectually gifted?"

They stared at him.

Okay, he'd try a different approach. "What was the issue around Brenda taking her daughter out of class?"

They studied each other with mouths ajar.

Bewildered by their reaction, Reece asked, "What's the problem?"

"Brenda Harris isn't their mother," Sally said.

Reece was so stunned he couldn't respond.

"How come you don't know that?" Eric asked with suspicion. "She's their stepmother."

"What?" Reece sputtered. "Who's their mother?"

"Caitlyn Franklyn," Sally answered, looking confused.

"Caitlyn Franklyn," Reece echoed. Why hadn't Roger or Brenda told them? This was outrageous.

"She's a frightening woman and deeply disturbed," Sally said with a shudder. "I don't know the details, but Graham Harris had a restraining order against her. That's why I couldn't let her take Jordanna."

"I did some digging," Eric said eagerly. "I found an online newspaper article. MIT in Cambridge gave her a full scholarship when she was sixteen. She's a technology prodigy. That's why we figured she hacked our computer. You see, her background was in a piece the *Toronto Sun* ran seven years ago during her trial."

"Her trial?" Reece repeated.

"She served four years for manslaughter," Eric said as though Reece were a bit slow. "She killed her own mother. How is it you don't know this?"

Reece was livid. Why hadn't Roger told them? It was impossible that Brenda hadn't mentioned her husband's murderous ex-wife to her lover. He felt like an utter idiot. Worse, this news left him completely unprepared to continue the interview. Reece took a deep breath and tried to centre himself.

"Were the police involved?" he asked. "I mean when Caitlyn came to the school." If there was a peace bond against an ex-con, surely the school had called the cops. Reece figured he could follow up and get the incident report. It would list an address for Caitlyn Franklyn.

"I don't know how the administration handled it," Sally said. "But we involved the police."

"You called the police because of what happened at the school?" Reece asked.

Sally shook her head. "We called them when... when she killed our dog, Betsy. But the police didn't believe us." She hung her head and wiped at tears that coursed down her cheeks.

Reece was completely confused. "Caitlyn Franklyn killed your dog," he repeated. "How did you know it was her?"

"Our neighbour saw a woman enter the backyard when we were out," Eric explained. "She wore a Toronto Hydro uniform, but we all have SMART meters. They don't come onto the property anymore. Our neighbour assumed it was a problem with the electronic meter. I showed him a picture of Caitlyn I found online. He said it looked like the Hydro worker."

"What happened to the dog?" Reece asked.

"She poisoned her." Sally buried her face in her hands and her shoulders shook. "The vet said it was in Betsy's water dish."

After a momentary hesitation, he asked Eric, "What was it?" Reece knew what the answer would be and mentally braced himself.

"Antifreeze," Eric said.

CHAPTER TWENTY

SAM

"SO I SPOKE with Detective Alston, the lead on Graham's homicide." Reece shoved his plate to the centre of the table and rubbed his face with his hands.

"And?"

"York Police have a history with Eric and Sally Alistair. The incident about leaving the baby in the car isn't the way Eric told it."

"Oh?"

She popped another cream cheese wonton in her mouth. Reece used lemon thyme and a ton of herbs, along with lemon zest and hot peppers. They were deep-fried, golden bits of decadent deliciousness. Sam had a huge weakness for anything deep-fried.

"The officer spotted the baby alone in a car," Reece explained. "He had to look for a parent and found Eric in a convenience store, chatting up a pretty clerk. Eric was belligerent, told the officer to mind his own business, and tried to leave."

"Okay," Sam said, "that's worrisome. Did they say anything about Jordan?"

Reece grabbed an open bottle of wine from the table and poured a second glass. She shook her head when he offered her the bottle.

"Two incident reports on file, but against Eric," he said. "Both times, he showed up at the Harris farm threatening Jordan. The second was the most serious. It was right after the fire. Graham said he understood the man's frustration and declined to press charges. Cops released Eric with a warning."

She mulled it over. Understanding that Reece was very upset over how the interview had gone, she picked her words carefully. "It could be Eric's perception of the events is skewed. It doesn't mean he lied with intent. During severe conflict, people's natural reaction is to be defensive and self-righteous."

"Well, Jordan couldn't have set the fire," Reece said in aggravation. "His dad took him to Chicago to watch the Bears play. Graham gave police a credit card receipt for the hotel room, plus pictures in the locker room with the team." He took a sip of his wine.

"How about the incident at the school?" she asked.

"Cops aren't stupid," he said sharply and put his wineglass on the table with deliberate force. "They did a thorough investigation and understood the cultural and familial ramifications for the girl."

She didn't appreciate his snotty tone and was about to snap at him when she noticed the dark bags under his bloodshot eyes. Reece was still recovering, physically and emotionally, from the poisoning. This case was personal for him now. He had the right to be discouraged.

"Didn't find anything to support the teacher's claim, eh?"

He rolled his eyes. "The football coach said he and Jordan were together until after seven o'clock. According to him, the week before, Sally had marched onto the field and argued with Jordan. Coach was crossing the field when he saw her hit Jordan and storm off. That's the record of inappropriate physical discipline that motivated the Board of Education to terminate her employment."

"Would the coach lie?"

Reece shrugged. "Maybe. He made racist comments about the alleged rape victim in his statement. He went on to joke— get this—that Muslim women wear too much clothing for anyone to bother trying to rape them." He shook his head in disgust. "Besides, the coach is a huge Argonauts fan and might lie to protect Graham's son. Also, without Jordan, the Lions didn't have a chance at winning the season."

Sam was skeptical. "Canadian high school football isn't a big deal like it is in the States. Tough to believe a gym teacher would lie about rape." She thought about it. "In addition to being a racist, maybe he's a misogynist who doesn't consider rape a real crime."

"In his statement to police, he said, and I quote, 'Alistair's a flirty bird looking for a tickle.'" Reece sighed and swirled the wine around his glass. "But the thing is, I spoke with Jordan's other teachers. Everyone liked him. They said he's a nice kid with a bit of attitude, but they couldn't fathom him raping a girl. They never witnessed any inappropriate conduct around younger kids." He gulped down the last of his wine. "In fact, Jordan tutors grade nine kids in math and chemistry and mentors rookie players during a summer football camp the high school runs."

"But you can't think the Alistair family poisoned their own dog."

"No, but their neighbours had plenty of negative things to say about the dog barking."

Sam clenched her hands into fists. "Meaning a neighbour could have poisoned the dog." The idea of someone killing an animal because of the owner's irresponsibility infuriated her.

"Eric Alistair is a difficult man, apparently. He complains about everything," Reece said. "If someone puts their garbage out on the curb too early in the day, Eric is over banging on their door. He sounds like a total dick."

"Did you find the guy who identified Caitlyn in the Hydro uniform?" she asked.

"The neighbour claims Eric was aggressive so he told him what he wanted to hear. What he told me was that he didn't get a good enough look at the Hydro worker to make a positive identification. The woman he remembers was blond and had a nice figure. It could be her, but it could be a hundred other women. The thing is Caitlyn has no motive to kill me, and where's her opportunity? I've never seen her before."

"Well, the court did convict her of manslaughter," Sam said. "I checked after you called this afternoon. She killed her mother."

"Geez," Reece muttered.

"Dolores Franklyn attacked Jennifer with a knife. She believed the devil had possessed her granddaughter. Jennifer was nine, I think. From the transcripts, it doesn't sound like Caitlyn had any option. Dolores had a documented history of mental instability. Police had charged her twice for aggravated assault, and she'd spent two years in a psychiatric hospital."

"Why wasn't it self-defence?" Reece asked.

"Because Caitlyn tested positive for heroin and stabbed Dolores fourteen times."

"Excessive force." Reece shook his head in confusion. "But if Dolores had a record of aggression, a good attorney could argue the situation required Caitlyn to protect her child. Panic and maternal instinct rendered her incapable of computing stop force. Something's not adding up here."

"My best guess is the drug angle influenced the judge," Sam said. "Caitlyn made a full confession, didn't appeal the sentence, or apply for parole. She offered Graham an uncontested divorce and gave him full custody of the kids. Grand Valley said she was an exemplary inmate. She taught computer courses, and, after her release, she volunteered at the prison twice a month to finish teaching the program."

"Eric made the mother's death out to be a vicious attack on an innocent person by a deranged woman." Reece shook his head. "Nothing Sally or Eric told me is credible."

Sam eyed the last wonton. She'd already eaten six, but it looked so lonely sitting there on that big plate.

"If Eric didn't dig deep enough, he would only have read biased articles." An extra half hour at the gym would balance the pig-out, she decided. She snagged the wonton. "Matricide should attract media attention, but there was surprisingly little, outside of a tabloid story that sensationalized the mother-daughter angle. That's probably what Eric read," she mumbled through a full mouth. "I don't think Eric's crappy research skills means he's a calculated liar."

When Reece didn't reply she added, "The details about the self-defence angle didn't come out until the sentencing hearing, which, by the way was unusually brisk. I doubt a regular citizen like Eric would know how to get their hands on court transcripts."

"Maybe," Reece muttered unconvincingly. "Why do you say the case was handled fast?"

"I dropped by Jim's office, gave him a rundown on the research I did on Caitlyn's trial, and asked his legal opinion," Sam said. "He felt confused by how quickly the court prosecuted Caitlyn and also by the harshness of the sentence." She shrugged. "A public defender represented her, so Jim figured the kid lacked experience."

"Did you find out anything about the restraining order Sally claimed Graham had against Caitlyn?" Reece asked.

"Yeah, he filed it six months after her release, about two and a half years ago."

"So she was in breach when she went to the school thirteen months ago," Reece said. "At least Sally didn't lie about that. Why did he want a restraining order?"

"Don't know. I meant to ask Jim's law clerk to pull the paperwork but forgot. I'll follow up tomorrow."

"Did you talk to Roger?" Reece demanded harshly. "What's his lame excuse for lying this time?" He pursed his lips together in dislike.

"Brenda never mentioned not being the kids' biological mother. She's thirty-five, and Roger assumed that the twins were a high school pregnancy, which explained—to him at least—why she never attended post-secondary school."

"Right, Roger never asked his lover how long she'd been married," Reece said sarcastically and shook his head in disbelief, implying Sam was a moron eagerly lapping up Roger's ridiculous lies.

"Enough with the attitude," she said sharply. "I get that you're frustrated, but it's not implausible that a man who's committing adultery wasn't keen on drilling his lover about her marriage. Come on, Reece."

"Convenient," he murmured.

Sam sighed and poured another glass of wine, not bothering to offer the bottle to Reece. She took a deep breath and then shoved the bottle over to his side of the table. Just because Reece was taking his bad mood out on her wasn't licence for her to act childish.

"Anyway," she continued in a pleasant tone, hoping to defuse the tension, "Roger was very shocked over the news. I asked him not to mention Caitlyn to Brenda or the kids. I'd like to spring it on them and find out why they didn't tell us."

Reece snorted in disgust. "I'm sure he called Brenda and spilled the beans." He smirked at her. "How about the pants that mysteriously disappeared? What about those?"

Sam ground her teeth together and ignored his snotty tone. "I picked them up yesterday. We should have the lab results in a few days."

She refrained from voicing her doubts about whether they were the same pants. Tan khakis were tan khakis. Roger could have destroyed the pants Jordan described to police and bought a new pair to submit for testing. All he'd have to do would be to have a random dry cleaner run them through the chemical process to ensure the lab found dry cleaning solvents. That would account for the delay in getting the pants to her.

"What about the DNA test?" Reece demanded. "Has he done it? I'd like to honour Abigail's final wish by helping Talia to get closure. I'd like to feel anything but incompetent." He slapped his hand hard against the table. "We should have known about Caitlyn Franklyn. We shouldn't have trusted Roger."

Sam knew Roger wouldn't do the test until they found something in Graham's murder to exonerate him. Looking at Reece's angry, judgemental face, she understood where Roger was coming from—didn't agree with it, but understood.

She disregarded Reece's question and asked one of her own. "About the money Brenda borrowed from Roger that she told us was to settle a property issue, did you find out anything?"

He laughed. "Big surprise, Brenda lied. An alleged dispute involving the Harris family surprised every neighbour."

She thought about it. "Maybe the person doesn't live there now. Did anyone sell their house since the Harris family moved?"

He nodded. "Two. I spoke with one and they didn't even know Graham Harris. The other relocated to Singapore with her daughter last year. The woman's a real estate attorney and lived at the end of the street. Sam, there's no way she had a property dispute with Graham Harris. Brenda's a liar."

"Or Graham lied to her to get the money." She cleared the plates from the table and leaned against the sink.

"Any luck finding an address on Caitlyn?" Reece asked.

"The cops did follow up with Caitlyn after Sally and Eric filed a complaint. The address they have isn't current and it's the same as Corrections had. I can't find a driver's licence, a health card, or any tax returns. She's living off the grid," Sam said. "I called Behoo. Maybe he can find creative ways to dig where I can't reach."

"I'm exhausted," he said. "Let's clean up and go to bed."

Poor Reece, she thought as she herded him to the stairs. "I'll tidy, you sleep. I'm behind on my case notes so I'll stay up for a bit."

He reached for her hand and gave it a little tug. "Leave it, come to bed. I haven't written up anything." He tapped his head. "It's all up here. We can worry about reports later."

She squeezed his hand gently, then let go. She wouldn't be able to sleep knowing the kitchen wasn't clean and orderly. "Just give me half an hour. I'll be up soon."

She watched him climb the stairs, feeling bad that he was so disheartened over the case. As he reached the top, she finally asked the question that had been on the tip of her tongue all night. "Reece? Did you forget to tell me about Lisa and Jim's dinner party on Saturday?"

He paused at the top of the stairs with his back turned. "Yeah. Sorry."

He hadn't forgotten, she knew. An explosion between Lisa and Reece hovered on the horizon. Worse, for some reason Sam didn't understand, Reece had decided he disliked Jim. She'd had enough. Dinner was the perfect opportunity for everyone to engage in a candid discussion and co-create resolutions.

"No worries. I told Lisa we'd be there at seven." She heard the challenge in her voice.

Reece didn't say anything, disappearing into the bathroom.

IT TOOK SAM a full minute to wake up and recognize the ringing was coming from their landline. No one ever called the home phone. They didn't even have an answering machine on it. Instead of hanging up, the caller stayed on the line. It rang and rang.

"It's two-thirty in the morning," Sam croaked, looking over at Reece's side of the bed.

He was already up, and he followed her down the stairs to the kitchen, where the phone sat unused. Brandy barked from the top of the stairs, unable to negotiate the steep staircase without help and mad at them for abandoning her.

Sam grabbed the phone. "If it's an international telemarketer, I'm going to lose my shit."

The number was blocked. She shouted a rude greeting into the receiver.

A drone of traffic hummed in the background. "Get Reece, put me on speaker," Behoo ordered without preamble.

Reece stood beside her, rubbing sleep out of his eyes.

Sam put the phone on speaker and placed it on the kitchen table. "What's going on?"

"Get your cells and mobile devices."

"Behoo, what's—"

"Shut up and listen to me," he ordered impatiently. "Take out the batteries."

Brandy continued to bark sharply from upstairs. Between the dog and the traffic noise on Behoo's end, it was hard to hear.

"Behoo, Reece here—"

"Hurry up! I remote wiped your hard drives, but she can run code to retrieve it. You gotta disable everything."

Reece ran up the stairs and returned with their cells. He fumbled the backs off and removed the batteries, while Sam flipped over her laptop and snapped out the battery.

"Your iPad," she reminded Reece.

He searched around and found it on the antique church altar. "Find my laptop," he told her. "It's by the desk."

Brandy was whining and pawing at the ladder. Sam located Reece's laptop and removed the battery. She raced upstairs, hoisted Brandy under her arm, and carried her down to the main floor.

"Is everything disabled?" Behoo demanded.

"Yes," Reece said. "Who's accessing our equipment?"

"Any webcams in your place? Do you have a home monitoring system?"

Sam glanced at the red flashing light by the front door. "Well, there's the ADT security."

"Where does it dump data? Is there a dedicated circuit in your apartment? Shit, your router. Unplug it and disable any modems."

On the other end of the phone, someone was speaking to Behoo, but she couldn't decipher the words.

Reece was already in the closet that housed the modem and wireless router, tugging plugs from the receptacle. Brandy was running between them barking.

"Behoo, you're scaring the shit out of me," Sam yelled over the melee.

"The security system. Tell me what it is."

"It's old." She pawed through the files she kept in the desk drawer and read him the serial number, make, and model. "I put it in years ago. They keep trying to upgrade it."

"Cameras?"

"No. Motion detectors, door and window alarms, and a panic button. Initiates a silent alarm. It doesn't digital record."

"What about the office?" Behoo asked, firing the question at her.

Reece put his arm around her shoulders and answered, "We don't keep a computer at the office, and there isn't a dedicated security system. The bakery downstairs has one, but I don't know the details. It's old, so I assume it's basic. What's going on?"

They heard the blare from a semi's horn. "Your banking?"

"Behoo, what—"

"Cancel all the cards. Do it now and fast."

"How, without a computer or phone?" Reece asked. "Can you do it?"

Sam tugged his arm and whispered, "What are you thinking? You're giving him our banking information?"

Reece patted her hand. "It's our only option. If we're at electronic risk, we need someone with the skills to intercept the banks' firewalls and freeze our accounts fast. Trust me. It'll be okay. He helped me with credit card fraud in the past."

Sam hesitated. She'd worked with Behoo for three years, and he'd been nothing but trustworthy. Reece was right: it would take too much time for them to reach the bank and credit card companies. Finally, she nodded and Reece went to the desk to pull the paperwork.

"Give me the details and make it fast," Behoo said in a clipped tone. "Bloody Widow's chasing Hybrid, but she'll figure out it's a red herring."

Sam had no idea what he was talking about. Hybrid must be a friend of Behoo's, probably the person he kept speaking to in the background. Was Bloody Widow the online handle of the person threatening her and Reece? Behoo must have moved from where he'd been when he'd first called. There was no traffic interference now. Sam strained to hear his conversation with this "Hybrid." All she heard was the thumping of her own heart, and, from the other end of the speakerphone, the fast clicking of computer keys.

Reece pulled a folder from the file drawer, opened it, and handed her a piece of paper. It listed all their banking details in a table, along with passwords and online account details for every site they accessed.

She recited the information and heard Behoo's fingers flying across the keys. He grunted twice, swore, and typed manically.

Through the phone, someone said loudly, "T-minus three, dude. There's the Widow."

"Got it!" Behoo shouted. "Shut it down, Hybrid. Get that bitch off your ass."

"Behoo, what's going on?" Reece asked.

The nonsensical technical gibberish that followed was incomprehensible to Sam.

"English!" she yelled over Behoo's explanation.

"She caught me up in her shit."

"Who caught you up in her what now?" Reece asked.

"Lanteka is safe," he said. "I set the IP address up in a maze of proxy servers but double checked that she didn't link it to me. But you guys? I dunno. Covered your gov docs. She's dope, and I don't know how long she shadowed. Get it?"

"No," Sam retorted.

"Need me to draw you a picture?" he shouted. "This Caitlyn Franklyn bitch you sent me after is protected by Bloody Widow, one of the most nefarious black-hatters on the deep web."

"Caitlyn is a technological genius," Reece stated with a sigh. "My guess is that she's not *protected* by Bloody Widow, she *is* Bloody Widow."

"And you didn't tell me?" Behoo's voice rose. "You sent me after the Widow blind?"

Dumb, dumb, dumb, Sam thought and her stomach dropped. It hadn't occurred to her to mention the technology aspect. She'd asked Behoo to find her an address on a woman who had served time at Grand Valley.

Behoo spoke away from the phone, rapidly shouting orders to whoever Hybrid was. Sam had never heard the laid-back hacker anything but serene and confident. He was brilliant, he was careful, and he was an outstanding hacker. As he scrambled to protect them from Bloody Widow, his uncharacteristic frenzy frightened her.

Reece sat at the table, crossed his legs, and casually linked his hands behind his head. "How at risk are we?" he inquired. Sam couldn't believe that he didn't seem at all upset or stressed.

"I think you're okay," Behoo said slowly. "But I warn you, I've never seen the mad skills I caught tonight." He paused before adding, "Look, we know Bloody Widow's handle and her rep. She's into bad shit. Scary people would love to shut her down permanently. Reece, you guys need to watch your backs. If the people who want Bloody Widow stopped find out that she was after you, they'll assume you have a connection to her real-world identity."

"And come looking for us," Reece said with another sigh. "Let's focus on the immediate problem. Will this Bloody Widow launch a cyber-attack?"

"No clue. I don't know why you were looking for her in the first place." Before Reece responded, Behoo rushed to add, "And I don't want to know. Look, I did what I could to make you ghosts. She can't touch what doesn't exist."

"Okay," Reece replied passively. "So we have no government identity, email, or social media accounts. No bank accounts or credit cards, and you purged all our documents, passwords, and contacts, yes?"

Sam's stomach flipped and sour bile rose to her throat. She tried to do a mental inventory of everything she kept on her computer and felt sicker.

Behoo's voice was hard when he said, "How you deal with the government and banks is up to you, but I got nothin' to do with it, nada. You don't know shit about me, get it?"

Reece stood and stretched out his back with a yawn. "You have my promise." Unruffled demeanour, pleasant tone of voice. "Thanks, Behoo."

"Gotta peace. Grab a pen." He gave them an address. "That's all I got for you."

"Appreciate it," Reece said. "I'll send you a grand for the trouble. Any chance she has your real-world identity?"

"No way. Bitcoin for the payment, some as usual. I suggest we all be extra diligent for the next little while. I'll contact you in the morning with a new cell number and email address you can use to reach me." Behoo hung up.

Sam flopped into a kitchen chair. "This is terrible! We have no money and no credit cards. We lost all our contacts, all our files. Behoo's pissed." Tears burned her eyes, which infuriated her.

Reece went into the kitchen and made coffee.

She'd had enough of his composed attitude. "What's the matter with you? This is a disaster!"

"Well," he said, extracting a T-Disc from the Tassimo and putting in another. "It's unfortunate."

"Unfortunate?" she screamed. "It's a nightmare!"

"Not really. We don't use social media anyway. Lanteka is safe, which is good since it skirts legalities." He passed her a mug of coffee and sat on a kitchen chair at the table.

"We're at risk of identity theft," Sam yelled. "Our reputa— shit!" She covered her mouth with both hands. "All my PhD notes for my dissertation. Eight months of work! Can she hack into the university database? Can she trash my record?" Panic washed over her, and she couldn't decide whether to cry or to punch something.

"Well, based on Behoo's impression of her skill, she can do whatever she likes. The question is whether she'll bother. But, no, you didn't lose anything." He thought for a minute. "Well, whatever you did today. Did you do anything significant today?"

She shook her head.

"You're fine. We're not broke, either. The accounts are frozen but the money's not gone." He chewed on his lip. "Explaining to the authorities how we managed to secure everything without speaking to the financial institutions will be tricky."

She didn't feel the least bit reassured. "And what do you suggest we do now?"

"The Financial Crimes Unit is the best starting point. We'll ask Bryce Mansfield for help," Reece said. "Not that this has anything to do with the homicide squad, but having a staff inspector in our court might grease the wheels with the police." He sighed and ran his hand across the stubble on his chin. "Since Behoo isn't one hundred percent sure how much Bloody Widow got before he shut her down, we better contact Trans Union Canada and Equifax Canada to put a fraud alert on our credit reports. I suggest we speak with the office of the Privacy Commissioner of Canada, too." He sipped his coffee. "Tomorrow, we'll replace our government documents."

"What about what Eric and Sally said about pornographic emails being sent to all their contacts?"

Her mother's critical face rose in her mind. That relationship was already hideous. She and her stepfather were close, but he disapproved of the strife between her and Grace, feeling strongly that Sam should make more of an effort. Sam shuddered to imagine what her stepfather would do if Grace received a disgusting email from her estranged daughter.

Uttering a small groan, her mind skipped to all of her professional contacts. If narcissistic, paranoid CEOs received an offensive email from her, how was she going to explain a massive electronic attack? It had taken years to develop those relationships and to convince them of her confidentiality. If Bloody Widow publicized confidential client material, the civil suits alone would cripple her business. She felt violated and homicidal toward the potential threat.

"Stop freaking out. I can see it in your face," Reece said, sipping his coffee. "Behoo cancelled our email accounts. It's doubtful she had time to send anything malicious. But we'll open new accounts and warn our contacts. Identity theft happens. People understand."

His passiveness just enraged her more. People who hire private investigators and entrust them with their darkest secrets did not understand horrendous security breaches.

"How are we going to warn anyone?" Sam retorted. "We lost all our contacts. Don't you understand the magnitude of what has happened? There was highly confidential material on my computer. What if she posts it online?"

"Behoo purged our files before she downloaded anything, Sam," he said, sounding a little impatient now. "He was online, along with whoever Hybrid is, and prevented Bloody Widow from getting the data. He deleted everything. I don't know much about the technology, but I know it's damn near impossible for a hacker to compromise someone of Behoo's talent when he's immediately aware of the threat. He took defensive manoeuvres." Reece took her hand.

She jerked away from him. "My PhD work is gone! I don't have any cash. What's wrong with you? Why can't you understand how devastating this is?"

He went to the closet and returned with a sachet, unzipped it, and handed it to her.

She peered inside and took out a block of paper-wrapped bills. "How much is here?" she asked in awe.

"A grand, give or take," he replied. "Three in the safe deposit box."

She pulled out a red My Passport portable hard drive.

"Most nights, when I remember," Reece said, "I back everything up. I forgot tonight, but I did it last night."

"My stuff, too?"

His smile was reassuring. "Of course. People rely on technology too much." He shrugged. "Hope for the best, but plan for the worse. I tried to talk to you about it last year, remember?"

She nodded. "I said you were paranoid."

"Who's paranoid now?" He arched his eyebrow and grinned.

"We're safe?"

"As safe as we can be." He gestured at the bag. "There are phones in there, too, and new SIM cards. The issue is how we explain to the cops what happened while protecting Behoo's identity. I need to sleep on that one."

"If it is Caitlyn Franklyn, her only motivation to hurt us would have to do with her ex-husband's murder," Sam said slowly, trying to assess the risk based on fact rather than emotion. "Even if she managed to grab data before Behoo wiped the drives, I didn't write up anything about this case. How about you?" she asked.

"Not a thing."

"If she reads the papers, she knows we're investigating her ex-husband's death." Rational thought was returning and Sam tried to think through Caitlyn's perspective. "She allegedly attacked the Alistair family after Sally accused Jordan of rape. Without those case notes, she won't know we suspect the twins in conjunction with your poisoning. Still, she could hack us for the hell of it." She checked her watch. It was nearly four in the morning and she was wide awake, riding an adrenalin rush. Reece, on the other hand, looked exhausted.

"From what Behoo said, she has bigger problems." He took their coffee mugs to the sink, speaking over his shoulder. "If Caitlyn Franklyn is Bloody Widow, protecting her anonymity is crucial. If she's cavorting with known cyber predators, guarding her identity is vital. She didn't know who Behoo was or why he was snooping into Caitlyn Franklyn. She attacked the threat. Now she knows it was just us, I doubt she'll care. She must have anticipated that we'd want to question her about her ex-husband's murder. Clearly, she doesn't want to talk to us, but I think she'll just ignore us."

Reece put the SIM cards in the phones, turned them on, and handed her one. "We need to call those emergency numbers. Grab that piece of paper."

On the back were the numbers for the agencies he'd recommended they call. While Reece called the police, filed an incident report, and obtained the number, Sam started notifying agencies and reporting the possible identity theft.

After half an hour, Reece hung up and ran his fingers through his hair. "We have to go to the pink palace and answer questions tomorrow." He sighed and closed his eyes. "That's not a conversation I'm excited about, but we're meeting at Bryce's office. That should offer some protection."

Having finished her own calls, Sam put down the cell she'd been using. "So, tomorrow, after we talk to the police, how about we check out Caitlyn's address?"

He nodded. "I'd like to talk with Bloody Widow."

Sam scowled. "You talk. I'm just going to beat the shit out of her."

CHAPTER TWENTY-ONE

SAM

BRYCE MANSFIELD SAT rigid behind his desk, with his hands folded on top of a file folder. He was clenching his hands together so hard that his knuckles were turning white. It looked to Sam as if he was also grinding his teeth. The man was furious and trying to hide it under a professional mask.

Sam had met the staff inspector once or twice when she was a police constable and wished that this reunion were under better circumstances. She felt terrible for Reece. The clusterfuck they were in could sully Reece's opportunity to join Bryce's homicide squad. Maybe it was for the best. Sometimes it was easier when circumstances made a tough decision for you, and Sam had felt for a little while that Reece's reluctance to accept the offer was because he didn't want to return to police work.

Bryce's tone of voice was neutral when he said, "I'm unclear on how you discovered you were at risk and how you hid or wiped out your identity so fast."

Knowing that Reece was a terrible liar, Sam leaned forward in her chair and spoke before he had a chance to answer. "I know someone in the US. I use her sometimes to gather information on cases." She held up her hand. "It's perfectly legal. You remember the Martina case. Jim Stipelli hired us to find Gabriella after she disappeared."

Bryce nodded.

"Well..." She paused and cleared her throat. "We needed to find her father, Quentin LeBlanc. He had dual citizenship and we had reason to believe he was stateside. Instead of collaborating with a PI in the US, I hired an IT specialist to get information we couldn't access." Not exactly true, but she thought that reminding Bryce about the excellent work they'd done on the Martina case might soften his attitude.

It didn't.

"A specialist who can infiltrate Canadian Government databases and financial institutions," Bryce said. "A hacker." He practically spat out the two words.

"Yeah, but one of the good ones," Sam said with a smile.

Bryce snorted. "There's no such thing. This one is a risk to national security. I want a name."

Lying in business situations usually wasn't a problem for her. It was unavoidable as a private investigator. You had to use whatever worked to get people to talk to you. But she was struggling today. Embedded in her DNA was respect for the chain of command. It wasn't only because of her short career as a cop; it was because she grew up with a dedicated homicide detective for a dad.

"I don't have a real name," she said.

"Yet she works for you," Bryce retorted incredulously. "How do you pay her?"

"Bitcoin."

Sam hoped he wasn't going to ask for further explanation. She had no idea what bitcoin was and didn't know how to get it or how to pay people with it. Reece paid Behoo, but the less he spoke in front of Bryce the better. If she was struggling in this interview, she didn't want to put Reece—who had followed the chain of command for over ten years—in the position of lying to a superior.

She could offer Bryce an online handle. This morning, when Behoo called with his new contact details, she'd asked for a name she could use. Behoo had supplied a legitimate handle to drop. He felt confident Canadian police would recognize the name but wouldn't know the hacker had died. All they'd discern was that Cereus had disappeared from the online world, and she'd been a white hat hacker, protecting innocent people from malware and invasion.

"Her online name is Cereus," Sam told Bryce. "It's a white cactus flower that blooms one night a year. Disappears when the sun comes up."

Too much information, a classic sign of lying. She clamped her lips together and placed her open palms on her knees, ensuring her eyes drifted off Bryce's from time to time. Liars maintained eye contact, often covered their mouths, and closed off their bodies.

There was a knock on the door, and a young man entered. He pushed his glasses up his nose and glanced at Sam and Reece. He leaned against the wall and hooked his thumbs through the belt loops in his jeans. "What's up, Inspector?"

"This is Detective Romero," Bryce told Sam and Reece. "He's one of our best cyber detectives. I invited him to sit in."

Bryce explained the situation to Romero, and Sam interjected a few times to correct the facts.

"I don't get it." Romero's eyes narrowed. "You're telling me that Cereus was online and Bloody Widow went after her?"

Sam nodded. "Cereus was trying to find information for us. We think Graham Harris's ex-wife is Bloody Widow. Cereus panicked, which was why she overreacted and wiped our data and identities."

"Cereus panicked?" He smirked. "If you say so."

"Do you know either handle?" Bryce asked.

Romero laughed. "Bloody Widow stole over six million from the financial sector alone. Over a year ago, there was a rumour that she'd branched out and hit racketeers." He scrutinized Sam. "Weird someone like that randomly hitting you."

"Well," she said quickly, "she didn't exactly hit us. She attacked Cereus. Like I said, we believe Caitlyn Franklyn is Bloody Widow. We got caught in the middle."

Romero's eyes lit up. "Is that so? Cereus tell you that?" He sniggered.

"Franklyn has a record," Reece said to Bryce. "Manslaughter. I dropped off everything we have for Detective Alston at York and have copies here for you. Including an address north of Toronto." He handed Bryce a file folder. "With your permission, we'd like to speak with her. Obviously after Detective Romero here and York Police conclude their investigation."

Bryce's lips thinned with displeasure. "Reece, York Regional Police know about Caitlyn Franklyn. Alston's investigating the murder of her ex-husband. If you'd spoken to him about the progress of your investigation, as I requested, you'd know that."

"I did speak to Alston," Reece said firmly. "He was rude and uncooperative. I've left three messages for him over the past week to update him on what we learned. He hasn't called back."

Romero stepped forward to stand in front of her. He leaned his back against the front of the staff inspector's desk. "I wanna get back to this online angle." His brown eyes drilled into Sam's face, and she struggled not to squirm around on her chair under his scrutiny.

He crossed his arms against his chest and smiled down at her. "Caitlyn Franklyn, a convicted murderer, is the notorious Bloody Widow, one of the best hidden hackers in the virtual world." He chortled. "And Cereus discovered this revelation *last night*. How about you run through it from the start?"

Sam outlined their investigation to date, explaining the online connection. Watching the amusement on Romero's face as she spoke, her nervousness increased.

Bryce sighed and addressed Romero. "Are either Sam or Reece at risk?"

"Of what, breaking the law?" He sneered at Sam. "Over my pay grade. If you mean electronically, nah. It was lucky *Cereus* moved so fast. Remarkable, under the circumstances."

He knew Cereus was dead. Sam quickly ran options through her head. She'd plead ignorance, suggesting that someone else was using the handle. She waited with tense anticipation, but Romero didn't challenge her. Yet. Sam suspected he would at some point.

Bryce stood. "I'd appreciate your help with this, Detective. Until York clears Franklyn in their homicide, keep this quiet. If she's Bloody Widow, the cybercrimes fall under our jurisdiction.

I'll speak to Alston and ask him to keep the cyber angle out of his interview with her. I don't want her tipped off that we've made the connection."

Romero shrugged. "Whatever you say, Inspector."

"We'll talk more about this later," Bryce warned Reece and pointed his finger at him to emphasize that the talk wasn't going to be a pleasant experience. "For now, get out. I have a staff meeting." He turned his back to them and browsed through a file cabinet.

"I'm going to the parking garage," Romero told Sam and Reece as they walked out of the office. "I'll ride down with you."

They followed Romero to the elevator. When the door opened, he glared at two constables who were waiting to get into the empty elevator car. "Take the next ride."

Inside, he stared up at the numbers descending. "Oleander."

Sam exchanged a look with Reece but said nothing.

After a beat of silence, Romero said, "Hybrid."

He was fishing but that was too close to home for Sam's comfort. She decided a flippant response was the best strategy. "Oh, I've always wanted one of those," she replied. "I have a restored 1973 Grand Am. What a pig on gas."

The elevator stopped, and Romero politely shooed two civilians away. After the doors slid closed, he said, "Belladonna."

She ignored him this time, deciding a snappy comeback wasn't advisable.

At the ground floor, he turned and put his hand on Reece's arm to prevent him from exiting the elevator. "Behoo."

Sam tugged Reece's free arm and they stepped off.

Romero leaned his shoulder against the elevator door to prevent it from closing and smiled unpleasantly, studying Sam's face with hard eyes. He held out his index and middle finger, cocked an imaginary hammer with his thumb, and clicked his teeth while jerking his outstretched fingers upward. "Watch your backs, amigos. You're in over your heads."

"Makes life interesting," Sam replied with a bright smile.

"True dat." He released the door and it slid closed.

CHAPTER TWENTY-TWO

SHE NEVER TOUCHED me, not in that way, but she'd come into my room late at night.

"A little cuddle?" she'd whisper through the darkness.

I'd lay still and silent, willing her to go away. It never worked. She'd crawl in beside me and coil her thin, cold body around mine.

She'd cry. Not the soft weeping of private despondency, but gut wrenching sobs that tore from her throat. How I hated the smell of her misery and the feathery touch of her fingers trailing across my forehead. A warm layer of snot from her running nose would coat my cheek, and tears would drizzle down my neck and soak the collar of my pajamas. The rancid odour of fried onions would drift across my face as she gasped and wailed, clinging to me as she drowned in her weakness.

I wouldn't move. I'd concentrate on counting the spaces between breaths, mimicking the even flow and ebb of deep sleep. Even then, I was good at pretending.

When the first hint of light from the rising sun inched across the windowpane, she'd disentangle her body from mine and lean over to tuck the damp sheets beneath my chin.

"Such a sweet child," she'd murmur. "Everything I do is for you."

I'd watch the sunrise and think about how to kill her. I'd imagine sticky blood staining my hands, and the expression of shock and betrayal before the light died in her eyes. I'd wonder how long her heart would beat after I tore it from her breast, and if her entrails would squish between my fingers when I spilled the spongy ropes from her withered body.

"Everything I do," I'd say to the sun while it rose from a shimmering pool of blood, "will be for you."

CHAPTER TWENTY-THREE

REECE

THERE WAS ROGER'S car snuggled tight against Brenda's in the yard of the Harris farm. Immediate distrust washed over Reece. Before they visited Bryce yesterday morning, Reece had called Roger to warn him about a possible hack. In the course of his explanation, he'd let it slip they had an address for Caitlyn and were speaking to the police before confronting Brenda and the kids today. Reece had quickly reiterated Sam's previous warning of not mentioning Caitlyn. They needed to gauge the family's spontaneous reaction to the discovery that Graham's ex-wife was a suspect. And here was Roger, where he wasn't supposed to be. Again.

Reece laid his hand on the hood of Roger's vehicle. Cold. He'd been here for a while, enjoying a tête-à-tête. Everything about the man made Reece angry and suspicious.

"What are you doing?"

He joined Sam on the front porch. "The engine's cold."

With an indifferent shrug, she knocked on the door. Roger— new master of the house, apparently—answered.

"Hi, we're in the living room." He stepped aside so they could enter.

Brenda, who had been standing and wringing her hands when they entered, perched on the edge of a loveseat. Roger settled in beside her, patting her trembling hand.

Jordan was slouching against the arm of a sofa across from them, putting as much distance as he could between himself and Jennifer, who sat in the lotus position on the middle cushion. Jordanna sat on the other end of the couch with her long legs crossed. Today, she was wearing a tight T-shirt with a scooped neckline that showed enough cleavage that she could carry a good-sized cell phone between her breasts, if she'd been so inclined. A thin gold chain circled her waist. She'd threaded the ends of the chain through a pierced belly-button hoop on her naked midriff. Arrow charms decorated the chain ends and fell into her crotch. Jordan's surly expression implied he'd rather be anywhere than with his family. Jordanna's bright smile looked staged, and Jennifer wore no expression. In her hands, she clutched a grubby white bible.

Reece eyed the three teenagers sitting in a row in various positions of displeasure. *See no evil, hear no evil, speak no evil*, he thought.

Sam sat in an armchair, and Reece leaned against the wall beside her chair. Short of sitting on the floor, it was his only option.

"Oh, that outfit is the bomb-dot-com." Jordanna widened her artificial grin and pointed a crimson fingernail at Sam.

A flicker of annoyance crossed Sam's face. Considering she was wearing a black Alter Bridge band T-shirt and a pair of jeans, Reece figured the false flattery pissed her off.

"We're here to discuss Caitlyn Franklyn." Roger blushed, avoiding Reece's glare.

Son of a bitch!

"I have an ethical requirement to disclose information to protect people from harm," Roger said in a sanctimonious tone. "After much consideration, I felt your directive to remain silent over Caitlyn to be incompatible with my code of ethics, and I divulged the potential threat."

Brenda's cheeks flushed with colour, but her eyes remained on her lap, where she once again twisted the fabric of her skirt into a rope.

Jennifer studied Roger with a strange expression Reece couldn't identify. Jordanna's fake smile stayed firmly in place. Her eyes were cold when they flitted between her sister and brother. Jordan twisted his head to the side and muttered something under his breath that Reece didn't hear.

Foregoing small talk, Sam turned to Jordanna. "When you and I talked, why didn't you tell me Brenda wasn't your biological mother?"

She shrugged. "I thought you knew. Why did you think I called her Brenda instead of Mom?"

"Brenda, why didn't you tell us?" Sam asked.

"I also thought you knew. You're investigators, after all."

Reece could see the frustration in Sam's face when she caught his eye, suggesting he take over.

"How old were you when your mother left?" he asked Jordan.

"Didn't leave, she—"

Jordanna shot him the evil eye, and he clamped his mouth shut. She answered for her brother. "Jordan and I had just turned twelve and Jennifer was nine. Mom killed our grandmother. We were there when she stabbed her over and over." Her tone was nonchalant and she absentmindedly picked a piece of lint off her shorts.

"What was your mother like?" Sam asked.

"Overprotective." Her expression suggested it wasn't a positive attribute.

"She came to my class," Jordon blurted out. "What an epic fail!"

"Was that last year?" Reece asked him. "In Mrs. Alistair's class?"

"She sent me perverted Snapchats." His nose crinkled in disgust.

Sam looked as puzzled as Reece felt over Jordan volunteering this information.

"Who did? Your mother or Mrs. Alistair?" Sam asked, clearly confused.

He rolled his eyes. "Mrs. Alistair. There's something wrong with her. I kept telling her to fuck off, but she wouldn't leave me alone. She'd photobomb pics of my friends and me. You know, sneak up behind us so she'd be in the picture. Who does that?" His harsh laughter grated against Reece's ears.

Sam leaned forward and put her elbows on her knees, studying Jordan. "Really? Do you have copies of the pictures she wormed her way into?"

"Nah, trashed them." His eyes darted to Jordanna.

"How about the Snapchats?" Sam asked. "Did you take a screenshot?"

Jordan sneered at her. "Right, like I'd keep disgusting shit a pervy teacher sent me!"

"Really? You didn't want to share it with your friends and make a fool out of your teacher. That seems odd, what with you being so disgusted and upset," Sam said sarcastically, leaning back against the chair and shooting Reece a doubtful look.

Reece understood her skepticism. Sending a provocative picture on social media was risky, and it was unlikely that a teacher would put her job on the line by using it to lure a student who had made it clear he wasn't interested. But, then again, Snapchat wasn't like other social media applications. Reece didn't personally use Snapchat but understood a bit about it. It was possible that Mrs. Alistair had believed it was a safe means to entice a student. Since the video messaging app allowed users to set a time limit of mere second for their recipients to view the snap, many people believed that the content completely disappeared without leaving an electronic trail.

Reece didn't see the point in challenging Jordan. He'd like to know Caitlyn's motivation for breaching a restraining order and risking arrest by going to the school.

"Why did your mother come to the school and what did she want?" he asked.

"It was awful!" Jordanna exclaimed with Academy Awards–worthy dramatics. "Mrs. Alistair spoke to her in the hall, but Mom shoved her way into the classroom and grabbed me." She rubbed her arm, presumably where her mother had seized her. "She was yelling I had to go with her. Jordan tried to get her off and she totally freaked, yelling horrible stuff at him. Mrs. Alistair got in between us and my mother hit her. One of the kids called the office, and the principal went on the intercom and ordered lockdown."

Jordanna trembled and scrunched up her face, fighting tears. The emotion felt over the top to Reece, but the one thing he understood about teenage girls was they loved to be in the centre of a good drama.

When he didn't comment on her harrowing experience, she said, "Everyone was freaking out, like she might have a gun. It was *sooo* embarrassing."

"Then Mrs. A got all weird and up in my shit," Jordan said.

Reece turned to Brenda, ignoring Jordan's attempt to focus the conversation on Sally Alistair. "Did Caitlyn ever have visitation rights?"

"When they released her, we had sole custody." Brenda's voice was so low Reece had to strain to hear her. "Graham let her see them about a month after her release. She kidnapped them. Then claimed it was a misunderstanding. Said she thought it was okay to keep them overnight. That's when Graham filed the restraining order. We never heard from her again."

"Yet she went to the school eighteen months ago in front of multiple witnesses," Sam said, "and you have no idea why she did it?"

Brenda nodded.

Sam's tone of voice was tinged with annoyance when she asked, "Has she contacted you since?" She looked between Brenda and the kids.

Jennifer didn't appear to be listening at all. She sat perfectly still, staring at the cover of the bible she held. The twins exchanged a look before shaking their heads.

Brenda cleared her throat. "We never saw her again."

"Did you or the school press charges?" Reece asked.

"My husband didn't want Caitlyn to go back to jail." Brenda glued her eyes to her skirt. "Graham made excuses because his ex-wife and her sister had a terrible childhood. Their mother was abusive and mentally ill." She glanced at Roger. "Paranoid schizophrenia, I think."

Roger nodded. "The night Caitlyn..." He glanced at Jennifer. "The night of the crime, Caitlyn's mother had a psychotic break. Based on Dolores's medical file, she'd suffered from homicidal ideation since adolescence. Given her psychopathology, a psychotic episode would pose a dangerous threat."

Reece again wondered why Caitlyn had pled guilty to manslaughter. Based on what Roger just said, it sounded like an open and shut case of self-defence.

"How did Graham meet his first wife?" Sam asked Brenda.

"They grew up together, married right after high school, and moved to Boston," Brenda said. "Caitlyn graduated high school at sixteen and received a full scholarship to MIT. Emerson accepted Graham for communications. They stayed for three semesters, and then Caitlyn became pregnant with the twins. She quit school and Graham transferred to the University of Toronto to play football."

It must have killed Caitlyn to give up a full ride to MIT. Reece wondered why she hadn't deferred for a year to have the babies and return. He didn't know much about US university scholarships. Maybe deferring wasn't an option.

"So she was eighteen when she had the twins," he said. "That's young."

Brenda nodded. "Then Jennifer was born when she was twenty. Caitlyn went to prison nine years later, but there were problems before that. Drugs maybe. Graham didn't talk about his ex-wife. I know he believed Caitlyn hated him." She picked at the wrinkles in her skirt. "My husband felt he deserved her contempt. He cheated her out of MIT, took away her children, and abandoned her." Her eyes roamed around the room. "But there was something else, something he refused to talk to me about. I always thought that the secret, whatever it was, made him feel guilty." She sighed. "But I have no idea what it was. He'd always get angry if I asked." A tear dripped down her pale cheek. "Did she kill my husband?"

"Is it possible she was in the house without your knowledge?" Reece asked.

Brenda swallowed and gave a little shrug. "I guess. We don't keep the doors locked out here."

Something wasn't adding up to Reece. If Caitlyn had tried to take her children when the prison released her, why wasn't she seeking full custody now Graham was out of the picture? Maybe she'd legally relinquished her rights to her children.

"Did you adopt the kids when Caitlyn was in prison?" Reece asked.

Brenda shook her head. "No. We tried, but Caitlyn refused to sign the papers." She paused before saying, "After she got out of prison, she kept calling Graham and saying terrible things. A week before his death, Graham had a terrible fight with her."

Sam frowned. "You said the last time you heard from her was eighteen months ago when she went to the school."

"I meant we didn't see her." Colour rose in Brenda's cheeks. "Caitlyn called. Maybe she did something to the sump-pump so Graham would have to go downstairs." She dabbed her eyes with a tissue she took from the pocket of her skirt. Roger put his arm around her shoulders.

"Since the incident at the school, have any of you spoken to your mother? Maybe on the phone?" Reece scrutinized the three kids, watching for classic signs of lying.

Jordan continued to look bored, Jordanna flipped her hair with a provocative smile, and Jennifer stared into space. Reading teenagers was next to impossible. He hoped Sam was having more luck.

Speaking for her siblings, Jordanna finally answered, "We didn't want anything to do with her after she embarrassed us and we had to deal with psycho Mrs. A."

Bringing the conversation back to Sally Alistair again. Since they were determined to tell their side of the story, Reece decided to hear them out. He supposed he understood. Jordan was denying that he did anything to deserve having his teacher accuse him of rape.

Reece spoke to Jordan. "Why do you think Mrs. Alistair made such a serious charge against you?"

Jordan snorted but refused to respond. Brenda glanced at him and he looked at Jordanna before nodding his chin at his stepmother, as if indicating she had permission to speak. The exchange bemused Reece.

"Well, she said she was experiencing behavioural problems with Jordan and asked to see Graham." Brenda's voice was soft, and there was a strange intensity on her face. "The conversation upset my husband. He was good friends with the football coach, so he asked his advice."

Her eyes darted up to Reece's and then fell to her lap. "Coach told him strange things he'd witnessed between Jordan and his math teacher."

"That's when my dad talked to me." Jordanna spoke to Reece. "Mrs. A seemed... I dunno. She told me once my brother was hot." She shuddered. "She texted Jordan that her son was sucking her dry but there was some left for him. Then she kept texting him sick stuff about what she wanted him to do to her. You know, like sexually."

Reece might be able to buy a Snapchat, but he found it difficult to imagine a teacher texting an illicit message to a student. It was easy to trace text messages to the sender. Everyone knew that. Reece fully understood why Sam was smirking.

"Can we see the text thread?" Sam asked Jordan.

"Nah, trashed them," he muttered.

"Jordan, why didn't you keep the text?" Reece demanded, losing his patience. "Why wouldn't you show your father?"

"Dad would make a big deal and everyone at school would find out. I showed my sister." He glanced sideways at his twin. "Then Mrs. A showed at practice. I told her to leave me alone or I was telling the principal. She punched me, like right in the face. It was wacked."

"A week later," Jordanna continued, "she accused Jordan of raping a grade nine girl. After cheerleading practice that day, Coach said he'd drive Jordan home so I could take the car. There was no way my brother was in the parking lot."

"As if I need to rape a chick," he declared. "I get plenty."

But Reece knew that rape wasn't about sex. It was about fear and control. Raping a Muslim girl heightened the thrill of humiliation and shame. Observing Jordan's angry face and clenched fists, Reece had no problem imagining him capable of rape. He was a scary, entitled kid who was a hair away from being a full-blown narcissist.

Reece caught Sam's eye. She tapped her index and middle fingers casually against her cheek. A gesture they'd used for the past year as a non-verbal signal to wrap up a meeting. Because of Roger's interference before they arrived, the interview was a waste of time. No spontaneous reaction to Caitlyn Franklyn's involvement or the complaints of Sally and Eric Alistair. Roger had given the family plenty of forewarning. Lots of time to get their stories straight.

Sam stood. "Jennifer, that's a nice bible. Was it a gift?"

"*The wolf also shall dwell with the lamb, and the leopard shall lie down with the kid; and the calf and the young lion and the fatling together; and a little child shall lead them,*" Jennifer quoted deadpan. "Mother believes that the passage means that a child will lead the way to heaven or to hell. She's wrong. I go to bible camp every summer, Sunday school every week, and bible study on Thursdays."

"No one cares, you bed-wetting Jesus-freak," Jordan yelled.

Reece jumped a bit at the sudden outburst. It was the first time he'd heard Jordan, who strived hard to act cool and in control, raise his voice.

"Jordan, please," murmured Brenda, and Reece couldn't tell if Jordan's attitude toward his younger sister surprised her or not.

"Who wets the bed at sixteen?" Jordan retorted with a mean laugh. "A bible-thumping loser, that's who!"

Stone-faced, Jennifer replied, "I told Mother you killed my cat."

Brenda's face sagged in shock and Jordan leaped to his feet. "You lying skank! I didn't touch your fucking cat and you know it!"

The vet's autopsy had confirmed that a human eviscerated the animal. The evidence was inconclusive as to whether the cat was alive during most of the attack. There was no ambiguity about the missing eye, though. Someone had meticulously gouged out the eyeball first, while the cat was very much alive.

Reece had considered Jordan a prime suspect in the heinous crime, but felt unsure now. The young man's outrage and disgust over the allegation were genuine. The more troubling revelation was that Jennifer had spoken to Caitlyn recently.

"How often do you speak with your mother?" Reece asked her.

"All the time." Jennifer stood and went around the coffee table.

Reece thought she was going to leave the room, but she turned back and faced them.

"When Brenda was in the hospital," Jennifer said, speaking to Sam, "I told Mom you think one of us killed Dad. My mother's angry with you."

From the corner of his eye, Reece saw Brenda's lips narrow. Her face became uncharacteristically hard and ugly.

"Why do you think we suspect one of you?" Sam asked

Reece studied Brenda's face, which had returned to its usual bewildered expression. Maybe he'd imagined the moment of fury.

Jennifer didn't answer Sam's question. Instead, she said, "I wish you hadn't involved Mom." She turned her head to look at Roger, sitting on the sofa beside Brenda. "Thanks for letting me know they figured out who my mother was." She grinned. "And thanks a lot for telling me they knew where she lived so I could warn her and she could leave."

Goddamn your insufferable interference! Reece glared at Roger, who had the good sense to drop his eyes.

This explained why the police hadn't found Caitlyn at the address. Jennifer warned her. She'd vanished because Roger couldn't keep his damn mouth shut.

"Can you reach your mom?" Reece asked Jennifer. "It would help if she'd talk to us."

"She doesn't want to speak with the police."

"We aren't the police," he replied.

"Does it matter?" she asked. "Because of you, I won't get to see my mother again." Jennifer left the room and the back door slammed.

"I didn't know," Brenda said. "She must be sneaking out."

Considering the medicated daze Brenda was in, it didn't surprise Reece that the teenagers were coming and going as they pleased.

"I don't even know where Caitlyn lives," Brenda hurried to add, looking flustered and upset. "She had an apartment on Yonge and Eglinton when she got out of prison, but she left it. She never told us where she moved."

Sam's face was angry as she stood and walked over to where Roger sat on the sofa. She put her fists on her hips and stared Roger down. "What about you? You want to explain why you offered up confidential information on our case to a sixteen-year-old?" she demanded.

Finally! Reece thought. He was sick of pointing out Roger's suspicious interference to Sam.

Roger folded his hands against his knee. "Jennifer overheard me talking with Reece yesterday morning. My sense was she feared her mother would hurt her." He paused and returned Sam's hard stare with one of his own. "Obviously, I didn't know she was in contact with her mother. I simply told her she didn't need to worry. You had found an address and were sharing it with the police. It was a perfectly reasonable thing to do, and I don't appreciate your tone."

She pointed her finger at his chest. "You and I are going to talk about this later."

Reece considered the timeline. Caitlyn had caught Behoo online the night before they went to speak to Bryce. She knew Reece and Sam suspected she was Bloody Widow. No wonder she ran before the police could question her. She had every reason to believe they would arrest her for cybercrimes.

Reece glared at Roger who sat nonchalant on the sofa with a smug little grin. Reece wanted to punch him in the face.

Sam had turned to face Jordanna and Jordan, who were standing together beside the sofa across from Roger. "Where's your mother?" she demanded.

"Jordan and I are stunned Jennifer was visiting her," Jordanna declared with wide-eyed innocence. "I can't believe it. I can talk to her, if you like. Maybe she'll tell me where she is."

"Like she's gonna tell you anything," Jordan muttered. "I have a calculus test tomorrow, and this hasn't got anything to do with me." He sauntered across the living room to the stairs, leaning down to pick up a backpack from the base of the staircase.

Jordanna arched her back with a sigh of pleasure. "I'll call if Jennifer talks to me," she promised. "See y'all later." She waved her fingers at Reece before prancing up the stairs behind her brother.

"I'll walk you out." Roger offered, leading the way outside.

He stopped them before they got into the car. Roger took out his cell phone and turned it to face them. "Do either of you recognize this woman?"

Sam looked. "Well yeah. It's a better picture than we've found, but that's Caitlyn Franklyn."

"Have you seen her before?" Roger asked Reece.

He glanced at the photo. "No." The resemblance to Jordanna was striking. "Why?"

"That's the nurse who went into Brenda's room when we were at the hospital," Roger said impatiently. "Remember? You and I stepped into the hallway for a private talk. A nurse went into the room."

Reece replayed the chain of events in his mind. Roger's back had been to the doorway. To the best of Reece's recollection, Roger never had sightlines to the nurse. Funny how he could make a positive identification when Reece, a trained cop, couldn't. If he pointed out his suspicion, Roger would just come up with some lame excuse that would increase Reece's desire to smack him. He took a deep breath and unlocked the car door.

"Caitlyn went to the hospital?" Sam was asking Roger. "Why didn't Brenda say anything?"

"Brenda was catatonic and unaware of visitors," Roger replied tersely. "You're missing the point." He put away his phone before saying, "What was Caitlyn doing in a locked-down psychiatric ward? Dressed in a nursing uniform. In the room of her murdered ex-husband's wife. A woman Caitlyn hates for taking away her kids." He raised a questioning eyebrow at them.

If what Jennifer had said was true, she'd spoken to her mother after their first interview. That meant Caitlyn was aware he and Sam were investigating the murder of her ex-husband a day or two before someone poisoned him. Reece retraced the afternoon he'd visited Brenda. It would be simple for Caitlyn to research their firm and find pictures of him and Sam. Maybe she'd intended to poison Brenda but reconsidered when she recognized him in the hospital, sucking on a banana smoothie. A drink he'd left unattended. But that theory didn't sit right with Reece. It felt too random for someone as deliberate and intelligent as Caitlyn.

Roger was interfering in their investigation—continuously and unnecessarily. Brenda could have told Roger about the Alistairs' poisoned dog and the witness who put Caitlyn on the scene. If Roger had wanted to kill him, using a poison that police suspected Caitlyn of using in the past would point the finger of blame right at her. Roger just had to wait for Reece and Sam to talk to the Alistairs and make the connection to Caitlyn.

Deflection and multiple suspects established reasonable doubt. It was a clever murderer's best defence. And Roger was a clever man.

CHAPTER TWENTY-FOUR

SAM

"I DON'T WANT to go." Reece's petulant pout was not attractive.

"We can't cancel last minute. Lisa's brother and sister-in-law took Kira." Sam searched through their wine fridge and selected two bottles.

He marched over and studied the labels. "This Dugat-Py is over a hundred and fifty dollars. I was saving it for a special occasion."

Sam sighed. "Then you pick something."

"Never mind. Take it."

"Are you ready?" Keeping her tone neutral was a struggle. Reece was wearing track pants and hadn't showered. They were running late, and her temper was running hot.

Yesterday, he'd bitched all the way home from the Harris farm, insisting Roger was up to "shenanigans." He refused to relinquish his suspicion that Roger had poisoned him, even though the evidence now pointed to Caitlyn, and he regretted taking the case, claiming Roger's situation had nothing to do with the letter Abigail had sent him.

"Call and say I'm sick." There was a definite whine in Reece's voice.

"You're the one who preaches honesty," she retorted. "What's the big deal? It's dinner. I'm not asking you to donate a testicle to medical research. Can you *please* go shower?"

He stood with his arms crossed over his chest. "I don't like your friends. Roger attacked his sister with a hammer and has sex with patients. Lisa's a passive-aggressive witch, and Jim's a sanctimonious bore who defends rapists and murderers."

She closed her eyes and took a deep breath. "Wow. I'm not even going there with you. Can you please go shower?"

"So I can share a meal with a man who puts killers and child molesters back on the street."

She stared him. "Why are you so angry with Jim? Did something happen when he was over on Monday?"

His lips thinned and his eyes shone with anger. "Why does Jim think I'm manipulating you into not seeing Kira? Did you blame me for that zoo screw-up?"

"Of course not. Did he say something?"

Reece turned his back and went to the base of the ladder stairs, leaving her in the kitchen. "Detective Romero told me Caitlyn's house is a state-of-the-art fortress," he said. "He's offered to meet us and explain the oddities."

"He didn't mean on a Saturday night." She rummaged through a closet to find a gift bag for the wine. Finding one that wasn't in too bad shape, she went back to the kitchen island to package the wine.

"I suppose I can suffer through Roger's company one more time. Tell me, did he book the DNA test?" His upper lip curled up, and the snarly expression that showed his rogue eyetooth was a major turn off.

"I don't know." She kept her tone impartial.

"I'm sure he didn't. Probably has some new excuse." He sighed heavily. "The man is an outright liar. I bet those pants he gave you weren't even the ones he was wearing the afternoon Graham died."

She'd had the same suspicion, but kept it to herself. The lab results had come in, and she didn't know whether to feel relieved or apprehensive that they hadn't found biodegradable waste on the pant legs.

"He's not rushing to do the test because he thinks you won't follow through on the murder investigation if he gives you what you want." She gave him a steely look. "Is he wrong?"

"He's reluctant because it'll prove he's the father." His nose and forehead crinkled with disgust. "Slept with Abigail—an informal patient, but still a patient—and drove her to suicide. All while he was sleeping with Brenda, another ex-patient and a married woman. He's a sketchy, dishonest man and probably a murderer."

Sam just shook her head. "I'm leaving. Are you coming or not?"

He leaned against the railing to the stairs and picked at his thumbnail. "Please don't accept any more invitations on my behalf. It's disrespectful."

Despite his less than ideal behaviour, he did have a point. Relationships were partnerships, and one person shouldn't make unilateral decisions that affected the other.

"You're right. I'm sorry," she said. "I'm going and I hope you come with me, but I understand if you don't."

Her apology seemed to break the tension between them. Reece ran his fingers through his hair, leaving a tuft sticking up at the back of his head. "No, I'm the one who should apologize." He sighed. "It's important to you, so I'll go."

He trudged up to the bedroom loft, and, a minute later, she heard the shower.

Her new cell rang while she was tucking the wine into a gift bag. Only a few people had the number—the police, her stepfather, Lisa and Jim, and Roger. No one else. And this caller had blocked their number. With a feeling of unease, she answered and waited.

There was breathing and a low, unvarying beat that resembled a very slow tempo on a metronome but reverberated like shallow, even hits on a drum skin. Whatever caused the sound was either away from the caller or very quiet. It was hard to hear it, and impossible to identify. She was about to hang up, when a robotic, genderless voice started singing.

"*Red rover, red rover, I call Sam on over. A life or death type game. The purpose is to maim. You'll be the first to play, then Reece another day.*"

The caller was using a voice modulator. That explained the mechanical, toneless singing.

"Who is this?" Sam demanded.

"*See the blood on Sam's face, as her skin's carved to lace. See her look of surprise, as she painfully dies. Red rover, red rover, I call Sam on over.*" There was a moment of silence before the voice said, "Keep that white blouse on so I can watch the blood drip from the silk." An ominous chuckle followed and the caller disconnected.

She frantically turned out all the lights, crept to the south wall of windows, and gazed down three floors to the bustling city street. Pedestrians strolled along the sidewalks on both sides of Queen Street. People sat at outdoor tables on the patio of a corner bistro. Lights glowed from the windows of a building across from hers, where a small advertising company operated. Streetlights lit the street, but she couldn't see into the dark alleys that ran between the buildings.

She'd been wearing her white silk blouse all day—a visit to the library, coffee with Roger, lunch with Reece, and various errands around the city. It was possible the caller wasn't outside but had seen her sometime during the day. Still.

"Turning out all the lights to hurry me along?"

Reece's voice made her jump.

He wrapped his arms around her. "I'm sorry I was such an asshole. I washed off the grumpy and sprayed on some charming, I promise."

She opened her mouth to explain about the call, but paused. Roger had her new cell number. They'd had coffee this afternoon, and he knew what she was wearing. Did she believe he'd threaten her? For just a moment, she did. She remembered how uncomfortable she'd been at his house on the day she'd gone over to get the pants. Ridiculous. Yet she couldn't bring herself to dismiss the notion.

She pulled away and headed for the door before Reece could read the fear and confusion on her face.

"It's okay." Her voice cracked and she cleared her throat. "Let's go. Lisa's a great cook so at least you'll enjoy the food."

AFTER SAM FINISHED updating Lisa on how they'd found Caitlyn, she hesitantly told her about the death threat. It wasn't the first death threat she'd received—there had been plenty after she'd shot the fifteen-year-old gangbanger who killed her police partner—but Lisa's preoccupation with the pots on the stove annoyed Sam.

When Lisa shut the oven door, still without commenting, Sam asked impatiently, "So, what do you think?"

Lisa dropped an oven mitt to the counter. "You didn't recognize the voice?"

The men were in the living room, so Sam led Lisa through the kitchen to the patio doors, where she hoped she'd have her friend's full attention. They stepped out of the house to the side deck. Across the street, stars speckled the sky above High Park, and the southern breeze drifting inland from Lake Ontario was warm. The air was redolent with the scent of burning wood from a neighbour's outdoor fire pit. Along the side of Lisa's property, maple trees shielded the yard from the four-hundred-acre city park across the street, and tall cedar bushes hid the neighbours on either side. Still, Sam's eyes roamed over the area, hunting for anywhere an interloper could skulk. A warble of laughter reached them from the street and she flinched.

"The caller used something to disguise their voice. A modulator is my guess." She wrapped her arms around her body.

"It was just a silly song. Don't overreact." Lisa's voice was impatient, and she flipped her long black hair over her shoulder.

"They knew I was wearing a white blouse. They may have had sightlines into the loft," Sam said. "What worries me is no one has the number except for this group and the police."

Lisa gazed across the yard. "I didn't give the number to anyone. I'm sad you're blaming me, but I guess that's where our relationship is now."

"I never accused you of giving out the number," Sam said, caught off-guard by her friend's accusation. She thought they'd finally been having a friendly conversation, like they used to. "Lisa, what's going on with us? Why are you so difficult all the time?"

Lisa's lips turned down. Perma-frown was her new expression and it drove Sam crazy.

Instead of answering, she said, "Jim wouldn't publicize your number, but you can ask. Talia's overseas and I can't see her taking a break from fighting terrorism to make a threatening call to you. Roger's acting peculiar, but..." Lisa didn't finish her thought.

"Peculiar how?"

Lisa shrugged and pulled her cardigan across her chest. "Never mind. Roger has the bad habit of leaving his phone places, and he unlocks it with a flourish so it's easy to see the swipe pattern. Brenda or her kids could take your number off his cell."

"I thought of that."

"What's the possibility of this Caitlyn woman finding it?" She looked off into the distance, a pensive expression on her face. "You said she's an IT genius, couldn't she hack into one of our accounts and scroll through our contacts?"

"Maybe."

In the dim moonlight, she felt Lisa's eyes on her.

"You think it was Roger."

Sam remained silent.

"But it was so childish," Lisa argued. "The red rover thing is weird. We all associate that game with Abigail getting hurt, and this whole mess started with her suicide. This has been such a terrible time for me. I wish everything could get back to normal."

"No, this started when someone killed Graham Harris. The husband of Roger's lover," Sam said firmly. Immature behaviour must be contagious. After dealing with Reece's temper tantrum earlier, and now Lisa's self-involvement, Sam felt like adding a resounding "duh" to make her point.

Before Lisa could argue with her, she hurried to say, "Jordan knows the game. He and Reece talked about it. Brenda does too—Graham played it with some of Jordan's football friends."

"There you go. It wasn't Roger," Lisa said with a dismissive wave of her hand. "Brenda, Jordan, or Jordanna are your best suspects." She paused before adding, "Or this Caitlyn person."

Sam agreed, but the vision of Roger lurking outside her loft would not leave her mind.

"Well," Lisa said, "I'm not surprised you don't want to tell Reece." Her tone was cold.

"Why's that?"

Instead of answering, she turned to the door.

Sam took her hand. "Lisa, why don't you like Reece?"

"I never get to see you, and you're never around when I need you. He keeps you on a short leash and that scares me. I fear controlling men, and you know why."

"Why do you think Reece is controlling?" Sam asked evenly

"It doesn't matter, you won't listen. I don't know how you can be with someone who doesn't like Kira." She pulled her hand away and went into the house.

Sam followed, locking the patio doors behind her. "He likes Kira. It was Reece's idea to take her to Canada's Wonderland. Remember? I asked you when I dropped off the stuffed llama."

Lisa didn't reply, busying herself with the food preparation. Sam leaned against the island and watched. The room wasn't hot, but a sheen of perspiration coated Lisa's face. At five-foot-eight with tiny bones, Lisa had always been thin and fragile, but she looked like she'd lost some weight. It was probably the cut of her dress. Front pleats bunched across her middle, and the fabric created the illusion of a potbelly.

"Are you okay?" Sam asked.

Lisa transferred pasta to a bowl. "I've gone to a lot of trouble. I'm here by myself without any help or company. You used to pop over before Reece moved here. Now you don't have time for anyone but him."

"Well, I'm sorry dinner was so much effort. You could have cancelled."

Lisa collected plates from a cupboard and handed them to Sam. "Can you finish setting the table? We'll eat family-style."

Sam took the plates to the dining room and set the table. Preoccupied with her own thoughts, she absentmindedly opened the two bottles of wine she'd brought. Then she noticed that Jim or Lisa had already opened two bottles and had left them on the bar to breathe.

"It smells fantastic in here." Reece was smiling and seemed to be enjoying himself, which was a relief. He gave her a kiss. "Where do you want me?"

She pulled out a chair, and he chuckled when she tucked him into the table and kissed the top of his head.

Jim arrived from the kitchen with a heaping platter of osso buco and a gigantic bowl of fresh orecchiette pasta smothered in a white wine sauce. Lisa followed, balancing a platter of green beans with pancetta and a basket of homemade rolls. There was enough food to feed twelve people. Reece's eyes widened with admiration as he gazed at the pasta dish.

"Lisa, the pasta is amazing," he said, and Sam could hear the sincerity in his voice. "It's been years since I've seen osso buco this tender. You outdid yourself. Thank you."

"I'm Italian," Lisa replied with a flat voice. "Pasta isn't special." She sat down. "Jim, pass the veal. Roger, start with pasta."

Undeterred, Reece reached for the red wine. "We brought a 2011 Dugat-Py Burgundy. I hear it has dark fruit and finishes with sweet, horizontal tannins. The balance should be excellent." He stood and circled the table, poising the bottle over Lisa's glass. "Compliments to the chef," he exclaimed with a wide smile.

She covered the top of her glass with her palm. "No thank you."

"It's supposed to be fantastic," Reece coaxed good-humouredly, turning the bottle so she could see the label.

"I said no," she snapped. "Not everyone has to drink to have fun. I see you opened four bottles for five people. A little excessive, don't you think?"

Reece froze on her left side and his smile faltered.

Jim glanced at him. "I'll try some."

Reece moved to his side and poured. He filled Sam's glass and passed the bottle to Roger without speaking.

"Lisa, I opened the extra wine," Sam told her. "Didn't notice you had some breathing." She took a sip. "This is delicious, Reece. Excellent pick."

Based on Lisa's angry expression whatever she planned to say wasn't nice, but Roger spoke before she had a chance.

"So you're an oenophile," he said to Reece. "I'm a member of Vintage Conservatory, the private wine club. I'd be honoured if you'd accompany me to a tasting."

"I'm sure Reece would enjoy that," Lisa retorted. "I don't recall ever seeing him without a glass in his hand."

Shock prevented Sam from saying anything, and she dropped the platter of green beans she was holding to the table.

Roger arched an eyebrow at Lisa. "Shall I assume your ungracious opinion extends to me?" he asked magnanimously. "After all, I'm the one who pays to belong to a club whose mandate is to consume wine."

Lisa shrugged, moving her pasta around on her plate. "Some people hold their liquor better than others."

"Lisa—" Sam said sharply, but Reece interrupted.

"Excuse me, but have I done something to offend you?"

She glared at him. "You drink too much," she stated tersely.

Sam didn't bother to disguise her anger. "That's a nasty thing to say. Just because you experienced issues with your dad doesn't mean everyone who drinks is an alcoholic."

"If you say so," Lisa replied condescendingly. "Roger, pass the beans please."

Roger passed the dish and held up his glass. "Let us offer libations to appease the gods." With his glass raised, he turned to Reece. "My ambition is to become a modern day god of wine." He clicked his glass against Reece's glass. "We'll gather women to hold secret meetings and hope Lisa doesn't evoke the 186 BC *Senatus consultum de Bacchanalibus*, ordering our execution." He chuckled.

Lisa turned on him. "I'm glad you find humour in the destructive properties of alcohol!" she said, her tone scathing. "I'm sure your flippant attitude would thrill your self-help fans."

"My darling, there's a monumental difference between guzzling moonshine and partaking in wine as splendid as this vintage while consuming ambrosia prepared by a goddess. Your meal is sublime." Roger smiled over the rim of his glass, tipped it back, and finished the half glass in a single gulp. Rolling his eyes upward, he sighed with pleasure. "Magnificent."

Lisa threw her napkin on her untouched food. "It's wonderful you're all enjoying yourselves at my expense."

"Lisa—" Sam began, but her irate friend cut her off.

"Made any interesting phone calls recently, hmmm?" Lisa scowled at Roger and held out her hand. "Let's see your phone."

Roger looked mystified. "Pardon me?"

"Your phone! Unlock it and give it to me."

He reached into his pocket, swiped his password, and passed her his cell. "What's going on?"

She snatched the phone and scrolled through. She smiled triumphantly. "You have it set to clear your call log." She tossed it on the table. "Convenient."

"Lisa, don't do this," Sam begged.

"What's this all about?" Reece asked.

"Oh nothing," Lisa said airily, waving a hand in the air. "Just that someone is threatening to kill Sam." She broke into a cruel smile. "Ah, she didn't tell you, did she? She's in danger, and she's hiding it from *you.*"

Colour drained from Reece's face.

"It was one call, while you were getting ready," Sam hurried to say. "I was going to tell you tonight."

Roger pushed back his chair and stood. "And you have the unmitigated audacity to accuse me?" He spun around to face Sam. "Are *you* accusing me too?"

"No! I just thought it was possible someone may have gotten my number off your phone." It sounded lame to her ears.

"You told Lisa but you didn't tell me," Reece cut in.

"I—"

"Because you're controlling," Lisa shouted at Reece. "You'd lock her in a dog crate under the guise of protecting her if you thought you could get away with it."

"I'm controlling?" Reece said and laughed at her. "Lisa, you're impossible. You're rude, self-centred, and lack compassion for anyone. Do you even care that someone's threatening your best friend?"

"Reece, that's en—" Jim started.

Lisa turned on her husband. "I don't need you to fight my battles." She turned and glared at Reece. "You're closed-minded and arrogant! Sam told me that she tried to talk to you about controlling her life. You went on the offensive and attacked."

"No! Lisa, I never said any such thing." Sam took Reece's hand. "I promise."

"May we get back to the matter at hand," Roger said, still standing. "I'm outraged you've accused me of helping someone to make death threats!"

"Calm down," Reece told Roger, giving Sam's hand a reassuring squeeze before letting go. "We're in the middle of a murder investigation. Caitlyn and the rest of the Harris family all have reasons to play with us." He stood and laid his hand on Roger's shoulder. "Let's talk it over and figure it out together."

Relief flooded over Sam. She'd half-expected Reece to lose his shit, too.

"No one touched my phone," Roger insisted, bristling.

"The evening is ruined," Lisa said. "Enjoy the wine, everyone. When you run out, feel free to raid the liquor cabinet." She glared at Reece and angry tears flooded her eyes. "You need to face the truth and make yourself well. I'm concerned for Sam." She abruptly stood and her chair fell over with a clatter. With a final scathing look in Reece's direction, she stomped upstairs.

Jim, who had barely spoken a word during the disagreement, slowly stood and followed his wife. His shoulders were slouched and he didn't look at any of them.

Roger sat back at the dining table, and Sam ran her fingers through her short hair.

"Is she always like this, or is it me?" Reece righted Lisa's toppled chair and circled the table to take his seat beside Sam.

"It's not you per se, but there's something about you that up-sets her," Roger said. "Her accusation about you being control-ling is interesting. Lisa's dad was tyrannical toward her and her mother."

"What has that got to do with me?"

Roger held up his hand. "Let me finish. Once a week, her dad drove Lisa and her mom to Knob Hill Farms to shop for grocer-ies. He gave them a signed check made out to the grocery store. The cashier wrote in the amount. Mrs. Altieri had no access to money." He reached for the other bottle of wine and took Lisa's unused glass from the table.

Sam didn't care about getting a clean wine glass just because it was a new bottle. She held out her empty glass for Roger to fill. "He'd wait in the parking lot and they had twenty minutes to shop and check out," she told Reece as Roger frowned at the used glass she waved in front of him.

"One day, they were two minutes late and he left," she said, taking the bottle from Roger's hand and pouring herself a half glass, since he clearly wasn't going to. "They had no way to get home. Her mother didn't speak English, and Lisa had to pan-handle to get money for the payphone. Lisa was eight. She called my house, and my dad and I picked them up. Mrs. Altieri invited me in, and my dad went home. "

Roger leaned back in the chair and swirled his wine. "Another excellent vintage. You have extraordinary taste."

"Her father was drunk when they got home," Sam continued. "He beat up his wife, and his son had to drag him off before he killed her. I ran home to get Dad. He found Lisa locked in the closet. Her father had blackened her eye and broken her wrist."

"That's awful." Reece reached for Sam's hand. "What a frightening thing for you to deal with at such a young age. But what does that have to do with me?"

"Reece, you're not the real problem," Roger said, twirling the wine around in his glass. "Sam's the problem."

The revelation stunned her. "What?"

"She's obsessed with the idea she's losing you, and her fear of abandonment is manifesting into anger she's projecting onto Reece," he said. "She's violating your boundaries because she's struggling with painful emotions she's incapable of sharing. If Reece leaves, you'll be despondent and need her support, but, more importantly, she'll have you back in her life full-time."

Reece put his arm around her shoulders. "Tough, I'm not going anywhere and Lisa needs to accept that so we can all move forward."

Roger smiled. "Well, I suspect Lisa does know that and is concerned that you're influencing Sam to abandon her."

Sam saw a blush creep up Reece's face. He dropped his eyes and took a sip of his wine.

"But there's something else going on with her." Roger frowned. "I wonder..."

"What?" Sam asked.

Roger sighed. "I was not the father of Abigail's baby, but I wonder if Lisa knows who was. She and Abigail were close."

"Would she keep that a secret? Would she hurt Talia that way?" Reece asked.

Sam nodded. "Yes. If Abigail asked her not to tell, Lisa wouldn't." She sighed, beginning to understand part of the problem. "If Lisa was Abigail's confidant, it would hurt her that you were the one to receive Abby's final letter." She chewed on her lower lip. "Maybe I should try to talk to her."

Roger shook his head. "Ill-advised in her current state. Let Jim handle it. In fact, we should leave. But before we go, I need to understand this threatening call."

Sam explained the phone call and watched Reece's face grow dark.

Roger held Reece's eyes. "You don't like me and suspect I killed Graham. I did not. You believe I seduced Abigail and drove her to suicide. We need to engage in a frank discussion. Otherwise, your bias toward me will continue to cloud your judgement. It's absurd to think I would call and threaten Sam." Before Reece had a chance to respond, Roger said, "For now, let us focus on the matter at hand. I think Jennifer took the number off my cell and gave it to her mother."

Sam tried to see things from Jennifer's point of view. "She wants her mother in her life. Keeping her updated on the case would be a way to stay in touch while Caitlyn's in hiding."

"Jenny's unhappy." Roger sighed and leaned back in his chair. "She spends too much time alone. Bright but her marks are not reflective of her capabilities. Brenda ignores her, the great-aunt is peculiar, Jordan is cruel, and Jordanna is stuck in the middle between her siblings. The relationship with her mother is important to Jennifer, and I suspect it's important to Caitlyn," he said. "Sam, with your experience in juvenile psychology, you might have luck establishing trust with her. She needs a friend."

Jim came downstairs and scowled at them sitting around the table.

"You should leave." He picked dishes off the table.

Sam stood and gathered the napkins. "I'll help you clean up."

"I'd prefer you didn't." He avoided her eyes.

"Jim, I'm—"

"Please, just leave." He disappeared into the kitchen.

"Well," Roger picked up his coat, "it's been a delightful evening." He gave them a sardonic smile. "We must do this again. Remember, Reece, my door is always open. Call me when you're ready to talk."

CHAPTER TWENTY-FIVE

REECE

"ANSWER YOUR PHONE," Reece grumbled and poked Sam, which netted him a grunt and a slap before she rolled over. With a sigh, he reached across her body and snagged her cell from the bedside table.

Before he had a chance to speak, he heard toneless, mechanical singing. An electronic voice distorter was his guess.

"Red rover, red rover, I call Sam on over. A life or death type game. The purpose is to maim. You'll be the first to play, then Reece another day. Red rover, red rover, I call Sam on over."

The low-frequency thump, thump in the background reminded him of blade slap when a helicopter pilot applies too much power during descent. A generator, maybe. He strained to hear. Tough to tell if it was knocking or thumping. Whatever was causing it was too far away from the caller's phone. Frustrating because he recognized the sound but couldn't put his finger on it.

"See the blood on Sam's face, as her skin's carved to lace. See her look of surprise, as she painfully dies. Red rover, red rover, I call Sam on over." The eerie sound of robotic laughter disturbed Reece more than the macabre chant did.

He took a chance, to judge the caller's reaction. "Hi Caitlyn. This isn't Sam. Want to hold while I get her?" he inquired. "What a fine ditty. Worked hard on the rhyme did you?"

From his experience, nothing annoyed a cowardly intimidator who hid behind the anonymity of a crank phone call more than aloofness.

There was a pause before the voice said, "Enjoy your antifreeze cocktail?"

If it was Caitlyn, calling her by name didn't bother her at all. "You didn't succeed." He kept his tone pleasant.

Again with the disturbing laughter. "Assuming that was my plan. Nice dog, by the way. Carrying her upstairs every night must be a chore. I should take the burden off your hands. We'll meet soon. I'll play with you after Sam loses the game."

The caller disconnected and Reece climbed out of bed, taking Sam's cell with him. He glanced at the clock. Five-thirty. He tucked the blankets around her and went downstairs.

When she came down two hours later, she sniffed the air and grinned. "Breakfast! Is that bacon?" She glanced at her cell on the kitchen table and took the mug of coffee he handed her. "Why do you have my phone?"

"It rang in the night. I picked up."

The coffee mug froze halfway to her mouth. "Same caller?"

He nodded and set a plate of Belgium waffles and sliced strawberries in front of her. "Was there any background noise when you received the first call?"

"Yeah, actually, a pounding. It reminded me of a drum," she mumbled through a mouthful of bacon.

He carried his plate to the table and reached for the syrup. "No, I don't think so. It's tickling the back of my mind, but I can't place it." He repeated the caller's words.

"So he or she was watching the loft again." She reached down and patted Brandy, offering a chunk of bacon that disappeared with a tail wag of thanks.

"Maybe," he said. "But if you knew the loft design, you'd know an animal Brandy's size couldn't negotiate the ladder. It's too steep and too narrow. We're assuming the caller is watching. That may not be the case. Yesterday, you wore that white blouse all day, and someone could have seen you earlier. Even if you weren't wearing it when you received the call, it would still freak you out because you own one that matched the description. See what I mean?"

The other alternative—one he didn't want to share—was that someone didn't need to be physically present to spy. Reece had spent the morning searching for cameras hidden in the recessed lighting, around the wireless speakers mounted in the ceiling, and any other spot where someone could conceal a tiny device. After ninety minutes of futile hunting, he'd called Detective Romero to ask him to send someone out to scan the space for electronic signals.

For now, Reece was keeping his suspicions to himself. Sam didn't need to worry about cameras invading her space, recording her most intimate tasks. Although she was acting blasé, he knew her well enough to know the calls spooked her. The implied threat to him and Brandy would unnerve her more than any danger to herself.

"Whoever is making the threat knows what the inside of the loft looks like," she said, glancing around the interior of their home with a troubled expression.

"Not necessarily," Reece said. "Your contractor filed renovation plans with the city when he got the building permits. The public can access records held by the City of Toronto."

"But that's restricted to three months after the building inspector closes the file."

"So? That wouldn't stop Caitlyn. She'd hack the computers and find what she wanted." He picked up his plate and went to the dishwasher. "Detective Romero is meeting us at Caitlyn's house in an hour," he said. "I have directions. Kleinburg, backing onto Boyd Conservation Area."

She studied the address and directions. "That's not far from the McMichael gallery, you know, the Group of Seven art."

"Be warned," Reece said and rolled his eyes. "Romero also told me that Alston at York Regional is blaming us for Caitlyn disappearing. Claims we interfered with an ongoing investigation and tipped her off so she ran."

Reece didn't like pissing off the lead detective in a homicide investigation. It made him recall his own bias to private investigators when he was with the OPP.

Sam shrugged. "He'll get over it. We never spoke to the woman, so it's not like he can arrest us for obstruction."

"I already took Brandy out, so I'm ready when you are," he said.

She eyed the dog sitting by her feet. "I want to bring her."

Reece expected her to say that. He agreed that it was too risky to leave Brandy unprotected until they closed the case. "Okay, but we're taking my car," he said firmly.

Stuffing Brandy into the back of her two-door coupe was a struggle. Last time they'd taken her car, she'd suggested— seriously suggested—that Reece sit in the back so Brandy could have the passenger seat.

He grabbed his keys from the church altar, but Sam remained motionless by the table.

"We shouldn't take Kira to Wonderland until this is re-solved," she said.

"Lisa will be angry," Reece warned.

"I know, but I'm uncomfortable with someone seeing Kira with us." She joined him at the door, clipped on Brandy's leash, and went out to the hall.

Reece engaged the alarm and locked the door. Sam was right but Lisa would freak out. And she'd direct that anger squarely at him. Again.

WHEN THEY PULLED up to the address, Detective Romero was sitting on the front steps of a small house located on a cul-de-sac. The bungalow backed onto the conservation area and the land on the left, adjacent to the perimeter fence, was barren, also part of the protected acreage. There was a neighbour to the right, but a high fence and tall cedar bushes separated the two properties. It was a gorgeous location. Surprisingly secluded, considering the proximity to the city.

Rather than greeting them, Romero stopped throwing a baseball between his hands and crouched to rub Brandy's ears. Brandy sniffed the ball and Romero smiled. "You like fetch? I'll throw you a couple later." He stood and walked to the house.

Reece couldn't see anything special about the brick bungalow. The steel roof was nice, but many homeowners were opting for steel due to durability. A high, thick bush ran the height and length of the house and shielded the front and sides from the street. Not great for curb appeal. A four-foot space in the greenery accessed the steps to the porch. The door lock was unusual. There was a video intercom, a keypad, a strange deadbolt, and, mounted on the exterior wall about five feet above the ground, a metal box with a raised, circular glass screen that resembled a camera lens.

Romero must have noticed him examining the box. "One of many weird things," he stated.

"How so?"

"*Patience, grasshopper.* Our team spent hours investigating all the gizmos, but I'll walk you through the most interesting bits." He gestured to the window. "Tell me if you notice anything."

Sam peered through the window. "The glass is tinted so you can't see in." She tapped her knuckles against it with a bewildered expression. "It doesn't sound or feel like glass."

Romero hurled the baseball.

Sam gasped and dropped to the ground with her arms over her head.

Reece watched in awe as the ball bounced off the surface and fell to the porch. There was a mechanical whirling noise. Behind the glass, steel shutters closed.

"We've determined that the glass is one-point-six-inch aluminum oxynitride transparent armour that will stop a point fifty BMG round." Romero knocked on the window. "Automatic half-inch steel shutters close when impact is sensed. In the event you kept firing at exactly the same place and managed to penetrate the exterior armour, you wouldn't get through the steel shutters between the two pieces of armour."

With a click, the hurricane shutters locked in place behind the transparent armour.

"Every window in the house is outfitted with the shutter gizmo." Romero waved his hand around the property. "CCTV cameras with a twenty-foot, overlapping arc protect the building and surrounding area. I won't bore you with the technical setup, but suffice it to say you can't disable the cameras, motion detectors, or sensors. Cut the electricity to the house, no worries. It has an independent generator contained in a cold room in the basement. Our people are still figuring out a lot of the details." He waved at the door security. "This bit is the same on the back as well as on the garage and the gate to the backyard."

"What's the box?" Sam asked, reaching down to take the baseball out of Brandy's mouth.

"A retina scanner," he said. "I know, right? Three-part entrance process. Key in a thirteen alphanumeric code on the pad. You have twenty seconds and one chance before it locks you out and generates a new code. Key it in right, and it activates the scanner. Once you pass the retinal scan, the slide across the keyhole opens. I had our IT guys turn on the system and add me so I could demonstrate."

After keying in a code, he held his eye to the box. A green light flashed on the optical scanner. On the door itself, a metal panel slid aside to show vertical and horizontal slits that formed a cross against the face of a weird deadbolt set flush against the door.

Romero held up a bizarre, metal gadget. "No matter how you hold this key, it fits the lock. But woe is you if you don't insert it correctly the first time."

There were no markings on the key or the lock, but there must have been a trick because Romero examined it and turned it to a specific angle before inserting it. The sophistication of the security fascinated Reece.

"Not a house to come home to after a night in the bars," Sam remarked.

Romero laughed. "If you insert it wrong, it freezes, closes the shutters, and engages metal tube locks on the top and bottom of the doors. If it's correct, you have seven seconds to follow a pattern."

He turned it all the way around, flipped it two-thirds to the right, straightened it, flipped it right again and then halfway to the left. There was a sucking sound, and the door swung open an inch.

"But this is ridiculous," Sam said. "It's a wooden door. You could kick it in."

"*Not to understand a man's purpose does not make him confused*," Romero recited, once again quoting Po from *Kung Fu Panda*.

He stepped back so they could inspect the door.

"The wood is window dressing," Romero explained. "The guts are four inches of reinforced steel. You heard that sucking sound, right? There's a device to open it because it's too heavy. Similar design to a bank vault door."

Reece looked through the doorway. The door opened into a sterile looking white windowless foyer. Another door—no wood window dressing on the interior door—accessed the house. He immediately thought of SWAT teams' multiple methods of contravening doors. Assuming they could even breach the first door, finding the second door would remove the shock value and significantly slow their efforts to gain entrance. Reece couldn't help but be impressed by the ingenuity.

Romero shut the door and they followed him to the back gate with Brandy trotting between them. "See anything odd about the fencing?" Romero asked, crouching down to pat the dog.

Reece ran his hand across the wood of the fence. The fence was taller than he was, maybe seven feet. He reached up to hoist himself to see over the top.

Romero jumped up and grabbed his arm, pulling him back with a laugh. "You don't want to do that, amigo."

"What is it?"

"Behind the cedar wood facade that circles the property is re-inforced steel that runs three feet below the ground. There are motion sensors and cameras in the post caps. Running across the top is an electric fence that delivers sixty-three joules of output. Essentially, it's what they use to contain big game in Africa and Australia." He grinned. "Without the disguise of normalcy."

"Jesus, how much did this cost?" Reece asked.

"We estimate the security is over a million, maybe two," Romero answered with a shrug. "It was divided between numerous companies, some we haven't identified. They're prohibited features, in direct violation of fire and building codes. This fence, for example, is illegal, and we have no clue who installed it."

"How would you build this without getting caught?" Sam's gaze drifted across the street to the neighbours' properties.

"That we know," Romero said. "Neighbours were told there was a drainage problem, and the contractor had to dig a trench to access the water lines. The workers put up a barrier to hide the work, like the ones you see downtown during commercial building. They claimed concern about children or pets falling in. Lots of transparent chats with neighbours and fuzzy hugs to keep everyone happy."

"Didn't the neighbours see company identification on the equipment?" Reece asked.

"Sure, but the company doesn't exist." He gestured to the neighbouring house. "That woman died a week before construction, and the property was vacant during probate. Folks across the street said it stunned them how fast they completed the work."

"Did they know Caitlyn?" Sam asked.

Romero shook his head. "Never saw her. They saw the car a couple of times, but the windows are tinted and she entered the house through the garage. The car is here, but it's worth pointing out she has an exit built into the back fence. If Caitlyn had added specific people to her system and provided them with the codes, her guests could come and go through the conservation area without the neighbours seeing."

In the Windsor suburb where Reece grew up, the residential neighbours were curious creatures. It struck him as odd that sneaky and unfriendly behaviour by a new buyer wouldn't concern the neighbours.

"Didn't they think it was strange they never saw her?" he asked Romero, assuming the police had questioned everyone on the cul-de-sac.

"Maybe yes, maybe no. People pay for privacy. All the folks on the street said she was quiet and maintained her property. A landscaping company mows the front and clears snow in the winter. They cleared the cul-de-sac whenever bad weather delayed the municipal plows, which the neighbours loved. A grocery delivery service drops off food."

"Did you speak with either service?" Reece asked.

"Yup. She paid them online and they didn't meet her. Landscaper didn't have access to the back and the grocery service was instructed to leave the boxes inside the mudroom." They returned to the front, and Romero went through the process of opening the door. He waved them through the entrance.

"What about Brandy?" Sam asked.

Romero shrugged. "Bring her in. Forensics is done so it doesn't matter."

Sam signalled to Brandy that she could enter, and the dog trotted into the mudroom and looked up, wagging her tail. Sam pointed down and Brandy sat.

"Every week," Romero continued, "Caitlyn buzzed the grocery delivery driver through the first door and left an envelope on the bench with a twenty-dollar tip."

Reece nudged Brandy aside so he could enter. Attached to the wall above a white metal bench was a box similar to the one on the exterior.

"So this house is impregnable," Reece said.

"If you had technical knowledge of the system and expert skill, you could get inside. It wouldn't be easy, and the occupant would have lots of forewarning," Romero said. "There are industrial grade metal grates protecting the ventilation routes. Water and utility line entrances have safeguards to stop access, similar to what you'd see in meat processing plants to prevent rodent infestation. I suppose a tank could get through the walls, which, by the way, are also reinforced from the inside."

"Why would she do this?" Sam asked, clearly bewildered.

"If Caitlyn Franklyn is the real-world identity of Bloody Widow, she has scary enemies," Romero explained. "This level of paranoia isn't a surprise given her profession." He looked around. "Hell of a way to live. With her IT skills, she could have made six figures working for a cyber security company."

Not the same adrenalin rush as ripping off cyber criminals and international financial institutions. Reece kept his opinion to himself. "And there's no sign of her?" he asked.

Romero shook his head. "She's in the wind." His expression was wistful. "Shame to let all this technology go to waste. Must have hurt to run."

"Unless she didn't run," Sam said slowly. "Maybe she didn't leave by her own volition. Can you open this door?"

He held his eye to the box and opened the second door. They entered a large space with shiny white walls and white aggregate-poured flooring. No light fixtures, only recessed pods in the ceiling. A cluster of module, metal desks that resembled a NASA command centre took up the entire space.

A small kitchen ran across the back wall with a metal table and four metal chairs to the right of a shiny stainless steel stove. Leaving Sam and Brandy with Romero, Reece went down the short hallway to the left of the kitchen. It ended at the doorway to one enormous bedroom suite.

Terrazzo flooring, which ran throughout the house, gave the bedroom a hospital feel. The bedroom walls were the same shiny white as in the main room. There was a king-sized bed in the middle of the empty bedroom. A thick plastic sheet encased the mattress. When Reece leaned down and sniffed, it smelled like ammonia-based disinfectant.

He went into the walk-in closet. Empty. So was the built-in dresser. In the hallway, he rejoined Sam, Brandy, and Romero.

"There's nothing in the bathroom or the kitchen and everything smells like bleach," Sam told him.

Reece sauntered into the large, open-concept main area, turning in a small circle to take in the space. "I worked for a chemical flooring company one summer in university. Epoxy flooring is what hospitals use because it's non-porous, which means it's highly sanitary." He pointed to the glossy white walls. "Also epoxy coating."

"I'm a clean freak, but this is a whole new level," Sam said. "I'm assuming forensics didn't get anything."

Romero nodded.

Reece gestured at the impressive computer equipment. "How about those?"

Romero cringed. "She modified code similar to Rombertik malware, which is already an advanced obfuscation technique. I assume this Trojan is how she infiltrated the banking computers she stole money from." He blushed. "I triggered the self-destruct. She'd installed a fail-safe device that altered the BIOS, over-clocked the CPU, and a piece of hardware that essentially fried the motherboard."

Now that he knew, Reece could smell a hint of corrosion. "You mean a bomb?"

"Of sorts. It was highly sophisticated. She didn't design it to hurt anyone, just to destroy the computer and ensure the data was unrecoverable." He glanced at his watch. "I've got to split."

Once outside, Reece threw Sam the car keys as Romero collected his baseball from the front porch.

"How about you get Brandy settled," Reece said to Sam. "I'll be right there."

She gave him a strange look but took the dog to the car.

Reece put his hand on Romero's arm to keep him from leaving. "Can you check to see if your sweepers found anything in the loft?"

The detective took out his phone and made a call. He listened, then thanked the person on the other end and hung up. "Nada, not a thing. Your crib's clear and the key is back where you hid it for them. Have you updated Alston at York Regional about the calls?"

Before Reece could answer, Romero held up his hand. "Forget I asked. I don't want to get between you two. He's one unhappy camper. Besides, I have my hands full with Bloody Widow."

Romero headed to his car, turning back to repeat the imaginary gun gesture with his hand. "If whoever Franklyn stole from and tried to secure her home against is after you, I'd consider changing careers, amigo."

"Do you have any idea who it is?" Reece asked.

Romero's expression shifted and became serious. "Our best guess," he held Reece's eyes, "the Russian mob."

CHAPTER TWENTY-SIX

SAM

"I'M SORRY. THERE'S stuff going on and—"

Sam listened to Lisa yelling at her. When she could slip a word in, she spoke in as reasonable a voice as she could muster. "It's not like that. Look, how about I come over tomorrow and explain?"

Her best friend—if she could even still call her that—hung up on her. With a sigh, Sam put her phone on the table.

Reece picked it up and attached it to his iPad. "Didn't go well, eh?"

"Lisa thinks you don't like kids and don't want to spend time with Kira. I'm not taking her to Wonderland because I do everything you say and swoon over you to the detriment of everyone else." She put her elbows on the table and cupped her chin between her hands. "I'm irresponsible, dismissive of her feelings, and—get this—*penis-whipped.* I shit you not."

He burst into laughter. "Well, I told you she'd be pissed off."

It suddenly occurred to her to wonder why Reece had connected her phone to his iPad. "What are you doing?"

"Setting up GPS tracking on your cell, and I installed the Google app that allows you to tape a call in process." He tapped on the keyboard. "You know how it works. You taped Quentin LeBlanc's call last year."

An in-process recording app was fine, but the GPS? Less fine. "You're going to track my location?"

"Temporarily. I also put a GPS tracker on your car." He held up his hand to ward off her objection. "Don't make that face. It's just until we figure out what's going on or they have Caitlyn in custody."

She went to the fridge, standing with her back to him. She didn't know quite what to say.

"And I'd like you to carry your gun."

She spun around. "What! No way."

"You have a carrying permit. You've done it before when the situation required it. Again, Sam, it's temporary."

She slammed the fridge door shut and yanked a box of cereal from the cupboard. "I'm not toting a gun around like Annie Oakley."

"First of all, yours is a Glock, not a rifle. You were a cop and carried a gun all the time. Besides, you're better on the range than I am. It's not a big deal."

She sat at the table and took a fistful of cereal from the box. "I'm not a cop now. I'm a citizen." She munched on Cap'n Crunch and dove her hand back in for more.

She wanted to change the subject. "Why would someone leave heavy plastic on her mattress?" she asked between handfuls of cereal.

"You shed skin when you sleep. Removing DNA from a mattress is next to impossible." He handed her the phone. "I'll put the GPS tracking on my cell, too, and set it up on your laptop so you can access it from your phone." He grabbed her computer from the desk.

She'd never look up the whereabouts of his cell. It felt like a breach of privacy to her. But she knew the death threats she'd received were psyching out Reece. If being able to find her made him feel better about her safety, she'd drop it. Until the case was over, at least.

"Or Jennifer didn't just visit her mother, she had sleepovers," Sam suggested.

"The plastic was because of her bladder problem?"

"Maybe. I called Brenda to ask if Jennifer ever stayed away overnight. She did. She's been having lots of sleepovers at her great-aunt's house, the religious woman we met the first time we went over."

"Let me guess. She wasn't there."

"No, Rachel said she was. But I think she lied."

"Why?"

"I don't know. Just a feeling." She put the cereal on the table, wiped her hands on her jeans, and stood. "Caitlyn trusted her daughter."

Reece closed the computer and stared at her in disbelief. "You can't be suggesting Jennifer did something to her mother."

"No, but Jordan or Brenda might." She returned the cereal box to the kitchen cupboard. "Maybe someone cajoled Jennifer to lull her mother into a false sense of security." Pondering the idea, she turned to face him. "Or, maybe Jordanna also visited her mother and snuck in Jordan or Brenda."

"That's a lot of maybes," Reece said skeptically.

"Well, here are some more," she said with a grin. "Maybe that's why Jordan was so angry when Jennifer told us she saw her mother. If he swore his sisters to secrecy about their visits, it would explain those looks he kept exchanging with Jordanna." She tapped her fingers against the top of the island. "Maybe it wasn't Jordan. Brenda's the one who outright lied to all of us about Caitlyn's existence. Did you see the look on her face when Jennifer told us she'd talked with her mother? It wasn't surprise. It was fury. She covered it fast, but I saw it."

Reece waved her over to the table. "What makes you think Caitlyn didn't leave on her own accord? She was into illegal shit. The hits on the banks would send her away for the rest of her life, and Romero said she stole from cybercriminals. He told me police suspect it was the Russian mob. They have exactly one way of dealing with threats." He ran his finger across his throat.

He got up and returned her laptop to the desk before continuing. "The cops know Caitlyn Franklyn is Bloody Widow, so it's only a matter of time before her online enemies find out too. Jennifer warned her about us, and she ran because of them." He crossed the loft and sat beside her at the kitchen table, leaning the chair back on two legs. He linked his fingers behind his head. "If I were her, I'd run."

Sam had no idea why he liked to sit precariously balanced on a chair's two legs. He did it all the time, and it bugged her. She reminded herself that she probably had bad habits that drove him nuts and resisted the urge to grab his shoulder and jerk him forward so the chair settled onto four legs.

"I don't think Caitlyn ran," she insisted.

"You think she's dead," Reece said.

She nodded. "I just don't think the person who killed her was the same person she tried to protect her home against." She hadn't realized she thought this until she just voiced it. A hunch that defied explanation.

"Romero said she rarely left the house." Reece lowered the chair with a clatter that made her jump and put his elbows on the table. "I think she ran, but I'll play devil's advocate with your murder theory." He made horns with his fingers that he waggled on top of his head. "If you don't think it was connected to her cybercrimes, then why would Brenda or one of the kids kill her? Where's the motive?"

"Why would Jordan kill his father?" she countered.

"I thought you believed it was Brenda."

"Maybe they did it together. Brenda engaged the electricity and Jordan held his father's head in the sewage. He was there when Graham died," she reminded him. "Roger watched him go into the house and heard arguing from the basement."

"You mentioned the glances the twins exchanged during our interview," Reece said. "I felt Jordan was seeking permission from Jordanna."

Sam shook her head. "No, Jordan was intimidating her. Maybe Jordanna knows he helped Brenda kill Graham, and he's threatening her."

Jordanna struck her as a normal teenage girl. Exploiting the newfound power of sexuality and enjoying melodrama were age-appropriate human development traits. Besides, Jordanna had an alibi for the afternoon her father had died. Reece had spoken to the boy, Steve, who had confirmed he was with her.

Jordan, on the other hand, gave Sam the creeps. His belligerent behaviour felt staged because his face was just… dead. The juxtaposition disturbed her. So did the vicious disembowelment of the cat, which she believed he had done.

"Remember what Jordanna said about Caitlyn coming to the classroom?" she asked.

He nodded.

"Her mother was yelling terrible things about Jordan. She was there to protect Jordanna."

"Sally Alistair isn't a credible witness, but the school's security officer confirmed that bit," Reece said. "But it had to have been Caitlyn who caught Behoo online."

Sam raised her eyebrows. "Yes, but if she's Bloody Widow, how's that relevant to Graham's murder?" she asked. "We've been working on the assumption that Caitlyn targeted the Alistair family because she was protecting her son after the rape allegation. Protecting Jordan doesn't make sense, based on her behaviour around him at the school." She got up and paced the room, trying to work out the incongruities that bugged her.

After a minute, she said, "Caitlyn isn't the only hacker in the world, and the neighbour couldn't positively identify her picture as the Hydro worker who entered the yard the day the Alistair's dog died. I don't think Caitlyn had anything to do with what happened to the Alistair family."

An important part of the investigation process was to brainstorm and poke holes in respective theories. For the first time, Sam realized how much she'd miss these exchanges if Reece decided to pursue other interests.

"So you're saying Bloody Widow attacked Behoo simply as a defensive tactic, to protect her anonymity, and it had nothing to do with the case?" Reece didn't look convinced.

"I don't think it had anything to do with Graham's murder, if that's what you mean," Sam said, warming to her theory. "I do think it had to do with her cybercrimes. Think about it. She'd stolen money from the mob. Catching another hacker digging into her online would immediately panic her."

Reece studied her with a frown. "I get that the mob would try to find her and they'd want her dead, but we're back to my original objection. The mob wouldn't bother to move the body," he insisted.

"Because they didn't kill her," she argued. "Let's back up and look at the motive for the home security. Someone as smart as Caitlyn would understand the risk involved with stealing from the mob," Sam said, taking short strides around the room. "We can agree that the excessive security had to do with her black-hat hacking. She might have recognized Behoo's online handle, but she didn't know who hired him. All she'd know was that a talented hacker was on the deep web, digging into Caitlyn Franklyn, and she'd want to know why. Behoo started deleting data because Bloody Widow was looking into *him*. Think about it, he assumed it had to do with us because *we* hired him."

"Yeah, you're right. That makes sense," Reece conceded.

Sam stopped pacing and sat at the table. "The one piece of hard evidence is that she went to the school. What happened a year before Graham's murder that made Caitlyn risk arrest by violating the restraining order?"

The spark of inspiration glowed and took form. She slapped her hands on the table and smiled. "I think Jennifer told Caitlyn something last year. Something awful. Something about Jordan."

Reece stretched his arms over his head and yawned. "Maybe but what has it got to do with Graham's murder?" He stood and cleared a few remaining dinner dishes from the table. "I know you don't want to hear it, but Roger has lied to us from day one. He was in the house, in the stairwell leading to the crime scene. He has a severe anger problem and low impulse control."

She didn't say anything, but privately she disagreed. She was certain that, at the very least, Roger would have had the common sense to retrieve the bouquet of roses from the garden. He wouldn't leave a time-stamped credit card purchase at a murder scene.

Reece was wandering around aimlessly, gazing up to the bedroom loft, and making a point of yawning. Loudly.

"Jordan's involved," she said. "I need to talk to Jennifer alone. If I can figure out a way to convince her she's protected, maybe she'll open up."

Reece nudged her toward the stairs and stooped to pick up Brandy.

"Murder is straightforward," he argued. "Money, revenge, or love. Brenda, Roger, and Caitlyn all had motives."

Upstairs, he popped Brandy into bed and went into the bathroom.

Sam flopped onto the bed beside the dog and thought about the tortured cat. "Some people kill because it's fun," she called out.

He grunted while brushing his teeth but made no comment.

Long after they'd settled into bed, Sam lay awake while Reece's breathing evened out. When she still couldn't fall asleep after an hour, she got up and crept to the back of the walk-in closet. She reached above her winter coats and removed her gun box from the shelf. The Glock was clean and oiled. She grabbed the spare clip and box of ammunition, before tucking the empty gun box back on the shelf. In the bedroom, she put the gun and accessories in the drawer of her bedside table.

There was a custom gun mount under the driver's seat of her car in a space between the springs. Hard to find if you didn't know it was there. Tougher to release it without knowledge and practice.

She wasn't going to carry the gun around on her hip, but it couldn't hurt to keep it handy.

CHAPTER TWENTY-SEVEN

SAM

BRENDA'S CAR WASN'T in the yard when Sam arrived at the farm. No one answered her knocks, and the property had that vacant feel. She wandered around the house and pounded on the back door. No answer. A woodpecker tapped a message against a tree in the copse where she'd found Jennifer traumatized, cuddling her murdered cat. In the distance, a tractor rumbled and burped, but sound travelled on a clear day, and it could have been a kilometre or more away. It wasn't working on the Harris farm, which wasn't a surprise since no one had sown those fields in decades.

Stupid to have driven all the way out to the farm without calling first. She'd taken her car to her usual service station in north Toronto to have the oil changed. Afterwards, she'd made the decision to continue north to visit the farm. Now here she was, wasting time when she had a mountain of schoolwork. She strolled aimlessly around the property, wondering where everyone was. It was three-thirty and the kids should be home from school.

"Damn phone," she mumbled. Her cell was dead and she couldn't call Brenda to find out when they'd be home.

Worse, since the trip was impulsive, Reece didn't know where she was and expected her to meet him at the office. She'd intended to call him from the car, but the car charger wasn't working again. Reece had borrowed the portable charger from the glove compartment and had forgotten to put it back. Regardless, he'd chirp at her about being inconsiderate. This morning, he'd made a big deal out of staying in close contact, and she'd bitched about having a babysitter.

She was turning to leave when something caught her eye. A twinkle. She peered across the fields. There seemed to be something on the ground that was catching the sunlight. It was between the barn and a large shed that wasn't in bad shape. Fresh black shingles protected the roof, and someone had spruced up the exterior. No windows, but white trim and a yellow door with brass fixtures. Sam cheered up and smiled. Maybe the trip didn't need to be a write-off. The deserted farm offered the perfect opportunity to snoop. It was closer to trespassing, since she hadn't sought explicit permission to poke around the outbuildings, but no matter. Encroaching on people's privacy didn't faze her. She headed for the barn.

Between the house and the barn was a weed-infested field that was about the length of a football field. Brenda—or Graham before his death—had hired someone to aerate the field. Sam recognized the cylinders of grass-topped dirt that littered the ground. Her mother had hired a landscaper to aerate their back yard every spring. Sam's chore had been to collect all the dirt chunks, a tedious job that she'd always resented. Simply looking at those clumps of dirt dissolved her excitement over snooping. It was funny how childhood memories had the power to change your mood. As she clumsily picked her way across the field, avoiding divots of soil, she grew irritated and impatient. It took nearly five minutes to navigate the terrain and reach the barn.

Beside the barn was a stone structure. Sam thought it was probably a grain silo. Stones had collapsed on the right side, and someone had heaped crumbling rocks next to a full wheelbarrow. A weather vane lay in a rusted tangle adjacent to the wheelbarrow. It retained a clean spot of metal that reflected the sunlight, and she figured that was what had caught her eye.

The barn was even uglier up close. The wood was rotting, and a large gap at the bottom of the door testified to the many trips people had made over the years. Footprints had worn down the earth, and the middle of the sill had crumbled, leaving a six-inch space at the base of the door. Handy for rodents and small animals. There was a padlock attached to a crooked safety hasp, and heaving on the lock didn't loosen the screws that held the hardware to the door. She swore in frustration and pounded her fist on the closed door. With a sigh, she walked around to the other side, and it delighted her to find a large sliding door that was slightly ajar. She tugged and the door opened further.

Before going in, she decided to walk around the barn, checking to make sure the structure was sturdy. There were half-inch gaps between some of the timbers in the wall. She cupped her hands and peered inside. Not much to see, but sunlight streamed from the fissures and produced sufficient interior light to explore. Good news since she didn't feel like trudging all the way back to the car to fetch a flashlight. She returned to the sliding door, shoved it open three feet, and stepped into the barn.

It was warm and quiet inside with swirling dust floating in the sunbeams. One wide cement platform ran the length of the building, divided into corrals by metal frames. The long platform sloped up on a gradual angle to rusted metal stanchions designed to hold animals' heads. Her grandparents had been dairy farmers, and her father had taken her family to Nova Scotia to visit when she was young. Her mother had hated the trips and the farm, but Sam had always looked forward to playing with the cows. They were like big, dumb dogs.

Graham's ancestors were dairy farmers, from the look of it. The building interior was clean. Someone had removed the straw and hosed down the cement platform, but the space retained the gamey odour of fermented grain, sour milk, and linseed oil that sealed the ash and earthen floor.

To the left of the padlocked door that led outside was an old tack or feed room. As she moved closer, she smelled fresh paint. Taking a cautious step into the gloom, she glided her hands down the walls on either side of the door. Her fingers hit a switch on the right side. Light flickered and there was a whirring noise. Twelve feet above her head, suspended from a beam that connected opposite rafters, was an old ceiling fan with a wrapped electrical wire that ended in a naked bulb. The light swung in the downdraft from the oscillating blades. A dull thumping resonated from the unbalanced fan every time it hit a certain point in its rotation.

Sam closed her eyes and listened to the sound, counting seconds between the soft thumps. It was definitely the background noise from the threatening calls. The caller had been in the barn, meaning it was someone from the Harris family. Then again, the calls were late at night. If Reece was right and Caitlyn was somehow involved in Graham's murder, she could have crept onto the property under the cover of darkness. Maybe she'd intended for Sam or Reece to identify the background sound, hoping it would implicate Brenda.

Excited to see what else she might discover, Sam entered the room. There was an old wooden desk in the corner with a narrow centre drawer and two file drawers banking a kneehole. She searched through the right drawer. Mould and mildew wafted from old file folders. Nothing but ancient receipts for grain and a handwritten accounting journal that recorded purchases and milk sales from 1955.

While rummaging through the second drawer, there was a loud clang from outside and she jumped. A second clang followed. It sounded like something hitting metal. She hurried from the office and stood in the centre of the barn, looking around. A shadow moved across the wall to her left. She sprinted to the sliding door. Closed. No matter how hard she pushed, the door refused to budge. Someone had locked her in the barn. He or she probably hadn't known anyone was inside, had noticed the open door, and had closed and locked it. There wasn't any reason to panic.

She ran to the back of the barn to hunt for another exit. If she stayed calm and didn't jump to conclusions, she'd be able to get out. Explaining what she was doing in the barn might be tricky, but so long as she didn't tip anyone off that she'd connected the fan to the threatening calls she'd be fine. Taking a deep breath, she peered through an opening in the boards along the back wall. There was definitely a person out there. But the hole was too low and all she could see was a pair of denim-clad legs.

"Hey! It's Sam McNamara. Open the door," she called.

There was a scuffing noise—feet shuffling along the ground—and a nasty odour. Gasoline. Her heart dropped to her feet and she felt a flutter of panic. Locking her in wasn't an accident. She pounded against the wall, her heart racing. "Hey! I'm still in here."

The shadow retreated. Sam ran to the right side of the barn. The stench of gasoline was stronger. She tucked her fingers into a gap between the wallboards and pulled. No give. Pressing her face against the slit, she started shouting at whoever was out there.

"Brenda? Is that you? Let me out, now. I've called the police!"

The terrifying sound of crackling wood stopped her in her tracks. She immediately felt a flight, fight, or freeze sensation that made her legs turn to jelly. Her heartbeat thundered in her ears. Fighting to stay calm, she moved slowly to the centre of the room, concentrating on taking even breaths to control the psychological need to run aimlessly.

Think, she willed herself. Panic killed people.

There had to be a way out. If she could find a tool, she could pull apart the rotted boards. She tore into the office, tugged out the centre drawer, and spilled the contents to the floor. Nothing. A quick check of the drywall seams confirmed that multiple screws mounted it tight against the frame. Impossible to pry it loose with her bare hands. Staying in the room, closing the door, and trying to barricade the bottom to reduce the smoke was too risky. Flames would roast her alive if smoke inhalation didn't kill her first.

She dashed through the door and searched for something to use as a jimmy to wrench away a board. At the dairy stalls, she yanked at the metal stanchions. They held fast.

Smoke billowed while flames sucked oxygen from the air. Fire spread against the back wall, licked the upper trusses, and ignited the roof.

"Stay calm, don't panic," she said aloud. Her voice shook and she closed her eyes to concentrate.

She'd dated a firefighter years ago. She tried to remember stuff he'd taught her. Air circulated through the wall cracks. Dry wood burned hot and quick, but it wouldn't create a lot of smoke right away. When the smoke turned thick and black, her chances of surviving smoke toxicity would decrease.

"There's time. Stay calm," she repeated. There must be a weak spot on the decaying walls.

To her horror, the smoke was getting thicker much faster than she'd predicted. The temperature was skyrocketing and sweat poured down her face. She stripped off her T-shirt and tied it around her mouth and nose. Carefully, she examined the right wall, avoiding the back where the fire roared strongest, and hunted for a spot to break through. The flames at the point of ignition were burning blue.

"Don't look at it," she yelled.

Crouching low to the ground, she duck-walked along the wall at the front of the barn, where the flames hadn't reached. There wasn't sufficient wood rot anywhere. She stood and kicked the wall as hard as she could, but the boards held. The fire was advancing fast. Feeding off the dry wood, it was consuming everything in its path. She gasped for air and stumbled to the centre of the large space away from the flames. She had to try the other side. There had to be a weak point she could get through. A tie beam from the ceiling crashed down. She dropped and rolled, narrowly avoiding the burning joist. The floor of the hayloft crumbled, raining down fiery particles of hay, and she screamed. A smouldering ember fell on the edge of the T-shirt she held against her mouth. She tore it from her face and dropped again, rolling frantically to extinguish any sparks on her jeans. She managed to climb to her feet, gasping and choking on smoke that filled her lungs and seared the inside of her nose. Between the smoke and the tears streaming from her stinging eyes, she could barely see.

Getting out took a backseat to finding fresh air. She had to get to the padlocked door. There was a large gap at the bottom. It was at the front. Away from the ignition point. Weaving around clumps of burning hay, she moved as fast as she could toward the front of the barn. Her head throbbed. Her thoughts were a jumble. Her lungs ached with the need for clean air. She fell and dragged herself across the floor. Finally, she glimpsed a flicker of light through the smoke. Crawling on all fours, she held her breath and fought her way to the light.

Lying on the floor by the padlocked door, she gulped oxygen from the six-inch crevasse. After each huge inhalation, she popped onto her knees and dug under the door like a dog to widen the space.

A horrific crack thundered behind her. She whimpered and cringed against the door. The moan of collapsing wood behind her sounded almost human. Terrified to look back, she lay flat against the ground and stuck her lips and nose into the door gap. Heat pushed at her back and the smell of her own burning hair mingled with the ever-thickening smoke. A glowing splinter fell on her forearm and she shrieked. Frantic, she brushed it off and swatted at another sudden scalding pain on her neck. Sticking her face against the door gap again, she tried to suck in more air. She choked and spit out a mouthful of dirt. Sitting up, she grabbed handfuls of loose dirt from around the opening and hurled them over her shoulder. After she'd widened the gap another inch, she dropped to her stomach, stuffed her face against the opening, and breathed deeply. If she could keep her strength, maybe she could widen the gap enough to wiggle underneath the door.

As she dug manically at the dirt, she thought she heard something from the other side of the door. A yell that sounded panicked. Was someone out there? Someone other than the person who had lit the fire?

A female voice shouted outside the door but Sam couldn't make out the words. Something hit the door hard.

"Help, I'm—" A stabbing pain pierced her temple. She couldn't yell, could barely even speak. Tears streamed from her burning eyes. She spat up a wad of sooty, dirty phlegm. Hitting the door with one hand, she waggled the fingers of her other hand under the door. "In here," she croaked.

Cringing against the floor, sucking clean air, she felt someone caress the tips of her fingers.

Behind Sam, she heard a deep cracking sound. A thunderous reverberation deafened her. The world went black.

CHAPTER TWENTY-EIGHT

REECE

"WHERE ARE YOU? Call me when you get this." Reece put down the cell and tried to squash his irritation. Sam couldn't *still* be on the phone. He'd been trying to reach her for over an hour, and it kept going straight to voice mail.

He studied his iPad. It might be intrusive and controlling, but he'd track her cell. They were in the middle of a murder investigation, and if she didn't want him "spying" on her, as she saw it, then she should be more dependable.

Scrolling through his applications, he double-clicked on the GPS tracking for her phone. It showed her on the Don Valley Parkway, headed north. Ten minutes later, it was still there. Stationary on a major freeway.

A few clicks and he had a traffic cam image of the city highway. Cars travelled along at a good rate. Enlarging the image, Reece traced the lanes of traffic. No cars broken down on the shoulders. He had a pretty good guess what the problem was. That useless car charger wasn't working again and her cell was dead. The application was showing her last known location before the cell crashed.

Chewing on the corner of his lip, he switched applications and checked the GPS tracker for the device he'd attached to her car. He studied the map. The car was at the Harris farm. Grumbling under his breath, he picked up his cell.

"Hi, Brenda, it's Reece Hash. Sorry to disturb but can you put Sam on the phone?"

"I'm at Roger's house," she replied. "Sam's not here." Some type of bird was making a racket in the background. They must be sitting on Roger's *fantastic* deck beside his *magnificent* barbeque.

"I'll try your landline."

"Why would Sam be there? No one's home." She sounded perplexed. "Jordan's in the city, I dropped him off at the Rogers Centre to attend a Blue Jays game. Jordanna has detention all week, and Jennifer is with her aunt." She paused before rushing to add, "I checked on her this time and she's there."

Reece stared at the flashing dot on his screen. Sam's car was definitely at the farm. She must be snooping. Hopefully she hadn't broken into the house. During an active investigation, Sam's scruples about obeying certain laws—such as breaking and entering—were shady.

"Ah, my mistake." He kept his voice matter-of-fact. "Enjoy your evening and say hello to Roger."

The red dot flashed at him. He couldn't shake the feeling that something was wrong. When he'd worked with the provincial police, he'd learned to respect his instincts—except for once. He'd neglected to act on his suspicions about Bueton Sanctuary. What happened that winter would forever haunt him.

With a sigh, he grabbed his keys and attached Brandy's leash—the dog wasn't staying home with Jordan gallivanting around Toronto. Who knew if the little creep was actually attending a baseball game? Maybe he'd ditched his squad and was on his way over to make good on the threat to kill Brandy.

During the day, Reece had considered Sam's hypothesis from the night before. She was right. There was something off about Jordan. The more Reece examined the facts, the more convinced he was that Jordan was behind the threatening telephone calls. He remembered the smug expression on the kid's face when they'd chatted about football coaches using red rover to measure players' strength and agility. Reece wasn't convinced that Jordan had killed his father—Roger was his main suspect, followed closely by Brenda or Caitlyn—but the telephone calls felt like a prank. But, with or without intent, a nasty prank could accidentally turn deadly in a heartbeat.

After he set the alarm and locked up the loft, he and Brandy went to the parking lot and Reece settled the dog in the back seat. He drove to the Don Valley Parkway, hoping it was early enough in the afternoon to miss the joy of Toronto's infamous bumper-to-bumper rush hour traffic. Heading north, he made good time and was able to avoid all but two traffic jams on his way out of the city.

After exiting the 400, he caught a glimpse of a tendril of smoke curling into the distant sky. Someone was burning spring lawn waste. The sight reminded him of working in the backyard of his old Uthisca home—he actually missed the everyday chores that had been part of his country life.

As he gazed at the horizon, he realized it was more than just a whiff of smoke. It was billowing and the cloud was black. Something was burning hot and fast. A troubling sense of urgency overwhelmed him. He stepped on the accelerator and sped to the farm.

Sam's car was in the gravel lot, and Reece pulled up beside it, got out of his car, and opened the back door for Brandy. The dog hopped out and whined. The odour of smoke was prominent, and it was rising into the sky from the back of the property. A high-pitched scream mixed with the crackling roar of fire that floated on the wind. Reece's blood ran cold and he sprinted around the house. He stared with horror at the flames that engulfed the barn, too astonished to move.

Jennifer was running toward him from the direction of the fire, waving her arms over her head and yelling something he couldn't hear. Reece closed the distance, and Jennifer fell into his arms. Her clothing reeked of smoke, sweat ran down her soot-covered cheeks, and her eyes roamed everywhere, never focusing on one spot.

"Are you okay?" He took her hand. There was an ugly, blistering burn on her forearm.

"There's someone in the barn! We can't get in. There's a padlock and the other doors won't open."

Reece's stomach dropped. He let go of her hand and thrust his cell at her. "Call 911. Get an ambulance and fire trucks."

He tore around the house to his car, popped the trunk, and rummaged under the trunk pad. Blood pounded in his ears, his hands shook, and he couldn't find the damn crowbar.

"Jordanna called them when we got here ten minutes ago. She's trying to get in." Jennifer grabbed his arm. "There's someone in there!" In the grips of panic, she looked like a scared little girl. "They're gonna get all burned up! You gotta do something!" She was near hysterics as she tugged at his arm, urging him to hurry.

Reece cupped her chin and held her eyes, trying to get her to focus. "Where's Sam?"

Confusion flooded her face. "What? Sam's not here." Her eyes fell to the car beside his. She looked stricken and clamped her hand over her mouth.

When her legs gave out, Reece grabbed her shoulders and propped her up against the hood of the car, making sure she was able to stay upright before he returned to the trunk and snagged a crowbar.

He circled the car and found Jennifer collapsed. Reece knelt beside her. "I need you to stay here with Brandy." He held her eyes and fought to keep the panic from his voice. "Can you do that? Can you take care of Brandy for me?"

She nodded mutely and he sprinted to the barn, tripping on a divot of soil and twisting his ankle. With a roar, he struggled to his feet, ignoring the searing pain in his ankle, and ran. In the distance, sirens warbled from the west, but he couldn't tell how close they were.

As he closed the distance between the house and the barn, he saw Jordanna beating on the east wall where the flames hadn't reached. Reece hollered at her and she turned.

"Someone's inside," she screamed at him. "I saw her fingers. But something happened. There was this horrible crash and now I can't see her. I can't get the doors open!"

Sam! Reaching the barn, Reece shoved Jordanna aside harder than he intended. "Go to the house," he shouted. "Wait for the fire trucks."

Reece positioned the crowbar against the lock and threw his weight against it, popping the screws that held the lapse. Even without the lock, the door still wouldn't budge. He got on his hands and knees and tried to see under the door. Something was blocking the door from the inside, but he couldn't tell what it was.

He stood and raced to the sliding barn doors, put the crowbar in the narrow gap, and pushed. They inched apart but the space was too narrow for him to get through. Black smoke billowed out, and he grunted as he tried to wedge the door open. Something was stopping the rollers from sliding.

Stepping back, his eyes searched the top of the door. A piece of rebar blocked the rollers. He would need a ladder to reach the top to dislodge it from the tracks. There was no ladder in sight. Chaotic thoughts crowded his mind and he took a deep breath to gain control. He had to think. He had to get inside.

"Sam!" He pounded on the door with his fist and tried to force his body through the narrow opening. "Sam! Are you in there?"

Please God, don't let her be in there. But he knew that she must be.

He turned away to grab fresh air before circling to the other door to try to force it inward. It wouldn't budge. Feeling helpless and infuriated, he ran back to the sliding doors. There had to be a way in. He needed to calm down and think.

Before he knew it was happening, Jordanna had shoved by him and squeezed through the gap he'd created in the sliding barn doors. He peered through the narrow opening. The sound of coughing and choking reached him, but he couldn't see through the smoke.

"No! Jordanna, get out!" He pressed his ear to the gap but couldn't hear anything.

Returning to the padlocked door, he slammed his shoulder against it. "Get out! Jordanna, get out!"

Her fingers grasped the edge of the door from the inside, and she yelled something he couldn't hear over the roar of the inferno. Her fingers disappeared.

"Jordanna! Get out!" He pressed his ear against the crack and heard dragging and coughing.

Reece had never felt so useless. He backed up and charged the door, lowering his head, and throwing his shoulder against the wood. It flew open and he lost his footing, plummeting into the barn and spinning to avoid the flames. Jordanna staggered into him. He had to wrench his arm from her strong grasp and shove her through the door.

When he turned back, Reece saw Sam. Her body must have been what had blocked the door. Jordanna had managed to drag her away, but, in the confusion created by the smoke and lack of oxygen, she'd accidentally pulled Sam deeper inside the barn. Closer to the raging inferno.

With a howl, he raced toward her, choking on smoke and struggling to see.

A rafter collapsed in front of him, obstructing his path. A chunk of burning wood glanced off his shoulder. White-hot pain flooded his arm. He tore the burning shirt from his body, stomped on it to smother the flames, and ripped off a strip of fabric. He shoved it against his mouth and nose and tied the ends behind his head. He circled the burning rafter and squinted through the smoke.

Where was Sam? He searched the ground through the billowing black smoke. Finally, he spied her and lurched over with his hand pressed against his mouth and nose.

"Sam! Sam, can you hear me?" He slapped his hand gently against her cheek, but she remained unconscious. The pulse in her neck was weak under his fingertips. Fumbling the cloth away from his face, he tried to tie it around her mouth and nose. Reece flung her limp body over his shoulder. A sharp, stabbing pain in his ankle made him waver. Gritting his teeth in agony, he limped toward the exit. Something hit his shoulder and he faltered under the assault. He staggered and nearly dropped her before regaining his footing and lurching for the door. He cleared the door just before the entire wall burst into flames.

Jordanna was standing a few feet from the door. Her mouth was open wide as she fought to catch her breath, and her eyes were wide and glazed with fear. Reece snatched her wrist with his free hand and dragged her from the blaze.

Just then, the roof caved in and a shower of glowing splinters projected across the field. Jordanna shrieked and grabbed tightly to his hand. She flung her arms over her head, screaming and crying. He couldn't yank his hand free from her grasp. Her frantic movements unbalanced him and he staggered back. Sam slipped off his shoulder. He tried to grab her body and they fell together into a heap. Reece jumped to his feet, stamping out grass fires around Sam. From the corner of his eye, he glimpsed Jordanna. Confused and in shock, she was wandering blindly back to the barn. Adrenalin rushed through him, masking the pain in his ankle. He ran over and grabbed her.

Terrified and confused, Jordanna fought against him. Reece wrapped his arms around her waist and lifted her off her feet. With the last of his strength, he spun around and hurled her as hard as he could away from the burning barn. She flew across patches of burning grass, landing far enough away to be safe. A glittering shard of wood landed on his thigh. He brushed it off and smacked his palm against the burning fabric of his jeans.

Crawling on all fours, he reached Sam. He used the width of his body and outstretched arms to protect her from sparks and projectiles that flew from the disintegrating barn.

Sirens pierced the air and deafened him as they drew closer. Someone yelled. Between the roar of the fire, smoke inhalation, and Reece's utter exhaustion, he couldn't understand the words. Water suddenly soaked his back and pounded his head. He collapsed to the grass, watching a fire truck fly across the field to the rear of the barn. Fifty feet in front of him, a second truck was stationary. Two firefighters had their feet braced against the weight of the water rushing through the spewing hose they held. A third firefighter ran over while his partners kept the hose flowing, spraying high above their heads, ensuring the force of the water didn't hit them. The downpour was like needles piercing Reece's skin. Still, he relished the pain, filled with gratitude that help had arrived.

A firefighter threw Sam over his shoulder, and Reece shuffled to his feet. The adrenalin rush was leaving his blood and his muscles felt loose and difficult to control. When they reached the safety zone, Reece sank gratefully to the ground beside Sam. He could hear Jordanna screaming hysterically in the distance. Turning his head, he saw her sitting on the back of the ambulance. A paramedic was trying to fit an oxygen mask over her face.

Reece huddled on the ground beside Sam, wiping burned curls from her forehead. "Hang on," he whispered.

A paramedic tried to move him. "Sir, you need oxygen and we need to see her."

"I'm okay," he said. "Help Sam."

They attached an oxygen mask and an IV to her. When the EMTs tried to move her onto a gurney, she opened panic-filled eyes and swatted at them.

"It's okay," Reece's voice was hoarse from the smoke. "I'm here. You need to let them help you." He leaned over the stretcher so his face was in her line of sight.

Recognition flooded her bloodshot eyes. She pawed at the oxygen mask.

"No, Sam, you need to leave it. Everything's okay. Just let them help you now." Reece removed her hand from the mask and held it against his chest, studying the colour of her forearm.

He tried to recall the signs of carbon monoxide poisoning. All he could remember was that the colour of the victim's skin changed. He spit on his finger and rubbed away some soot and dirt from her arm.

Desperate for reassurance that she was okay, he turned and spoke to the paramedic. "Her skin colour isn't bad." Quivering fear rolled over him and he couldn't prevent the tremble in his voice. "How much carbon monoxide do you think she inhaled? Do you think she's okay?"

"Sir, step aside."

A firefighter grabbed Reece's shoulder. "Anyone else inside?"

"I don't know. I just got here." He couldn't bring himself to look away from Sam.

The female firefighter leaned over Sam. "Ma'am, is anyone inside?"

She shook her head and the woman nodded, leaving them with the paramedics.

Over his shoulder, Reece watched the firefighters. Half of them were fighting the actual fire. The other half was drenching a huge circle around the blaze to prevent the fire from spreading to the tree line that separated the Harris farm from the neighbouring property. There was nothing left of the barn to save.

Sam fumbled again with the oxygen mask. Her face was turning bright pink from the effort to speak, and she was gesticulating wildly.

Reece lifted the mask.

"Brenda?" she croaked.

"She's okay. She's in the city with Roger. Sam, you need to leave the mask." He tried to fit the oxygen mask back on her face and she slapped at him.

"No!" The word was a grunt of anger. "Set fire. Jordan?"

She was telling him that someone had intentionally locked her in the barn and set it on fire. Not wanting to upset her more than she already was, Reece tried to keep the rage from his face and answered in a neutral tone. "Brenda said he's at a Blue Jays game."

"Jordanna?" she whispered, her eyes beginning to close.

He shook his head, leaning close so Sam could hear him. "If she hadn't gone in, I wouldn't have gotten to you in time. She and Jennifer risked their lives trying to save you."

Her eyes rolled back and her hand dropped.

Alarmed, Reece turned to the EMT. "What happened? Is she okay?"

"We need to get her to the hospital." He glanced over at Reece and frowned. "Someone needs to take a look at you."

Fear froze Reece to the spot and he clutched Sam's hand in his. "I'm fine. Can't you tell me if she's going to be okay?"

The paramedic took his upper arm and moved him away from Sam's side. "You can ride with us, come on."

He couldn't leave Brandy by herself at the farm. Paralysed with indecision, Reece watched them roll the gurney to the ambulance. His mind felt slow and dull. He'd have to leave Sam alone in the ambulance and follow in his car. It was hard to concentrate and he couldn't figure out another option. When his legs obeyed his brain's command to move, he limped toward the ambulances to where Jennifer stood, holding Brandy's leash in her hand.

Jennifer was clutching the lead so hard that small drops of blood dripped off her hand from where she'd dug her fingernails into her palm. The dog's tail was between her haunches. She growled low in her throat and nudged Reece's leg. The leash twisted around his knees when Brandy moved to his other side.

"Is my sister dead?" Jennifer's skin looked mottled with bright spots of red high on her cheeks. There was something odd about her eyes, and her upper lip kept twitching.

Reece suspected she was in shock. "Jordanna's going to be okay. She's a hero." He wrapped his arm around her thin shoulders. "So are you."

Brandy's growl deepened and she cowered on his opposite side. Fire frightened animals, and Reece needed to get the old dog back to the car. He took the leash from Jennifer, patted Brandy, and made soothing noises to try to calm both the dog and Jennifer.

"Did you smell it? Did you smell the burning skin?"

Preoccupied with the dog, Reece thought he'd misheard. He looked up and her face was without expression.

He waved over a paramedic. "She's in shock," he whispered.

The man nodded. "I have her sister in my ambulance. I'll take her with us." He said something to Jennifer that Reece didn't hear. Jennifer grinned. On her soot-covered face, the smile was unsettling.

A different paramedic than the one who attended Sam marched up to him. "Sir, my partner's dealing with your friend, but I need to take a look at you before we leave. Come with me."

Reece shook his head in defiance. "I'm fine."

"Sir, refusing treatment is your right, but I strongly advise you to let me examine you."

Irritated by the delay in getting Sam to the hospital, Reece looked pointedly at Brandy. "Go, please. I'll follow you guys and check in at emergency."

The woman frowned at the car keys in his hands. "Sir, I can't allow you to drive until we've cleared you."

"Reece, can you drive?"

He turned to find Detective Alston from York Regional standing behind him.

Reece nodded curtly.

"Let him go," Alston told the paramedic.

The woman glanced at Alston's badge, shrugged her shoulders, and left.

Alston gazed pensively at the burning barn. "This is one unlucky family," he commented to Reece. "At least there wasn't another fatality. My case load is high enough."

Offended by his flippant tone, Reece retorted, "Sam was inside. Someone had barred the doors. This is arson and attempted murder."

"Is that so?" the detective said with a condescending smirk.

Reece clenched his fists at his side. "Someone stuck rebar between the sliders so the rollers jammed. There was a new padlock on the side door."

"How'd Sam get in?" Alston asked pleasantly, seemingly unconcerned by a near homicide.

"That's the point!" Reece shouted. "Someone blocked the sliding doors and padlocked the other door *after* she was inside." He pointed at the firefighters. "They'll find an accelerant when they investigate. Probably gasoline."

Alston studied him. "You know you have a major burn on your shoulder? What's wrong with your leg? Are you sure you're okay to drive?"

The man's lackadaisical attitude infuriated Reece. "Are you going to bother to investigate this?" he demanded forcefully. "I remind you, Detective, that I outranked you when I was with the OPP. You want a political nightmare on your hands, I'm happy to call in a few favours and oblige you."

The detective folded his arms and stood aggressively with his feet wide apart. His face was rigid with anger. "Contrary to your belief, Mr. Hash, I'm proficient at my job. If this is arson, I assure you we'll discover the underlying cause. If we're dealing with attempted murder, we'll apprehend the perpetrator. The same as we'll find the person who killed Graham Harris."

"Well," Reece said with disgust, "you haven't had much luck on that front."

Alston's face darkened. "If you hadn't interfered in an active investigation, we'd have Caitlyn Franklyn in custody." He pointed at Reece. "You and I are going to have a serious discussion over that, Mr. Hash." He turned his back. "I'll see you at the hospital."

The detective started to leave and turned back. "By the way, we contacted Brenda Harris. She's on the way with your good friend, Roger Peterson." His smile was ugly. "The key suspect in a homicide. You should pick your friends more carefully."

Reece glared at Alston's back as he walked away. His shoulder throbbed, and he couldn't put weight on his ankle. Ignoring the pain, he limped to where he'd parked his car beside Sam's Grand Am. He'd have to figure out how to get her car back to Toronto, but that could wait. All he wanted to do now was to get to the hospital so he could be with her.

What was he going to do with Brandy? He couldn't leave her in the car for hours while they were in the hospital. His mind cleared for a split second and he saw the solution. He used his key to open Sam's trunk. What he wanted was in plain sight, which was a relief.

After he put Brandy in the backseat of his car, Reece sat in the running vehicle, waiting for the ambulance to leave with Sam. His impatience rose as the paramedics spoke with the driver of the second ambulance.

"Hurry up! What are you waiting for," Reece muttered and slapped his hand against the steering wheel.

Finally, they closed the ambulance doors. The frustration from just a moment earlier faded. Reece felt helpless and terrified as he watched the flashing lights on top of the ambulance. Sam was inside. Alone. Probably scared. A sinking feeling of dread and loss made his limbs weak as blood pounded in his ears.

He was twenty-four again, holding the phone to his ear while an Illinois State Trooper told him his parents and brother had died in a car accident. A car Reece should have been in, but he'd fought with his father that day.

This is an unattractive quality in a grown man, son. I'm disappointed in you.

The last words his dad had spoken to him. He couldn't lose Sam, too.

At the end of the lane, Reece followed the flashing lights as the ambulance turned right onto the country road. The driver put on the siren and raced toward the hospital. Within seconds,

Reece had lost sight of the vehicle that carried the only family left to him.

CHAPTER TWENTY-NINE

SAM

"OH BOY." SAM laughed as she reached for Brandy. "I haven't seen that vest in ages."

The golden retriever trotted over with a big doggy grin. Her tail wagged so hard it made a slapping sound every time it hit the side of the hospital bed.

The red St. John Ambulance vest was snug around her middle. The white embossed letters spelling *Please Pet Me* and *Therapy Dog* had yellowed with age, and the SJA logo was tattered from too many spins in the washing machine. Wrinkled black letters spelled out Brandy's name across the collar of the faded vest. There was now more grey than gold fur around her snout, and her left eye had a milky cataract, but Brandy still looked proud and fetching in her old therapy vest.

"How did you get her in the hospital?" Sam asked Reece. "The vest doesn't work if they don't recognize the dog, and her ID tag expired last month. Didn't they ask for your photo card?" She tugged at Brandy's floppy ears and leaned down to have her cheek slobbered.

"Roger and Brenda arrived while the nurse was arguing with me about it," Reece explained. "Roger flashed his spiffy, impressive medical credentials and vouched for Brandy." There was more than a touch of sarcasm in his tone. "Anyway, I didn't want to leave her in the car and remembered that you kept the vest in your trunk. I thought *Eureka* and grabbed it."

"Well, I'm glad to see my golden beauty. But be forewarned: If it's the same nurse I've had all evening, you better make sure she doesn't check Brandy's toenails." She rolled her eyes. "They aren't regulation length. Hospitals were strict about that back in the day when we did friendly visiting."

"She won't be going anywhere else, so we're fine."

"Aw, you should take her down to pediatrics. The kids love her. Don't they, sweetheart?"

Shifting her focus off the dog, Sam studied Reece. "I'm also glad to see you. What on earth have you been doing for the past six hours?"

Exhaustion had carved lines in his face, and the edge of a dressing protruded from the filthy sleeve of his charred T-shirt. "How bad is your shoulder?" she asked.

"Second degree, but on the low end of the spectrum. It'll take a couple of weeks to heal, and I have antibiotics." He grinned. "Guess you'll have to change the dressing since I can't reach. Want a nursing outfit from the adult store?" He wiggled his eyebrows at her but sobered when his eyes came to rest on the bandage on her forearm and the oxygen tubes in her nose that gave her voice a slightly nasal sound. "How about you? How are you doing?"

"Also second degree." She patted the bandage on her forearm. "Can we go home?"

Reece ignored her request for escape. "And your lungs? Any permanent damage?"

She flicked the oxygen tubes attached to her nose. "Not severe enough to intubate. They didn't schedule a bronchoscopy. I overhead some chatter about hyperbaric oxygenation, but they're waiting to review carbon monoxide levels in the latest set of blood tests." She reached out her hand. "Stop worrying. I'm fine. The fire was in the back and there was enough fresh air through the bottom of the door. I'm okay. Where are Lisa, Jim, and Roger?"

He shrugged. "I left two messages for Lisa and Jim on their cells and a voice mail on their home phone, but neither of them called back. Roger's here, but he's with Brenda, Jordanna, and Jennifer at the moment."

Her best friend hadn't bothered to come to the hospital or even to call. Her other childhood friend was right down the hall and hadn't checked on her. Disappointment formed a hot ball in the pit of her stomach.

Reece perched on the side of her bed and ran his fingers through her hair. "The ends are singed. You must have been terrified." He kissed the palm of her hand. "How are you doing on an emotional level?"

A year ago, she would have lied and downplayed her feelings. Sharing honest emotions was important to Reece, his compassion was genuine, and he was her biggest cheerleader. He was the one person she could count on to love and support her unconditionally.

"I'm upset my friends don't care," she confessed, swallowing hard and blinking back tears. "As far as the fire, I'm angry. It wasn't an accident. Someone was lurking outside."

Reece listened intently as she told him about hearing clanging, seeing someone through the wall gaps, and smelling gasoline.

She concluded by saying, "I never saw the arsonist, but I'm telling you whoever it was knew I was inside, locked me in with intent, and lit the barn on fire to kill me."

He didn't say anything for a few minutes. His voice was quiet and deadly when he said, "They jammed the track with a piece of rebar and took the time to hide the ladder."

"That must have been the metal clanging," she said. "I did find out what made the background sound we heard on the death threat calls. There was an old, unbalanced fan in the makeshift office. It made a *thump, thump* sound while it oscillated. The caller was in the barn office."

Reece raised his eyebrows. "I remember thinking it sounded like muted helicopter blades."

"If Jordanna risked her life to save me, I guess we can eliminate her as an arson suspect," she said.

The troubled expression on Reece's face deepened. "Unless she saw me and realized she'd be caught unless she did something to deflect blame. The thing that bothers me is no one knew you were going to the farm. Whoever did this saw an opportunity and acted spur of the moment. But it took time and materials to set it up. That's deliberate and calculated."

"Diabolical," Sam said. "But if it was Jordanna, wouldn't that mean Jennifer knew her sister started the fire? She was there, right?"

"She was there," he agreed. "But I don't know the circumstances. Brenda said Jennifer was at her aunt's house. Could be she crossed the field and found Jordanna on the scene of a raging fire."

Sam frowned. "Speaking of Aunt Rachel, where was she? Wouldn't she have seen smoke from her house?"

His face was grim. "I hadn't considered that."

"How sure are you Jordan was in the city?"

Reece shrugged. "Until Detective Alston checks alibis..." He trailed off and his lips thinned. "Assuming he bothers. Anyway, we can't be sure anyone was where they claim they were." He held her eyes. "That includes Brenda and Roger. Could you tell approximate age or gender based on the size of the legs and the type of pants? What about shoes, did you see them?"

She shook her head. "No. It was a flash of denim. What were Jordanna and Jennifer wearing?"

"Jeans. Same as Brenda and Roger. I called Brenda's cell before I drove out to the farm. She said she and Roger were in the city, but who knows."

Already upset about her friends' lack of concern, Sam didn't want to consider the possibility that Roger had lit the fire. Could misplaced loyalty have blinded her to the fact that one of her childhood friends was a multiple murderer? The concept terrified and sickened her.

The door opened and a doctor entered. "Hi, Sam." He reached out his hand to Reece. "I'm Dr. Kulkarni. You're the fiancé from the ER, I assume."

"Reece Hash."

They shook hands and the doctor turned to her. "I have the ABG results and your blood gases are good. The high flow oxygen the paramedics administered at the scene, in addition to the treatment you've received with us, reduced the CO in your blood. Your ECG and chest X-ray are normal." He glanced up from the chart. "We'll need to do a second X-ray in a day or two to check for atelectasis and pulmonary edema, which can develop later. From all accounts, you are a fortunate young lady." He closed the chart. "On a scale of one to ten, how's the pain?"

"I have a high tolerance for pain," she replied truthfully.

"Any trouble breathing?"

She shook her head.

"Okay, we'll keep you overnight and—"

"Nope, not happening." She flung off the blanket. "Where are my clothes?"

"Sam—" Reece said.

"Don't waste your breath. I'm not staying." She got up, clutching her gown closed. Her smelly clothes were in the closet but she didn't have a T-shirt anymore.

"You need to stay overnight," Dr. Kulkarni insisted.

"I'll sign a waiver that I'm leaving against doctor's orders. I need to borrow the gown since my T-shirt went up in smoke." She closed the bathroom door behind her.

In the other room, she heard a mumbled conversation between Reece and the doctor. They could chat all they wanted. It was her legal right to refuse treatment and leave.

When she came out, the doctor wasn't there. "Ready?" she asked Reece as she attempted to tuck the ends of the gown into her jeans.

"We need to wait for prescriptions. An inhaler, antibiotics, and some pain meds."

"He gave up faster than I expected," she said and grinned.

"I told him it was pointless. You're the single most pigheaded person I've ever met." He wrapped his arm around her waist. "Besides, Brandy and I want you home." He tilted her chin up with the tip of his finger. "But if I see *one* sign of respiratory distress or suspect any complication, I'm taking you to a Toronto hospital, and I mean it. He told me what to watch for. You'll tell me if you feel unwell, right?"

"Sure."

He gave her a stern look. "Don't lie to me."

She stood on her tiptoes to kiss him. "I promise." She pulled him to the door with Brandy trotting along between them. "Let's grab the prescriptions and split before he changes his mind."

They met Dr. Kulkarni at the nurses' station, took the prescriptions, and listened to a last-ditch lecture.

On their way out, they ran into Roger, who made a cursory inquiry into her health. It felt dismissive to Sam. Then he offered to drive her car to the loft, stating that he'd driven to the farm in Brenda's car and didn't have a way back to the city.

Roger's attitude completely pissed her off. But the Grand Am had been her father's pride and joy. Sam didn't like the idea of leaving it unattended at the farm. Seeing little option to get her precious car safely home where it belonged, she threw Roger the keys.

He caught them and she circled his wrist with her hand. "Where were you this afternoon?"

Roger glanced at her hand in confusion and tried to tug his arm free. "At my house. With Brenda. Why?"

"Can you prove it?"

His arm went limp. "You're kidding! You can't be suggesting we attempted to incinerate you alive."

"Roger, I've made excuses for you because of Suzanna's overdose, your mother's mental break, and your estrangement from Veronica," she shouted. It was all pouring out now, and she couldn't stop it. "It's time for you to deal with your anger. You've become an embittered, entitled little man. Ever since Abigail's suicide, you, Lisa, and Jim have been selfish and unreasonable. No matter how hard I try to support you, it's not enough, and I'm fed up with the lot of you."

"You've been through a terrible ordeal," Roger said soothingly, "we can talk—"

"Don't you patronize me, *Doctor*," she snapped. "I'm through talking. You're taking that DNA test. I want to put Abigail—the only real friend I ever had—to rest. That requires knowing if you took advantage of her right under my nose. On top of being a scumbag, who hustles everything in a skirt, I'm inclined to believe you and Brenda murdered Graham."

His eyes widened with shock. "I didn't sleep with Abigail. I didn't kill Graham Harris. What's the matter with you?"

She released his wrist and crossed her arms against her chest. "Detective Alston told Reece you're his prime murder suspect. Cops aren't stupid, Roger, and I'm sick of you implying they are. The entire time I was with Toronto Police, you treated me like I was a clinical experiment on the intellectual development of the simple-minded."

"Now wait just a—"

She held up a hand to silence him. "Look, it's simple. Don't take the test, and we're off the case. Take the test and even if it turns out you are the father, regardless of how disgusting a human being that makes you, I'll finish the murder investigation."

His face paled. "I don't know where this hostility is coming from. It's unseemly."

Sam laughed. "It's been coming for years. It just took another ignored near-death experience to open my eyes."

"I'll drop your car off in the parking lot of the loft and put the keys through the mail slot." Righteous indignation filled his tone. "Good night."

He left with an overconfident swagger, and Sam felt a weight lift from her shoulders.

After a moment of stunned silence, Reece let out a low whistle. "That was... something else. Nicely done."

"Yeah, well, it's probably something I'll regret tomorrow," she said. "Come on, let's get home."

He took her hand and they strolled out to the car. "What's next?" he asked as he put Brandy in the backseat and held the passenger side door open for her.

She shrugged. "Find the asshole who keeps trying to kill us."

CHAPTER THIRTY

MY MOTHER'S DESPERATION to find love in a house that would never be a home amused me. I'd taunt her, poking at her festering wound of abandonment. The pain that would flood her eyes was satisfying. I'd watch her tears with a burning in my groin, yearning to cut her flesh to see physical agony mingle with the sting of neglect.

I wonder if my mother crept into my sister's room at night. Did she whisper through the gloom, 'a little cuddle, my sweet child" or was that degradation mine alone? I never asked because it doesn't matter.

Whether it is nature or nurture is irrelevant. I embrace what I am and know many of us exist in plain sight. I catch the eye of a kindred spirit in a park, and it shines with needs that match my own. We're not burdened by regret, shame, or pity—emotions that stunt the human mind. We have no need for love or empathy. We detest compassion.

I've learned to fake humanity and to mask my yearning to witness misery. Creatures like me are safe from detection because the weak-minded refuse to accept the truth. We stand alongside you in lines in supermarkets. We chat about the weather and imagine blood pouring from the cavity we long to claw into your chest. We pump gas with charming smiles that disguise our desire to witness your charring flesh constrict and suck away from pristine bone. With bovine eyes, you deny there are those of us born without a soul. You see the best in everyone. You are easy prey—the prey on which we hone our skills.

I cautiously circle, watching for the like-minded. I wait for a partner and for a worthy opponent. There is no fear. There is only the pulsing beat of the game.

Red rover, red rover, I call Sam on over. It's time we play a game.

CHAPTER THIRTY-ONE

REECE

THEY SPENT THE next three days recuperating from their ordeal. Sam accompanied him on his Saturday morning jaunt to the St. Lawrence Market. Getting her up at six in the morning wasn't easy, and she didn't care for the farmer's market, but she'd put on a brave face and remained cheerful while he visited kiosks. In exchange, he suggested pizza for dinner, her favourite meal, rather than preparing the coq au vin and baked Alaska he was itching to master.

Over pizza and chicken wings, they watched the recording of Abigail's last dance performance. It was getting easier to celebrate Abby's life, rather than focusing on the darkness of her death, but Sam remained irate with Lisa, Jim, and Roger.

Lisa had called six times, Jim had dropped over, and Roger had sent flowers and emailed. Sam refused to speak to any of them, even after Detective Alston verified that witnesses put Jordan at the baseball game and Brenda with Roger at his house on the day of the fire. That left Caitlyn as the arson suspect.

Sam was having a hard time accepting that her theory about Jordan was wrong. She was questioning her instincts, and her sudden lack of confidence worried Reece. She missed her friends and Reece wished he'd stayed out of her relationships. Now she was unhappy and had lost faith in herself. He felt like a dick and didn't know how to fix it.

The next day, he was disinfecting the kitchen and cleaning the six-burner gas stovetop when someone tapped at the door. It was either a neighbour or the visitor had followed a resident through the security door again—a regular happenstance that bugged Reece who felt strongly that people should be security-minded in such a big city. He stripped off his rubber gloves, shoved Brandy out of the way, and opened the door.

"Hi Reece."

His stomach dropped when he saw the visitor. "Sam's at the university."

"I came to speak with you," Lisa said.

There was something different about her, but Reece couldn't put his finger on the change. One thing was that she appeared less grouchy than usual. She was smiling, at least.

Left with no option but outright rudeness, he invited her inside. It was six o'clock in the evening, and he was opening his mouth to offer her wine when he caught himself.

"I can make coffee," he said instead.

"No thanks." She seemed nervous as her eyes flitted to his while she fiddled with her necklace and shuffled her feet.

"What's up?"

She took a deep breath. "You deserve an explanation for why I've treated you the way I have." She hesitated before adding, "I don't want you to think that what I have to say is an excuse. I don't mean it that way."

Lisa had treated him poorly, and he wasn't going to pretend she hadn't just to be polite. "I'd appreciate an explanation, thank you." He ushered her to the sofa and sat in a chair across from her.

She ran her tongue across her upper lip and her eyes shifted around the room before landing on his. "When we graduated high school, Sam and I planned to share an apartment downtown. University of Toronto accepted her for her undergraduate degree in psychology, and Ontario College of Art and Design accepted me."

He didn't know Lisa had studied with the impressive OCAD University. He also didn't care. What did ancient history have to do with how she'd been treating him?

She fiddled with her necklace again before dropping her hands to clasp them in her lap. "We found an adorable one-bedroom in Grange Park, a minute walk to the art gallery and the campus." Her voice was wistful. "I was so excited. Jim was finished law school and articling, so he also lived downtown. It was going to be amazing."

Reece snuck a peek at his watch. "Didn't work out, eh?" He hated to leave a chore incomplete and had the fridge to tackle.

She shook her head. It looked like she was fighting back tears. "My father said he wouldn't pay for his daughter to whore around an art school filled with hippy degenerates."

Harsh.

"Sam said to defer, save money, and I could apply for loans for winter admission. Not even a year, everyone said."

Good advice that she didn't take, or maybe something stopped her. Reece waited out her silence.

"My mother got sick. I had to quit my job. She wasn't safe alone with my father."

The pregnant pause made Reece uncomfortable. "Tough break," he mumbled.

"Six months turned into three years," she said. "My mother went into remission and Detective McNamara got my father into recovery. He talked him into letting me reapply."

Lisa's grim expression told him that things probably hadn't worked out. He made a point of lifting his arm to examine his watch. Rude, but he didn't care. She deserved it.

She blushed and spoke faster. "Detective McNamara died and my father started drinking again. I had to be there for my mother and for Sam, so school wasn't an option."

At the mention of Sam, Reece got defensive. "Sam did continue her education after U of T. She went to Queen's for her masters. Her father's death didn't prevent her from living her life." He was getting that "poor me" vibe from Lisa that he hated.

"I know," she agreed quickly. "And Dad's sponsor got him through the relapse. But before I knew it, I was pregnant with Kira." Her voice was low and trembled slightly when she continued. "I love Jim and adore Kira. I decided to postpone my studies until Kira started school."

Kira was five, turning six. Reece didn't know much about preschool education but assumed kindergarten was over, which meant Kira would attend grade one in the fall.

"Have you applied?" He was sure she'd manufactured some adversity outside her control.

She nodded. "They accepted me on condition. I have to present my portfolio and fill in some paperwork."

"Congratulations," he mumbled.

"It's just that, well… I'm pregnant." There was no expression on her face. No joy, no regret, nothing.

Reece didn't know how to react. A baby was happy news, if you wanted it. If you didn't, well, that was a different story. What was he supposed to say? Not understanding what she wanted made him uncomfortable and annoyed.

"I realize how bitter I've felt over the years, watching my friends grow and become independent people," she said with a sigh. "They left me behind."

No one left you anywhere. You made different choices.

Reece squashed his aggravation and linked his hands between his knees. "Why can't you be a mother and go to school? The key to happiness is adaptation. Everyone has challenges."

"I counted on Sam's help, like with Kira," she said. "But then I realized how much has changed over the past six years. That's when I knew school was a pipe dream."

Here comes the victimization.

He leaned back in the chair. "Why's that?"

"Because of you," she stated simply.

Reece couldn't believe she was blaming him! What did *he* have to do with whether *she* attended school?

Seeming to sense his indignation, Lisa rushed to explain. "You are the best thing that's ever happened to Sam. You're her highest priority."

He shook his head in frustration. "So you can't go to school because Sam and I love each other?"

"You're twisting everything around." Almost as soon as the words came out of her mouth, she was shaking her head. "No, you aren't. I'm not communicating clearly again." She sighed. "I did blame you. I resented the fact you talked Sam into doing her PhD. Between school and your relationship, she doesn't have time for me." She lowered her eyes to her hands. "I projected all my loneliness and confusion onto you."

She laid her hand on her stomach, where he now saw she had a little baby bump. It surprised him he and Sam hadn't noticed.

"I've treated you horribly," she said. "I want to change. I'm asking for a second chance."

Most people can't change without sustained effort. If she was on the level, he needed to understand her motivation.

"What made you decide to talk to me?" he asked.

"Jim and I are in therapy. It was his idea. At first, I said no. It was easier to blame everyone, convince myself they had the problem. They were too emotionally unavailable. They were selfish. They neglected and rejected me. That same old dance." Her expression was regretful. "When Sam nearly died in that fire, I had an epiphany." Her voice quivered. "I looked in the mirror," she whispered, tears dripping down her cheeks, "and saw my mother. Always the victim."

Reece saw her sincerity and wanted to trust her but was skeptical. For over six months, he'd tried hard to connect with the woman in front of him. Truth was he didn't like Lisa. It wasn't her dehumanizing conduct toward him. It was her parasitical feeding off Sam. Adjusting behaviour to become a different person took courage and stamina. He didn't believe Lisa had either.

"Change is difficult," he muttered, unwilling to commit to anything at this point. "What's motivating you to try?"

She was crying hard now and he felt bad.

"Growing up, my mother was an angry woman who complained about my dad but bought him bottles of gin." Lisa wiped her hand across her nose. "I have to break the cycle. I don't want my children growing up with a mother who blames everyone else for her own broken dreams. Do you see?"

A mother's love and desire to protect her children was a strong instinct. A chunk of his resistance melted. Coming here was far outside her comfort zone. She was nervous and scared but was pushing through her discomfort and apologizing.

If it were just about the two of them, Reece would accept her apology to be gracious but drop the relationship. It wasn't just about him and Lisa. The woman was important to Sam.

Reece stood. "Is it okay if I sit beside you?"

She nodded and he moved from the chair and sat beside her on the sofa.

"Are you happy about the pregnancy?" he asked directly.

Her face lit up and her smile was brilliant. "Yes. I'm nearly five months and I'm feeling much better. The first little while was hard. Morning sickness, you know how it is." She studied him with nothing but sincerity on her face. "I really do want to change for Kira and the baby."

"Then you will. Recognizing the consequences of our actions is the single most important tool to facilitate change. Can I ask you something?"

Her brown eyes held his, and Reece realized how beautiful she was. Wide-set, large eyes with smoky lids. High cheekbones on a flawless Mediterranean complexion. Thick, glossy hair fell in waves over her shoulders. She was stunning. He'd never noticed. All he'd seen was her negative disposition.

"Why don't you begin your undergraduate degree part time?" He pointed at the painting she'd given him that hung above the desk. "You're a talented artist. Can't you juggle part-time studies with motherhood?"

"Jim wants me to try in September. The baby will be so young, I'm not sure if I'll want to be away for even a few hours a week."

"Well, you don't know what your schedule will be or what you can arrange with the university. There may be online lecture options. Remember, fathers enjoy alone time with babies. Mothers don't get to have all the fun." He patted her hand. "Explore your options and make the right decision for you."

"I'm going to try again to speak with Sam," Lisa told him.

"If you want, I'll mediate," he said.

"Would you? Thank you." She paused and chewed on her lower lip. "Can I ask you to do one more thing?"

He nodded.

"Can you share something personal with me?" She blushed. "You see, for me, mutual sharing establishes trust. I want us to be friends, not because of Sam, but because we share our own relationship. Does that make sense?"

Reece wasn't sure how he felt about it. But he wanted to know if Roger was right—if Abigail had told Lisa the name of her baby's father. Maybe if he told her something personal, it would create trust, and he could encourage Lisa to recognize that keeping Abigail's secret posthumously was hurting people. Regardless of the murder case, Reece would feel better if he could honour Abigail's wish and conclude his commitment to Talia.

"Okay," he agreed. "One sec." He stood and went up to the bedroom loft. When he returned, he laid his father's gold Rolex on the table in front of her.

"If I have a glass of wine, are you going to accuse me of being an alcoholic?"

Lisa laughed. Reece had never heard the sour woman make that sound.

"I'd join you if it wasn't for the baby." She patted her stomach. "God, I was such a bitch at that dinner party." Her cheeks flushed with colour. "And I'm sorry I bought you a skunk costume," she added with a sheepish grin. "Jim was furious."

He'd misjudged the man. Reece believed Jim dismissed his wife's passive aggression, perhaps even enabled it by not confronting her about her behaviour, which was why he didn't enjoy Jim's company.

Reece went to the kitchen to get his wine and returned to sit across from her, feeling a tad more open to sharing. "That watch belonged to my father. He was a federal court judge."

"I know," she said with a curious expression. "Jim told me."

"I had a twin brother, Ray. Growing up, Ray was the wild child. He balked at the idea of attending Western University, our dad's alma mater. Dad's hope for a protege landed on me, the hard-working, studious son who obeyed all the rules and did what Father expected. Until I didn't."

He took a sip of his wine. Telling the story was hard, but it was a mistake to try to control Sam's relationships rather than working on his own. Sometimes, it's easier to speak your truth to people you don't know well, which was part of the reason group therapy worked.

Reece cleared his throat and continued. "I quit law school, joined the Ontario Provincial Police, and didn't tell my father. Six months later, I went home to accompany my family to a cousin's wedding in Chicago and broke the news." He winced at the memory of his father's reaction. "It didn't land well, and the ensuing argument was brutal. Instead of trying to work things out, I left pissed off. My whole family died in a ten-car pileup on the I-94 West outside Michigan City."

She gasped. "I'm so sorry."

He swallowed hard. Embarrassed that tears burned in his eyes, he stood and shuffled to the kitchen, brushing the back of his hand across his cheeks.

"If I hadn't fought with my father before he got behind the wheel of the car, he'd have avoided the accident. The argument distracted him and he lost focus."

"I'm sure that's not true." She followed him to the kitchen. "It was a terrible tragedy. What caused the pile-up?"

"A hitch on an RV released. Drivers couldn't avoid hitting the trailer, and the cars behind couldn't get out of the way."

"How old were you?"

"Twenty-four."

It touched him to see her eyes fill with tears.

"That's awful," she murmured. "I'm so sorry."

"I tell you this because I experienced similar emotions to what you've described today. I was angry all the time. I felt like no one in the world could understand what I was going through. I couldn't find joy. I couldn't even find a reason to be kind to people," he said, remembering how his pain had changed the way he had interacted with friends who had tried to help him. "If you're invested in therapy, it works. Well," he rolled his eyes, "maybe not if it's with Roger."

She laughed. "It's not."

Taking advantage of their moment of bonding, he placed his hand over hers. "Lisa, did Abigail tell you she was pregnant? Did she tell you who the father was?"

She dropped her eyes, pulled away her hand, and picked at the beads on her necklace. "Yes." It was a sigh more than a word.

"Was it Roger?"

"Abby made me promise not to tell anyone, even Jim. I've struggled with it since her suicide. Watching how much it hurts Talia and the chaos it's caused is driving me crazy. But I promised. Don't ask me to betray her, please."

There was only one reason Abby would be so adamant that no one found out the truth. Disgust rolled across his stomach.

"It was Roger. That miserable son of a bitch!" He pounded his fist against the kitchen island.

Lisa jumped and quickly said, "Wait, I—"

Reece barely heard her. "He deserves whatever Talia does." He paced in a circle, taking angry strides.

"Reece—"

"Thank Christ, Sam has finally accepted that Roger is a piece of shit."

"Stop, please!"

He stopped his furious pacing and turned to her.

She licked her lips and raised her eyes to meet his. "Abby wouldn't have wanted this," she whispered.

He snorted with contempt. "This is exactly the outcome she'd want. She was violated in a weak moment by a bastard."

"I don't disagree." Tears dripped down her cheeks. "But it wasn't Roger. It was an executive from New York. He was here on business and saw Abigail dance. He became, I don't know, relentless, I guess. Eventually, well, his attention wore her down. She was so lonely while Talia was overseas. They spent a weekend together. She never heard from him again. Abigail didn't want anyone to know what she'd done."

A wave of sadness tainted with rage flowed over Reece. He remembered Talia saying that conquering a lesbian would give some men a sense of accomplishment.

Lisa took his hand. "I know how you feel," she said softly. "I can see it on your face. That's why I'll never disclose the man's name." She squeezed his fingers. "It's over. I understand now that we have to let it be over."

The door opened and Sam looked between Reece and Lisa. "What's going on?" Her voice was terse. "Reece, why are you upset? Lisa, what are you doing here?"

Reece put his arm around Lisa's shoulder. "We've worked everything out."

Sam looked flabbergasted. "What?"

"And now," he announced, "Brandy and I are leaving you ladies to reconcile your differences." He took his keys from the church altar, clipped on Brandy's leash, and kissed Sam's open mouth.

He turned to Lisa. "You'll tell her your news and the other piece?" he asked. "You're right. We need to let it end. We need to remember Abby's life, not her death."

Lisa nodded.

"What news? What other piece? What about Abby?" Sam's eyes darted from him to Lisa and back to him.

"How about you and I take a trip to OCAD on Thursday?" he asked Lisa. "Bring Kira, I'll treat for lunch."

"I'll take you up on that," she agreed with a wide smile.

Sam stood speechless but she was smiling now, and the flicker of light in her green eyes that Reece adored had returned.

"I have a few ideas on how you can thank me tonight," he whispered, and winked at her before leaving the two women to stitch together their torn friendship.

CHAPTER THIRTY-TWO

REECE

THE MAIN BUILDING of the OCAD University was an ordinary brown brick Georgian. But The Sharp Centre for Design—the fifth addition, according to Lisa—was something else. Straddling other buildings that made up the college, the Centre looked like a giant's black and white checked table with coloured legs, which Reece supposed was the idea because people referred to the Centre as the "tabletop." The two-storey structure, speckled with black squares and windows, perched on twelve yellow, purple, and blue stilts that resembled coloured pencils. The steel supports ran from the bottom of the rectangle addition to the sidewalk.

The massive table loomed above the original building that squatted underneath. To Reece, the contrast was jarring. Clearly most people disagreed with him though, because the addition had won prestigious design and engineering awards.

Lisa took him on a guided tour through the university and its galleries. Her excitement was contagious and the exhibits intrigued Reece, although he found it a little sad how well she knew the school. He imagined her wandering the halls, year after year, fantasizing about attending someday. He hoped she'd find the courage to pursue her dream, but it was her journey to take. Watching her waffle and make excuses not to try was a challenge. Maybe he *was* controlling, because he wanted to march her in by the elbow to collect and fill out the paperwork to accept her admission. Instead, he kept his mouth shut and pretended not to notice her procrastination.

After an hour, Reece could tell the tour was boring Kira. She was adorable, trotting along at his side in pink overalls, a frilly white blouse, and a tiny pair of pink and white high-top Adidas. Pink stones set in gold teardrops decorated her plump earlobes and matched the colour of her rosebud lips. A lump formed in his throat when she slipped her small hand into his and gazed up with big brown eyes.

Reece handed Lisa a portfolio he was carrying for her. "How about I take Kira across the street to McDonald's while you meet with the admission counsellor?"

Lisa glanced at her daughter's hand in his and smiled. "Are you sure?"

"If it's okay with Kira."

"Can I have a Happy Meal with a toy and a pop?" Kira asked her mother.

Lisa frowned. "Milk, no soda."

"Cookies?"

"Only if you drink all your milk, and it has to be white milk, not chocolate."

The five-year-old nodded and tugged Reece to the door.

"I'll be about half an hour," Lisa said. "I'll find out what they expect in the portfolio. I doubt I have sufficient material." She plucked at the handle of her portfolio, lowered her eyes, and shuffled her feet. "Maybe I should come back another day."

Reece patted her shoulder. "May as well get it done today. See you later." He tugged Kira to the door.

"Have fun," she called after them. "Kira, listen to Uncle Reece."

Reece held open the door and ushered Kira through. When they were outside on the sidewalk, Kira said, "Mommy's scared to go to school."

"How about you? You're starting grade one soon."

They waited at the corner for the streetlight to change. Reece didn't want to set a bad example by jaywalking, even though there was a break in traffic.

"I wanna go. I have lots of friends in kindergarten," she said.

Reece laughed. "Maybe your mom will make new friends too."

"What toy will I get?"

The sudden change of subject confused him until he realized she was talking about the Happy Meal. "Guess we'll find out."

They crossed the street and the scrumptious aroma of French fries and grilled meat greeted them. Students milled around the tables and the ambiance was bright and cheerful.

Once the cashier gave them their food, Reece led Kira to a table. Across from them, a young woman took out a sketchpad and leaned over to speak to Reece.

"Can I draw her? Your daughter's so cute."

He felt a blush rise to his cheeks. "Ah, yeah, I guess if it's okay with her."

Kira shrugged and grabbed her toy from the tray. Reece had no clue what it was, but it thrilled the five-year-old. He opened her carton of milk and eyed the small bag of cookies on the table in front of her. Was he supposed to hold the cookies hostage until she finished her milk? Reece sneaked peeks at her while he stirred sugar into his coffee. Kira was wolfing down French fries between sips of milk. Feeling confident that she'd finish her milk, or at least most of it, Reece left the cookies where they were.

Staring at the cardboard box containing his Big Mac, Reece felt a ridiculous pang of guilt. Sam loved McD's. For some reason, he had the need to hear her voice, so he called while Kira dug into her bag of chicken nuggets. It was disappointing that Sam didn't pick up, but it wasn't a surprise. She always turned off her phone in the university library. He let Kira leave the voicemail and smiled while the little girl chatted confidently to dead air.

Just as he finished stuffing the last chunk of his Big Mac in his mouth, his cell rang. Expecting Sam, he answered with a full mouth.

"It's Romero. We have Caitlyn Franklyn. We're at her house."

Reece glanced at his watch. Lisa would arrive in a few minutes. He didn't like ditching her and Kira, but they needed a break in the case. Lisa's reaction would be the first test of their new relationship. Based on the success of the day so far, if she understood his need to leave for work, it would signify trust and friendship.

"Give me an hour. Will you still be there?"

Romero laughed. "Oh yeah, amigo, I'll be here for some time." With that, he disconnected the call.

Reece called Sam again and left his own message, letting her know about Romero's call and inviting her to meet him at the house in Kleinburg. By the time he finished, Lisa had joined them. She was juggling her portfolio, purse, and a bound catalogue. She fell into a chair, wearing a brilliant smile.

"My portfolio is good—*impressive* was the word," she said with pride. "The interview went well and I have a follow-up meeting to bring in the completed paperwork."

Kira tugged at her mother's dress and waved the toy, which Lisa examined in detail. Reece still had no idea what it was or what it did but gleaned it was a character from a recent movie.

"So listen, I feel bad about this but there's a development in the case," he said. "I need to cut our day short."

"A development? That's wonderful. Is it good news?" she asked.

"Police have Caitlyn Franklyn in custody," he said.

Her eyes widened with surprise. "What a relief! Go," she said with genuine understanding. "Don't forget I have Sam tonight for girl's night." She paused and then added, "But if she needs to reschedule, tell her not to worry. Right now, this case is more important. You've both been in dangerous situations before, but..." She sighed. "This feels different. I'm worried."

He smiled at her. "We'll be fine, promise. Look, I don't want to abandon you. How about I run you guys home?"

She laughed. "We're capable of getting home alone. Besides, I want to buy a new dress for tonight to celebrate." She flipped through the catalogue. "It's so exciting to take action." She smiled at him. "It's been a lovely day, and we've had a wonderful time, haven't we Kira?"

The munchkin studied him solemnly. "Wanna come over and have a teddy bear picnic?" she asked.

From the serious expression on her face, Reece suspected that she didn't invite just anyone to her teddy picnics. "I'd be honoured," he said with a smile.

"Auntie Sam plays with me," Kira said. "She sings the song the best."

Reece couldn't imagine Sam singing the nursery rhyme. That was something he wanted to see.

"Can the llama we gave you attend, even though he's not a bear?" he asked in mock solemnity.

Her eyes crinkled and her lips pursed before she nodded. "He can't sit at the picnic table. He's not a teddy. He can sit on a pillow on the floor with the beaver and Brandy. Brandy gets doggy treats. Do llamas eat doggy treats?"

Reece stood and gathered up the garbage from the table. "I'm sure they do," he agreed, giving her a kiss on the head.

Her eyes narrowed. "But you gotta sing the song with Auntie Sam."

Laughing, he put the trash in the bin across from their table, dug in his pocket, and turned to the girl with the sketchpad. "Can I buy that from you?"

The artist's mouth opened in surprise when she looked at the fifty-dollar bill in his hand. "It's not worth that much."

"It is to me." He handed her the money and took the pencil sketch. "It signifies a good friend's accomplishment and commemorates a great day. One of the best I've had in years."

Lisa reached for his hand and squeezed his fingers gently. "Me too."

Seeing the smile that lit her face, Reece finally felt that Sam's best friend had accepted him.

CHAPTER THIRTY-THREE

SAM

SAM SLUNG HER book bag over her head and across her chest and ran for the streetcar. She felt a tug and suddenly the strap was pressing into her neck and strangling her. Fumbling to get her fingers underneath, she yanked on the strap too hard and it tore off the bag. Reeling as she tried to grab the bag before it hit the ground, she accidentally released the clasp. Her books tumbled out, and her fresh pack of mints rolled into the gutter and dropped through the sewage grate.

"Goddamn it," she muttered with growing frustration and crouched to collect her books.

Pedestrians crowded the sidewalk, jostling her and kicking the books out of reach. A man nearly stepped on her hand as she grabbed the final book and stuffed it into the bag. Just as she stood and tucked the bag under her arm, the streetcar started to leave.

"Hey! Wait!" She slapped the door.

The streetcar jerked to a stop. The door opened and the scowling driver impatiently waved her inside.

Flustered and out of breath, Sam flung herself onto the nearest seat she could find in the crowded streetcar. It had been one annoyance after another all morning. First, she'd gotten to the library and realized she'd forgotten her data stick. Once she fetched it from the loft, she had to reverse the half-hour transit ride back to St. George Street. Ninety minutes of wasted time.

She was checking email and trying to focus on something other than her bad mood when her phone rang. Roger. Again. He'd been calling all morning. It was driving her nuts. At some point, they needed to have a conversation, but it wasn't going to be today. She was in a foul mood and didn't want to try to talk to *Doctor* Peterson, who would twist the conversation into a therapy session designed to point out all her issues. She let the call go to voicemail.

A dude with a purple Mohawk, neck tattoos, and too many facial piercings to count sat beside her. His body odour was overpowering. She clamped her finger under her nose, pressed against the window, and scowled at him. She was beginning to understand why Reece hated public transportation.

Her cell tweeted. A text message. She ignored the text and gazed out the window at the passing shops and restaurants. The phone rang again.

Goddamn it, Roger.

She sent it to voice mail. A second later, it tweeted. She experienced the spontaneous urge to hurl her cell to the ground and stomp on it. Taking a deep breath, she tried to find one positive event in this exasperating day. Nothing came to mind, and, when the phone rang again, she wished she'd stayed in bed.

"Popular chick." Purple Mohawk eyed her up and down with a lazy grin. "How you doin', pretty lady?"

Suppressing a shudder, Sam answered her phone. The alternative was to engage with her streetcar companion, and Roger was tenacious when he felt slighted. He'd keep calling until he wore her down.

Instead of Roger, it sounded like a woman, but Sam couldn't understand a word. She held the phone away and checked the caller ID. Brenda. She was hysterical, jabbering about a story and pictures and a shed. In the background, Roger's melodic "therapist" voice was telling her to slow down. Eventually, he took the phone.

"Sam, can you and Reece come out to the farm?"

Reece was out with Lisa and Kira, where he was making a gallant effort to overcome his awkwardness around kids. Interrupting their outing wasn't happening. Especially not because Roger dictated it. Besides after weeks of procrastination, her neglected academic commitments chewed at her like a ravenous rat stripping meat off a bone.

"We're busy," she told Roger brusquely. "What's going on?"

"Brenda found papers in the shed."

"What kind?"

"You know, the yellow shed that survived the barn fire," he said impatiently.

"Not the fucking shed, Roger," she barked. "The papers. What kind of papers?"

"Oh right, well, it's a dark graphic novel," he said. "There are disturbing illustrations."

Something about drawings prickled her brain. "Who wrote it?" she asked.

There was a beat of silence. "That's the issue," he said. "It's typed."

Brenda was screeching in the background, and Roger covered the phone. A mumbled conversation ensued before he returned.

"Brenda is positive the writing is reflective of desires. I'm dubious because of the accompanying illustrations."

"Okay, scan and email it to me," she said.

"Sam," Roger lowered his voice, "Brenda's distressed. She's afraid Jordan is the author."

After their first interview with the twins, Reece had joked that Jordan could ink inmates in prison. It made sense he was the illustrator, but Sam didn't consider it a big deal. Creepy teenagers wrote creepy stories. Who cared?

"Where are the kids now?" she asked.

"Jennifer is here with us. Jordanna's with a friend, and we don't know where Jordan is." Roger paused. "There's something else."

She waited but he didn't continue. "Am I expected to guess?"

"Brenda's having flashbacks of the afternoon Graham died. They're distorted and confused, but I might be able to help her back at the office. Can you come? I was hoping you could stay with Jennifer. Brenda's afraid to leave her alone."

She could grab her car and drive out to the farm rather than returning to the library. But her mountain of schoolwork lurked like a predator. On the other hand, if she could end this case, she'd have time to focus on her studies. Jennifer could hold the key to unravelling aspects of the case, and Sam wanted to speak with her alone.

She jumped off the streetcar at Sumach Street. "I'll be there in forty minutes."

While she jogged toward her building, she tried to decide whether to text Reece. He'd want to meet her, which would ruin his outing with Lisa and Kira. But he'd be angry if she went alone. With a nod, she thought of a decent compromise.

Instead of going to the back parking lot, she trotted into the building and up the three flights to the loft. She retrieved her gun, checked the clip, and strapped on the new ankle holster Reece had given her. Carrying the Glock was a reasonable precaution after what had happened in the barn. After a quick peek to confirm she had her possession licence, she took the stairs two at a time to the back parking lot.

The drive was pleasant, but her thoughts kept drifting across the coalescing stresses of her PhD. She needed to nail down a new research question and redesign the premise statement for her thesis. The subject had to be unique, relatable, and something she'd embrace because of the arduous research the dissertation necessitated. She considered options. Nothing distinctive came to mind. Not a single idea.

In the crystal blue sky, the sun was a shimmering yellow ball, and there was a warm breeze from the open car windows. Along the side of the highway, wildflowers bloomed, and, when she exited onto the country road, she spied chubby cows munching new grass in pretty pastures. There was a whiff of manure in the air, and tractors bumped along the fields that lined the road. Spring was in full swing. She wished she could enjoy it rather than fretting over life's mundane problems like the cost of her

PhD studies and her limited progress... And who killed Graham Harris and tried to poison Reece and set her on fire.

Roger and Brenda were waiting on the front porch and stood when she exited the car. Brenda's face was puffy and her nose was bright red. She had a moist tissue in one hand and was clenching Roger's upper arm with her other.

Much to Sam's dismay, Brenda threw herself into her arms. Roger strolled over and pulled her off, tucking Brenda under the protection of his arm.

"The story's on the porch." He led Brenda back up the porch stairs. "We didn't want Jennifer to know about it. She's inside." He plucked a sheaf of paper from a decrepit table and handed it to Sam.

She sat on one of the rickety wicker chairs and perused a few pages. She could feel Roger and Brenda's eyes drilling into her as she read.

The graphic violence and hideous images made reading the text difficult to stomach. This wasn't creepy writing by a creepy teenager. Clinically speaking, it depicted a disturbed mind fixated on torture and murder. The paragraph that described shoving a stun gun up a woman's vagina was so gruesome that Sam had to stop reading. Living under the same roof as the author explained Brenda's hysteria.

"It's a sad attempt at horror or perhaps a dark, graphic novel," Roger proclaimed with confidence, squeezing Brenda's shoulder. "No reason to overreact. Cool heads need to prevail."

Sam's irritation ratcheted up a notch. "When you review it in conjunction with Graham's murder, the tortured cat, and the attempt on Reece's life and mine, the logical hypothesis is mental illness. Antisocial personality disorder, if I took a stab in the dark."

"Well, now," he sputtered, "let's not get ahead of ourselves."

"This isn't gratuitous violence, Roger," she snapped. "It's a well-conceived, practical guide to torture and homicide. It's terrifying to think an eighteen-year-old created this." She tossed the papers onto the table.

Brenda's voice fluttered with panic when she shrieked, "It has to be Jordan." Her eyes were wide with fear. "What the hell am I going to do? I can't stay here! The girls can't stay here! Did you read the piece about cutting off the woman's nipples?" Brenda burst into tears.

Roger held her close against his chest and made soothing noises in her ear.

When she'd calmed down a bit, he said to Sam, "The day Graham died, Brenda remembers finding me in the house and asking me to leave. After I left, Jordan stormed into the basement and confronted his father. That's all, she can't see the rest."

Roger was now shamelessly admitting he'd entered the house and lied throughout the investigation. Sam closed her eyes and tried to focus on the matter at hand instead of giving in to her urge to throttle him.

Brenda was wiping the soggy tissue across her nose. She made a strange growling noise deep in her throat. When she looked up at Sam, the frightened expression that she'd worn only a second earlier had changed. Brenda's face was a hard mask of fury. "Jordan can't stay here. I'll kill him myself if he comes near me or the girls."

The suddenness of Brenda's shift from fear to rage disturbed Sam, and she raised her eyebrow at Roger.

He hurried to say, "Look, we need to figure out what happened the afternoon Graham died. I think hypnosis may open Brenda's mind and uncover the repressed memories. Would her testimony against Jordan be sufficient for the police to charge him?"

Sam shrugged. "It depends on what she remembers and if there's any way of corroborating it with physical evidence." Her cell rang and she glanced at the caller ID. Reece. She'd call him back. "I'll speak with Jennifer first and then Jordanna."

"Jenny's inside," Brenda said. "I told her you were coming and she seemed relieved. My sense is she knows something and is afraid to tell. Jordanna's at a girlfriend's house. I can call and have her come home, she took Graham's car."

Sam checked the time. "I'm concerned about where Jordan is and when he's coming home." The weight of the gun on her ankle was a small comfort. "I can handle him. So long as he doesn't suspect you're regaining your memories or that you have these papers."

"No one knows. The memories started coming in flashes after I read that." She pointed at the sheaf of papers. "I found it this afternoon when I was in the shed looking for the pruning shears. He'd taped it under the potting bench. I wouldn't have seen it except I dropped the shears and hit my head on the shelf. That loosened the tape and the plastic folder fell." She shuddered. "I wish I hadn't opened it."

Sam gazed at the house. "Do you keep any weapons? A hunting rifle or a shotgun?"

Brenda shook her head.

"What should we do with this?" Roger picked up the sheets of paper and bent to grab the plastic envelope.

"Don't touch it!" Sam hollered and he dropped his hand.

They'd handled the stack of papers too much but there might be viable prints on the plastic folder.

She turned to Brenda. "Can you get a large freezer bag?"

When she returned with the sack, Sam picked the plastic cover up by the corner and tucked it into the bag. In the event Jordan arrived, she'd rather the evidence not be available for him to find and destroy.

She handed the freezer bag to Roger. "Take it with you, I'll talk with Jennifer, and we'll meet you back at your house."

"What about Jordanna?" Brenda asked sharply.

"Wait half an hour, call her, and tell her to come home," Sam said. "Don't mention I'm here. I'll deal with it when she arrives." She held Brenda's eyes. "You need to act normal. Cheerful, even. It's imperative she doesn't call her brother and tell him something's wrong."

Brenda was clutching Roger's arm in a death grip and he was wincing.

"Get in the car," he told her and kissed her cheek. "I'll be right there."

After she was out of earshot, he took Sam's hand. "We need to talk. Lisa told me she and Reece had an honest discussion. I'm hoping we can do the same."

She pulled her hand from his grasp. "Not now."

Sadness touched his eyes. "I wasn't the father of Abigail's baby. I sent Talia the DNA results. She arranged a video chat from her base overseas. We're good, Sam, and I want us to work out our issues, too." He sighed. "The things you said about me are true. Anger over the past has taken over my life. Veronica and I spoke last night. I want to fix the relationships I've destroyed and am going to see my sister. Please, give me one more chance."

Lisa had already told her Roger wasn't the father, but she hadn't believed it. The test confirmed it, and Sam was glad they could put that piece behind them.

"We'll talk," she promised. "But I'm not sure we can repair the damage. You've lied to me throughout this investigation and I don't understand why."

He lowered his eyes with another deep sigh. "Because I'm in love with Brenda. I referred her to another psychiatrist because of my feelings. I didn't want you to judge me, so I lied." He gazed at Brenda sitting in the car. "The day Graham died, I heard someone yelling at her in the basement," he said. "I thought he hit her. I picked up a pipe from the yard and went into the house." He swallowed hard. "I considered killing him."

"Why? Why didn't you just take Brenda and leave?"

"Because I overheard him threatening to lodge a complaint with the College of Physicians," he said.

A second complaint would cost him his medical licence and destroy his reputation as a self-help expert. A hard knot formed in Sam's stomach.

"Did you kill him?" she asked.

He looked off into the distance, avoiding her eyes. "I went down the stairs and into the cellar but I didn't touch Graham. He didn't even know I was there. Brenda came around the alcove from the laundry room and caught me standing at the bottom of the stairs in the water. We went up to the kitchen before Graham saw me. She was crying but she said Graham struck Jordan, not her. Upstairs, we talked for a few minutes and she told me she was done. She loved me and she was leaving her husband. I offered to wait, but she told me to go, that she'd pack and follow me in her car."

Sam thought about it. "While you and Brenda were talking in the kitchen, did you hear anything from the basement?"

He nodded and held her eyes. "Metal hitting metal. But Brenda and I only talked for a few minutes. I... I left her there." His eyes drifted off hers and he picked at the pleat in his trousers. "Graham was alive when I left," he said softly.

"You thought Brenda killed him after you left."

He cleared his throat and looked up at her. "I told her that money wasn't important. We'd be fine without her proceeds from the sale. I told her that I'd take care of her." He paused and then hesitantly added, "I just don't know. She was so upset."

"Did she kill him?"

"We've talked about it. I don't believe she is capable of such a heinous crime. She wouldn't drown him in sewage." He hung his head. "But then I began to have doubts because of the catatonia and episodic amnesia. If the violence of the argument had triggered a psychotic break... well, in that case, I can't say with any medical certainty what she'd be capable of."

He looked up at her with tears in his eyes. "I had to protect her," he said. "The trouble with Graham was because of me. I love her. I want to marry her, if she'll have me. I'm so sorry. I should have trusted you and Reece and told you the truth."

Sam didn't know what to think. He'd lied, and he and Brenda both had motive, opportunity, and means.

"If she did kill him, will hypnosis expose that?" she asked.

"Maybe. She's agreed to have the session witnessed and recorded. If it incriminates her, she's willing to face the consequences."

"Okay," Sam said with an exhale. "We'll talk later." She turned for the house.

His voice called her back. "Be careful," he said. "Brenda's fragile and I need her to remain calm for the hypnosis so I underplayed how concerned I am about that grisly story." He shuddered and wrapped his arms around his body. "Sam, the author is a psychopath."

She nodded. "I know."

"If it's Jordan, if he comes home and finds you with Jennifer, you'll be at serious risk. Do you have your gun?"

"Yup."

Relief flooded Roger's face and he squeezed her shoulder. "Thank God. Whatever you do, don't let Jennifer out of your sight."

She shrugged out of his grasp. "We'll meet you in the city in a couple of hours."

After Roger and Brenda drove away, Sam knocked on the door and poked in her head. "Jennifer? It's Sam McNamara."

"In here."

Sam followed her voice to the kitchen. The back door was open, and the screen door had fallen off the top hinge. It sagged against the wall and flies were enjoying free access to the house. Jennifer was sitting on a ladder back chair at a table, facing the open door. A half glass of milk was in front of her, and a plate with chocolate crumbs.

Sam took the seat across from her. "I hear you want to talk to me."

"It's about my brother." She ran her fork through the crumbs on her plate. "He scares me."

"Why's that?"

"Sometimes," her voice caught, "he comes into my room at night."

A cold shiver of disgust ran down Sam's back. "Does he touch you?"

She shook her head. "Not like that. He gets in bed with me. He asks for a little cuddle. That's how he knew I started having accidents at night. He teases and bullies me."

Terror and emotional turmoil explained the loss of bladder control, but Sam left that discussion for another time. "Have you told your stepmother about your brother's nightly visits?"

"No, Brenda would confront Jordan and he'd be angry. He killed Midnight when I told him I didn't like him in bed with me. Then—" She choked on tears and hung her head.

Sam reached across the table and took her hand. "It's okay. You're safe now, I promise."

Long hair fell in a sheet across her face and her thin shoulders shook. "I think," she paused and sucked on her upper lip, "I think he hurt my mom."

"Why? Did Caitlyn know about your troubles?"

"She was angry."

A strange expression crossed her face, but Sam couldn't put her finger on it. Trying to force kids to talk by hammering them with questions never worked well. She waited out the silence.

After a few minutes, Jennifer said, "I told her last year, and Mom went to the school. Jordan went to see her the next day and beat her up. He told her he'd kill her if she interfered in his life again. She put lots of stuff in her house so he couldn't hurt her. She said I was safe there, but Dad wouldn't let me live with her." Her lips clamped together and she ran her finger through a streak of icing on the plate.

Caitlyn's house construction began before the visit to the school, and the level of security was overkill if the only threat was her teenage son. Then again, she probably hadn't told her daughter about her cybercrimes, and Jennifer had drawn her own conclusions.

"If your mom was that scared, what makes you think she saw your brother recently?" Sam asked.

"Because, two weeks ago, I told her he was still coming into my room." Tears dripped down her cheeks. "Mom called him. Jordan went to her house and convinced her I was a liar. He told her I killed Grandma."

Her eyes focused on Sam's face. "I didn't. Honest. He told me Mom was mad because she wouldn't have taken the blame if she'd known it had been me. Everything he said made sense. Like, the police wouldn't have arrested me because I was too young. Mom was angry over all the time she spent in prison. I believed him. You know, that she didn't want to see me."

"I don't understand. If your mother didn't kill your grandmother, who did?"

"Jordan."

"Why?" Sam asked.

Jennifer shrugged. "I don't know. I was in the other room. They were arguing."

"Where was Jordanna?"

"With me. We didn't see what happened. When we heard screaming, we ran out but Grandma was already dead. My mom was out. When she got back, she told us to say Grandma attacked me. We had to rehearse the story. Mom picked up the knife and put blood on her hand and her clothes. She told my brother to change. She burned his clothes before she called the cops and took the blame."

Jordan had been twelve. The *Youth Criminal Justice Act* dictated that the court could sentence youths over the age of twelve but under the age of eighteen as adults under certain conditions.

That was why Caitlyn had pled guilty to manslaughter rather than claiming self-defence. It was why she hadn't appealed the harshness of the sentence or applied for early parole. To protect her twelve-year-old son, it was imperative there be no major investigation. A full confession eliminated the need for ironclad evidence. But the timeline didn't add up.

"Jenny, you told us the other day you warned Caitlyn that the police had her address. She must have been okay when you talked to her."

Jennifer hung her head. "But I didn't talk to her. The day after Jordan told me my mother hated me, I went over. Mom wasn't there. I had the access codes and a key. All her stuff was gone. When Roger said you had Mom's address, I called but she didn't pick up. I left a message that you were coming. She never called back. My mother wouldn't leave without telling me. No matter what."

"How about your sister?" Sam asked. "Have you talked to her about any of this?"

"Jordanna's scared, too. She tried to talk to you in the city, but Jordan followed her to your office." A sob caught in her throat. "We think he killed our dad."

"Why?"

"He was in the cellar the morning Dad died. I asked him what he was doing and he got mad. Then the sump-pump stopped working and the septic system backed up through the basement drain."

That made no sense, but Sam couldn't grab hold of the incongruity. It hovered just outside her conscious thought, just beyond her reach.

Jennifer must have recognized doubt on her face because she added, "When we were waiting for the bus, he said the old man should have given him what he wanted. He wanted to live in the city, but Dad made us leave because of Jordan."

"Do you know why?"

She slouched lower in her seat. "Jordan did something bad to a girl who lived on our street. Brenda gave her money and tried to make it right with the mother so we didn't have to move, but Dad said we couldn't trust them not to say anything if we stayed. Brenda wanted to sell the farm and go back to Toronto. Jordan said if Mom and Dad were dead, Brenda could sell, and we could live with her in the city."

Jordan was eighteen and free to move out. According to the terms of Graham's will, the three kids shared in the proceeds from the sale. Jordan would have his own money, and a large sum of it. He didn't need to kill Caitlyn to avoid having to live with her, but he'd have to kill his father to get his hands on the inheritance.

Sam grasped the discrepancy that troubled her. Reece had confirmed with the school that on the day of the murder Jordan had taken the morning bus, attended all his classes, and was with the football team until he came home and discovered Roger in the yard. If Jordan intended to electrocute his father, why would he sabotage the sump-pump and the septic in the morning and disappear to school? If his father had attempted the repairs in the morning, Jordan wouldn't be on-site to complete his murderous plan. Something wasn't adding up.

Before Sam could challenge her, Jennifer asked, "What happens now?"

"Now we leave," Sam said. "You can stay with Roger until the police sort things out. Gather up what you want to bring, okay?"

Jennifer's eyes snapped to something over Sam's shoulder. Sam was about to turn when there was a blinding pain in the back of her head. She fell face-first to the tabletop and tried to stand. Her brain refused to send the signal to her legs. Her chair fell to the side with a clatter.

The last thing she was aware of was a whistling sound and a gush of air on the back of her neck.

CHAPTER THIRTY-FOUR

REECE

OFFICIAL VEHICLES CROWDED Caitlyn's cul-de-sac and people loitered on their lawns with worried expressions as they strained to see what was going on. Reece's heart dropped when he passed the coroner's van.

He parked behind a forensic identification vehicle. When he got out of the car, a man in a hooded white jumpsuit and blue gloves turned to face him.

"This is a restricted site."

"Reece Hash, here for Detective Romero."

The man waved over a uniformed constable. "Hash for Romero. Wanna radio him for me?"

The officer turned away and spoke into his radio. He turned back and waved at Reece to join him. "Follow me and don't move from my path. Understood?"

Reece nodded and carefully followed the officer through the side gate and along the fence line until they came to the yard's back gate, which opened to the Boyd Conservation Area.

About fifty metres into the nature park, Romero was approaching, pulling off a pair of latex gloves. He nodded to his colleague. "Thanks, Officer."

When they were alone, Reece asked, "Where is she?"

Romero gestured over his shoulder. "Off the Humber River. The perp dumped her in a shallow grave about a hundred metres from her backyard. A jogger's dog uncovered her this morning."

"How long has she been dead?"

"A week at least. The coroner will know more when he gets her on the table."

Caitlyn couldn't have started the fire that nearly killed Sam. She was already dead. Reece glanced over his shoulder at the house. "Was she killed where you found her?"

Romero shook his head. "No, not enough blood. We suspect the perp attacked her in the house, transported the body, and returned to clean up."

"That would be why the place smelled of bleach the other day," Reece said. "Cause of death?"

"The killer gutted her and cut her throat. Messy and amateurish. York Regional Police will know more after the postmortem."

"Any evidence?"

"Not my case. The homicide took place in York's jurisdiction. Caitlyn's cybercrimes fall under Toronto, which is why I'm here. All I can tell you is that this isn't the work of organized crime."

Reece agreed. The mob wouldn't bother moving the body, and the kill would be clean. If they'd wanted information, there would be signs of torture. The evisceration didn't fit. Neither did Romero's description of the murder as amateurish.

A voice behind Reece called out, "Look who it is. You keep turning up at the most opportune times, Mr. Hash."

Reece turned to find Alston strolling toward him. "I'm investigating Graham Harris's death. You know that, Detective."

Alston was studying him with no expression. "So you think this has something to do with the Harris homicide. Enlighten me."

"Someone disembowelled the Harris cat," Reece said. "Now, I haven't seen the wounds on Caitlyn Franklyn, but I doubt it's a coincidence her perpetrator mimicked that event. He practised on the cat. He killed Graham Harris and murdered Graham's ex-wife. When did cops give up on victim profiling?"

Alston raised an eyebrow. "What makes you think the perp is male?"

"The killer moved the body." Reece waved at the house. "There are no tracks or divots in the grass leading from the house to the back gate, meaning someone carried Caitlyn into the woods."

Alston glanced behind his shoulder and then looked back at the house. "There also isn't a wheelbarrow or wagon anywhere around the property and we've interviewed the neighbours. They all have locked sheds and garages, as well as security lights. It's unlikely someone could access their equipment without drawing attention." He sighed. "Could drag her on a tarp or blanket."

It surprised Reece that Alston seemed to be agreeing with him, but Reece doubted that the murderer dragged the body—there would be impressions in the ground because the spring grass was wet and loose.

"Jennifer said her brother killed the cat," he told Alston. "I think Jordan Harris killed his father, poisoned me, and tried to murder Sam. I think he killed his mother too."

"Three witnesses put Jordan Harris at a Blue Jays game the afternoon the barn caught fire," Alston replied.

Reece put his hands on his hips. "Don't be stupid. If the witnesses putting Jordan at the game were his friends, they lied. He could easily have made his way back to Vaughan before Sam arrived at the farm." He immediately regretted calling Alston stupid. The man wasn't going to offer up details on Caitlyn's murder if Reece kept antagonizing him.

Before he could think of something to say to defuse the tension, Alston demanded, "What evidence do you have? In fact, what are you even doing here? This is an official crime scene."

Romero stepped between them. "Enough. I called Reece. If you're pissed, blame me."

A forensic technician and an officer stopped to speak with Alston before he could reply. The tech handed him an evidence bag and the cop whispered something. When they completed their conversation, the detective's eyes followed the tech to where yellow tape cordoned off the crime scene. In preparation for the loss of sunlight, cops were setting up lights.

Reece checked his watch. It was later than he'd realized. Sam and Lisa had tickets to a play in a couple of hours, but it was strange she wasn't calling him back. Maybe she'd decided to go straight from the library to Lisa's house.

Reece felt Alston's eyes on him and looked up. The detective's face was grim.

"Jordan Harris is a big guy, I'll give you that," Alston said. "But Caitlyn was about one-twenty. Could he cart that much dead weight alone?"

Reece shrugged, curious over Alston's change of attitude. "If he took breaks. The kid is strong and in excellent physical condition because of football." He wondered what the technician had brought to Alston's attention a minute earlier.

"You've spent time with him," Alston said. "Any theory on why an eighteen-year-old kid is killing off his family? Is he capable, in your opinion?"

"Jordan's an angry kid," Reece said. "Caitlyn embarrassed him in school last year. The brutality of both this crime and Graham's murder implies frenzied anger. A killer who lacked control and experience. There was trauma in his childhood—you know Caitlyn killed her mother in front of the children. Graham had a restraining order against her."

"What about the girl?"

"Jordanna?"

Alston nodded curtly.

Reece frowned. "How could Jordanna move a hundred and twenty pounds of dead weight?"

Alston took a plastic evidence bag from his pocket. "Recognize this?"

It was a gold lapel pin with a crest of a lion's head.

"No. Should I?"

"It's an award that's presented to students at the secondary school the twins attend," Alston said. "We found it about ten metres from the river bank on a piece of white fabric."

"Have you called the school for a list of recipients?"

"An officer just got off the phone with them. Jordan won MVP last season. Jordanna received one for a cheerleading routine she choreographed that placed the squad in the city finals."

Before Reece could respond, his cell rang. Roger. "Hold on, I need to take this."

He moved five paces from the other men and answered.

"Reece, Roger. I'm here with Brenda. We're waiting for Sam to bring Jennifer and Jordanna but she hasn't arrived and I can't reach her or the girls." Roger filled him in on the afternoon events, concluding by saying, "I'm worried something's wrong."

A sensation of cold fear gripped Reece's heart as his eyes strayed to the evidence bag in Alston's hand. "I'm with the police now. We'll head over there."

Alston's face darkened as Reece explained the situation. While Reece spoke to Alston and Romero, he dialled Sam's cell. It went to voice mail. He immediately sent a text and received no response. He tried not to overreact—maybe her phone battery had died again, or she'd left her cell in the car. He quickly opened the GPS tracking app on his phone and traced her car to the Harris farm. He called the farm. No one answered.

"I can't reach Sam," he said to the two detectives and swallowed hard. "Her car is still at the Harris farm."

"I'll grab a unit." Alston clamped his hand on Reece's shoulder. "I'm not going to try and order you to stay put, but if you arrive before us, you stand down. Understood?"

Reece didn't agree or disagree.

Alston jogged over to an officer. The two men spoke for a moment and then hastened to a cruiser parked at the bottom of Caitlyn's driveway.

Romero's eyes met Reece's. He moved to let Reece pass. For the first time since they'd met, Romero didn't have a snappy parting comment.

CHAPTER THIRTY-FIVE

SAM

WITH THE RESURGENCE of consciousness came terror. Keeping her eyes shut, Sam waited for the disorientation to fade and for her faculties to sharpen. A vicious, barbed pain surfaced in her wrists, and the back of her head throbbed in harmony with her increased heart rate. She concentrated on gaining mental acuity. The spiralling kaleidoscope of colours slowly stopped dancing against her eyelids.

She opened them a slit. Shadows bobbed across the floor. Uneven light bounced on the walls—a flashlight or a halogen lantern. No sound but she sensed she wasn't alone. On a visceral level, she grasped the need for stillness and fought the urge to scream and thrash against her restraints.

She was sitting on a hard surface with her back pressed against something. A wall maybe. Her knees were to her chin, forcing her bent thighs against her chest. Coarse rope bound her crossed wrists tight behind her back. The binding on her hands snaked beneath her buttocks and secured her ankles to her wrists. There was no give to the rope tethering her wrists and ankles. Attempting to straighten her legs or to shift them to the side pulled on the rope, forcing her arms down until her shoulders shrieked in misery under the pressure. The taut rope that trussed her arms to her legs wedged itself between her butt cheeks.

Biting her lip to silence her moan of agony, she pushed her ankles as close to her butt as she could in order to slacken the rope that connected her ankles and wrists. Her shoulders relaxed slightly and the burning lessened. She slowed her heartbeat by inhaling in measured breaths. The acidic odour of scorched wood, mildew, and rot engulfed her. Extending the tips of her fingers, she felt the ground on which she sat. Moist and rough. Packed soil. The room was damp. She grazed the wall behind her with her fingertips. Unfinished lumber.

Images collided, orbiting her conscious mind but refusing to take logical form. She mentally retraced her steps during the day. She'd looked up psychogenic voice disorders at the library, but realized she'd forgotten the data stick with her PhD research. There had been something about hypnosis. But that didn't make sense. Her research had nothing to do with hypnotherapy.

Her memories were a jumbled mess and she was struggling to focus. The flashes of light she kept catching from her half-open eyes made the pain in her head worse. She was dizzy and the taste of copper in the back of her throat made her gag.

Breathe, just breathe, she thought and tried to slow her galloping heart.

An image of grazing cows materialized beneath her lids. Her memory solidified and took shape. She and Jennifer had been talking in the kitchen. She'd left her back to the door, a rookie mistake, and someone hit her. She hadn't seen the attacker, but

Jennifer had. Based on the expression Sam recalled, Jennifer knew the assailant.

Sam snapped back to the present when she heard a soft chuckling pierce the darkness. She opened her eyes and saw a light moving toward her. When she could make out her captor, she was too astonished to react.

"Look at you all surprised." The cheerful tone was in mocking contrast to the hard eyes that met hers. "And look what I found."

Sam stared at her gun in Jordanna's hand.

"We're going to play a game. First, we have to wait for someone. Wanna guess who?"

"Jordan," Sam mumbled. Her mouth felt like cotton. "Where's Jennifer?"

Jordanna giggled. "Around."

A phone rang. It was her ringtone.

"Your blue-eyed baby has called five times. Aren't you allowed out by yourself?" Jordanna walked away and disappeared into the gloom.

The sudden glare of fluorescent light caused a piercing pain in Sam's head. Her stomach cramped and vomit filled her mouth. Choking, she spit it out and exhaled hard through her nose to clear the acid burning her sinuses.

Jordanna laughed and strolled back to face her. She waved the cell phone enticingly in front of Sam's face and gripped the gun in her other hand. "Interrupting is so rude. Let's lose the battery."

The dead phone land on the floor about six feet from Sam. For the first time, she felt grateful that Reece was overprotective. When she didn't reply, he'd track her cell, but how long had she been here and where was she? She'd never reviewed the app and didn't know if the software showed the last known location of a disabled device.

Her eyes had adjusted to the bright light that filled the space from the overhead fixture. She snuck surreptitious peeks around the room as her heartbeat thundered in her ears and she fought to control her mounting fear. There was a potting bench littered with cracked pottery and dead plants. Long-handled tools leaned against the bench. The room was about five hundred square feet without windows. The door was yellow. She was in the shed behind the stone farmhouse. That's why she smelled char. It was from the incinerated barn. She was still on the Harris property.

The door swung open, clanking against the side of the shed.

Jordan froze in the doorway, his eyes wide with shock when he saw Sam. "Oh my God," he whispered. "What's she doing here?"

"Close the door. You weren't raised in a barn," Jordanna said in a scolding tone.

Very slowly, he shut the door. He took a step toward his sister. "You have to let her go. You can't do this."

Jordanna ignored him. "You're just in time to play a life or death type game. Now, Sam has agreed to be *it*. The rules are simple. Whoever wins survives. Fun, eh?"

"No." The word was a moan of despair. Jordan crossed the room but stopped when he saw the gun in his sister's hand.

"In for a penny, in for a pound." Jordanna glanced at Sam. "That's the saying, right?"

Jordan took another hesitant step forward. "Give me the gun," he said.

His sister swatted his outstretched hand away. "Gimme, gimme never gets." Her voice deepened and became menacing. "We'll put her in her car, drive back to the city, and make it look like suicide."

"You're going to have to come up with something better," Sam rushed to say. "No one will believe I committed suicide. Brenda and Roger were here and know I was with Jennifer." She tried to keep her tone measured and reasonable but heard an edge of hysteria in the high pitch of her voice. "When we don't meet them, they'll know we're still here. Where's Jennifer? What did you do to her?"

She pressed her ankles against her butt to loosen the tension on the rope and rotated her hands, trying to slacken the bindings around her wrist. Realizing again that she couldn't move her arms created a primal wave of panic. She bit hard on her lip to keep from screaming.

"She's right," Jordan said rapidly. "Let her go. You haven't done anything. We can walk away from this." His voice was persuasive and urgent.

A glimmer of hope shone through Sam's terror. If Jordan held the power in the twins' relationship, he'd be able to convince his sister to let her go.

Jordanna put her hand on her hip, and her authority over her brother was suddenly evident in the insolent gesture. Sam's heart sank. Jordanna was the stronger sibling.

"We can't explain any of this." Jordanna waved the gun around and Sam cringed against the wall. "We can't explain

Mother, we can't explain Father. Unless..." She clenched her fist and cold, dead eyes scrutinized her brother. "You want to tell the truth?"

"We need help." Jordan sounded whiny rather than influential now. He reached for the gun again.

His sister sidestepped his grasp, and he stuffed his hand into his back pocket.

"I can help you," Sam desperately promised over the deafening beat of her heart in her ears. "This doesn't have to end badly for anyone. Tell me what you need and let me help you."

Completely ignoring her, Jordanna licked her lips and smiled at her brother. "Hey, I know. You could take one for the team," she said in a pleasant tone. "What do you say?"

His voice trembled when he said, "I didn't kill anyone." He edged away from his sister and punched his fist against the side of his thigh. "I tried, Jordanna. I did everything you said. When you called from Caitlyn's house, I came. I helped you."

"I'm not suggesting you talk to the police." She cocked her head to the side, and regarded him coyly. "That's not the object of the game."

Keep them talking, keep them bickering.

"Who killed Graham?" Sam broke in, pausing in her attempts to loosen the ropes when Jordanna glanced at her.

"What do you think, brother dearest? Should we satiate her curiosity?"

He lunged for the gun.

Jordanna easily avoided him. Anger flooded her face. "Get on the floor!" she demanded, aiming the weapon at his head.

Jordan raised his left hand in submission and slouched to the ground beside Sam, so close their shoulders touched. He ran his fingers through his hair with his left hand and shoved something behind her back with his right. His eyes never left his sister's face.

The object fell between the wall and her back, but Sam knew what it was the second her fingers found it. A small pocketknife, maybe four inches in length. What she didn't know was how she could finagle the task of releasing the blade. Her wrists crossed over each other and she couldn't bring her hands together.

"I went to my room that afternoon," Jordan said. "There was yelling from the basement. Jordanna came home and went downstairs. When she didn't come back, I followed. Brenda was on the stairs zoning and Dad was dead." He swallowed. "I ran upstairs, called 911, and waited outside." He shuddered and self-consciously brushed a tear off his cheek.

"Crying?" Jordanna said with contempt. "You're *crying* over that son of a bitch. You are such a fucking loser. If you'd manned up, none of this would have happened." Her face became a mask of fury. "This is your fault. All of it!" she screamed.

Sam had the closed pocketknife between the middle and index fingers of her left hand. With her thumbnail, she tried to push out the blade. Her fingers grew clumsy with panic. It took her a second to realize she had it upside down. She could feel the pivot and locking mechanism. She had to flip it and try to pull the tip of the blade outward from the casing. If she could keep them talking, she might have enough time.

"You killed your father," Sam said to Jordanna. "Why?"

"I did not!" Jordanna retorted. "I wouldn't be sloshing around in raw sewage like an animal," she said with a grimace.

She paced back and forth in front of them, but the gun never wavered. If anything, her rage had made her more focused. "I was handling things until Caitlyn got involved. I told her to stay away from Jenny, but the stupid bitch didn't listen."

"Is Caitlyn dead?" Sam asked.

Much to her horror, the knife dropped. Sam shoved her butt against the wall in a feeble effort to silence the noise but the metal scraped against the wall.

Jordan's eyes flickered to her side and he screeched, "Yes!"

His sister frowned and suspicious eyes drilled into Sam's face.

Sam sat still and held the girl's steady gaze.

After a few seconds that felt like hours to Sam, Jordanna turned around and took two steps away from them.

Jordan slumped closer to Sam's side and flicked the knife with the end of his finger. "I buried Caitlyn in the conservation area behind her house," he said.

Sam grasped the knife and felt the edge with the tip of her thumb, located what she thought was the right end, and positioned it between her fingers.

Spinning around to face them, Jordanna said in a haughty tone, "Don't bother asking. I didn't kill her either. Well," she paused and shrugged her shoulders with a sigh of displeasure. "I had to finish the job, but I didn't plan to kill her. The whole thing ended up much too messy for my taste. At least that sterile home was a breeze to clean. No irritating stains on carpets or fabric. Still, bleach is horrible for your nails." She glared at her brother. "Because you bought bargain basement gloves, I broke two nails."

If it hadn't been Jordan or Jordanna, it could only have been one other person. Sam felt a wave of overwhelming sadness. "Jennifer. Why?"

"Ever since Caitlyn got out of jail, Jennifer spent the night once a week," Jordan said. "Great-aunt Rachel set it up in secret and wanted Jordanna and me to go, too. She quoted this bible verse and told us we wouldn't reach the kingdom of heaven if we dishonoured our mother."

Jordanna rolled her eyes, an expression of exaggerated annoyance on her face. "*Do not forsake your mother's teaching. Bind them upon your heart forever.* Blah, blah, blah. Can you believe that religious old bitch thinks everyone's a child of God? She didn't recognize the devil when she stood beside her. What a joke."

"I threatened to tell Dad," Jordan continued. "Jenny went and told Caitlyn awful stuff about me. Stuff that wasn't true and then she showed at the school and Mrs. Alistair got all up in my shit and told lies." He stared accusingly at his sister. "I couldn't handle Jenny. You said you'd take care of it."

"You did rape that girl outside the school. Mrs. Alistair didn't lie about that," Jordanna commented. "And who helped you out of that mess, hum? I had to give Steve a blowjob to get him to hack their computer. Thank God that fat neighbour identified Caitlyn when he saw me poison the dog. That was a lucky break."

She leaned down and poked a manicured nail into her brother's shoulder. "It was because of the dog that Mr. Alistair freaked out on Daddy and nearly got himself arrested. The police figured he was a nut case and a liar. I managed to discredit everything the Alistairs said about you. Did you thank me? No, of course not. I protect you and I protect Jennifer." She stepped back and studied him with disapproval.

"I've done lots to keep Jenny safe," Jordan sputtered.

Jordanna laughed at him. "Like what, nearly getting her arrested after she killed Daddy? If you had talked Daddy out of sending Jenny to a shrink, she wouldn't have had to kill him at all."

"I stopped those tests that Roger was doing. I told Dad that Brenda was sleeping with Roger," Jordan argued.

"Daddy made an appointment with an adolescent psychiatrist the school recommended!" Jordanna shouted.

"Ask Jenny why she had to play with that English teacher! When Jenny asked for my drawings, I didn't know about the sick shit she was writing." There was a defeated slump to Jordan's shoulders now. "She didn't need to kill Dad. She could have tricked any shrink he sent her to."

"You're her big brother. It's your job to protect her. Everything pointed to Roger killing Dad. All we had to do was get them to back off." She waved the gun at Sam. "Once everyone thought Caitlyn poisoned the Alistair's dog, killing Reece should have been a breeze," she said in aggravation. "I got him out of the office, just like I promised Jennifer I would. You raced in and stopped Jenny before she put enough antifreeze in his drink."

Jordanna threw a nasty look Sam's way and then glared at her brother. "And where were you when Jenny lit the barn on fire? When I got home, Reece was already there. Jenny had to try to delay him long enough for me to get inside and drag Sam further into the flames before her blue-eyed baby saved her."

The blade required too much pressure to open. She'd have to nudge it, get her nail under the edge, and push up. It would cut her, but it was the only option. She needed time. She had to try to turn Jordan against his sister.

"You're innocent of murder," Sam said to him. "You probably saved Reece's life when you stopped Jennifer."

He scowled at his sister and nodded. "I didn't rape that girl either. She wanted it. It's not my fault she changed her mind."

Jordanna rolled her eyes. "What about that girl who lived down the street before we moved here?" She turned to Sam. "Brenda freaked out but Daddy said 'boys will be boys' and it was a misunderstanding." She laughed. "Not that he cared what happened to Jordan, but he was worried about his reputation if his son was labelled a rapist. Brenda borrowed money and compensated the girl behind Daddy's back, but we still had to move out to the boondocks because of Romeo over there."

Get the focus away from Jordan's crimes, a voice yelled through the chaotic thoughts circling Sam's mind. She concentrated on how to manipulate Jordan. The most important thing was to make him feel protected from prosecution. She had to get the topic back to murder.

"Why did you kill Caitlyn?" Sam asked Jordanna, gritting her teeth to hide the pain of the honed metal slicing through her thumbnail while she pushed against the blade, coaxing it open.

"I didn't kill her. Just like this afternoon, little sis called me. It's always me she calls." She waved the gun at her brother and uttered a frustrated sigh. "Jordan can't do anything right. We've covered for Jenny for years, but he freaked out over the cat."

"She blamed me," Jordan shouted. "Just like before. If you'd helped when I told you what I saw her do to Midnight, we could have stopped her. When I got to Caitlyn's place, I told you to call the cops. She was into illegal shit. We could have said we found her like that."

"Jordan," his sister said with a show of great patience, "we couldn't call the police. How would we explain it?"

Her attention shifted back to Sam. "Jenny had made such a mess of Mother." She shook her head in exasperation. "She was up to her elbows in blood."

The blade snapped open, and Sam rotated it against the rope. Once in place, the challenge was to apply enough pressure to score the heavy rope. She couldn't get a firm enough grip on the handle because of her fingers' limited mobility. The rope was thick. Sawing through it would take time, time Sam didn't think she had. Worse, the binding on her wrists was beginning to cut off the blood circulation to her hands. Her fingers were numb and tingled painfully.

There has to be another way, Sam thought in desperation. *Think.*

If Jordan didn't hold sufficient power to talk Jordanna out of killing her, Sam had to create dissonance between them and trigger Jordan's temper. Maybe he'd attack his sister. He might be able to disarm her.

"Why did Jennifer do it?" Sam asked Jordan.

Jordanna glared at her brother and answered for him. "Because Mother figured out Jennifer had killed our grandmother.

You see, Mom wasn't there when it happened. Mother had a little problem." Jordanna formed a needle out of her finger and mimed putting it in her arm. She rolled her eyes with a euphoric expression that mimicked a stoned drug addict.

"When she came back, she thought I did it," Jordan said.

Jordanna smiled at her brother. "I admit I helped her reach that conclusion. You had Grandma's blood all over you. All I had to do was clean up Jennifer before Mother got back."

"I pulled Jennifer off," Jordan shrieked. "I tried to stop it."

Jordanna shrugged. "I made up the story about crazy Grandma attacking Jennifer because the devil told her to, and you saved Jenny by killing her. You were Mom's favourite, and I knew she'd protect you."

"I warned you it was too dangerous to have Jennifer visit Caitlyn," Jordan said.

Jordanna gazed into the distance with a speculative expression. "It surprised me she wanted to spend time with her." She giggled. "Guess it makes sense now. She wanted to kill her."

"But you said *you* killed Caitlyn," Sam argued. "You made Jordan an accessory to murder by forcing him to help you *after* you killed your mother."

Jordanna's brow creased. "I slit her throat because she was making terrible noises. I put her out of her misery." Her mouth puckered with disgust. "If Jennifer hadn't tried to tear out her guts like she did to Midnight, we could have claimed we'd found her like that. But she figured everyone would blame Jordan."

Her attention focused on her brother. "You were becoming a problem, tiptoeing into her room at night. She told me all about it. All about the sick things you did to her under the cover of darkness."

"It wasn't me," he yelled. "Jenny's a liar and you know it. Before Caitlyn went to prison, she used to go into Jenny's room at night. Maybe she was still doing it, I dunno, but it was fucking sick! I was the only one trying to help Jenny."

Jordanna stormed over and smacked him across the side of the head with the butt of the gun. "I helped Jennifer! You made a mess out of everything." She raised the gun and brought it down on his shoulder.

Sam heard a crack and Jordan squealed. She cringed against the wall while Jordan submissively covered his head with his arm and whimpered. Any hope Sam had of Jordan overpowering his sister dissolved. He was the subservient partner, completely under the control of his twin. The realization that she was powerless to prevent her imminent death made Sam's bowels feel loose. She was going to die. Die at the hands of a demented teenager. The need to scream was so overpowering that she had to clamp her lips together. A groan of fear emanated from between her pressed lips.

Jordanna leaned down and shouted in her brother's face. "I'm the one who got Jenny out of the house after she killed Daddy." Her spittle sprayed Sam's cheek. "You called the police and hid upstairs!"

She straightened and kicked Jordan in the ribs with vicious force. "If I hadn't come home and found her hiding in the basement closet covered in sewage and wearing Daddy's rubber boots, she'd be in jail. I was the one who took her over to great-aunt Rachel's house and told that dotty old bitch Jennifer had been in her disgusting prayer room all afternoon."

She stomped across the room, standing with her back to them. After a moment, her shoulders relaxed and she returned to where they sat. Her face was calm and her voice was soft. "I love you, Jordan. I'm the only one." She crouched down and ran her hand across his cheek. "You don't want me to leave you, do you? Do you want to be all alone?"

He clasped her hand against his face and shook his head.

"Why do you have to make me so angry? You know I don't want to hurt you," she whispered. "I'm the only one who has ever understood you. Those girls, it wasn't your fault. I know that. They asked for it."

He nodded and smiled at her.

She stood. "I helped you and you want to help me, right?" She held out her hand.

Jordan took her hand and stood.

She tilted her head to the side. "Do you love me?" she asked softly.

"Yes, you know I do."

"Then you need to kill her."

In the harsh light, Sam saw the colour blanch from Jordan's face, but his head bobbed in agreement. "I will. I promise." He held out his hand. "Give me the gun," he said eagerly.

His sister's laughter was hard and mean when she dropped his hand. "Didn't I just say we can't trust you?"

"You can. I'll do it," he said speaking urgently.

She marched to the other side of the shed and grabbed a piece of rope from the gardening shelves. "Here." She threw the rope at him. "Strangle her."

"Jordanna—" he began.

She jutted out her hip and interrupted him. "Since *you* love me and *you* do everything to protect Jenny and me, *you* can get rid of this problem."

He stood holding the rope.

A tear leaked from the corner of Sam's eye. "You don't have to do this," she said to Jordan. "There's another way. Take my car."

Jordanna aimed the gun at his head. "Kill her. Now," she said coldly.

"Please," he whimpered and dropped the rope to the ground. "I can't do it."

Jordanna nodded. "I didn't think so." She sighed. "I'll kill her and tell the police you did it. All of it. By yourself."

He looked at Sam. His expression was sad and there were tears in his eyes. "I'm sorry," he whispered.

"Please, Jordan," Sam begged, unable to stop the tears that coursed down her face.

She couldn't give up. She had to think. There had to be a way to manipulate him. She didn't want to die trussed up on the dirty floor of a potting shed. The blood from the gash on her thumb made it difficult to hold the knife, but she was almost through the rope. If she only had a few more minutes, she'd be able to free her hands.

"It doesn't have to end like this," Sam said. "Think about it, Jordan. Do you want to spend the rest of your life in prison?" She turned to Jordanna. "You need help. You won't go to prison.

You'll get the help you need and so will Jennifer. Please, think about it."

Jordanna ignored her and stroked her brother's hair. "I'll say you killed Daddy and Mother. You threatened Jenny and me. You told us what you did to Mother and where you put her body."

She lifted his chin and gazed into his eyes. "Jenny and I are the only ones who have ever loved you," she said tenderly. "Dad didn't love you. Remember when he took that other boy's side when he was playing red rover with you and your football friends?"

Jordan's Adam apple bobbed in his throat as he swallowed. "He never practised with me after that," he murmured. "He never even went to my games."

Jordanna was nodding sympathetically. "It was so sad. Your own father didn't want anything to do with you. Without Jenny and me, you'll be all alone forever. If you do this, we'll be safe. That's what you want, right? You want to protect us. You want us to love you, don't you?"

"Yes." He grasped her hand, brought it to his lips, and kissed her palm. "I'll tell them anything you want."

She pulled her hand free from his grasp. "You play the game so poorly." She wiped her hand against her jeans. "Don't you see? The only way this will work is if you shoot Sam and I wrestle the gun away and shoot you in self-defence."

Confusion contorted his features. He took a step behind him, away from his sister. "What?"

Jordanna gazed at her twin with affection. "Jenny's right. You're a liability."

She raised the gun and shot her brother in the head.

CHAPTER THIRTY-SIX

REECE

SAM'S CAR WAS parked in front of the Harris farm. Reece raced into the old house, Alston calling after him to stop. A glass of milk and a plate were on the kitchen table. A chair was overturned. There was blood on the side of the table.

He flew down the stairs to the cellar. Empty. He leaped back up the stairs two at a time and stopped dead when he heard a shot. His eyes scanned the backyard. The burned-out barn. The yellow shed. He sprinted toward the shed with Alston right at his heels.

Flinging the door open, Reece charged inside and assessed the scene at lightning speed. Jordan dead on the ground, Sam lying on her side hog-tied, and Jordanna aiming a gun at Sam's head.

Reece felt detached as he rapidly ran through scenarios to predict responses and reactions. The first option was to tackle Jordanna, but she had the gun pointed at Sam. It could go off when he hit her. Sam would die. Yelling at Jordanna could distract her and she'd turn. He could charge her. Sam would live but Reece knew Jordanna would most likely shoot him before he covered the twenty feet between them.

Alston's breath was hot on Reece's neck. The detective shoved him aside, aiming his gun at Jordanna's back.

"Police!" he yelled, and the girl stiffened her back but her hand didn't flinch. The gun's ominous black eye remained aimed at the side of Sam's head.

"Drop the weapon and get to your knees," Alston ordered.

Jordanna didn't move, not even to glance over her shoulder.

"*Red rover, red rover, I call Sam on over,*" she sang, and the hair rose on Reece's arms.

"Jordanna, it's Reece Hash." He kept his tone expressionless. "We know Jordan killed your dad and Caitlyn. We can help you." He took a step toward her.

"*You'll be the first to play, then Reece another day.*" A trill of laughter. "I wish you'd worn that white blouse."

Reece took three long strides. Fifteen feet separated them. If she turned, she'd kill him.

"It wasn't supposed to be this way," she said in a lazy voice. "If it wasn't for Jordan, we wouldn't be here."

"Reece, find Jennifer," Sam shouted. "She killed Graham and Caitlyn. It wasn't Jordan."

"You're lying!" Jordanna screamed. "Jennifer didn't do anything."

"You can't protect her any longer," Sam said. "We can help Jennifer."

Reece detected panic and fear under the persuasive tone of her voice.

"Jordanna, you're all Jennifer has left," Sam continued. "The police are here. You know it's over. If you kill me, the police will kill you. You don't need to die. I understand why you've done this. Please, let me help you."

"You understand nothing!" she yelled, putting the palm of her left hand under the pistol grip. "It was all Jordan. My brother was going to kill you. I saved you. Tell them the truth!"

"They can see the truth," Sam said. "You're holding a gun on me. Let me help you."

From over Reece's shoulder, he heard Alston whispered, "Look."

When Reece turned, Alston nodded his head behind him, keeping his gun aimed at Jordanna's back. A uniformed officer stood in the doorway with his hand clamped on Jennifer's shoulder.

Reece took another step toward Jordanna's back. In the strong florescent light that flooded the shed, he could see trails of tears through the dirt on Sam's face.

"They've arrested Jennifer," he said. "If she's innocent, you have to help her. If Jordan killed your mother and father, police will believe your statement. Let Sam go," he said with as much authority as he could muster.

Jordanna swung around, levelling the gun at his chest. Her eyes flickered to her sister in the doorway.

Reece used her moment of distraction to ram into her knees. The gun flew from her hand and clattered against the wall behind her. She tore at the back of his neck with her fingernails, kicking her feet to dislodge his body. He grabbed her wrists and pulled her toward him, forcing her body beneath his. Letting go of her wrists, he straddled her body and tried to climb over her to reach the gun. With a wail of fury, she wrapped her fingers in his hair and yanked him to the side, rolling out from underneath him and scuttling forward on her hands and knees.

Reece tried to grab her ankle as she crawled on all fours. She kicked him hard in the face. Blood spewed from his nose. He latched onto her leg and pulled as hard as he could. She fell flat on her stomach and he managed to drag her away from the gun. She kicked at his body and reached down, grabbing his arm in a steely grip. Sharp teeth sank into his forearm and he howled when she ripped away a chunk of flesh. Reece kneeled with blood streaming from his arm. She rolled to her back, kicked him in the gut with both feet, and scrambled to her hands and knees to crawl for the weapon.

Reece dropped flat against the ground, giving Alston a clear shot.

A gun roared.

Jordanna froze. Her mouth opened and the life faded from her eyes. Her body fell across Sam's curled torso. Blood from the wound in Jordanna's head ran across the side of Sam's face and spattered the ground around her.

Sam was screaming, straining helplessly against the ropes that tethered her arms and legs. She was frantically bucking her body, trying to dislodge Jordanna's corpse so she could roll from beneath it.

Reece crawled across the distance separating them. He shoved Jordanna's body off. He wiped blood off Sam's face and gathered her in his arms. She cried out in pain. He quickly released her, and she toppled over, landing on her side again beside Jordanna's body. Against the wall, Reece spied a pocketknife. He sawed at the rope connecting Sam's wrists to her ankles and then tugged the rope free.

Alston crouched beside them. "The ambulance is on the way."

Sam rubbed her bruised wrists and tentatively stretched out her legs with a moan. Reece gently embraced her, kissing the side of her face and tasting Jordanna's blood on his lips.

"It took you long enough," she whimpered, burrowing her face against his chest. "But I knew you'd come."

"Always," he promised.

CHAPTER THIRTY-SEVEN

SAM

ONE MONTH LATER

SOMETHING HEAVY PREVENTED Sam's legs from moving. She couldn't breathe. Apocalyptic dread suffocated her and she thrashed her arms. A subtle scent of citrus pulled her awake, and her eyes snapped opened. In the moment before full consciousness, primitive panic insisted she was still in the shed, hog-tied and helpless, held captive by a murderous eighteen-year-old. Jordanna's face floated in front of her eyes. She blinked rapidly, expelling the vision. Her heart rate slowed and her breathing evened. She was home. She was safe. It was over.

Sam sat up and the silky Egyptian cotton sheet slid against her bare arm. The fingers on her right hand twitched, and she focused on controlling the muscles. When the twitching stopped, she held her bedsheet to her nose and inhaled the aroma of clean linen. Familiar smells helped, a bit. In the back of her mind, a phantom stench of blood lingered. She worried it would never go away.

Reaching across Reece, she plucked the lighter from his nightstand and lit the lemon candle beside her. The wick flickered and caught, and the aroma of citrus began filling the room.

Reece rolled over and moaned. She didn't want to wake him, not again. Against the shadowy backdrop of her bedroom, hallucinatory images suddenly coalesced in a technicolour assault. She reached for the bottle of acetaminophen with codeine. Two tablets fell into her hand. They were the last of a bottle of one hundred Reece had picked up for her ten days ago. How had she consumed so much? It did nothing to alleviate the constant pain in her head or the spasms in her back.

For a month, she'd had trouble sleeping, waking disoriented and terrified from nightmares. It felt like someone had punched her in the stomach while she slept, leaving her winded and breathless. Impending doom would engulf her, the same nasty feeling you experience when you reach for your wallet and discover it missing or turn to find the child that had stood beside you gone.

During the day, she'd see Jordan. His face would appear in a streetcar window or she'd catch a glimpse of him from her peripheral vision. Understanding it was her imagination didn't help. Attending the funerals hadn't helped. Nothing stopped him from appearing to her at random times.

Sometimes, blood covered his face and he looked as he had in death. Often, he simply stared at her from outside the library window or from the street below the loft, dressed in his football kit and holding his helmet. His sad eyes reminded her of all the things he'd never do. The scholarship to UBC he wouldn't accept, the career he'd never have. Remembering that Jordan had raped at least two girls didn't dispel the guilt. Away from his sisters' influences, psychiatrists could have helped him. Maybe. She didn't know. Everything was a jumbled mess in her head.

Brandy snored at the bottom of the king-sized bed, and her hind legs jerked in her sleep. Above the six-foot partition wall that circled the bedroom loft, streetlights twinkled through the southern windows. She was home. She was safe. It was over. The three phrases had become a silent mantra.

But it didn't help. She didn't feel safe.

Not giving in to paranoia was important, but it was a struggle not to put on the light or wake Reece. The need to check the loft for invaders, to search every closet and corner, was overwhelming. Her jaw hurt from grinding her teeth in her sleep, and she was thirsty again. The water bottle beside her was empty.

Get up, go into the bathroom, and fill it.

The idea of crossing the dark loft to the bathroom caused her stomach to cramp.

There's no one hiding in the bathroom. Brandy would have barked.

Reasonable, but rational thought was on holiday. Her emotions were a turbulent mass of insensible contradictions. On an intellectual level, she knew her subconscious mind was sorting out the trauma. The nightmares and panic attacks were normal. They'd disperse with time, if she didn't allow post-traumatic stress to get a foothold. She understood the psychology, and it infuriated her she couldn't employ the tools to overcome her problem. It should be easy for her. She was earning a PhD in psychology. Why couldn't she help herself?

Critical incident stress management hadn't helped and neither had the York Regional Police debriefing. She'd tried talking unremittingly about the events in the shed to anyone who would listen. Half the time she spoke in non sequiturs that were incomprehensible while her audience's face turned confused and their eyes filled with pity. She'd feel no emotion as she babbled on about Jordanna, Jordan, and the shed. If someone interrupted to ask how she had actually felt in the moment, she'd act flippant and return to reporting the facts. She couldn't face her feelings of utter helplessness or the residual anger that chewed at her without mercy.

But the worst feeling—the one she couldn't understand and couldn't talk herself out of—was shame. She berated herself over the amateurish stupidity of sitting in the kitchen with her back to the door. Her inability to use her psychology skills to manipulate Jordan into disarming his sister disgusted her. There was a constant simmering sense of self-hate that she couldn't get past. For a day or two, she'd be okay before an intermittent backslide flipped her into more night terrors, panic attacks, and self-loathing.

"Want me to get you water?"

Reece spoke in a soft tone and didn't touch her. She felt guilty that he'd learned the hard way that a sudden motion or a loud noise caused her to react violently. She couldn't control her instinct to lash out at whatever startled her.

"Thanks."

He climbed out of bed and shuffled to the washroom, scratching his back. Her heart pounded. She clutched the sheet tight, waiting for his grunt of pain when a home intruder attacked him.

He returned with the water and got in bed. After she sucked on the bottle, he pulled her into his arms.

His skin was pliable and soft yet protective. "Want the light on?" he asked. There wasn't even a hint of exasperation to his voice. Only kindness and understanding.

Against his chest, she shook her head.

"I put *Harry Potter and the Goblet of Fire* on the e-reader. Do you want to read for a bit?"

For some odd reason, the only thing that offered some relief from her memories of the shed was J.K. Rowling's books. She didn't usually enjoy the fantasy genre, and her love of the novels had taken her by surprise. Reece had bought her an e-reader so she could read whenever a nightmare woke her. He knew she felt guilty over interrupting his sleep by putting on the light.

"I'm fine," she said.

"Since you're awake, I want to get your opinion on something."

"What's that?"

"How would you feel if I went back to school?" he asked.

She sat up. "What for?"

"Law."

It was a great idea but she was wary. He'd said he'd never finish his law degree.

"Why?"

"It's not because of my father," he said, a little quickly. "I mean, it is, but it isn't."

For the past six months, Reece had waffled over whether to join Toronto homicide until their screw-up with Caitlyn had forced Bryce to rescind the offer. She had known for some time Reece wasn't keen on working as a private investigator either. He'd been a bit too involved with her school work and had assumed an unattractive parental role. He scolded her about deadlines and offered unwanted advice on her dissertation. Now it made sense. Meddling in her academic world came from a desire to experience university vicariously. Reece wanted to go back to school.

"How long have you been considering it?" she asked.

"Well," he said, rolling over to face her, "I guess it was when I took my dad's watch out for Lisa's urban animal party."

The night they'd discovered Abigail's suicide.

"When I accompanied Lisa to OCAD," he said, "I felt this tug, you know?"

She nodded.

"So, I thought if Lisa had the guts to go back to school maybe I should consider it. I spoke with Osgoode Hall Law School to see if it was possible to transfer my credits from Western Law School."

"And?"

"It is." He rolled to his back and smiled. "I can finish in a year. Now, I'd have to article or complete the LPP and write the bar exam. That would take another year or so." Enthusiasm rang in his voice.

She snuggled against his chest. "So what type of law do you want to practise?"

"I'd like to be a prosecutor."

She laughed. "Oh boy, that puts you and Jim on opposite sides."

He squeezed her shoulder. "It does, but his win record as a defender is too high. I'd enjoy taking him down a notch. Healthy competition and all that."

Reece had once confided in her that he quit law school and joined the Ontario Provincial Police because he couldn't fill his father's shoes. The man was a brilliant prosecutor who had earned a position as a judge with the Ontario Court of Justice by the time he was in his mid-forties and advanced to Justice of the Supreme Court of Canada by fifty-two. His father's success intimidated him. Confronting fears took guts, and Sam was proud of Reece for realizing he could be his own man, even if he chose a similar profession.

"You'll make a fantastic prosecutor. After all, you were a fantastic cop, and that experience is going to be priceless." She kissed him and pulled away to add, "I know this has taken a lot of soul searching, but you've made the right decision. The Crown Attorney's Office is going to be lucky to have you."

She recalled the words of Nelson Mandela—*I learned that courage was not the absence of fear but the triumph over it.* Her experience inside the shed was a part of her now, but it didn't need to be the defining moment on which the rest of her life pivoted.

If Reece could overcome his fear and move forward, maybe she could too. "I'm going to the hospital tomorrow." Once the words left her mouth, she felt something loosen in her gut. "To see Jennifer Harris."

He sat up. "Are you certain?"

A peace settled over her. She needed to face the monster that had instigated the horror.

"Yeah." She closed her eyes. "It's what I need to do to be free."

CHAPTER THIRTY-EIGHT

Sam

SAM STOOD IN the viewing room on the psychiatric floor at Toronto's SickKids Hospital and stared through the one-way mirror at the teenager sitting cross-legged on the floor.

Jennifer's long blond hair framed her pretty, heart-shaped face. Her clear complexion had spots of colour high on her cheeks, and her blue eyes were wide and earnest. An English rose, precious and fragile.

Her lips moved when she spoke to the female psychiatrist who sat on the carpet beside her. Roger didn't have the audio turned on in the room they watched from, but the doctor laughed at something Jennifer said and patted her shoulder. The intimate gesture made bile rise in the back of Sam's throat and she clenched her jaw. Jennifer blushed and smiled up at the doctor. The perfect image of a sweet adolescent doing her stoic best to overcome horrific tragedy. Sam didn't buy any of it.

Roger hadn't uttered a word since she'd entered. He was shuffling his feet, and, with a soft sigh, he crossed his arms against his chest. His expression was neutral while he studiously watched the girl behind the glass. Sam knew his intense concentration was a ploy to avoid looking at her.

"Detective Alston spoke with Jennifer's teachers," she said. "They denied she's capable of writing the hideous story about kidnap and torture that Brenda found. Her English skills aren't good enough, they say. She's fooled them." She took a breath and wrestled with her emotions.

Roger's shoulders stiffened but he made no comment, and uncomfortable silence hung between them. Sam couldn't tell whether Jennifer's mask of virtue had seduced him as well.

"Jordan's art teacher produced samples of his work," she said. "Experts confirm he drew the illustrations. Police identified only his fingerprints on the plastic folder that contained the story. There weren't enough match points to compare the rest. Too smudged. The conclusion is that Jordan wrote and illustrated the despicable comic."

Roger's eyes didn't move from the scene through the mirror. "Brenda remembers Jordan in the cellar, squabbling with his father," he said. "She recalls the electricity coming back on, which was why she returned to the basement. There was a figure in rubber boots standing over Graham, but she can't bring the face into focus. I've tried everything." Regret filled his voice. "I can't retrieve the memories. They're gone."

"Jordanna wasn't lying," Sam retorted. "She had no reason to. Jennifer murdered Graham."

"She claims Jordan did everything." Roger's voice was impartial. "She was in the cellar looking for a soccer ball the day of her father's murder. Her brother came home and accused Brenda of having an affair with me." He swallowed hard. "Brenda stormed out and Jennifer hid in the closet. Graham slapped Jordan and enraged him. She claims she watched from the closet when her brother engaged the master switch on the fuse box and electrocuted Graham. After he shut off the power, Jordan put on the rubber boots that were at the bottom of the stairs, waded into the sewage, and held down his father's head until he stopped moving."

Sam knew that. Police had substantiated there were sight lines from the closet. In her interview, Jennifer had explained she went into the sewage to try to save her father. Her sister found her and misunderstood. Jennifer had been too scared of Jordan to tell Jordanna what she'd witnessed.

When they'd asked about Caitlyn's murder, Jennifer had become distraught, claiming her sister was jealous of her relationship with her mother. Jordanna had assumed the role of mother, and it infuriated her when Jennifer turned to Caitlyn. Jennifer wouldn't accuse her sister of murder. At the suggestion, she became hysterical and a doctor had to sedate her.

"She's lying." Sam felt so detached that her voice sounded dim to her own ears, as if it originated in a tunnel. "She knows how to manipulate the neuropsychology tests." A wave of heat engulfed her, and sweat trickled down her back to the waist of her jeans. "She's lying about everything."

"Her story is consistent, Sam." Roger's tone was supremely condescending. "She has a reasonable explanation for everything. Jennifer hasn't diverted once from her version of the truth." He turned to face her and raised his hand to ward off her objection. "I know you believe Jordanna told you the truth, but do the police have any evidence to connect Jennifer to Caitlyn's murder?"

"No," Sam said through gritted teeth. "Rachel Harris insists Jennifer was with her at a church event. She's admitted she went behind Graham's back and allowed Jennifer to visit with Caitlyn over the past three years. According to Rachel, Jennifer and her mother had a wonderful relationship. Rachel told police Jennifer is a good Christian girl and incapable of violence."

Sam clenched her fists at her sides. Blood rushed to her face and her heartbeat quickened in response to her anger. "Her friends from bible study signed statements that Jennifer was at the church the night Caitlyn died."

"So she didn't kill her," Roger stated. "She has an alibi. You have to let this go and leave it to the professionals."

Sam grunted. "The naive church women lied to protect a teenage girl they believe authorities are using as a scapegoat. A child who lost her entire family to violence. A girl who stood helpless and terrified while police gunned down her eighteen-year-old sister."

The police had found Jordanna's school pin on the lapel of her cheerleader sweater. They hadn't found her brother's pin, but they did find a white shirt with a torn collar and bloodstains hidden in the back of his closet. DNA matched the blood to Caitlyn.

They'd found Jordan's fingerprints on a shovel in Caitlyn's garage and on the plastic tarp that he'd wrapped her body in before dumping it in the grave. The direct evidence convinced the Attorney General that Jordan Harris murdered Caitlyn Franklyn and Graham Harris. Case closed.

Sam had spent hours trying to convince the authorities that although he disposed of the body, Jordan had not killed his mother. The more insistent she was, the more Detective Alston looked at her with pity. Now he didn't return her calls.

From the corner of her eye, she felt Roger staring at her. She couldn't look at him.

"Doctor Weinstein is one of the best child psychiatrists in North America," he said with confidence. "She has experience working with juvenile sociopaths and psychopaths. Jennifer won't be able to trick her."

"She's doing a fine job, so far."

Even though Jennifer couldn't see them, Sam experienced a creepy sensation that the girl knew they were watching.

"Maladaptive patterns of behaviour that impair social functioning originate within the gardens of childhood," she said. "After their grandmother's murder, doctors should have been involved. The Harris children could have been stopped." The bitterness was sour in her mouth.

Roger shrugged. "Without a parent advocating or co-paying, it's not a surprise that people missed the signs of antisocial disorder. An aging population is crippling the Canadian health care system. You know that. Mental health has taken a backseat because of limited resources."

A mistake that would continue to prevent the detection of pre-existing psychiatric disorders in children and put society at risk. Sam realized she had the premise for her thesis.

"How are you doing?" Roger asked. "Should I be worried?" His expression betrayed the fact that he was already worried about her psychological well-being.

"No one's going to stop her." A hard ball of hate took up residence in her gut. "She's going to get away with everything."

Roger sighed and turned back to the glass. "Doctor Weinstein recommended an inpatient program. Jennifer will be confined for at least two more months."

"What happens then?" Sam asked. The repugnant, singsong verse that never stopped playing in her head for more than an hour at a time began again.

Red rover, red rover, I call Sam on over. See the blood on Sam's face, as her skin's carved to lace. See her look of surprise, as she painfully dies. Red rover, red rover, I call Sam on over.

"Brenda sold the farm to a land developer," Roger was saying. "She's giving Jennifer her siblings' proceeds of the sale. There's a trust that holds the money until Jennifer's twenty-one. Rachel Harris is the trustee. Brenda wants nothing to do with the girl."

"Why twenty-one? Shouldn't she have access at eighteen?" Sam asked, trying to hide her bitterness. The girl would be a millionaire. A murderous, psychopathic millionaire.

"That's the best Brenda and her lawyers could do. Rachel can release education funds and plans to send Jennifer to a private prep school to prepare for university." He sighed. "If it's any consolation, Brenda agrees with you. It's her hope professionals will identify Jennifer's mental illness and rule her as a risk to society before she turns eighteen."

"How likely is that?" she asked. "Psychopaths can pass lie detectors and manipulate test results. They're brilliant, charming chameleons." Her jaw clenched while she stared through the glass at the monster on the other side. "She's the best I've ever seen."

Jennifer and the doctor had moved to a round table with art supplies. The teenager was drawing a picture. A large yellow sun on a purple horizon and pink and gold streaks across a navy sky over a still blue lake lined with pretty trees. An innocuous sketch by a stable adolescent. In and of itself, that struck Sam as ominous. Jennifer had lost both of her parents to violence, had witnessed her sister shot, and had seen her brother's bloody corpse.

"If there's anything to find, Doctor Weinstein will break through to the truth. Trust me." Roger's tone was dismissive. "Let's go." He held open the door. "Coming?"

"In a minute," she said.

After Roger left, the doctor glanced at the door to the room she shared with Jennifer. She said something and Jennifer nodded, smiling up at the doctor. Dr. Weinstein left the room and Jennifer continued to draw. A moment later, she lifted the coloured pencil from the paper and her head swivelled. She stared at the mirror that separated her and Sam. All the pretence disappeared from her face, leaving nothing but malevolence and evil.

"You can fool them, but you'll never fool me," Sam whispered to the glass. "I'll be waiting for you."

EPILOGUE

THEN THERE WAS one. I let my thoughts drift as they did in the past. I remember the feel of my sister's hands when she braided my hair and hear my brother's guffawing laughter from the backyard. It doesn't bother me, the fact they're gone. They served their purpose.

When I first arrived here, I didn't believe someone was always watching. I'd treat myself to the special memories and free my fermenting imagination. The rush of anticipation when blood slithers between my fingers and cascades across my wrists. My omniscient power when a victim's eyes first register fear. The way my heart quickens when life fades. That empty gaze of death confirms we are all just lumps of soulless meat.

Once, Dr. Weinstein caught me reminiscing. She'd entered with stealth to spy. Reliving the pleasant memories had painted my face with angelic joy. She had spoken with suspicion, asking me what was on my mind. I affixed the auspicious, vulnerable mask I wear so well and opened my eyes. With spontaneous ease, they filled with tears and I jutted my lower lip to a trembling pout.

"I was remembering," I said and started to weep. "I was at the beach with Daddy, Mom, Jordan, and Jordanna. It was such a lovely day."

I witnessed doubt in her bovine eyes, and so I held out a nugget of progress to appease her. I offered an expression of survivor guilt I knew her archaic therapy methods were endeavouring to coax to the foreground.

"It's so hard to remember them. I feel so bad that I'm still here." I sniffled. "What Jordan and Jordanna did was awful but I still love them." I howled. "I miss my parents so much."

We talked, and I spoon-fed her responses she wanted to hear. Careful, always careful to play the proper psychological victim until the game shifts and the time is right.

I understand the signs she's watching for and what she wants. My cognitive understanding of her and her methodology outweighs her comprehension of me. What she fails to grasp is we're all different. There are many of us among you, but we have unique styles and abilities. Professionals will never learn the key to identifying us, because there isn't one. We will always be two steps ahead. We are smarter. Our survival instincts are stronger.

Dr. Weinstein left my room that day with a smug expression that made me smile behind her back. It's almost too easy. I will dole out my recovery in tiny morsels. I will regress to darkness and race back to the light under her skilled guidance. Before I turn eighteen, I will convince her of my recovery. She will write a paper on her brilliant treatment. I will be free.

Dr. Weinstein almost catching me for what I truly am taught me the necessity of diligence. Someone is always watching. They lurk behind the mirrors and hover in shadowy corners. They wait for the mask to slip and for me to show my true face. But I know the tricks to the tests they administer.

Hidden beneath this shell of an average teenage girl, my intellect is superior. I will change my mood at a moment's notice. I'll befriend the other girls and flirt with the boys. I will cry from a purported broken heart and exhibit appropriate remorse and emotions. I will ask Dr. Weinstein for news of celebrities and fashion trends. I will test a notch above average but never too high for them to suspect manipulation. I will win the game. I always do.

I can hear kids crying at night. Some scream and rage against the walls. But one boy understands the game. We rarely speak. We exchange clandestine gazes from across the room. We recognize each other and long to be together.

"Someday," he whispered to me when I passed him in the hallway last night, "we'll hunt together."

THE END

ACKNOWLEDGEMENTS

NOTHING WOULD BE possible without the support and skill of my editor, Sadie Scapillato, and my proofreader, Elizabeth West.

Mike Doyle did a fantastic job on the cover, and I owe him a debt of gratitude.

Thanks to US Author Joseph Hirsch for critique partnering and to Paula Henderson for beta-reading.

Fuzzy hugs to my husband and sons for putting up with me. It isn't easy to live with someone who spends hours researching monsters. If society doesn't pay attention to mental health, I fear we're going to see a lot more of them.

Most of all, thank you for reading *Red Rover, Perdition Games*. I appreciate the time you invested. I'm requesting a bit more kindness by asking you to write a review on Amazon and Goodreads to offer your feedback. Good or bad, your opinion is priceless, and I hope you catch me on social media.

Haven't read *Simon Says, Perdition Games* yet? Turn the page to read the first chapter.

Thank you,
Lori

www.perditiongames.com
Twitter: @perditiongames
Facebook: perditiongamesseries

SIMONSAYS
PERDITION GAMES

By L.E. Fraser

Amazon reviewers are saying...

5* The prefect thriller, with a number of ups and downs.

5* This is a must read!

5* ...forward moving, fast paced plot...

5* This is not a novel you can predict throughout.

5* Incredible writing and editing.

Where will you be when the sun sets in the sky,
when the children's games are done and all their laughter dies?
When the Pacific Loon finally takes to flight,
which saviour will you bribe to stand guard throughout the night?

The emaciated wolves bay at your door.
Have you travelled far from Babylon, my virgin whore?
Hear their heartbeats through the silence of the woods.
They howl for you, my child, and they wait where you once stood.

L.E. Fraser

PROLOGUE

SYLVIA SHOVED THE hem of her sackcloth robe into the twine around her waist. Her heart was racing, and, every time she tried to breathe, there was a stabbing pain in her chest. She ran.

Thorns sliced open the vulnerable skin of her arms, and she swiped her right hand against the sharp twigs to try to protect her face. Blood dripped from the end of the middle finger on her left hand where the detached nail hung to the bed by a string of bloody tissue. Still, she ran.

Without warning, a piercing pain shot through her chest. Her stomach convulsed and bloody vomit spewed from between her cracked lips. She stumbled and choked on the blood that ran down her throat. She stopped running.

From directly behind her, she heard a pitiful whimper and a soft swishing sound, like air escaping from a balloon. The noise of breaking branches was intrusive in the dark forest. She froze and waited in fear, expecting to hear the gleeful shouts of their pursuers.

After a moment of absolute silence, she whispered through the darkness, "Get up, Mandy, we have to keep moving."

"I can't."

She leaned down and felt around the rough ground until she hit flesh. She ran her fingers along the girl's forearm, grasped Mandy's thin wrist and pulled hard. The body barely shifted. "We can't stay here."

"I can't run any further."

Mandy was making little meowing sounds that broke Sylvia's heart. If they rested, he'd catch them. They couldn't give up. They were too close to freedom. She took a deep breath. "The road is at the top of the escarpment, we can make it."

"I can't," Mandy repeated through her tears.

Sylvia sat down hard, and her knee smashed against a boulder. Agony shot across her kneecap, and a spasm seized her calf muscle, forcing her to bite on her tongue to keep from crying out in pain. Shuddering tremors ran down her legs. She curled into a fetal position on the ground beside Mandy and wept in pain and frustration.

She was twenty-eight and had volunteered to be Mandy's mentor when the sixteen-year-old had arrived at the sanctuary six months earlier. When she made the decision to try to escape, she took her protegé with her. Now, the responsibility weighed heavily on her shoulders.

They'd left just before ten o'clock at night, and she'd struck the sentry with a plank stolen from the lumberyard. Fear had weakened her grip and coated her hands in sweat. The club slipped at the point of impact, and her blow had barely slowed the man's attack. He'd thrown her to the ground, hurled aside her weapon, and savagely kicked her. He would have killed her, but Mandy had grabbed the makeshift club and bludgeoned the man. Together, the women had dragged him to the side of the shed, but Sylvia couldn't commit murder. That was her first mistake. They would discover him. Mussani would know what she'd done, and there would be no mercy if he caught them.

"Go on without me," Mandy whispered.

She dug deep to find the strength to go on and slowly sat up, groaning in pain. "We stay together. It's our only chance. Get up." The desperate words echoed loudly through the forest, and she pressed together her split lips. She could see Mandy's eyes shining with fear.

They waited in tense silence and then Sylvia whispered, "He's coming. He's close now. I feel him. We can't stay here."

"I'm so scared." Mandy grasped her hand. "Why did we do this? We shouldn't have done this." Hysteria laced her voice and she was gasping for breath.

"We're going to be okay," Sylvia promised. "The road is at the top of the escarpment." She wiped the back of her hand across her mouth, and it was sticky with bloody mucus. She was thankful that the darkness camouflaged her injuries. She was not okay and knew she didn't have much time left.

She removed the tie to her robe and shivered when cold air rippled against her naked flesh. She made a slipknot at each end of the rope, gliding one circle over her injured hand. The rough hemp caught the torn nail and ripped it free from her finger. The intensity of the pain made her cry out.

"Sylvia?" Mandy whimpered, with a pitiful hitch in her young voice.

Fumbling to find Mandy's hand, Sylvia secured the other slipknot around her wrist and squeezed the girl's hand. Now the rope connected them for better or for worse. As the clouds parted and the half moon looked down on them, they ran.

JB WATCHED MUSSANI light a cigarette, and the misshapen flame from the lighter bobbed in the wind. The moonlight turned his dark eyes into mirrors that reflected the cigarette ember. A reddish orange dot glowed in the middle of the pools of darkness in his face. JB turned away, alarmed by what he glimpsed in the disembodied eyes.

"Whatcha wanna do?"

Mussani took a deep drag from the cigarette, and the red ember shone again in his eyes. JB shuddered and dropped his gaze to the ground.

Father Mussani nonchalantly leaned against the front grill of the Jeep. His tone was calm and melodic when he said, "We wait."

Toeing the gravel at the side of the road, JB tried to emulate his companion's casual stance but his brow broke out in perspiration, and the pits of his chambray work shirt were sticky with sweat. Unable to endure the darkness and silence, he asked, "What if th-th-they don't c-c-come this way?"

Mussani flicked the burning cigarette into the woods. "They'll come."

"Could head s-s-south," JB suggested.

"To the lake?"

He felt his cheeks flush with embarrassment. "C-c-could have a b-b-boat," he stuttered, ashamed of the difficulty he had in spitting out the four miserable words.

Father Mussani ignored the stuttering, and gratitude washed over JB. Father never commented on the speech impediment or suggested the stutter meant he was stupid.

Mussani pulled a flask from the inside pocket of his ceremonial robe, unscrewed the top, and put the bottle to his lips. The smell of whisky tainted the wind. He didn't offer the flask, and JB didn't expect him to.

The road was north, the lake was south, the valley was east, and the woods were west. The sanctuary farmland ran between, with its buildings along the east border beside the valley. As usual, Mussani was right. The sisters would walk north to civilization, but they'd have to travel through the acres of woods that hugged the road. There were no paths through the thick brush and mature trees, and they'd need to climb a steep escarpment to reach the road. JB didn't think they could negotiate the trek without light. It had been raining for a week, and the forest ground was slick and treacherous. At least one of the sisters had a serious injury. A shiver of shame scurried along JB's spine.

"W-w-what should we do when they g-g-get here?" he asked.

"She has lost the vision. If possible, she will transcend. That's the only way to achieve self-realization."

"She's my friend." JB pulled at the crotch of his pants, a nervous habit his father had beat him for when he was a kid. He'd tried to stop but he couldn't. One of the reasons he'd joined Bueton Sanctuary was because people didn't laugh at him over his bad habit, his stutter, or the birthmark that scarred his right temple.

"She's a sister and has broken the oath. Are you questioning the Creed?" Mussani asked.

The clouds broke apart, and the silver crest of the half moon winked. For just a moment, the moonlight illuminated Mussani's face. What JB saw in those dark eyes made him look to the ground and exhale a single puff of fear.

With his head lowered submissively and his hands clasped tightly against his chest, he said, "I'd never disobey the Creed." Although shamed by his quivering voice, he was proud that his passion had empowered him to speak the words without stumbling over the first syllable. Feeling doubt and confusion, JB gazed up at the heavens to hunt for a star to wish upon, but there were none.

SYLVIA HAD MANAGED to lead Mandy north along the irrigation tracks, so crossing the acres of fields was easy. The orchard had been tricky. When they hit the woods that crested the land, they were both confused about what direction they were going. If they fell off course, and Mussani sent out the dogs, the animals would tear them apart. The road was their only hope.

Mandy had stopped crying, a small mercy for which Sylvia was grateful. The trouble she was having breathing, the unsecured robe, and the freezing temperature had forced her to slow to a shuffling trudge, but the gentle tug on the rope indicated that Mandy was still moving behind her.

As she towed the terrified adolescent, Sylvia accepted she'd made a terrible mistake. What she was putting the girl through was worse than the initiation ceremony would have been. Her decision to take Mandy and run, without a plan to ensure they escaped, was stupid. If he caught them, he'd kill her and, although he probably wouldn't kill his pet, Mandy would pay a high price. There was no turning back. She had to get the girl to safety.

The half moon's light in the cloudy sky was now stingy, and the frigid wind was merciless. Their feet were bare, and the escarpment was becoming harder to climb. In places, they had to crawl in single file. At a spot where they could walk upright, she shoved aside jagged branches and held her arms behind her to try to keep the sharp twigs from slapping Mandy's face. Each time she stumbled, Mandy grasped the loose fabric of her open robe and pushed on her back to steady her. Under the indifferent eye of the moon, they slowly ascended the steep hill.

She turned to glance over her shoulder, slipped in a puddle of mud, and lost her balance. She grasped at the trees in an effort not to fall back down the hill. With a startled cry, Mandy's hands pawed and pushed at her back to try to balance her. Sylvia swayed for a moment and then pitched backwards, rolling over Mandy and sliding downhill. Dragged by the tethering rope, Mandy tumbled after her and crushed Sylvia's face into the moist, decaying leaves.

A rainbow of light exploded in front of Sylvia's closed eyes. She could feel the warmth of her blood streaming down her chin, and her mouth filled with the coppery taste. Every time she tried to breathe, there was a crackling sound in her chest. She felt like she was drowning, and the night air tasted metallic. She was certain one of her broken ribs had punctured her lung. If she died in the woods, Mandy wouldn't make it out. They had to get to the road. She fought against the pain and focused on Mandy's hysterical yelps.

"Get off," she whispered, forcing the two words from her bruised lips.

The girl pathetically whimpered, and her breath was hot and wet against Sylvia's neck.

"Get off," she grunted.

Mandy rolled over and the tethering rope stretched taut across Sylvia's back. They lay together on the cold ground. Above them, the moon slithered beneath a cloud. The darkness was a black velvet blindfold. In that moment, Sylvia knew God had finally turned His back. He was showing them their destiny, and it was hell.

JB TRIED TO keep track of time by the number of cigarettes Father Mussani smoked. Ten minutes was the average time to smoke one, and Father had puffed on five. He figured there were about thirty minutes between butts, so that meant they had waited at the side of the road for nearly three hours.

JB wished he had the sense to leave. He had nowhere to go. He wished he had the courage to save Sylvia. He knew he did not. He sensed Mussani coming into his space and took a small, involuntary step back.

"Problem, JB?" The voice came from his immediate right.

"I was wondering b-b-bout the ceremony."

"Why?"

He struggled to stay immobile, hoping Mussani couldn't smell his fear. "H-h-how can she be initiated?"

"She'll be initiated here."

"What about the w-w-witnesses?"

"Two, Brother, we only need two," remarked Mussani.

JB asked the question that had nagged at him ever since Mussani's second cigarette. "Who will g-g-guide Sylvia?"

Father didn't answer. His silence spoke volumes to JB.

"I c-c-can't. Sh-sh-she's my friend."

Several moments elapsed before Mussani spoke in a slow, even pitch. "You've been initiated, Brother, and cleansed to guide the metamorphosing of the worthy. Sister Sylvia is a traitor."

JB remained still and silent at the side of his Messiah.

"Are you questioning the Creed and the ordinances, which you swore had saved your miserable soul? Don't you believe that the doctrines of our existence are absolute loyalty, confidentiality, and—"

"And obedience," JB interrupted, anxious to redeem himself in the eyes of his mentor. He felt sweat trickle to the loose waist of his sackcloth pants.

"And obedience," Mussani agreed. His voice filled with enthusiasm, "Look, Brother, a shooting star!"

"SYLVIA, LOOK A shooting star!" Mandy's voice sounded so young and innocent. "Wishes come true on shooting stars. Make a wish, quick before the tail fades."

Sylvia tried to focus on the star blurring and flashing before her eyes. She wished for Mandy to make it to safety. Her eyes rolled, and she opened her mouth to let the bloody saliva run from the corner of her swollen lips. She placed her palms on the ground and pushed her broken body to its knees. Agony exploded in her chest, forcing her to bite hard on her lip to keep from screaming. She tucked one foot underneath her and stood.

"Come on, Mandy. Road, over the hill."

"Did you make a wish?" Mandy asked as she stood up and followed along behind.

"I made a wish," Sylvia agreed and closed her eyes against the tears.

FROM THE DARKNESS, JB heard them. He knew they were very close, but he couldn't see them. Sister Sylvia was advising Mandy to stay in the ditch, and her voice was thick and wet sounding. He heard her pain, and it made the hair rise on his neck.

Mussani ignored them and continued to lean against the front bumper of the Jeep. He was merely waiting, like a lion carefully stalking its prey. After several motionless moments, he reached into the Jeep and switched on the headlights.

In response, JB heard Mandy cry out, "Sylvia, I see a car!"

They watched in silence as she crawled up the ditch, standing at the top to wave her arms. A frayed piece of braided hemp circled her right wrist.

Mussani slid through the darkness to the girl. "Find the other one."

JB reluctantly jumped into the ditch, walking ten metres before his boot hit something solid. He carefully slung Sylvia across his shoulder and trudged up the steep slope to the road where Mussani waited.

"Move her by the tree and wake her."

JB lowered his friend to the ground, and, from the corner of his eye, he saw Mussani take Mandy's hand. She blinked and shaded her eyes from the glare of the car's lights but stood silent and still. Her eyes widened with horror when she looked from Mussani to Sylvia, who was now visible in the harsh light.

JB propped Sylvia against the thick trunk of an elm tree and groped for her hand. She tensed at his touch but didn't open her eyes. He pinched her arm and wept.

His pinch drew her back to consciousness, and she struggled to stand before giving up and slumping weakly against the tree trunk.

He studied her in the harsh light from the Jeep. Her lower teeth and gums were visible through a gaping tear in her lip. Pink foam coated her lips and dark blood stained her chin. It had flowed down her neck to pool in the hollows of her collarbones. Her left eye was black and swollen closed. Blood covered the hand he held, and one of her fingernails was missing.

Her head slowly turned toward him, and recognition flickered in her eyes. They'd been friends and lovers, and he could tell she believed he'd betrayed her.

JB grasped her hand hard and tears dripped down his cheeks. "I d-d-didn't t-t-tell. He knew."

"It wasn't her fault," she whispered. "Swear you'll protect her." She gasped for breath. "Swear you'll get her home to her sister."

He turned away from her and stared at the dismal scene in front of the Jeep. Mandy was sprawled on her back against the gravel, with her robe around her neck in concertina folds. Her young, lustrous skin was translucent in the cruel white light from the Jeep. Mussani knelt before the girl, anointing her trembling flesh with the initiation oil, pinching her nipples and forcing her legs apart. He grabbed her hips, thrusting himself inside her. Mandy's screams cut JB's heart. He covered his ears to block out the terrifying cries. After a few minutes, Mussani violently turned her to her stomach, grabbed her around the waist and pushed himself inside her from behind, pressing her naked body against the sharp stones on the road. She was no longer screaming, and JB prayed she was unconscious. He dropped his hands from his ears and held tightly to Sylvia's hand, averting his eyes from the brutality he'd vowed to witness.

Sylvia raised her head to the heavens. "Lord, we are still your children. Why have you abandoned us?" The light faded from her eyes. Her broken body drooped to the ground.

A bolt of lightning lit the sky, and a single star, lonely in solitude, twinkled in the darkness. JB watched the star blink once and twice, and then it vanished like an angel's tear.

When Mussani completed the initiation ceremony, JB stood and went to the Jeep. He felt sick to his stomach, and his skin was crawling with goosebumps. Mussani tightened the gold, braided rope around his thick waist, lit a cigarette, and smiled.

"What about h-h-h-her?" JB nodded toward the dead woman sprawled at the base of the giant elm. He swallowed the sour saliva gathering in his mouth and wiped the back of his hand against the clammy sweat on his forehead.

Mussani unscrewed his flask of whisky. He took a long drink and shrugged.

JB swallowed hard and let grief wash over him. Sylvia had never teased or rejected him. For the first time since joining the life at Bueton, he felt doubt.

As if aware of his disloyal thoughts, Mussani laid his arm across his shoulders. They stood together in the artificial light from the Jeep's headlights.

"It's sad," Mussani said, and his expression showed deep sympathy. "Her death was an accident, Brother. The woods are dangerous and off limits."

"There w-w-was blood on her l-l-lips."

"Sylvia was a traitor. Brother, hold tight to your faith and remember that not everyone is worthy of rising to the next level."

Mussani flicked the cigarette toward the Jeep, and the smoldering filter fell on Mandy's grubby robe. She crawled across the road toward her Messiah, guttural whimpers tearing from her throat. She reached for him.

He grasped her hand and pulled her to her feet. "My poor child, look at how betrayed you were by Sister Sylvia. Come, it's time for you to go home." He was smiling, but JB saw no kindness in the expression.

JB turned his back and went around the front of the Jeep to the passenger door. "I swear," he whispered to the wind.

With a final glance at his lover's dead body slouching against the giant elm tree, JB climbed into the Jeep and closed his eyes.

Amazon – *Simon Says, Perdition Games*
Kobo – *Simon Says, Perdition Games*
Barnes and Noble – *Simon Says, Perdition Games*
iBooks – *Simon Says, Perdition Games*